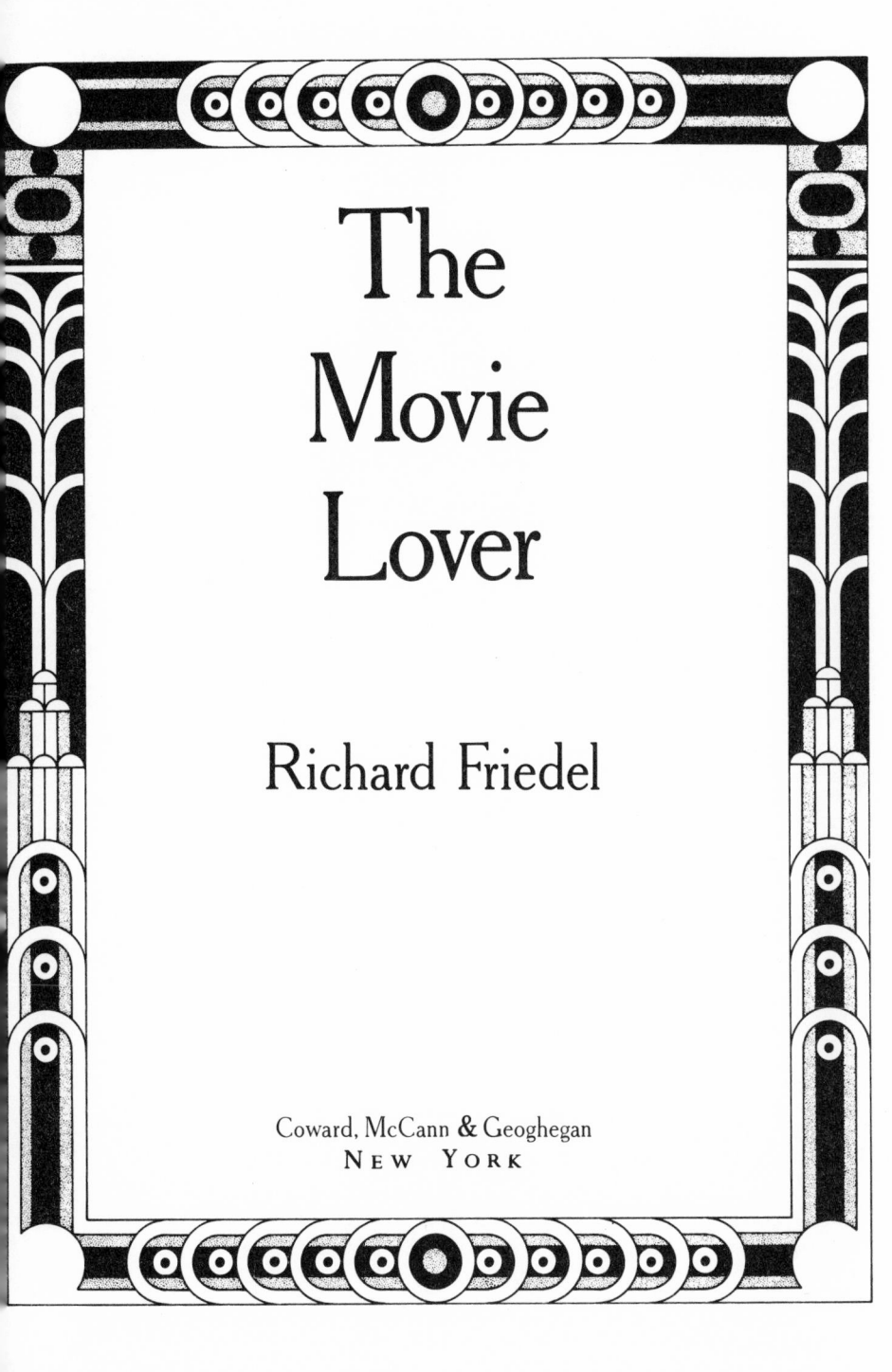

The
Movie
Lover

Richard Friedel

Coward, McCann & Geoghegan
NEW YORK

Library of Congress Cataloging in Publication Data

Friedel, Richard.
The movie lover.

I. Title.
PS3556.R489M6   1981   813'.54   80-28720

ISBN 0-698-11068-4

The text of this book has been set in Perpetua.

Printed in the United States of America

For my extraordinary mother, father, and sister

I wish to thank:
Jeffrey; for his affection, understanding and support—but for him this novel would not have been written.

Thomas Miller, for the generous application of his intelligence and taste in editing this manuscript.

Charles Ortleb, for the chance that allowed me to develop as a writer.

Thomas Steele, for the effervescent encouragement that gave me the confidence to attempt this novel.

The Movie Lover

Odd Man Out

The smoke ring floated through the air. Illuminated briefly by the glow of the table lamp, it brushed against the Tiffany stained glass shade and disintegrated. I produced another, savoring the exquisite flavor, and jettisoned it in the same direction. This one sailed over the lamp with ease, expanding to an appreciable size, but finally it suffered a similar fate, and crashed softly against my mother's head.

"I do wish you'd open the curtains," she said from across the pink marble table. "It's such a nice day."

Remarks of this nature and the persistent cry of an infant down the hall were the only disconcerting sounds to puncture the pleasant dimness, reinforced by maroon velvet drapes, of the rococo sitting room that connected our suites. Just outside, a view of the cobalt blue Mediterranean and swaying palm trees was ruined by an especially sunny day.

I tapped the gray ashes from the tip of my cigarette and sent a smoke ring hurling in the direction of my father, who was seated at a writing desk.

Four tapestries hung halfway down each oak wall. A centaur was being hunted down in one, a feast was being served to an unruly mob of aristocrats in another, a king was being crowned in the third and a virgin being serenaded in the last. Below them, oval mirrors framed in elaborate patterns of shellwork and vegetation reflected the delicate chairs and tables that filled the room in discrete groups. *Cannes.* The hotel manager had personally installed us here and, with a pride that is rare in our modern age, told us of the famous guests who had slept in our beds before us.

"The Countess de Rouville lived for years in these very rooms. *With the Baron de Guivellure,*" he had added confidentially—as if the illicit affair had taken place last week rather than one hundred years earlier. "Then there was President Franco. Eleanor Roosevelt. And, of course, Frank Sinatra."

This was our third day here; it was two o'clock and we were all busy waiting: I for my breakfast of two flaky croissants and a bowl of café au lait; my mother for me to play the hand of cards I was holding; my father for the hotel manager to be brought to the telephone.

Putting his hand over the receiver, he asked my mother irritably, "Is he still there?"

She glanced over to the ornate door that led to the hall. The door boasted plaster cupids at its upper frame, gilt-edged panels on its face, and an oldfangled keyhole. The eye that had been looking at us through this keyhole and the shadows cast by the two knees bent in genuflection at its sill were the reasons for my father's telephone call to the hotel manager.

"Yes, dear," my mother replied, looking back at her cards. "I'm afraid he's still there."

I blew a smoke ring up toward a ceiling of tiny frescoes. "What happened to the guy you hired, daddy?"

"I don't know. Probably downstairs in the bar," he replied, rapidly depressing and releasing the cradle. "Allo? Allo? What's wrong with these people?"

"Have you discarded yet, Burton?" my mother demanded. She was the type of woman who took gin rummy seriously.

I sent a smoke ring hurling toward the door. "No," I replied.

"What are you waiting for?" mother asked.

I leaned sideways in my seat toward the door and waved at the eye in the keyhole. It blinked, then disappeared; the muffled groan of someone rising to his feet could be heard, and the shadows at the base of the door slid out of view. "He's going to another room," I said. The paparazzi were so resourceful.

"Damn these people!" my father yelled at the small porcelain statue of Mercury on the desk. "Allo! Allo!"

In a movie there might have been a close-up of the moist eyeball framed behind the keyhole—perhaps even a cut outside to a tight shot of a tongue licking eager lips. The camera might have followed my father into the next room where he would secure a revolver or wrought-iron poker and then sneak up behind the intruder for a final confrontation. He might have killed him, or a wild shot might have gone through the door and killed me. In either case, my mother would have looked glamorous screaming in the black cocktail dress that she had put on this morning. Appropriately, she was a Debra Paget lookalike. But real life being the pale, plodding substitute it is for the brisk-paced, tidy world of the movies, all that happened was that my father slammed down the telephone receiver.

"Dammit!" he yelled.

"Shouldn't we do something?" my mother asked.

Daddy frowned. "Well, Lucy will be coming back from the lobby with my cigars. She'll scare him away. They scare pretty easily."

Lucy, my younger sister, was a beauty in her twenties, a Natalie Wood type who had taken after my father in color and temperament: brown hair and black eyes. Chromatically, I was more aligned with my mother: auburn-haired as a child, I had matured into a blond. Genetic commingling had also produced a strongly wrought jaw, green eyes outlined with luxurious black eyelashes, and a respectable slender nose. In earlier days, I had been likened to Johnny Sheffield. In certain lighting now, I was compared to Paul Newman. Both observations were somewhat specious, but I found neither offensive. I am a vain sort of person, but not conceited. I think everyone should show a certain amount of discrimination at his clothier and deliberation during his morning toilet. An attention to personal appearance will not lessen the strife of oppressed peoples around the world, but its impact on daylight hours cannot be underestimated. At the same time, I find an exaggerated estimate of one's own physical arrangement the most unbecoming of characteristics.

"Gin," I said to my mother, placing a fan of cards on the table. As she picked through them in astonishment, the child who had been crying down the hall suddenly hit an unprecedented decibel.

"Oh, God! What else!" my father cursed as he opened a tattered copy of *Variety*. MARIETTA BOFFO IN CANNES, the headline proclaimed.

"It *is* annoying," my mother said, glaring at me.

"I hope I never carried on like that when I was a child," I offered by way of compensation.

"You, Burton," my mother said, gathering up the cards in an uncharacteristically peevish manner, "were never a child."

I let go with a small smoke ring which dangled in the air between us. My mother destroyed it with a wave of her hand. She was being somewhat less than accurate about my never having been a child. Of course I had been; she had proof in her wallet. She was referring to the fact that in those dramatic first years of my life I had met her and my father's expectations less often than they would have liked. Among my earliest recollections of my parents is the bewildered expression my actions often brought to their faces. I have seen that same puzzled look on different faces all my life. It is the one constant against which I judge all personal vicissitudes.

I think the problem then was that I never *thought* of myself as a child. My parents, however—seeing that I embodied several of the appropriate characteristics: shortness, limited vocabulary, and a decided preference for chocolate pudding over lima beans—did. For a long time, no matter how much evidence was presented to the contrary, they made the mistake of confusing me with the rest of the wagon-pulling set.

Unlike the standard toddler, I was always quite content to amuse myself without the help of adults; I was happiest looking through magazines in my playpen, undisturbed. One might think that this would have been considered a laudable attribute, but it seems that parents prefer to see one laughing through one's formative years rather than thumbing. Hence, they take it upon themselves to provide entertainment: shaking a rattle in one's face at every opportunity or hoisting one into the air at terrifying heights.

I could never work up much of a mania for this sort of thing and my parents grew worried.

"Not a peep out of him for hours," my mother would whisper to my father. "He just sits there with my *Vogue*. I don't like it."

"What he needs is a playmate," my father decided after studying a child psychology paperback.

Thus, in the hope of providing an alternate source of amusement, my parents lowered a succession of children into my playpen. Notable among these annoyances was a child of dubious pedigree who belonged to a next-door neighbor.

"This, darling, is little Butch."

When this diapered demon first appeared, I was in the midst of a nap and did not appreciate being disturbed. Observing *little Butch* from a distance, I noticed that he had little going for him aside from a marked ability to fit his entire index finger into his left nostril. Not wanting to play, I graciously pointed out the rubber toys with which he could amuse himself. He seemed appreciative and I turned over and started counting sheep.

My mother, unhappy that we weren't interacting, picked up little Butch and placed him adjacent to me.

"Now play nice."

Seeing him at this uncomfortable distance did nothing to change my attitude. I was repulsed by his inability to control saliva production and crawled to another corner, resigning myself to wakefulness.

"Patty cake, patty cake . . ." my mother sang, moving little Butch close to me once more. I could smell the pureed carrots on his breath.

Exasperated, I rattled the bars of my playpen and screamed. Mercifully, she got the idea and returned him to his owner.

Unfortunately, that was only the beginning.

There were also my relatives (a group of strangers with whom, ostensibly, I had some connection). When I learned to speak, they were as perplexed as my parents by my inappropriate responses. There was no end to the throat clearing when I would stamp my foot and say things like, "For the tenth time! I do *not* want to be a fire chief when I grow up!" But they'd smile politely and suggest to my parents that they supplement my diet with prune juice or something equally as vile.

My mother wasn't prepared for this at all. After all, she had *planned* to have a child: If it was a girl, she wanted a Margaret O'Brien; if a boy, she preferred the Huckleberry Finn model. During her pregnancy, she gave up everything that might sabotage these desired results. Smoking and drinking were completely abandoned. Priests were consulted. What, then, had happened? Why wasn't I making a raft in the backyard or wearing a straw hat and shredded pedal-pushers? She had wanted a child whose coat she could button and whose nose she could wipe; instead she got a short little man who seemed quite capable of handling his own affairs.

As time passed, I did little to meet her original expectations except grow taller. Conversations with other mothers provided little consolation.

"You should see Sidney's room. Clothes all over the place, tuna fish sandwiches under his bed. He takes after his father," Mrs. Molson would say proudly.

What could my mother say? I had been instrumental in helping her pick out the bathroom wallpaper.

"My Harold is into everything. He loves to rip paper. I haven't been able to get one recipe out of the *Ladies' Home Journal* since he discovered his fingers," Mrs. Anderson would say.

I was licking *my* fingers to facilitate turning the pages of the *Saturday Evening Post.*

"Belshazzar, Junior, loves to play outside," Mrs. Ahmou would crow.

This was a particularly sticky point. For some peculiar reason the maternal instinct includes the feeling that it is of paramount importance that little boys spend a great deal of time *out of doors*. When my mother told them that I refused to set foot outside, their respective eyeballs popped out.

"Won't go outside!"

It wasn't that my mother didn't try. She was always nagging me to fraternize with the neighborhood riffraff. "They are *not* morons," she insisted. "Go outside."

"No."

"Please."

"No."

"But your skin is turning *gray.*"

"I don't care."

"For five minutes?"

"No."

"For chocolate pudding?"

"No."

"For me."

"Forget it, mother!" She had a way of finally getting on my nerves.

Most of our conversations ended without incident, but once in a while she would become adamant about my itinerary for the day.

"OUTSIDE!"

With arms crossed, she'd watch me slowly, begrudgingly put on my shoes and jacket. "Leave the book here, young man."

Then, with her finger pointing the way, I'd walk out the door, dragging my feet and mumbling warnings about how sorry she would be for forcing me into this. Just wait, I'd think to myself, I'll start hanging around these local yokels and then I'll start picking my nose at dinner and then I'll go *deaf* from her recriminations.

Slam!

With a sigh of relief, she would go on with her domestic business. I think she hoped I would meet some kid, who would teach me to play some game, which other kids, whom I liked, would join, all of which would make me late for dinner. Her naïveté was touching.

After a while, curiosity would get the best of her and she would stop separating laundry and go to the window to check my progress. Searching the horizon for a sign of her firstborn, she would wonder, Is he climbing a tree? Is he doing handstands? Is he running and laughing wildly? Her hopes would be dashed when she saw me standing on the welcome mat waiting to be readmitted into the house.

"Don't you want to play with children your own age?" she would plead upon opening the door. "Don't you want to explore the neighborhood? Swing a baseball bat? Catch frogs?"

Questions. Questions. One would think she had enough vacuuming to keep her busy.

"Running is good for your health," she would say in one of her sarcastic moods. "I can teach you if you'd like. It's like walking, but you do it faster."

This went on for years. My only relief from her badgering occurred on rainy days when I could curl up with *Look* magazine quietly in a corner. To this day, whenever I'm depressed, I prefer a clap of thunder to a dose of Librium.

With my father gone all day, I spent a lot of time with my mother.

"Come on, Burton. Let's go to the store."

I loved to be chauffeured. Most children enjoy sitting in the front seat of a car and throwing bubble gum wrappers out the window. I preferred riding alone, ankles crossed, in the back seat.

Tap. Tap. Tap.

"Driver, stop at the next drugstore you see. I seem to have run out of chocolate cigarettes."

My mother never got used to the idea.

Whenever we went out together, I loved to look for additions to my wardrobe. Most five-year-olds are as interested in developing a sense of fashion as they are in understanding history in terms of dialectical materialism. Even when their trousers are ripped to the point of immodesty they have to be dragged kicking and screaming to a clothier.

My mother, an impeccably dressed woman herself, and I often argued about what was suitable for me.

"This is adorable," she would say, holding up a sweater.

"Ugh!" I would reply, repulsed by anything with a choo-choo train print.

Given the limitations of preschool fashions, one couldn't help but be vulnerable to disappointment. "What do you mean, you don't have any capes, mister?"

When not on one of these excursions, I spent my time watching television. This pleased my father, to an extent; he was employed by a television network and headed the staff of a particularly popular children's program called the *Captain Dodo Show.*

"Look! There's your father's name on the screen!" my mother would yell once a day when his credit was rolled.

I was unimpressed. Captain Dodo indeed! I just wasn't interested in the regular programming on television. I was fascinated by the wonderful old movies from the 1930s and '40s. With all they had to offer, how could I possibly be content to watch this *Captain Dodo,* or confine myself to the rabble outside for whom the act of digging a hole could be considered overachieving? I had the world passing before me. Granted, an MGM version of the world, but nonetheless informative, entertaining and exciting. Definitely a vast improvement over throwing rocks at tin cans.

"Please go outside."

Why? I had all the adventure I could handle right in my living room. Spencer Tracy exploring the Northwest Passage. Tyrone Power building the Suez Canal with Loretta Young. Don Ameche spilling acid on his privates and inventing the telephone. Greer Garson deigning to discover radium.

I had become accustomed to a certain standard of glamour in my life, a criterion never met by the preschoolers on my block. Rita Hayworth. Linda Darnell. Alice Faye. The vertiginous Ann Miller and the noble Norma Shearer. What better way to spend a day than to be sprawled on the living room floor, basking in the radiance of Vivien Leigh or Marietta (my favorites). With their blue-black hair cascading from center parts, Vivien Leigh was primly feline, rubbing up against a cheek and dashing out of reach; Marietta was a cool, marble statue saddened at finding itself animated. Vivien had the edge as far as acting was concerned, but Marietta was the more gorgeous. She had utterly unique gray-violet eyes; it was said that she was so dermatologically endowed that her cheekbones were naturally accented with the slightest tint of amber; any application of makeup was prodigal. I was six when I saw my first movie starring Marietta, *The Waltz,* and when all that milk-skinned beauty appeared on the screen in a black sequined ball gown, I put aside my Wheatena and blueberries and fell madly in love. After watching those full, crimson lips part to whisper a warning to Tyrone Power, those sultry eyes beg for his forgiveness, how could I be expected to content myself catching frogs with the untidy children of my neighborhood?

"You need exercise!"

Why? Were my six-year-old arteries in danger of hardening? I got enough of a workout imitating Fred Astaire's tap dancing technique by leaping from bureau to nightstand to clothes hamper.

"Really, mother. Fresh air?"

My parents found my value system as inscrutable as my habits. For instance, one Christmas I specifically asked my mother to have Santa Claus deliver a picture book I had espied of various MGM movie stars.

"Wouldn't you rather have a football helmet?" she asked.

After giving her one of my icy stares, I was assured that Santa would be informed of my request.

She had a big get-together with all the relatives that year and presents were exchanged, but much to my dismay, no book. Before I could confront my mother, she clapped her hands, shushed everybody, and announced, "Oh, Santa Claus forgot a few things. I think I hear him on the roof."

That was the cue for daddy to come down dressed in his red suit and white beard.

"*Ho! Ho! Ho!*"

It was very effective, even though I knew it was my father (I recognized the shoes.) He began calling people up to sit on his knee and I thought, this is where I get restitution.

My two cousins, Danny and Joey, were there. I didn't care for them much. Santa Claus gave each of them a dump truck, which I thought quite appropriate, given their mental capacities. They squealed with delight upon receiving their windfall, then went off to a corner to break them.

"I think I have something for you, young man," my father finally said to me.

I played along. "Oh boy, Santa Claus! Wowee! Golly, did you get me what I asked for?" Jackie Cooper couldn't have given a better performance.

"Here you go!" he said.

Much to my dismayed surprise, he handed me a dump truck.

"What's this?" I asked.

"That's the nice shiny present Santa forgot."

I looked over at my cousins, who were busy sticking broken dump truck parts into each other's ears. What was I supposed to do now, I wondered, go over and play blue-collar worker with them?

"With all due respect, *Mister* Claus, I think there's been a mix-up," I whispered. "I distinctly remember asking my mother—she's that woman over there—for a picture book of movie stars."

"*Ho. Ho. Ho.*"

No. No. No.

I jumped off his lap and went over to my mother. "There's been a mistake," I said, gesturing for her to bend down. "Could you please tell *Santa* over there that he's ordered one too many dump trucks and not enough movie-star books?"

It turned out that she had had the book in her bedroom upstairs the whole time but thought it wasn't as substantial as a dump truck and had been afraid I would be jealous of my cousins. I couldn't *believe* her logic on that one. *Santa* went back to his *sled* and got the book for me, but the whole incident left my parents all the more confused as to what kind of little boy they had produced.

My father, like my mother, had a conception of what his son should be: intelligent, yet able to hit a baseball smack into the bleachers; someone who would get far in the world, yet never tire of saying "gee whiz." Sort of a cross between Felix Frankfurter and Spanky.

When he came home from the studio at night he would simply ask my mother, "Okay, which sound stage is he on today?" and she would indicate a room. He'd find me impersonating Ronald Colman or ducking mortar fire from the advancing German army, or dying on the bed from some mysterious Hollywood disease.

"Send for the specialist from Vienna," I'd moan.

"Don't you want to play catch?" my father would ask.

"Catch? I vant to be a-l-o-o-ne."

He succeeded in getting me into the backyard only once but he became so upset with my phlegmatic attitude toward running bases that I had to have a talk with him.

"Daddy, you're taking this *much* too seriously. It's only a *game,* for heaven's sake."

He gave up after that. He felt I would never be interested in physical activity, but later found out that was only partially true.

"He wants to take *tap* dancing lessons?"

Some friends of my parents had two kids who took tap at Miss Toledo's School of Tap & Toe. I was dragged to one of their recitals against my will but was gaga for taking lessons by the time it was over. The costumes (I was a sucker for sequins), the lights, the excitement and the applause had me tugging at my father's pants leg until he agreed I could do it.

"All right! But stick to the floor. I see one scuff mark on the étagère and you're through."

I eagerly agreed but, unfortunately, Miss Toledo had all the students she could handle. Instead I was enrolled with Mr. Parker's Rhythm Kids, the only other school in town.

Mr. Parker was sixty-eight years old and barely ambulatory. I'm sure all that was required of a dancing instructor by the state licensers was that he have a floor on which his pupils could dance. Even so, I was sure Mr. Parker had to resort to bribery. It took five of us to move the pool table out of the way before class could begin. My mother didn't want me to go through with it, but I insisted. *Got-ta dance!*

The Rhythm Kids were not memorable dancers. The girls concentrated more on pulling their leotards down from their crotches than on tapping. The boys were angry at their mothers for making them take dancing lessons and for diversion threw billiard balls at each other. More often than not, they miscalculated and came perilously close to hitting the piano player, Mrs. Potash, who, quite frankly, deserved the bombardment. She was terrible. One reason was that she needed glasses desperately but, I suppose, couldn't afford them on the salary Mr. Parker paid her. To perform her function, she had to bend over in her chair until her face was about four inches from the keyboard. Since the piano was an upright, this often saved her from getting beaned with the eight ball, but it simply *ruined* her posture. What posture she had.

She made a mockery of tunes like "Fascinatin' Rhythm." It didn't matter. The Rhythm Kids would have danced to the sound of a Con Edison jackhammer.

I was chagrined by all this, but I worked hard. I knew that each shuffle-ball-change was bringing me closer to dancing in costume on stage for a full audience.

After a few weeks, Mrs. Potash left. (She had stood to go to the bathroom and was clobbered with a cue ball.) Mr. Parker took over. He couldn't play the piano and didn't have a record player, so he provided verbal accompaniment.

"Ya-da, ya-da-da-dump." Etcetera. Supplemented by hand-clapping and foot-stomping. While the change of accompaniment had no noticeable effect on the Rhythm Kids, *I* often left class with a migraine.

Finally, after months of class, Mr. Parker announced, to the unabashed yawns of the class, that there would soon be a recital. My heart leaped! I had vision of flowers thrown at my feet as I stood on stage glittering in my costume.

"When, Mr. Parker? When!"

"Two weeks."

Wow! Two weeks to get my number down. "Where, Mr. Parker?"

I wondered what sets would be built for me. Maybe a half-moon would carry me down from the ceiling and deposit me on a floor of stardust. Or perhaps I'd do a military tap down the gangplank of a ship while twenty-one guns shot off.

"The recital will be quite a spectacle," Mr. Parker began.

Yes? Yes?

"The biggest I've ever had."

Yes! Yes!

"Sally Sue Damachio will be in charge of putting up the crepe paper decorations—"

Crepe paper decorations! There must be some mistake . . .

Ho! Ho! Ho!

"What about *costumes,* Mr. Parker?" I wanted a red silk cosmic jump suit with red sequins—a cape to match was optional. If I did a military tap, I wanted my shoes to blow up in a shower of red and silver sparks at the finish.

"The girls will wear white blouses and red skirts. The boys will wear white shirts and black pants."

I stood there in disbelief. When I regained my wits, I went up and poked him in the thigh.

"Yes, young man?" he said, smiling, his huge nose flattened on his face.

I put my hand on my hip. "You mean to tell me that I've gone through months of *ya-da, ya-da-da-dump,* and all I get to wear is a white shirt and black pants? No sequins, no rhinestones, *No exploding tap shoes!"*

Ignoring me, Mr. Parker continued to the class, "Mrs. Potash will return to supply the music. She's out of the hospital now—"

Mrs. Potash! I sat down on the floor. I had had my heart set on violins. I supposed that the crowds of adoring fans I had been counting on would be denied me as well.

"The pool table will be moved to the far corner to make room for the benches."

It's going to be *here,* I thought with dread, looking at the pegboard walls.

"You can each bring *one* parent."

Not having an agent, I complained bitterly to my parents that evening. They were sympathetic and asked me what I wanted to do.

"Sue!" I said. I meant it.

They countered that such action was quite out of the question; instead, they had me quit. They promised that if Miss Toledo had an opening I could join her school. That never happened. I did, however, perform magnificently for my mother's canasta club on several occasions.

So I've always had a tenuous relationship with real life. I've never quite belonged, never quite fit in. Though as a child I vaguely sensed my singularity, I was not consciously aware of it until I matriculated to kindergarten.

One day my mother informed me that it would no longer be possible for me to watch the *Morning Movie* on a regular basis. She was very gentle. "The jig's up, kid. You're going to school. Take off the kimono and get dressed."

Not wanting to lose contact with my celluloid friends, I tried reasoning with the woman, but she was immovable.

"Don't look so down, darling. Think of all the things you'll learn."

I handed her a piece of paper and asked if she would kindly list a few of these *things* so that I could determine whether they justified my getting up at the ungodly hour of seven o'clock. Pushing it aside, she said, "Well, you'll learn to write the ABC's."

Impatiently, I reminded her that she had already taught me the ABC's (to use her quaint appellation).

"You'll be taught how to count to ten."

Tapping my foot, I informed her that my frustration over inaccurate television listings had forced me to use that technique many times. "Is that it?"

"You'll learn to draw."

Satisfied with being able simply to draw my breath, I decided that none of these educational bonbons was sufficient reason for me to miss *Incendiary Blonde,* which was to air the day I was to start school.

"It's important for your future that you go," she whined.

I thanked her for all the concern, but preferred taking a rain check on the school business. The ball went into my father's court.

He implemented the you're-going-to-have-so-much-fun approach. I asked him briefly to describe one or two of the things that would precipitate all this fun. He explained that all the kids in the neighborhood would be going to the same school. Better yet, they would probably be in my class.

"Isn't that terrific?"

I showed him how overjoyed this bit of information made me by painting little red dots on my palms and dramatizing the scene at Calvary in the backyard.

My parents put all four of their feet down.

"You're going!"

But I persisted. My mother inadvertently came up with the solution. She bought me a little briefcase and pencil box and told me just to pretend that I was going to the office every day, like daddy. Being a mercenary soul, I liked getting the presents and started to think favorably about school. But instead of pretending to be daddy, I decided to be Jimmy Stewart (going to Washington) on Mondays, Wednesdays and Fridays, and Cary Grant, in *His Girl Friday,* on Tuesdays and

Thursdays. My mother was relieved when she saw me dressed and ready to go the first day.

I breezed into class and was told where to sit down. It was Thursday, so I unpacked my briefcase, took out the pencil box and waited for the first news story to break. I gave a quick look around at the people who, by coincidence of birth, were in my class. It took thirty seconds to see that my parents had copulated at the wrong time. The room was extremely noisy. We were told to quiet down but this had no effect whatsoever, except to make one girl burst out in tears. The teacher looked harried to the point of genocide. A boy stood in the corner holding his genitals and fidgeting but was completely ignored until it was too late. The teacher apoplectically directed him to the health office to wait for an emergency pair of trousers from his mother.

I didn't like all this disorganization so I got out of my seat and asked the teacher if I could come back tomorrow when she had everything a little more under control. I gathered this was the wrong thing to say when her complexion turned indigo.

I went back to my seat. There was a filthy-looking boy sitting next to me, a real *Tobacco Road* type. I gasped when I saw he was holding my pencil box. Trying not to embarrass him, I politely pointed out that he had mistakenly picked it up, but he paid no attention.

"*Your* pencil box is the ugly green one. *Mine* is the blue one in your hand," I said.

Continuing to ignore me, he opened it up and began banging the little plastic ruler on the desk.

"Don't do that, little boy," I warned, trying to control my temper. I'd have my mother wash it with hydrogen peroxide when I got home. "That doesn't belong to you. Give it back."

"*My wuler!*" was his glib retort.

"No, it's not your *wuler!*" I replied sarcastically, but before I could grab it he put one end in his mouth. Horrified, I said, "Consider it a gift," and grabbed the pencil box.

The boy sitting on the other side of me looked fairly intelligent so I decided to try to break the ice with him. I asked if he had seen the Norma Shearer film that had been on TV last night. He stared at me blankly. I asked him to tell me what he generally did like to watch.

"Captain Dodo," he replied.

So much for trying to mix, I thought. Marching back to the teacher, I asked if there had been some error in placement. "Do I really belong here? Is it possible my mother was given the wrong address?" This second confrontation made her equally choleric but I refused to be intimidated and insisted on a new seat assignment.

"Over there!" she snapped.

Now I was sitting next to a girl wearing a white dress. Perhaps, I thought, it will be easier to communicate with the female of the species. But apparently there was a law in the grammar-school jungle prohibiting such contact. Somehow an organism known as *kooties* was involved.

"Pardon me," I began, but before I was allowed to continue the girl in white frantically tapped her girlfriend on the shoulder.

"Mary Jane! Mary Jane! Euw! There's a boy talking to me! Euw!"

Mary Jane was equally repulsed.

One of the boys nearby picked up on my error in toddler etiquette and exclaimed, "Kooties! Kooties!"

I demanded to be promoted to the first grade.

That evening, I told my parents what a dismal experience school had been. They sympathized but reiterated that the law required I attend. I suggested they hire a tutor, but they refused.

"Can't you *afford* one?" I said, trying to shame them into it, only succeeding in losing out on dessert.

So I was stuck. Whether I liked my contemporaries or not, I had to tolerate them—there were too many to ignore.

I marched into school the next day and, to start things out on a better note, gave the teacher an apple. Apparently this was *also* the wrong thing to do.

"Teacher's pet! Teacher's pet!"

I wondered if there were a pamphlet on kindergarten protocol available in the principal's office.

The teacher, Miss Finklestein, was no help. She was a large woman without fashion sense. My desk was very close to hers and when she sat down I could see the stocking rolls just above her knees. This never failed to spoil my milk-and-cookie break.

The class adored her. She had a Billie Burke personality; she praised enthusiastically. The high-pitched tone of her voice could probably, on a warm summer night, attract bats.

"Oh, Tommy! You counted all the way to ten without any help from me," she'd shrill. "You're so smart! You might even be smarter than *me!*"

She had a point there. She was one of those instructors who spend a great deal of time preparing for their classes and just barely manage to keep one jump ahead of their students.

"Now then, who would like to spell 'cat' for me?"

This was to be my first taste of educational boredom.

Miss Finklestein took an immediate dislike to me. "Please be seated, Burton Raider! I'm sure the class has better things to do than listen to your Lionel Hampton impressions."

"*Barrymore,* Miss Finklestein," I'd say, rolling my eyes. A prescription for fruit-flavored Valium would have come in handy.

One day, Miss Finklestein clumped into the room with a bit of breakfast still stuck to her right front tooth and said, "Today, boys and girls, we are going to elect a cloakroom representative."

She went on to describe the position with such high-flown phrases that one would have thought a car and expense account came with the job. The actual function of the cloakroom representative was to open the door of a huge closet in the back of the room which contained, not surprisingly, cloaks. Then, later on, close the door while making sure that no cloaks and, I presume (it was never mentioned), children were left inside. It was not a high-stress employment situation nor would it ever look good on a résumé, but I was determined to make a place for myself in the class. I decided to run.

"Who would like to nominate someone?" Miss Finklestein asked. "Does anyone know what 'nominate' means?"

While five Liliputians simultaneously shared their definitions (all incorrect) with the class, I bribed the kid next to me for a nomination. I gave him a crash course in all my attributes and told him to keep his speech short but effective.

"All right," Miss Finklestein said, "Do I hear any nominations?"

My campaign manager spoke up first. *"Him!"* was all the idiot managed to get out, with supplemental pointing. I was chagrined but recovered in time to display the proper amount of surprise.

"Me?" I gushed. "Words are so useless at a time like this. Except, perhaps, for two little words . . . thank you."

Miss Finklestein was unimpressed. "Any other nominations?"

The girl in white who had taken such a dislike to me spoke up. "I'd like to monimate—"

Monimate?

"—Mary Jane Lincoln."

There goes the Protestant vote, I thought grimly to myself.

"Let's take a vote," Miss Finklestein suggested. She told each student to tear off a piece of paper and write the name of his choice on it. I immediately went into action by going up and down the aisles shaking hands and smiling. While doing so, I noticed that Mary Jane and her campaign manager tore off *seventeen* pieces of paper. I didn't say anything. I have a grudging admiration for deviousness.

"Pass them up!" Miss Finklestein collected all the votes, then sat down at her desk. I bit my lip. "All right now. That's one for Burton."

Lacking any grace, my two opponents scowled at me unabashedly.

"And one for Mary Jane."

The girl in white led everyone in hoorays.

"All right, children. I've finished," Miss Finklestein said finally, gathering up the scraps. The two girls held each other's shoulders while the teacher made a dramatic show of walking to the center of the room.

Holding up the piece of construction paper on which she had tabulated the returns in crayon, she said, "The cloakroom representative for this year is—"

My opponents squealed in anticipation.

"—Mary Jane Lincoln."

Assorted hoorays followed. I was appalled by the class's choice but, since the notion of the job bored me anyway, resisted spreading the rumor that Mary Jane had stooped to fraud. I was gratified later to see her finger crushed in the cloakroom door. I hoped that justice was served as well in adult life.

A Wing and a Prayer

One day in the 1950's in Washington, D.C., a bureaucrat was standing naked in front of his full-length mirror, contemplating the profile of his body. Earlier that day, his secretary, about whom he had been entertaining lustful thoughts, had witnessed a button pop off his shirt with orgasmic force. What was worse, she giggled.

"Sam! Come to bed!" his wife called from the next room.

It was the first time in years that the bureaucrat thought he had let himself go.

"In a minute!" he yelled back.

It's not *that* bad, he thought to himself, rubbing his paunch with his fingertips. His wife, annoyed by the glare of light from the partly opened bathroom door, rose and looked in on her husband. She watched with a slight feeling of repugnance as he vainly tried, by manipulating his diaphragm, to resurrect a form buried under twenty years of relentless fetuccine eating. Not bothering to hide her disgust, she said, "Christ, Sam, you're a pig."

After a week of thinking, the bureaucrat went to the White House.

"Mr. President," he said, casting a furtive glance at his stomach, "have *I* got an idea for *you.*"

So was born the President's Council on Physical Fitness, a program designed to reinterest a flabby nation in athletics and the benefits therein.

Just what I needed. It wasn't bad enough that one's worth was directly proportional to the distance one could hit a baseball; now being athletic had been legislated to the level of patriotic duty.

"All right, boys and girls," Mrs. Tanner, my third-grade teacher, said one day at recess, holding a government pamphlet. "The president wants to see how well you can all do in this list of skills."

She described fifteen events in which we were expected to participate.

Oh, God, a decathlon, I thought grimly to myself, and here I barely have the patience for Red Rover.

"The results will be sent to Washington," she continued. "If you receive a good score, you will be awarded a certificate and this nice green badge to wear on your coat." She held up a cloth patch with a pair of winged feet embossed on it—the kind of thing one wouldn't be caught *dead* in, let alone be *inspired* by. "Then you will be considered a member of the president's team."

I told Mrs. Tanner that I was too sedentary to participate. She replied that no medical excuses would be allowed without a doctor's note, so for the rest of the term I supplemented my statements with diagrams.

In the first event, the potential presidential team member had to climb a rope.

"Burton?" Mrs. Tanner said, poising pen to clipboard.

I grabbed onto the rope and pulled. *"Urrrghhhh!"*

"You're not *trying,* Burton," the teacher said, marking down a goose egg.

I lay on the ground, hand on heart, while the rest of the class racked up points.

Pull-ups were next. Discrimination, which sometimes has its advantages, although not in this case, required that boys do twenty, girls six. The class lined up. Feeling that one event per day was more than enough, I strolled to the end of the line when the teacher turned her back.

"Is that everyone?" Mrs. Tanner asked.

"Burton didn't go—" Sparks Compton jeered.

"Okay, okay," I said, shuffling up to the bar.

"Hold your hands six inches apart and pull," Mrs. Tanner instructed.

"*Grraaaaghhh!*"

"Burton, zero."

Clutching my stomach and panting, I asked Mrs. Tanner if there was something on the list with a bit more sophistication, like "number of machine-gun taps per minute."

"You're not *trying*, Burton," she said.

I asked her if a cerebral hemorrhage would be proof of my sincerity.

"Really, Burton, there's more at stake here than being able to perform these skills. Failure today could mean a lifetime of failure."

I wondered if my grade would be affected by offering Mrs. Tanner a bribe.

"I'm going to have to mark down an F," Mrs. Tanner said, shaking her head.

The rest of the class overheard her. "The weirdo's flunked! The weirdo's flunked!" they chanted.

What a time not to have a gun.

Well, I wasn't about to let this bunch of cornhuskers think they were superior to me simply because they could raise their weak chins above a pipe a couple of times. My mother had taught me to turn the other cheek when things got out of hand. Raising her eyes upward, she would say, "It will be taken care of later." Man's inhumanity to man might very well be reconciled in some heavenly court, but God had failed to bless me with the patience to wait until after my demise for restitution—a terrestrial revenge was in order.

My father unwittingly provided the means. He had been appointed talent coordinator for children's programs at his television network and it was his job to see that the various performers were happy.

One day my mother informed me that the station was having trouble with a host of one of the morning shows and that, in an attempt to rectify matters, my father had invited him to spend the weekend at our house.

"Who's coming?" I asked.

"Captain Dodo," she replied matter of factly.

I paused, wondering if I could occupy the same house for forty-eight hours with a man who made a living wearing a Prince Valiant wig and baggy coat, a man who moralized on the air to puppets and conversed with animated pieces of furniture.

I telephoned my father. "Maybe it would be best if I weekended at grandma's," I said.

"No, no," he replied, "it's important that you be there. You see, the Captain doesn't think he's funny anymore."

An accurate self-analysis, I thought to myself.

"The station cut the expense of having a live studio audience of children. Now he only performs in front of the camera crew. You can imagine how many laughs he gets from them. He's become depressed and it's starting to affect his work and the network expects me to do something about it. I figured if he saw that real children still like him he might snap out of it. So I'm counting on both you and Lucy to make a big fuss. I know Lucy's no problem. But I'm worried about you."

"Don't be," I said.

That evening I greeted my father at the door. The Captain was getting something out of the car.

"What's his real name?" I asked. "I can't very well call him *Captain Dodo* all weekend."

"That's *exactly* what you're going to call him, young man," my father said sternly.

"He's not going to spoil my meals by wearing that wig, is he?" I asked.

His answer was interrupted by Lucy, who was running down the hall yelling, *"Is he here! Is Captain Dodo here!"*

She almost succeeded in giving me a coronary.

"He's coming up the walk!" she yelled at the window.

Captain Dodo entered amidst Lucy's squeals. His face was pale; no doubt it was difficult to get all the meringue out of his pores. Quietly, he put down his suitcase, then handed me his coat, exhibiting none of the manic mannerisms for which he was known on television.

Lucy was not put off by how small and old he looked. *"Hello, Captain Dodo! Hello!"*

He looked at her dancing around his legs like a Navajo Indian. "Hi," he said in a subdued tone.

Excitedly, Lucy recounted how she had told her girlfriend Teresa that Captain Dodo was coming to visit but Teresa wouldn't believe her until she crossed her heart. "So I did and she still wouldn't believe me so I hung up on her."

For a few minutes, the Captain listened assiduously to Lucy go on. Finally he acknowledged her gushing with a nod of approval and crouched down to listen more closely. "Really? She wouldn't believe you?"

"No, she wouldn't and, oh, Captain Dodo, I watch you all the time—every morning! Even when mommy yells at me to come to breakfast, I won't till I see you!"

He chuckled.

"Sometimes mommy will let me eat in front of the TV. Then it's okay. I hate to miss Timothy the Tortoise or Sammy the Squirrel just to eat some dumb old cereal—or even French toast!"

I shook my head at her misdirected idolatry.

"I even have all your coloring books and won't let anyone else have them but me. I don't like the way Teresa colors. She makes faces blue and hands green."

The Captain chuckled but reminded Lucy that she should share with her friends. Lucy stood corrected and then begged him to do something. "Sing! Please sing!"

The Captain resisted for a moment but then surrendered to Lucy's cajolery. He hoisted her up in his arms and together they sang no less than three choruses of his theme song, "The Rainbow is Just an Upside-down Smile."

I thought I would retch.

My mother came in during the last eight bars and ran like a paparazzi to get a camera. For reasons of health, I decided to skip the rest of the saccharin scene and followed my father into the living room, where he proceeded to make cocktails.

"Well," he said cheerfully, "the Captain certainly has got your sister entertained."

What he's got, I thought to myself, is dementia praecox.

Sensing my disdain, my father said, "Don't you *dare* say anything that will upset the Captain."

I promised to be good and the Captain entered with Lucy attached to his leg like a rhesus monkey. "Your daughter is adorable!" he boomed. "And who have we here? I haven't met this young man yet. I hope he's not shy."

I thought for a moment. Perhaps going along with this incorrect psychological analysis was the best way to avoid a verbal confrontation. I blushed and looked at the floor.

"Aw, don't be afraid." He reached into his pocket and extricated a red nose. "Ta-da! Now you know me! Captain Dodo!"

I dug my fingernails into my palm and froze a toothy smile on my lips. "How do you do?" I asked glacially.

"That's the ticket!" he said, pinching my cheek.

Fearing trouble, my father spoke up quickly. "This is Burton. He just *loves* your show, Captain."

"Does he? Well, how would Burton like to see Sammy the Squirrel and Timothy the Tortoise?"

"Oh, he would just *love* that, Captain."

The Captain let go of my cheek and exited to get his puppets. I asked my father if there was any sign of a blood blister.

"You're doing fine," he said, "just sit down and enjoy his act."

"Well, I'll *sit* anyway," I said, taking the lotus position.

The Captain reappeared with two Dynel puppets: one was holding a mallet; the other's head was bandaged.

"YAY!" my sister cheered.

One puppet spoke in a falsetto voice: "Hello, everybody! My name is Sammy!"

"Where have you been!" the other indignantly squeaked. "I've been standing here for an hour!" To punish the squirrel for his tardiness, the tortoise bashed him over the head with the mallet.

"YAY!" my sister cheered.

Diarrhea is inevitable, I thought bleakly.

The Captain continued. Even though I feigned laughter, I think he realized I was unimpressed. He knew he had conquered Lucy, but like any ham, he wanted everyone to love him. Increasing his volume, he played directly to me.

"You think I'm stupid?" the squirrel raged in my ear.

Bam. Bam. Bam.

Only when my mother called dinner did the curtain go down on his puerile patter.

During dinner, the Captain again concentrated on me, pulling quarters out of my nose, making my tomato juice disappear and constructing a parakeet out of my napkin. Lucy had to be put to bed because of an upset stomach from overexcitement. I managed to stifle my yawns.

After dinner, the Captain tried a few more times to get me to laugh ("This is my impression of a coffee percolator") but I couldn't bring myself to do much more than grin. Without Lucy's exuberance to buttress his sagging ego, he again seemed to drift into a depression.

As the weekend progressed, his mood worsened.

"Jesus," my father complained worriedly, "he just mopes around and refuses to listen. What am I going to tell the network?"

I sighed, realizing that it was really up to me to set things right. I found the Captain in my father's den staring out the window. He looked tired and old.

"Captain?" I said.

His face brightened for a moment, then the drawn look appeared once more. "What do *you* want?" he said sullenly.

I climbed up on his knee and told him how unusual I thought he was and how awed I was by the fact that he entertained so many children. Using ambiguous phrases that did not compromise my aesthetic principles but seemed to suggest worship ("Just think, you do this stuff *every* day!"), I managed to get him excited again.

"Let me get my puppets!" he said, racing out of the room.

Peeling open a roll of antacid mints, I endured two more hours of his pugilistic rodent and amphibian.

"Amazing, Captain! Just amazing!" I said, popping another lozenge into my mouth.

By the time he was finished, I had not only succeeded in giving the Captain enough confidence to face the cameras again, I had also wangled a cameo appearance on his show. My parents and Lucy listened with open mouths as the Captain told them the news.

"This kid has really got something! We'll dress him up like a chipmunk and he can do a dance with me."

Lucy wouldn't talk to me for three weeks.

The day the show aired, Mrs. Tanner canceled recess and brought a television into the classroom.

Even Sparks Compton was impressed. "Gee, Burton, you actually *know* Captain Dodo!"

"Doesn't everyone?" I replied innocently.

"But he's your *friend!*" another, who enjoyed drawing caricatures of me in the sandbox, squealed.

Exclamations of envy went on until I finally got a review from Mrs. Tanner herself. "Burton!" she said, "I had no *idea!* I thought I'd *die* when I saw you do those fan kicks!"

Wouldst that were true, Mrs. Tanner, I thought.

Double Indemnity

I was fifteen when I had my first sexual experience. The event took place in one of Lucy's birthday presents, a pup tent, which she had abandoned in favor of a large cardboard box shed by our new refrigerator. One particularly dull afternoon, I was sitting in it on my wicker chair pretending to be Chester Morris during the leaner years of his career when Sarah Clarke, sixteen, black hair and hazel eyes, opened the flap and peered in.

"Well, hello there, Burton," she said seductively, wearing a candy-cane-striped sunsuit.

As a child, Sarah had been both pious and prim. In the heat of August she would walk about the neighborhood wearing a fussy velvet dress and white gloves and dangling a pink plastic pocketbook from her wrist while worrying about the salvation of her Jewish playmates. With the pretext of catching tadpoles, Sarah would lure her unsuspecting friends down to a nearby polluted lake, get them into a stranglehold, and baptize them amidst the upturned bellies of fish that had succumbed to an overdose of industrial chemicals. One day she was overzealous and almost succeeded in drowning Rachel Kleinsman. After washing the algae out of her daughter's hair, Mrs. Kleinsman telephoned Mrs. Clarke.

The punishment Sarah subsequently endured precipitated a meta-morphosis.

"What a nice sleeping bag," she cooed, batting her blue-eyeshadowed eyes. "Think we can both fit in it?"

Of late, she had begun a crusade personally to instruct all the neighborhood boys in the facts of life. I had been anticipating her pedagogical presence for some time now with sociological interest, so I bid her enter.

She unbuttoned her blouse and we slid into the sleeping bag together.

"Put your hands on my breast," she said. I did so. "Mmmmm. That's good. How is it for you?"

"Okay," I replied, shrugging.

"Now put your other hand there."

"Here?"

"Lower."

"Here?"

"Lower."

"Here!" It was moist.

"Mmmm. That's good. How is it for you?"

"Okay," I said, surprised at not feeling a thing.

"All right, now put this hand here. Move over on the other side and rub me there. Now, stick your tongue in there . . . no, *there,*" she said, choreographing our movements with the precision of Agnes DeMille. *"Mmmm.* That's *good.* How is it for you?"

I thought a moment. "Not quite as appetizing as I'd hoped."

"Maybe you're just nervous," Sarah said. "This is your first time, right?"

I nodded.

Interested in finding a skilled partner to share her convenient canvas motel room, Sarah proposed we get someone to join us. "Who lives next door?" she asked.

"Tommy Grahame."

"He'll do," she said, rebuttoning her sunsuit.

She must have yanked Tommy out of the deep end of his swimming pool because he arrived dripping in a pair of dark blue racer trunks.

"Hello, Burton," he said. His boyish tanned musculature rippled as he dried himself off.

"Come on! Come on!" Sarah said, tugging at him. "It's getting late. My mother's going to call me home for dinner soon."

Tommy Grahame was sixteen and had lived in Brooklyn most of his life. His father had been a poor delicatessen owner until he bought an indoor shooting range on Utica Avenue which he stocked with rifles and pistols. He made a fortune from the repressed hostilities of local welfare recipients. Tommy, because of the tempestuousness of his environment and the snare of his chestnut-haired good looks, had lost his virginity at eleven. "Do you mind us doing this?" he asked politely.

"No," I replied, sitting down. "Do you mind me watching?"

"Naw," he said.

"He could use a lesson," Sarah added. "Come on!"

Tommy got into the sleeping bag and took off his bathing suit. Sarah hopped around the tent on one leg trying to extricate an ankle sock. As I took a seat in the corner to take notes, I heard Mrs. Clarke scream from down the street. *"Sarah!"*

Sarah froze.

"Sar-ahhhh!"

"Oh, shit!" Sarrah cursed.

Din-nerr! Sar-ahhhh! Ham-burrgs!"

She redressed hurriedly. "I'll see you boys later," she said, taking a moment to pinch Tommy's cheek, then ran out of the tent.

"Com-ing, maaaa!"

Tommy and I laughed.

"God, she wants it bad," he said. He looked lepidopterous with half his naked tan frame sticking out of the thermal cocoon.

I expected him to slip his trunks on and leave after that, but he didn't. He just lay there smiling. We looked at each other for a while. I felt . . . anxious. Neither of us spoke.

"So!" I finally said, slapping my thighs, "*Captains Courageous* is on tonight."

"Is it?" he asked.

"Yeah . . ." I mumbled, watching him squeeze one of his rubicund nipples.

Uncomfortably hot, I stood up. The tent was terribly stuffy.

Tommy sat up. Tributaries of perspiration followed a path down to the pool of ripples shielding his stomach.

"Well, she's gone," he said.

"Yes, she's gone." Not quite knowing why, I walked over to the sleeping bag and crouched down.

He leaned back and put his hands behind his head. I felt . . . more anxious.

After a long silence he said, "Want to?" and I said, "Yes."

It was as simple as that. The sex was more affectionate than passionate, more superficial than intricate, yet it was important because it made clear to me exactly what I was, sexually, at least. I was . . . surprised.

It took less than two days of thinking to come to the conclusion that my sexuality didn't matter; it just was.

I cannot understand why being attracted to your own sex creates such a hubbub among those not so inclined. Physically, two arms, two legs, etc. are involved. A genital difference here, a gland difference there. What's the fuss?

There are, of course, heterosexuals who contend that propagation is the natural order of things. Admittedly, reproduction is not an *insignificant* pastime, but reproducing something that, progressively, cannot control its saliva manufacture, then demands its own apartment with Oriental rugs and subsidy, then forces its parents to live in a retirement village in another hemisphere does not strike me as being terribly natural.

Moreoever, sexual orientation is only one aspect of homosexuality, which is really a personality, a sensitivity. A spirit. It cannot be ignored like a pimple or repressed like the urge to eat a chocolate-covered cherry; it cannot be isolated from one's personality. It is an inexorable part of what makes one an individual.

Soon after the Tommy Grahame incident, my father decided to give me a lesson in the facts of life. Although it was difficult to tell the man about my sexual self-discovery with him busily illustrating the reproductive process with floral diagrams and hypothetical bees, I did anyway. I must say, he and my mother got used to the idea rather quickly. We talked for three hours. Dispelled myths. And ate cheesecake.

My family lived in upper-middle class comfort just outside of Oyster Bay in a cove of houses obscured from each other by a pine woods and connected by a long paved path which wound down to the main road. From my bedroom, I could just see the swimming pool behind Tommy Grahame's house.

The summer before I was to be a sophomore in high school, Gingold Secondary, Tommy Grahame's father franchised his shooting range and was able to parlay the bitterness of the five boroughs into a townhouse on Sutton Place. For several weeks, all sorts of people came to look at their house. At one point, the real estate agent told my father that an astronaut and his wife had bought it, but in the end a Mrs. DeMarco and her son did. I wondered how old he was. We gave them a week to unpack, then my mother, carrying an old-fashioned picnic basket covered with a checkered cloth, and I walked down our driveway and along the paved path to welcome them to the neighborhood.

When we rang the bell, a woman of about fifty, with a Claudette Colbert hairdo that was just beginning to gray and saucer-shaped earrings made of mother-of-pearl, answered the door. My mother introduced us—she had met Mrs. DeMarco briefly before—and, removing the sagging towel, gave Mrs. DeMarco a warm peach pie and some advice about the neighborhood.

"Has anyone told you the best place to buy fresh fish?"

While she passed judgment on a number of local entrepreneurs, I peered through the screen door into the dimness beyond. I could discern a carpeted stair directly ahead and, against its casing, a secretary.

On top of that stood a braced picture frame facing the other direction; I presumed this to be a picture of the dead husband the real estate agent had told my father about. Craning my neck slightly, I managed to see half the dining room, still filled only with boxes and corrugated cylinders.

"*Whatever* you do, Angela, *don't* go into Morcross's Dress Shoppe," my mother continued, ascending to Mrs. DeMarco's step.

My eyes drifted up the stairs. The landing was flooded with light from four windows. To my surprise, sitting at the top, cross-legged and chin resting on fist, was the son. A boy about my age, with nothing on but white underwear and a navy blue baseball cap. Although I couldn't see too clearly, he looked depressed silhouetted against the light. When he saw that I saw him, he got up and walked down the hall. Shy, I thought. I tried to pick up the threads of the conversation.

"I find if you put just a *little* ammonia in a bowl, then add—"

Forget that. I looked up again. The diaphanous white curtains hanging from just below the ceiling gently loomed out with the breeze from the windows. One panel had caught on a box that was spilling over with shoes and rubber boots. Only a few feet of a hallway that must have led to the bedrooms was visible. A white wicker flower box on legs was leaning empty against the wall.

I shrugged and turned around. The yard was in need of mowing. Yellow and white puffy dandelion heads jutted out above the shaggy grass; a hardier type of weed was encroaching on the walkway. It seemed odd, not seeing the Grahames' Chris Craft on supports or Tommy's cheap archery set at the end of the property.

Suddenly I heard someone bound down the stairs. Whirling around, I squinted through the screen again.

"Ma—"

The door was pushed open by a swarthy boy wearing a baseball cap and a pair of dressy gray trousers. Panning upward, I noticed he was taller than I and well muscled. His Rory Calhoun frame culminated in a face with the features of Tony Curtis: a thick tangle of black hair, Mediterranean blue eyes, voluptuous lips. Overwhelmed by what was supposed to have been a plain-looking astronaut's wife, I stepped backwards and almost fell off the porch.

"Ma, you said you'd find the shorts for me."

My mother stopped her diatribe on an overpriced local hardware store.

"Roman, I was talking to our new neighbors," Mrs. DeMarco chastised gently.

"But, ma, I can't do anything in these," he said in a deep voice, pulling the gabardine material away from his legs. "It's sticky."

I was immediately empathetic and looked at his mother impatiently.

"All right, all right." Turning to my mother, Mrs. DeMarco explained, "We're still getting organized here. Mrs. Raider, this is my boy Roman."

His face burst into a radiant smile. A muscle vibrated along the trough of his ribcage as he shook my mother's hand. I bit off a fingernail. "How do you do?" he asked her with the casualness of one who had long ago assumed good manners.

"Nice to meet you, Roman," my mother said.

"And this is Burton," Mrs. DeMarco added with a gesture.

We clasped hands. A clump of hair tumbled down over his forehead.

"Hello," I squeaked.

"Hi," he said, grinning.

It was like meeting a movie star in person, but my joy was short lived. While I wiped perspiration beads from my forehead, his mother told him where to find his shorts. I resumed breathing as he disappeared inside the house.

All About Eve, one of my favorites, was on later that day, but, try as I might, I couldn't get our new neighbors out of my mind. I wanted Roman and me to be friends. No. Brothers. Well, maybe best friends. From the bedroom window, I looked past the pine woods to the swimming pool in the DeMarcos' backyard.

Some men came one day to clean and fill the pool; thereafter in the mornings Roman would come out wearing his red swim suit to vacuum the submerged floor. I would wait for him to carry the stainless-steel device out of the shed and then let the video Mona Freeman or Anna May Wong dissolve to black before I scrambled through the woods between our houses. Hanging on the fence, I would talk to him, wondering if somehow my parents could adopt him.

At first, I had him all to myself, but then the neighborhood riffraff moved in.

"Come on, Ro! Let's play some ball!"

"You too, Burton," Roman would say, but since learning how to punt was quite out of the question at this late date, I'd wave good-bye and walk through the trees back to my house.

Though he looked more mature than I, Roman entered his sophomore year at Gingold Secondary with me that fall. The nitwits of Gingold took to him immediately. He began to pal around with Sparks Compton, Bob Monroe, whose father was the leading authority on financial investment on the East Coast and who had written a best-seller called *Invest with Success,* and Howard Joslyn. They sat with him at lunch, walked with him in the halls. The only time I was able to talk to him alone was when we waited for the school bus together.

Gym bag and books in hand, I would walk through the chaos of the English garden my mother tended in the backyard and shuffle down the incline of the driveway to the paved path. Mailboxes grew along it like metallic flowers arched at different angles toward the sun. Passing the garage of our neighbor Mrs. Ambrose, I would instinctively search the horizon for a sign of her German shepherd, Twinkles. A canine reject from the United States Army, he had been purchased as a watchdog by Mrs. Ambrose for next to nothing. Unfortunately, his aborted training cost the rest of the neighborhood plenty.

Twinkles terrorized small children as they disembarked from the grammar-school bus, leaving the road strewn with lunch boxes. He also gave Mrs. Constantinople's chihuahua a coronary and consumed almost every cat within a half-mile radius. Whenever confronted by irate neighbors, Mrs. Ambrose listened with arms akimbo; pleased by the aggressive streak in her watchdog, she would reply simply, "Prove it."

Confirmation was forthcoming when one day she was in the garage waiting for the spin dry cycle of her washing machine to complete itself. Without warning, Twinkles growled lowly and leapt for her throat. A quick thinker, Mrs. Ambrose was able to beat the dog senseless with a jumbo-sized box of Tide. Thereafter, he confined his reign of terror to the rest of the neighborhood, with increased gusto.

I passed the abandoned tennis courts which marked the halfway point to the bus stop; Lucy loved playing with daddy on their clay surfaces. In contrast to me, Lucy always relished the outdoors.

As a child, she ran, jumped and laughed with almost imbecilic intensity. My parents were thrilled that they had managed to produce a Rockwellesque type of child the second time around and they would stand by the kitchen window, tears welling up in their eyes, watching Lucy play.

"Look, darling," my mother would say, squeezing my father's hand, "she's got grass stains."

My trying to coax Lucy indoors so that I could teach her the proper way to lift her fingers to summon a waiter was so much whistling in the dark.

The last hundred yards of the path sloped downward to the telephone pole on the main road which marked the bus stop. Roman usually got there before me. Though I am not the sort of person who has difficulty engaging even the dullest relative in conversation, I found myself groping for subjects to broach with Roman. We had gone through family backgrounds at poolside—his father had drowned when he was three years old—and we criticized Gingold and its teaching staff early in the marking period. Since Roman's interests tended to be athletic, I assumed that recounting the joy I had derived from Mary Boland's performances would produce little in the way of conversational mileage. Roman wasn't a vociferous sort to begin with. And I have to admit that any determination I might have had at the top of the paved path to dazzle Roman with topical insights and witty anecdotes usually turned into a self-conscious report of Twinkles's latest atrocity at the bottom.

By October of our sophomore year, still determined to have our brief encounters evolve into a friendship, I put aside my pride and approached the bus stop one morning prepared. I could see Roman standing there. Putting down my gym bag and books, I quickly tucked in my shirt again. The night before I had given up watching a perfectly good movie starring Virginia Field and Warner Oland, *Charlie Chan in Monte Carlo,* to watch a baseball game and jot down information from the sports pages of the *Daily News.*

I unfolded a piece of notebook paper. The Yankees had won 4 to 3 against St. Louis. Willie Mays lined a single to right to score somebody else. The Cardinals had been held to one run for seven innings by a rookie who entered the game with a 10.13 ERA. I closed my eyes and repeated the information. Folding the paper and putting it back in my pocket, I looked at Roman's manly figure in the distance and took a deep breath. With an air of confidence that comes only from knowing who has the best batting average in the national league, I approached the bus stop.

"Hi, Roman," I said heartily.

"How're you doing," he replied.

Barely able to contain my excitement, I put down my gym bag and books and cleared my throat. Roman was squinting at the road looking for the bus. I began, "That Willie is really something, huh?"

Shading his eyes, he replied, "Willie?"

"Willie Mays! He was really something in the game last night. You saw it, of course."

"Nope," he replied and turned to look down the road again.

I gulped. "Well . . . er . . . what did you do?"

"I went for a drive. You got any gum?"

"No," I said, trying to think of a way to make a graceful transition to what I knew about earned-run averages. I looked nervously down the road. The rickety yellow school bus rounded the corner. I tried to assemble the fragments about the game that hadn't flown out of my head into a cohesive statement. The gears of the bus roared as it came down the road. Come on, come on, I said to myself, say *something*.

The bus came to a screeching halt in front of us.

In desperation I started to blurt out something about Twinkles.

"Watch your step!" the busdriver yelled, opening the door with a thump.

"What?" Roman asked as we ascended.

"Nothing," I replied. I followed him up the steps and the door closed behind us. The din of small talk filled the crowded bus. The air smelled of perfume and astringent.

"Hey, Roman!" I could see Sparks Compton waving to him. He had saved a seat in the back.

"See you later, Burton," Roman said, smiling.

"Yeah," I replied. So much for taking an interest in other people's perversions.

The bus was very crowded. I had two choices. I could either sit next to Leonard "Rubber Legs" Prousse, an accomplished clarinetist and chronic ankle scratcher, or Delilah Lutz, the class clairvoyant.

I chose Delilah, staring out the window with her legs drawn up to her chin. Though most people ridiculed her, it was obvious that she had a talent for communicating with some other dimension. She had once gone into a trance during home economics class. When the room emptied at the end of the period, she was left standing at a counter, eyes rolled to the back of her head, hands submerged in cake batter. A typical example of the narrow-mindedness of the school administration, she was given detention.

I had tried to get her to talk about her unusual perceptions, but she was reticent. Delilah was a terribly frail girl and I was sure that she had learned, more than anything else in high school, not to trust people. I knew something of what she faced. Perhaps the spirits of her netherworld were the counterparts to my black-and-white movie companions. Unfortunately, she brushed aside my platonic overtures.

The bus pulled up to school and I pulled my gym bag and books down from the overhead rack.

"Hey, Raider!"

I cringed and pretended not to have heard. Sparks Compton yelled that he wanted the answers to geometry homework. I had never bothered to hide my contempt for this loathsome creep, nor he his scorn for me—except, of course, when he could benefit from my knowledge of geometric progressions and sentence diagramming. I hoisted the bag onto my shoulder and inched my way to the front of the bus with the rest of the crowd.

"Hey, Raider! Wait up!" He cornered me outside the front door of school. Roman was with him. "Lemme see the answer you got to the fourth one in geometry," he said.

"Drop dead," I replied.

"Leave him alone," Roman said, grabbing his shoulder.

"Come on, Raider. I know you got it. Mr. Koenig said if I don't start handing in the homework I won't pass no matter how good I do on the final. Come on, pal. Gimme a break."

Sparks reminded me of Bud Abbott. Physically, he was tall and wiry, attractive in a seedy sort of way; his joie de vivre seemed to stem from tormenting others. He had acquired his nickname after burning down a house in his youth but, as with Twinkles, no one was able to prove anything. There was a staccato quality to him, a nervousness, as if he were always prepared to make a fast getaway. Needless to say, he was very popular in school.

"Piss off!" I said, somewhat envious of his proximity to Roman.

Roman laughed.

Sparks's eyes narrowed. "Shut up!" he spat. He ripped the gym bag out of my hands and threw it a few yards away. "Come on, let's go!" he said to Roman.

I pushed my way past them to pick up the bag. Sparks and I had gone to school together from kindergarten. In second grade I saw him push Delilah Lutz down a flight of stairs and I had detested him ever since.

He bothered everyone. My turn came during drawing period; Sparks decided it would be great fun to spill some red fingerpaints down my back. I was wearing a white silk shirt. While Miss Finklestein stood in disbelief, I went to the corner of the classroom, picked up one of those sticks tipped with a plastic horse's head, and knocked him cold. An unforgiving sort, he had tormented me ever since.

Now, as I was bending over, an arm came from behind and grabbed the handles of my gym bag.

"He shouldn't have done that," Roman said. "You know how he is." He handed it to me and smiled.

"Thanks," I said. The same fraternal feeling that welled up inside me when we had met on his doorstep reasserted itself.

Roman winked, then turned to catch up with Sparks.

Standing on a bus stop at the crack of dawn wasn't the only time I found myself close to Roman, though it was the only time we had any privacy. We shared a class during sophomore year.

"Get dressed, you idiots!"

Gym. The Gingold computer, to make matters worse, put me in Mr. Steele's class.

"Hut! Hut! Hut!"

Mr. Steele gave credence to my idea that when doctors pronounce psychotics incurable they release them and get them employed as gym teachers.

"Let's go! Let's go!"

Mr. Steele trained us as if the combined armed forces of the United States had just been defeated and the security of the Western Hemisphere depended on sixth-period gym class.

"Big day! Big day!"

He was a hulking figure of vanquished pro football dreams. His arms were lengthy; he was quite capable of scratching his shins without compromising his posture. If Charles Darwin had lived to see Mr. Steele, he would have said, *"Now* do you believe me?"

My indifference to physical activity had not changed over the years. I had spent the time developing not my solar plexus, but a catalogue of excuses:

MOURNING: "My great-grandmother died last night. I can't take gym."

CATASTROPHE: "My house burned down last night. I can't take gym."

SCANDAL: "I found out I'm illegitimate last night. I can't take gym."

It was especially important for me to have these excuses accepted this term: it was embarrassing to have Roman see me at my worst. Unfortunately, Mr. Steele was impervious to my heartrending fictions.

"Stop that limping, Raider, and get dressed!" He didn't have much patience. People lacking foreheads seldom do.

Opening my combination lock, I would mumble Hail Marys (I had been raised a Catholic) to myself in the hope that I might get through another fifty minutes of this without incident.

"Let's go! Let's go!"

Whistle in mouth, Mr. Steele would wave everyone into the gymnasium where he would lead us in calisthenics.

"Jumping jacks! Ready! One, two, three—"

The class would do five minutes of exercises, then line up to choose sides.

"DeMarco, pick!"

Roman was always one of the captains. He'd stride to the front of the gym and stand on a red foul line, his muscles straining his overwashed uniform.

Roman's first choice was always Sparks Compton; his last, usually me.

"Okay! Move out!" Mr. Steele always yelled, as if we were about to storm a beach.

One particularly horrid day during baseball season, I took my usual position in the outlying region of right field. Cautiously scanning the horizon for any sign of a left-handed batter, I also looked on the ground for quarters and communed with bumblebees. I tensed when Howard Joslyn, one of Roman's friends and a left-handed powerhouse, got up to the plate. But he bunted and I was able to uproot dandelions undisturbed.

Toward the end of the class period, the score was tied five all. The other team was up to bat with two outs and a man on third. Judging from the amount of whoops, hollers, and spitting, I realized that both teams were pressing hard for victory. I sighed and looked to see if the girls' gym class had started to go in yet; they had just broken up their more civilized game. I was watching them sling field hockey sticks over their shoulders when the crack of a bat echoed through the infield. I barely heard it.

"Raider!" someone screamed.

I turned in time to see the softball rise in an airy crescendo above my head. This one's got my name on it, I thought to myself. The blood drained from my knees as the ball reached its apogee and began to descend. I quickly picked up my glove from the ground. Everyone was yelling. *"Get it! Get it!"*

I could hear Roman shouting from the pitcher's mound. Oh, please let me catch this, I prayed, reaching out to the sky and closing my eyes.

"Go, Raider, go!"

As I stood there straining toward the heavens, the ball sailed over the tip of the glove and landed behind me with a thud, destroying an anthill.

"Raider!"

The opponent on third base ran home. Sparks Compton angrily threw down his glove. I was mortified. I picked up the ball and threw it, underhanded, to the first baseman, but the outcome became academic when Mr. Steele blew his whistle.

"Head in!"

I looked among the scurrying players in the infield for Roman. He was helping Mr. Steele put the bats and balls into a canvas gunnysack. Dejected, I turned and walked toward the gym.

"Nice going, Raider," my teammates said, jogging by and sealing their fate—they wouldn't get any homework answers from me for the next two years. I waved them away, not caring what they thought.

Halfway in, someone clapped me on the shoulder. It was Sparks.

"Can't you even catch a *ball*, Raider?" he said, seething. "Shit."

"Drop dead," I said, and kept walking.

He grabbed my shoulder and spun me around. "Say that again," he said, throwing down his glove.

I cleared my throat. "Drop . . . dead!"

"Come on, Raider," he said, breaking into a show of fancy footwork. He poked me in the stomach with his fist. Then my face. "Come on, Raider," he said, punching my stomach a little harder.

Rejecting pacifism as a course of action, I dropped my glove and prepared to be reduced to a tartarean puddle.

"Okay, Raider. Come at me. Come on." He bounced on the balls of his feet, continuing to throw jabs. I raised my fists in a pose I had seen Errol Flynn strike in *Gentleman Jim*.

"All right, break it up," a stern voice said a short distance away. It was Roman.

"Come *on*, Raider," Sparks continued.

"Cut it out!" Roman said, coming up to us.

I dropped my arms, trying not to show my tremendous relief.

"But Jesus, Roman. He lost us the game," Sparks complained.

"I said, leave him alone." Roman stopped and dropped the sack of equipment to the ground. Sparks looked at him.

"Shit," he said. "But he lost us the *game.*"

"Forget it," Roman said.

Sparks looked at me, then Roman. Frustrated, he picked up his glove and headed in. "Shit," he said.

"Come on," Roman said to me. We walked silently back to the gym.

Despite a summer of novenas, I was again put in gym class with Roman and Mr. Steele during junior year.

Senior year I got a break, sort of. I wasn't put in Roman's gym class.

But then I wasn't put in any of his classes. I rarely saw him in the halls—it was not through any lack of neck craning on my part. When I did catch sight of him ambling along, he was usually with Sparks, Bob Monroe or Howard Joslyn. At the beginning of October, a silver-gray used Volvo appeared in his driveway so we no longer had even our encounters at the bus stop.

I don't think anyone ever gets over an unrequited crush, especially the first one, until there is some sort of retaliation. Whether bad or good. Night after night during that last year, I stared at Jennifer Jones and Claire Trevor and Billy Gilbert and Franklin Pangborn, wishing I could be with Roman. Just once I would have liked to ask him over to my house for dinner or out to a movie, but I was afraid I might embarrass him—if he sensed my affection, he might have shunned me altogether. So I sat in my room, letting the magnificent Irene Dunne and the smarmy, tough Jack Carson dispel my malaise.

One day in mid-October, I seized an opportunity. I had been summoned to the Guidance Office. It was a rule that all students had to talk to their counselors at least once a year. Seniors twice. I hated sitting in Mr. Perdy's cheese box of an office, listening to him wheeze, suck on his dentures and suggest colleges. I felt that anyone who netted $182.76 per week at the age of fifty-seven was in no position to suggest career plans. As I sat dreading the pointless encounter in the waiting alcove of his office, Mr. Perdy's door opened and Roman came out.

"Thanks, Mr. Perdy," he said. He scratched his side.

I was thrilled at the coincidence.

Mr. Perdy emerged halfway. "Good luck, Roman," he said benedictorily. Peering over his gray safety reading glasses and Roman's shoulder, he said to me, "I'll be with you in a moment." His sentences were always accompanied by a hollow whistling sound as air found its way under his upper plate. He retreated into his office.

Roman was holding college bulletins and applications in his hand. "Hi, Burton," he said, smiling and sitting down next to me to put his bundle in order.

"Hi, Roman," I said, uncrossing my legs. "Applying to a lot of schools?" I asked, slightly anxious.

"Yeah. You?"

"Two in Massachusetts and one in Pennsylvania," I said. Tufts, Harvard and Penn, to be precise.

"Yeah, well, *you* don't have to worry about getting in anywhere."

"You shouldn't either," I replied, braced by the mellifluousness of what was shaping up to be our most fascinating conversation to date.

"Aw. I'm not so sure."

"What do you mean?"

"Well, Perdy in there thinks that I don't have enough activities to put on my application." He had said so last spring.

"You do, though." I gestured toward the varsity letter on his sweater.

"Yeah, but that's the wrong kind of stuff. That's good if you want an athletic scholarship or something. Perdy thinks I should talk to the head of the English Department about getting into the big Shakespeare thing they have before Christmas. Then maybe the musical in the spring." He brushed back a clump of his black hair.

The synapses of my brain began to sparkle with an idea. "Oh, he does?" I asked eagerly.

"I don't want to be an actor, you know. It's to get on the crew. I'm applying to film schools and—"

"Film schools!" I blurted, leaning forward like a piqued Phil Silvers.

"Yeah, but for the technical part, you know? My Uncle Hyam said he'd help me get into a union afterwards. He works in TV as a writer."

Mr. Perdy's head popped through the open door. "You can come in now, Burton."

I closed my eyes and bit the side of my cheek. "A writer, you say?" I prompted encouragingly.

"Yeah, uh—"

Mr. Perdy interrupted again. "Roman, I think the head of the English Department is in the teachers' conference room now. Why don't you see if you can talk to him." Damn him anyway.

"Right," Roman said, gathering up his materials.

"Burton?" Mr. Perdy stood at one side of the open doorway, waiting to admit me.

"I'll see you, Roman?" I said.

"Sure," he replied and left.

I turned a cold eye on Mr. Perdy and fumed silently in his office while he whistlingly talked about Ivy League schools. I ignored him, shook his hand, and left.

Then I headed for the teachers' conference room. The head of the English Department, Irving Jerome, was inside, playing cards with a colleague.

"Look," I said, "I want to direct the Shakespeare Plays Festival [five Shakespeare plays over the course of five evenings] again this year." He and I were friends. The many years I had spent watching old movies on television had by osmosis given me a feeling for staging, dialogue and timing, and had inspired me to get involved with Gingold's theatrical productions during my freshman and sophomore years. I had played Sebastian in *Twelfth Night* when I was a freshman and almost fell backwards into the scenery when my father popped a flashcube at the foot of the stage, trying to capture my entrance for posterity. The musical at the end of that year was *Camelot*. Since I couldn't sing, I was put in charge of props. I discovered I had a knack for organization. More importantly, I got the opportunity to watch the student director at work while I made papier mâché doublets at my workbench in the wings. I had talked to the head of the English Department about directing myself; it was his job both to pick and to supervise the student director. He let me assist the student director the following winter for the Shakespeare Plays Festival, and was so impressed with what he called my "intuitive sense of the boards" that he let me direct *As You Like It* in the festival by myself.

At the end of my junior year, I did the big musical, *Bye, Bye Birdie*. High school productions being what they are, it became a tedious experience toward the end. Confrontations with small-town temperaments and talents made me swear I'd never do another show—here, anyway.

"So what made you change your mind?" Mr. Jerome asked, not looking up from his game.

"I don't know," I replied. "Masochism, I guess."

"Any eights?" his opponent asked.

"So how about it?" I inquired eagerly.

"Nobody else wants it, so I guess it's yours. No eights! Go fish!"

I walked down the hall doing a little Cecil Kellaway jig every few yards. With the Shakespeare Plays Festival as my excuse, I could not only talk to Roman as much as I liked without fearing suspicion, but I would also have something at hand to talk about.

Auditions for female leads began two weeks later.

"Come on! Next!" I yelled, after three wooden auditions.

A member of the future nurses' club, Pam Wilson, took several baby steps to center stage, script in hand. She was reading for the part of Lady Macbeth, wearing a tight orange sweater and a poorly constructed, equally constricting red skirt. Her boyfriend, squatty Howard Joslyn, who had excused himself from math on a urological pretext to watch, whistled from the back of the auditorium.

"Oh, you!" she giggled, covering her breasts with the paperback version of the tragedy. A beautiful, not bright, girl, she nonetheless did surprisingly well in school. Male teachers were only too eager to extend the due dates of her term papers or tutor her in the uses of the Cartesian Plane after hours. Outside of Gingold Secondary, she was always being asked by veterans to lead local parades or by newspapermen to be photographed at the openings of new supermarkets, caressing a cantaloupe. She was Howard Joslyn's great love; though his simean form made him look incapable of human feeling, Howard had fallen in love with her in the fourth grade. He guarded her jealously, like an antique collector with only one sideboard. It was true that he had beaten up one of her tutors and afterwards, slapped her into a stupor, but by all accounts, she adored him.

"Could you read the lines marked in red please?" I asked politely.

A disciple of the Kim Novak school of acting, Pam cleared her throat and squinted at the page. "Out damned spot," she said in monotones, and smiled at Howard triumphantly.

"With *gestures,* please," I said, digging my fingernails into my palm.

She read the line again. This time she rubbed the sleeve of her blouse, suggesting that Lady Macbeth, rather than walking the halls of madness trying to remove the sanguine hallucinations of guilt, had instead been careless in drinking her morning coffee.

"How was that?" she asked brightly.

I slapped my hand against my forehead like Edgar Kennedy.

Male lead auditions were just as pathetic.

Leonard "Rubber Legs" Prousse read for the part of the petulant Tybalt in *Romeo and Juliet*. The talent was worse and worse each year and *this* year we had next year's crowd.

"What, drawn, and talk of peace! I hate the word, as I hate hell, all Montagues, and thee."

As he called for the blood of the Montagues, I thought of Leonard's biology class fainting spells.

"Stop scratching your ankles, Leonard!" I yelled. He self-consciously did so, but by the end of his audition was deep into a fit of eyelid pulling.

Aggravation notwithstanding, my decision to get involved again with the Shakespeare Plays Festival paid off. Though many of our conversations had to be shouted between the house and the lighting booth, Roman and I did become more friendly. Over a can of soda, we would discuss lighting cues; in the Band Room I would make him roar over my impression of a pretentious would-be actress in *Macbeth*. If we finished at the same time, he would give me a lift home in his Volvo. My excitement was ruined only when Sparks Compton waited around and drove back with us a few times. He didn't bother to hide his irritation over my presence and grew livid if Roman and I talked about the festival or anything else in which he wasn't interested.

"Will you two shut up about that horseshit!"

It was obvious—perhaps even to Roman—that he was fiercely jealous, though no one would have dared say so. It got to the point toward the end of rehearsals that Sparks would immediately push me into the back seat and would glare at me if I attempted to speak at all on the way home.

The Shakespeare Plays Festival was a tactical, if not an artistic, success. After it was over, things went pretty much back to the way they had been between Roman and me. But the rapport that had been established gave me the confidence I needed to do what I did next.

One Friday night when there were no movies on television and I was especially depressed, my aunt Hedy swooped down on her way to a group encounter session in Manhattan to deposit her two daughters at my house. She would be fondling the nipples and toes of strangers for forty-eight hours with her husband, so she wanted to make sure her offspring were properly fed and billeted.

My cousins were named Laura and Marlene. Laura was attractive, but rather silly; she had contracted hypoglycemia at a very early age and was prohibited from eating carbohydrates. Marlene was incapable of eating much else. Both were my age and vulgar. When they arrived, we went into the living room. My mother excused herself to tend to dinner. My father, Lucy and I stayed to chat.

"So how have you been, Marlene?" my father asked as she waddled to a chair.

"Fine," she said, diving into a nearby bowl of cashews.

Both girls wore brightly printed shifts. Their hair was teased as was the fashion; their lipstick was a currently popular white color.

"How do you like high school?" he asked.

She interrupted her stentorian chewing to warble, "Ifs, ukaw."

"How about you, Laura?"

"I don't know," she said, "it's hard. I'd really like to quit and get a job but my father won't let me."

"What would you do?" he asked.

"I haven't decided yet," she said, but added, "It's a toss-up between a Peace Corps volunteer and an airline stewardess." She leaned toward the airline stewardess.

Marlene grew tired of reaching forward to get at the cashews so she picked up the bowl from the coffee table and cradled it in her lap. Laura talked about stewardess school. As her fears of air pockets surfaced and the nuts disappeared, I thought how depressing my life was.

My depression did not lift at the dinner table. Laura talked about airplane safety statistics. The velocity with which Marlene brought fork to mouth threatened to blow out the centerpiece candles. Laura eyed the bib and tucker I was wearing and nudged her sister. They giggled. I threw down my napkin before dessert and retired to my room. I fell asleep watching the incomparable Eve Arden in *The Lady Wants Mink.*

The next morning, as I unhappily surveyed Roman unbolting the pool shed, I got an idea. I cantered across the pine woods and pulled myself up onto the fence. "Morning, Roman."

"Hi, Burton," he said, putting down the pole and coming over.

I explained the situation. "I've got these two girl cousins visiting. They're here for the weekend and my mother wants me to take them to the movies but I feel funny going with two girls alone. Do you think that maybe you could—"

"Sure," he said. "I'll double date."

My heart did a double lutz. "You get the better of the two and of course I'll pay for everything!" I was rapturous.

"Fine," he said.

"But we have to take your car. I don't drive, you know."

"No problem."

Roman went out with one girl at Gingold for quite a while but he had broken it off. Through high school, he went out with several others, but none for very long.

"See you tonight then, around seven," I said.

"Right," he said, returning to his suctional work.

I danced back through the woods to my house. Imagine enjoying an evening with my cousins!

At seven, he rang the doorbell. When I introduced Laura, she said hello and turned to her sister—eyes wide. They excused themselves for a last application of hairspray and ran up the stairs and loudly squealed over Laura's good fortune.

"I think they like you," I said, putting my fingers in my ears.

I wanted to go see *The Sound of Music* but was outvoted. We got into

Roman's Volvo and headed for *Easy Rider*. There was no way to change the seating arrangements in the car—Laura sat in front with Roman; Marlene in back with me—but at the theater, I pushed Marlene into the row of seats first so that Roman and I could sit together between them. Laura and Marlene waved to each other as we settled into our seats.

I asked Roman if he had heard anything about the movie. He described an especially gruesome scene involving shotguns and a pickup truck, which Sparks had enjoyed, while he took his navy sweater off; he leaned his shoulder against me while pulling off a stubborn sleeve. Tucking the sweater next to his leg, Roman settled back. His large frame expanded against the back and his arm pressed warmly against mine.

"Did you ever see *Dawn Patrol?*" I asked, pulling my collar away from my neck to let out some steam.

"Is that the one with that guy . . . uh . . . Basil something?"

"Rathbone," I said, turning toward him a bit more. "And David Niven. They play World War One pilots—"

"Yes!" Roman exclaimed. "They're all pals on the front lines. Oh, yeah. What a great movie! Remember the part when—"

He described, in detail, a party scene in which a presumed-dead David Niven appears. Thank you, I thought, looking toward heaven.

"Or how about when they crash!" I said.

"Yeah!" Roman said, becoming more and more animated. "And Erroll Flynn comes down and rescues him just when the Germans"—I felt a tapping on my shoulder but continued listening—"and David Niven's little brother drops in with only about an hour's worth of flying lessons and—"

"Burton!" Marlene said, shaking my arm.

I sighed. "Yes, Marlene?"

"Burton, could you get me some popcorn, please?"

"I got you some on the way in."

"But I finished it."

"Come on, Marlene," I said. "You couldn't have finished all that so quickly." The movie hadn't started yet. She thrust the empty bucket in front of me and shook the unpopped kernels in the bottom.

"And a Mars bar," she said.

I stomped up the aisle to the refreshment stand. The tuxedoed cashier was busy arranging Baby Ruths in the display case. "Sir, could you break your train of thought for a moment to get me a large popcorn, Coke, and Mars bar please?"

"One minute," he said, licking his lips.

I stood there drumming the counter while he put the Baby Ruths in neat, straight columns. After a few minutes I came to admire his patience and was pleased to note that society was becoming more successful at finding places for the mentally retarded. "All right, sir, what'll it be?" he asked.

With a Coke in one hand, popcorn in the other, and the Mars bar hanging from my teeth, I sidestepped along a row of knees to my place next to Marlene. The movie was just starting. Marlene was waiting with arms outstretched and mouth ajar.

"Thanks!" she said, tossing a kernel in the air and catching it in her mouth.

I sat back in my chair. Roman was listening to Laura talk about pressurized cabins. The momentum of our conversation had been lost for the moment so I took the opportunity to look about the theater. The teenagers around us kissed and joked and pawed each other. They took it all for granted.

"You ever go to Europe?" Roman asked.

I started out of my reverie. "What?"

He leaned closer. "Did you ever go to Europe?"

"No," I said. "You?"

"Nope. I'd like to, though. I'd like to go to France."

"Why there?"

"I've seen pictures of it. It's beautiful. The hills and the small towns in the provinces."

As he described a village he had read about, I imagined us jolting along in his Volvo up the mountains and stopping for a lunch of wine, oeufs à la Chimay, and cold cream of turnip soup. "Sounds wonderful," I said.

"I've heard that the people in the provinces are much more friendly than the Parisians," he said. My vision changed to a scene of us pulling into a gingerbread town filled with quaintly dressed peasants who sang and danced and called us by our first names. "My uncle Hyam was born in—" He was interrupted by a nudge of Laura's knee.

"*I'll* be able to go to France for twenty-four dollars," she said smugly.

Determined not to let our conversation be interrupted again, I quickly said, "Paris is a city that—"

"Shhhh!" Marlene said, punching my arm. "It's starting!"

I restrained myself from kicking her porcine shin.

The lights faded, along with my fancies. I settled back in my seat along with everyone else to watch Peter Fonda's protruding eyeballs in Cinemascope. I detest motorcycles; luckily I was not able to hear much in the way of revving over Marlene's crunching and slurping.

Roman put his arm over the back of Laura's chair and she nestled onto his shoulder. Although I had no intention of even sharing an arm rest with Marlene, she seemed to have other ideas. In the middle of a strangulation scene, I felt a hand on my thigh. When it started to move back, toward my ass, I whispered, "Marlene! *What* do you think you're doing?"

She leaned over to my ear and said, "Do you have any change? I want to get some Twislers."

After the movie, we drove to get something to eat. Along the way, I did my Hugh Herbert impression, which garnered quizzical looks, and then my Richard Burton impression, which was diverting enough to cause us to run a red light. Pleased with myself, I paid no attention when we pulled into the parking lot of Armando's, a pizza parlor in which Sparks Compton worked part time. I spotted him behind the soda machine through a screened window.

Roman walked in first. "Hey!" he yelled, waving.

"Hey!" Sparks shouted from behind the counter. His smile disappeared when he saw me push through the door behind Marlene.

The parlor was brightly lit. We all sat down at a red formica table. Sparks came over and put his hands on his hips. "What'll it be?" he said gruffly, looking at me.

Though I shifted uncomfortably in my seat under Sparks's gaze, Roman was oblivious to my tension. "Large pizza?" he asked, looking around the table. Everyone nodded.

"With sausages and meatballs," Marlene added.

The place wasn't busy. Roman told Sparks to pull up a chair.

"Nah. I got stuff to set up for tomorrow," he said and went back behind the counter.

Roman was quite talkative that evening. He filled us in on his pugilistic confrontations with the nuns at his parochial grammar school.

"They were all black belts," he said, laughing.

Laura flirted shamelessly with Roman. She actually *batted* her eyes several times, but he didn't seem interested.

Marlene almost choked on an ice cube.

Throughout the pizza, I could see Sparks standing in the back, twisting and untwisting a dish towel.

A Night to Remember

I looked in the mirror and studied the fit of the antique gray linen suit. The jacket was squarish; wide lapels fell from slightly padded shoulders to a double-breasted midriff. Six pleats adorned each hip of the baggy but narrowly cuffed trousers.

I had discovered the suit in a junk shop on Bleecker Street during Christmas vacation after convincing my parents that I would not be at all entertained watching my sister, Lucy, show off at the Rockefeller Center skating rink. In order to complete the outfit, I had also forfeited the opportunity to see and, of course, *smell* the circus; instead I had inventoried several pawn shops until I acquired the appropriate accessories: celluloid collar, vintage shirt, slender necktie, a stickpin faced with a geometric mermaid and a beautiful pair of pearl gray and white spats. When we had driven home that night, after I was picked up under the Washington Square arch, Lucy and I clutched at our respective treasures. She, still at an ambivalent age, had a dress from Saks, two pennants from the circus and a chameleon that dropped dead before we hit the Long Island Expressway. I had the survivors of an era as exanimated as the chameleon, the remains of a time when husbands and wives toasted each other with champagne cocktails in glittering cafés, girlfriends ran along train platforms waving pale blue hand-kerchiefs at their departing fiancés in uniform and movie stars sat on steamer trunks blowing kisses to the press without staining their white gloves with dark red lipstick.

A party was the occasion for the suit, thrown to celebrate the end of a more recent and less glamorous past: my long-awaited emancipation from a pedagogical snake pit. High school.

During the past week, I had felt light-headed, almost giddy at the prospect of ending my four-year run at Gingold Secondary. A summer could finally come and go without the prospect of a September rendezvous with the same two hundred and sixty-four blinking faces. I had practically romped through the halls for the last few days leading up to the graduation ceremony, disregarding tearful scenes between girls who had detested each other since kindergarten but whose imminent separation precipitated confessions of clandestine affection. I cheerfully acceded to the yearbook-signing demands of classmates whose names were as dim as their facial expressions would be a year later; I skipped through classes wishing luck to all those who were rumored to be leaving Gingold to enter colleges, technical schools, and abortion clinics.

I was going to Tufts. The party at Roman's house next door would be my last encounter with my classmates.

As I adjusted my dark gray necktie, a renewed feeling of glee came over me, and with it came my sister, Lucy.

"Jesus, that looks awful," she said, fondling a lapel.

Lucy was finishing her first year at Gingold Secondary. She was quite pretty; the Rubensesque chubbiness that had obscured her figure as a child had melted away so that now she stood tall, shapely and, unlike myself, draped in something inconsequential. A paisley skirt.

"You look like grandpa!" she complained. "You're not going to wear that junk to the party, are you?" she asked, circling and staring, the way children do when they discover something odd washed up on the beach. "Not in front of *Bob!*"

Bob Monroe, of all people, would be arriving soon to escort her to the party. Most of the girls at Gingold took a fancy to him at some time or other; he was quite handsome in a Stanley Kowalski sort of way. Most recently he had flattered Lucy with reciprocal interest. It unnerved me to think of Bob Monroe, a person who idolized Sparks Compton, dating my sister. His father was the leading authority on financial investment on the East Coast; Bob himself was planning a future in the care and maintenance of the internal combustion engine. To tangibly prove, I suppose, his sincerity toward Lucy, he had converted an old wood-paneled station wagon into a racing car and told her he had named it "Lucille."

"He's going to drive over in Lucille," she said with a straight face. "I'll *die* if he sees you wearing that stuff."

"It's just a suit, Lucy," I said, looking down.

"It looks ridiculous." She flung open my closet door, implying that enough had been heard in the way of discussion. I tried to explain the singularity of the outfit but she ignored me.

"How about this?" she asked, pulling out a revolting checkered shirt Aunt Hedy had given me.

"Really, Lucy," I said with the slightest disdain in my voice.

"Bur-*ton*—" she whined.

"No. I'm wearing this," I insisted, buttoning the jacket.

"Bob will be here any minute," she said, thrusting the shirt toward me.

"No!" I shouted, now quite irritated, smoothing a trouser leg.

"Oohhh!" she said, suddenly pulling at her hair as a missionary who had lost patience trying to tutor a native in the uses of the subjunctive case might. "Mommy!" she yelled and stomped down the hall.

As I finished buttoning my spats, I could hear her voice rising in an arpeggio of crankiness as she described to my mother the ignominy of being related to me. She expanded the complaint to include the chronic embarrassment she felt walking the halls of Gingold Secondary haunted by my reputation. The doorbell interrupted her monologue. Bob was here.

I looked through my bedroom window at the pool lights glimmering from Roman DeMarco's house. That was the one discordant note to this whole graduation business: I'd be leaving Roman behind along with everything else.

"Darling!" my mother called. "Come to the table!"

I smoothed and tugged until I achieved the level of nattiness generally associated with Zachary Scott. Graduation presents had been doled out after the ceremony. My favorite, a two-carat diamond ring set in white gold, sat amid loose change in an ashtray on the bureau. I put it on, rubbed the divine stone against my lapel and left the room.

In deference to the party tonight, a get-together with my benighted relatives had been postponed until Saturday. My mother had prepared a small auxiliary cake to mark today's event. Entering the dining room, I was blinded by a flashcube as my father took his forty-seven millionth photograph of the day.

"Sit down, darling," mother said, setting a cup of coffee at my place. Amid a flurry of black dots, I could see *Bob* seated across from me. Lucy was next to him, frowning.

"Bob," she said sullenly, "you know my brother."

"Burton," my mother added, cutting the devil's food.

Bob, I couldn't help noticing, was dressed in an undershirt inscribed with the name of the rock band Black Sabbath, and blue jean overalls.

"Sure! Hey there, Burt!" he said, pumping my arm as if he were jacking up a disabled car. His fingers were stained with the oily droppings of his academic study.

"Burton," I corrected. "Hello, Bob."

Some polite chatter followed as my mother distributed pieces of cake. I asked Bob if he had seen Sparks Compton. Scholastically, Sparks had not fared at all well this past year; he was not allowed to graduate with the rest of us. I was heartbroken. He had been conspicuously missing from school for over a week.

"Yeah. He's okay. He'll be at the party," Bob said. He went on to relate what Sparks had been doing since his expulsion: fixing pizza, mopping floors. As he continued, it was unavoidable to note that Bob did not believe conversation and the rapid ingestion of devil's food are acts that should remain mutually exclusive. "He says he's not going back next year," Bob concluded. He made a figure eight in the icing on his plate and sucked on each of his discolored fingers, loudly.

"I hear you're an automechanical genius," I said, trying to hide my revulsion with a change of subject.

"Yeah," Bob replied, scraping the last vestiges of icing from his plate with a piercing noise that prompted my mother to ask if he wanted another piece. "Why not," he replied without enthusiasm. Hoisting up his plate, he turned back toward me. "I love cars. I've always loved cars. I love cars more than anything else in the world."

Nodding at this confession of vehicular passion, wondering what Lucy thought of it, I said, "And I hear you've redesigned one."

Bob unloaded four teaspoons of sugar into his coffee and described in stupefyingly tedious detail the modification of Lucille's engine, the reupholstering of the old rotting seat covers, the replacement of camshaft, gears, pistons, points and out-of-line axles. I stifled a yawn. I have never liked automobiles nor understood the general public's fascination for them. In juxtaposition to Pullman cars and riverboats they merely seem to confirm the second-rateness of modern life.

"Took a long time," Bob said, wiping his mouth on his wrist. "But it goes like blazes now. I'll let you drive it."

I poured myself more coffee. "That's all right," I said. "I wouldn't want to put you out . . ."

"No problem! We can do it before we go to Roman's party."

"No, really," I reiterated.

"Zero to sixty in eight seconds!" he said, glinting at me.

"No, thank you," I said firmly. He looked at me quizzically and picked a cherry from the piece of cake on Lucy's plate. "Besides," I added, "I don't have a license."

Bob chewed vigorously for a moment. "Expired?"

"No. I never had one. Never wanted one, in fact."

Lucy looked uncomfortably at Bob.

"Oh, yeah?" he said, appearing not to know whether to take me seriously. Lucy clicked her tongue and looked down at her plate; Bob gazed around the table. Since this was his first visit to Lucy's house, he had been self-conscious and intent on making a good impression. The confession of my lack of driving skills and his knowledge of my lack of athletic prowess now set his thoughts running along a different path. His eyes drifted to my mermaid stickpin. I tried to express my philosophy of transportation—using the *Queen Mary,* as an example—but he just looked at me with a puzzled expression and cleared his throat. "It was a lovely graduation ceremony," my mother said, breaking the silence and passing Bob his third piece of cake.

I sighed and leaned back in my chair. Lovely indeed. Mr. Steele's jingoistic reputation and familiarity with the gymnasium had secured his appointment as commencement coordinator again this year. I smiled almost wistfully as he had shouted commands at everyone into the podium microphone in preparation for the ceremony. The French Club came through the gym with barrelsful of pink and green paper carnations, made at weekly French Club meetings, which were used to camouflage the basketball hoops; the cafeteria ladies got together and tried to poison everybody one more time with an appropriately inscribed FAREWELL CLASS OF '70 cake.

During the exercises, my esteemed peers had tripped over their gowns and lost their mortarboards. My eardrum was threatened by sound system feedback; my sanity by an athletic metaphor in the Student Council president's speech ("Life is like a track meet"). But at the bitter end, when my parents and I had walked through the parking lot to our car amidst the diploma-toting graduates and their . . . beaming parents, my mood could only be described as beatific.

Even now, watching chocolate crumbs fall from Bob's undulating lips, I felt almost intoxicated. High school was over. Only Roman's party remained.

"Don't you feel great now that it's over?" I asked Bob, smiling.

"Yeah, I was sweating like a pig under that gown."

"No, I mean school. Isn't it great that we don't have to go to Gingold anymore?"

"Yeah. No more Frau Krantz and her pop quizzes in German."

"And no more reading *The Bear* and *Our Town again* in English," I added.

"Yeah, that's another one. English!" He turned to Lucy. "If you ever get Mr. Lacey, switch! If he finds out you did a book report without reading the book he flunks you!" he said incredulously. Lucy acknowledged his advice with a nod.

"And no more Mr. Steele!" I said gleefully, raising my spoon for emphasis.

"I never had him," Bob said suspiciously. "But I heard he was a pretty nice guy."

"Ha!" I replied.

Chewing pensively, Bob regarded me.

"Better still," I continued, "no more gym!"

Bob stopped chewing and swallowed his mouthful with some difficulty. "What's wrong with gym?" he asked.

Lucy's fork clattered to her plate. "Come on, Bob. Let's go."

"But I'm not done yet," he protested, quickly picking a cherry from the cake in the center of the table.

"Come on," she repeated through clenched teeth.

The telephone rang in the kitchen and my mother got up to answer it. Bob gobbled down the cherry and the rest of his cake.

"I want you home by midnight, young lady," my father said.

"Dad-dy!" Lucy whined and clicked her tongue.

"None of that," he replied.

"But, daddy. Burton will be there. Let me stay till one. It's only next door."

"Midnight."

"Oh!" she huffed, throwing down her napkin. She stomped out of the room.

Bob almost took the tablecloth with him as he jumped up to follow her. "Thanks for the cake!" he called from the next room. The front door slammed and they went off to ride next door in his slaughtered station wagon.

My mother returned. "It's for you, Burton."

"Who is it?" I asked, surprised.

"She wouldn't say. Whoever it is sounds strange. I could barely hear her over the receiver."

I rose quickly and went to the kitchen. I couldn't imagine who would be calling me. "Hello?" I said eagerly. There was no reply. "Hello!" I repeated, louder.

"Um . . ." someone said. "Is . . . is this Burton Raider?"

"Yes."

"Um . . . this . . . this is Delilah Lutz. You sit next to me on the bus? Sometimes— Do you know who I mean? Delilah Lutz? I have brown hair?"

Shocked, I sat down on the stool in front of the telephone table. Why would she be calling me? "Yes, Delilah. Of course I know you."

"Hello," she whispered. I could hear a television in the background. She didn't say anything for several seconds. Then she coughed, fraily, like Garbo in *Camille*.

"How are you?" I asked, trying to encourage her.

"Fine," she replied faintly. There was another pause, then she abruptly got to the point. "I have this feeling. You'll probably think I'm . . . nuts . . . or something. But you've been— I like when you sit next to me. That's stupid. No. Anyway. I thought I should tell you. . . ." Her voice trailed off.

"Tell me what?"

"Are you going to Roman DeMarco's party?" she asked distinctly.

"Well, yes. I was just getting ready to leave."

She began to whisper excitedly. "I can't explain it. You'll think . . . I have this feeling. It started last night. Don't go. To that party, I mean." She paused.

"Don't go? Why?"

"Something. I saw you in a woods. I . . . Look, just don't. I'm sorry." She hung up.

"Hello? *Delilah!*" I said, tapping the cradle like a two-bit detective. What the hell was she talking about? I looked up her number and called her back. There was no answer.

"Who was that, dear?" my mother asked innocently as I reentered the dining room.

"Oh, just a friend wondering if I was going to be at the party." I sat down and poked at my cake. I wanted to see Roman, not listen to portents. "I should get going."

"All right, darling," my mother said.

"Keep an eye on Lucy, Burton," my father said sternly. "She's a little young to be going to one of these things. But you know how she carries on."

"I will," I said. My mother leaned over to receive a kiss.

"Congratulations again!" they called in unison after me as I walked out the back door.

I walked slowly through mother's English garden, turning Delilah's words over in my mind. When I stepped on the soft bed of pine needles that marked the end of our property, I stopped abruptly. *Saw you in a woods.* The pine woods rose before me, dark, fragrant and empty except for the faint sound of music and voices wafting from Roman's house. Saw me in a woods and what? Having watched the pragmatic characters in horror films scoff at reports of homicidal mummies and other supernatural phenomena only to be fatally punished for their skepticism, I was predisposed to turn back. Edging closer, I peered into the gloom. There was nothing menacing. But . . . With the caution of Stephin Fetchit, I walked on, straining to discern any movement or nearby sound. I pictured Gale Sondergaard behind a proximate tree, holding her breath and a silvery knife, waiting for my footfall with oriental calm. My heart was now beating quite audibly; my forehead was damp.

There was a rustle of leaves several feet to the left. I froze in alarm. The noise ceased. I imagined a trench-coated Richard Widmark watching me stumble along, smiling and rubbing the trigger of a black revolver, tired of toying with me, eager to give me the payoff.

"Ahhhh!" I screeched frantically.

A branch snapped under my foot and I fell backward into a bush as a wood thrush flew up into the dense pine ceiling, madly beating its wings. Relieved but still charged with adrenaline, I got to my feet and ran along the familiar path of gullies and stony mounds, hopping over saplings and scraping my hands against the jagged bark of old pines. The lights around the DeMarcos' swimming pool glittered through the thicket. I tripped over a rock and scrambled to my feet again. Out of breath, I stopped in a clearing near Roman's house and leaned against an elm.

"Hey, who's that?" someone said. I started but sighed with relief at the sight of several of my classmates hiding under bushes, clutching vodka bottles.

"It's me," I said, panting. "Burton Raider."

"Oh . . ." the voice said disappointedly. A girl giggled. I walked on and came through the edge of the wood, welcoming the assault of noise and lights.

The bulk of my class was jammed up against the hurricane fence of Roman's yard. Jimi Hendrix's "Purple Haze" blared from speakers perched on the roof of the house. I got a toehold in the fence, pulled myself up and over and wriggled into the herd of bodies on the other side. I felt braced by the crush of the crowd but a little angry at myself for allowing Delilah to unnerve me so easily.

Delilah never would come to have much of a rapport with people over the years. Those who did befriend her would stop calling after she trusted them enough to demonstrate her psychokinetic ability to bend paper clips and aluminum flatware.

I pushed my way through the crowd and ran right into Howard Joslyn and Pam, the would-be Lady Macbeth. "Hmmmmph!" she said, turning her back to me.

"Get lost, Raider," Howard elaborated. Their disdain had weakened over the months. When Howard first found out how I had dashed his girlfriend's hopes, he pushed me up against a lavatory wall at Gingold and threatened all of my appendages.

I pushed farther along to the pool. Mrs. DeMarco had set up a table for punch which had been variously spiked during the course of the evening; the ground was strewn with liquor bottles of assorted brands.

As I filled a cup, a cheer went up by the deep end of the pool. Cans of beer were raised into the air as Leonard "Rubber Legs" Prousse was helped onto the three-foot diving board. He was drunk and almost toppled over the other side but was caught and steadied. Sparks Compton jumped up with him.

"Let's hear it for Lenny!" he yelled, summoning more cheers. Leonard bowed grandly and nearly fell again. The people around me snickered. I drained my cup, tasting, among other cheap brands, the unmistakable Boone's Farm Strawberry Hill.

No one had seen Sparks all week. He had stormed out of school when he found out he wouldn't be graduating with the rest of us. It was *the* talk of lunch period. The police pulled the principal's car out of Long Island Sound several hours later. Lacking proof, the principal was unable to press charges against Sparks; being a principal of principles, he refused to reverse his decision.

Sparks cupped his hands around his mouth and yelled, "Let's go, Lenny!" Everyone cheered and whistled.

"Yay, Leonardo!"

"Come on, Rubber Legs!"

I filled my cup again, desiring inebriation, and wandered closer. This was the first party to which Leonard had ever been asked. Bolstered by the invitation and the liquor, Leonard surveyed the crowd, thinking that all the people who had pulled off his clip-on bow ties and knocked books out of his hands during the past four years had only been kidding.

"Go on!" they yelled. "Let's see a swan dive!"

The couples around me laughed at the scene and hugged each other tighter. Beer cans opened with a *ffzzztt!* Leonard waved at everyone, smiling stupidly.

"Yay, Prousse!"

Leonard weaved to the edge of the diving board and looked over. Sparks tiptoed up behind him, making faces and obscene gestures. The crowd roared. Mistaking the roars for camaraderie, Leonard jumped up and down on the end of the board and feigned diving movements. Sparks got a Budweiser from somebody in the crowd and, pulling Leonard away from the water, shoved it into his hand. He took Leonard's glasses off and gave them to someone else. Leonard sipped gingerly at the beer until Sparks pushed it into his face in an attempt to force him to drink it all down at once. It poured out the sides of his mouth and he gagged.

"That's it!" Sparks said, throwing the can into the pool.

Leonard brushed some suds from his shirt; Sparks pointed him in the direction of the water. Everyone yelled.

"Here he goes!"

"Hooray!"

"Go, R.L., go!"

Leonard grinned and again walked to the edge of the diving board. I circled behind. Roman was standing on the patio by a table of food, frowning.

"Come on, Lenny!"

Exaggerating his movements, Leonard drew his arms up over his head and bent his legs in preparation for a comedic dive. The crowd knew what was going to happen; Sparks teased them by creeping up very slowly behind Leonard. Hoots and whistles followed Sparks until he was standing right behind Leonard, red-faced and staring at the water.

Sparks tapped him on the shoulder. "Oh, *Rubber Legs*—" Smiling, Leonard turned. Sparks shoved him over the edge. Leonard didn't have time to catch his breath and his back hit the water hard with a horizontal splat. He came up sputtering and the crowd screamed with ecstasy.

"What an *asshole!"* Howard intoned.

He climbed out of the pool, shivering, and was handed a towel and his glasses, which somebody had smeared with potato chip dip.

"What a jerk!"

They pinched his cheeks and continued calling him names. Leonard looked up at them, bewildered for a moment; with the realization that he had misjudged the situation came a fury of ankle scratching.

Outside of real life, Leonard was much brighter. He just *seemed* to be an Eddie Bracken type. He was second in our class and had been accepted to MIT, where he would also graduate in the top of his class. The federal government would later recruit him as a chemical engineer and Leonard would gain distinction as one of the developers of the neutron bomb.

Sparks clasped his hands over his head like a prizefighter and everyone cheered. I pushed my way back toward Roman, who was talking to his mother through the window.

"No. Somebody just fell into the pool. It's okay."

"Are you sure?" she asked worriedly. "Do they need a blanket?"

"Nah. It's okay."

We shook hands.

"Do you believe this?" he said. "The place is a fucking zoo!"

Before I could agree, Sparks came bounding over with a can of beer in his hand.

"Did you see that?" he said, pointing. "Did you see Rubber Legs fall in the pool?"

"Yeah," Roman said.

"Did you see, Raider?"

"I saw."

"Wasn't it great?"

"Yeah. *Great.* What are you going to do next, asshole?" I said.

His smile faded. "Ya know, Raider. Sometime you're gonna—"

"Hey, Sparks!" someone shouted at him. We all turned to see Bob approaching. His hair was dripping wet.

"What the hell happened to you?" Sparks asked.

I stepped forward. "Where's Lucy?" I asked.

"Home!" he snarled.

"Home?"

"She's as crazy as you are, Raider. Look what she did to me!" he spat.

"Lucy did this to you?" I asked. Maybe Lucy had taste after all.

"What?" Sparks said, laughing.

"We left Raider's house. I have some beer in my car and I ask her if she wants to have some. She says yeah. So we're drinking and talking awhile. And all I do is try to get my arm around her and look at me!" Little droplets of Schlitz were falling from his earlobes. "That's all. I mean it. I'm changin' the name of that car. I swear."

"Here, have some potato chips with your beer," Sparks said, lifting up a bowl and dumping it over Bob's head.

"Christ, Compton!"

Mrs. DeMarco called through the screen window. "What's going *on* out there?"

"It's okay, ma!" Roman reassured her.

"How's the food holding up?" she asked.

"Fine, ma, fine." He peeked through the window at her and then turned to his friends. "You guys *are* assholes!" he hissed. "Come on, Burton!" He gestured to me and strode into the crowd.

"Hey, Roman, where ya goin'?" Sparks called after him.

"Come on!" Roman yelled. I put down my drink and went after him, the scowls of Sparks and Bob following us.

Roman and I chatted for a few minutes on the other side of his yard. The talk was superficial, about school, but he didn't seem at all himself. He kept muttering, "I can't wait . . . I can't wait," but only smiled wanly when I asked, "For what?" Furious when a cheerleader dragged him off somewhere, I nonetheless had a wonderful time the rest of the evening, talking and drinking with my dimwitted classmates until the party broke up at 2:00 A.M.

After thanking Roman and his mother, I climbed back over the fence. On the other side, I turned and looked at the dregs of the party. I raised my arm and waved a symbolic good-bye, then headed home.

The voices of lingering classmates followed me into the darkness and then retreated into memory, along with the rest of the preceding four years. I pushed aside a branch and trudged up the incline of the pine woods. The warning of Delilah Lutz was forgotten. Instead I thought wistfully of Roman and all my foolish schemes in that regard. Jumping over a narrow precipice which had been cut into the ground by spring showers, I resolved not to go out of my way to talk to him anymore: He would go to school and I would go to school and it was better to leave it alone. He was hopelessly straight. It was impossible.

I stepped on the exposed roots of an ancient, gnarled tree. I felt wonderful. Relieved! I jumped off, then froze with shock. Someone had spoken. Leaning against the trunk, I listened. But there was nothing to be heard except the last strains of a Cream song from the party.

Then I remembered Delilah's call. Suddenly terrified, I started to walk very quickly.

A branch snapped behind me. I whirled around in time to hear someone say, "Go!" A figure shot out from behind a tree, pulled me to the ground. I scrambled to my feet again and started to run, but two more came at me from the side. They tackled me and I toppled over into a bush, the prickly branches scratching my face. Someone punched me in the throat, then the stomach. I yelled, more angry than frightened. Then all three were on me, smashing my face, kicking me in the side. I swung and kicked back wildly, connecting with at least two noses. Then one of them held me down while the other two bludgeoned me with their fists.

The struggle interrupted two people nearby who had come into the woods to fornicate. They had just gotten out of their clothing when they heard us. They buttoned and zippered and ran back to the party.

"A fight! A fight!" they yelled delightedly through the fence.

Roman was cleaning up. He dropped a bag full of garbage and climbed over the fence to see what was going on. I had almost managed to get to my feet again when someone kicked me in the mouth and I fell, unconscious.

Roman ran up. "What the hell's goin' on!" he yelled. The sound of his voice stopped them from their massacre. Roman recognized them as they stood up in alarm. "What the hell—Sparks, what're you *doin'?"* Sparks didn't say anything. Roman stared down at me. *"Look* at him!" The three criminals retreated a few steps. *"Get away!"* Roman yelled. They stood watching as he leaned over to look at me. "Christ! His *face."* He turned to them. "You guys better get out of here fast!" They stayed there gawking, stupefied, as he picked me up in his arms and carried me up to my house.

"My God!" my mother screamed when he laid me down on the couch. My face was covered with blood and my lip was torn.

"His nose looks broken," my father said. He and Roman carried me out to the car and laid me across the back seat. Daddy drove to the hospital with no regard for pot holes or red lights.

I awoke the next morning to the blurred sight of three faces.

"Don't try to talk," mother said.

My nose had indeed been broken. So had my jaw. It was wired and I couldn't speak.

"If you have anything to say, use this," my father said, handing me a pad and pencil.

Roman leaned over. "Hi," he said hoarsely. He had been at the hospital all night.

Good News

I lay fallow in the hospital for three weeks. Blue patches of ruptured blood vessels stained my skin; bandages and wires obscured three-quarters of my face. Each morning my mother arrived with cheerful how-do-you-feels and Jane Austen novels, of which she gave passionate renderings until late in the afternoons. A less frequent visitor was my nurse, whose only apparent functions were to eat my get-well candy and thrust a thermometer into my rectum with an odd smile. Although the chocolate was imported, I'm not at all sure she didn't prefer the latter experience.

My father visited on many occasions. When he asked on the fourth day if I had any thought of pressing charges against my assailants, I pantomimed the act of locking a door and throwing away the key.

"All right," he said. "I'll call my lawyer and he'll have the police issue a warrant for their arrests. Roman gave us their names."

Sparks, Bob, and Howard Joslyn were arrested three hours later in the basement of Gingold Secondary, where summer school was in session. They were discovered putting a stink bomb in the central air-conditioning system.

The attempted assassins were interviewed separately at precinct headquarters. Sparks, despite lacerated knuckles, denied having been in a fight. Bob and Howard related contradictory stories. But Roman had been an eyewitness, so the three were charged with assault and battery—despite my attempts to have the charges changed to attempted murder. The case was quickly settled out of court by the parents of the accused who feared that an indictment might be looked upon unfavorably by college admissions officers. Sparks's and Howard's fathers paid ten thousand dollars each and Bob's, the leading authority on financial investment on the East Coast, having had little success during the past five years in following his own advice and therefore having nothing in the way of liquid assets, titled me a piece of property in Brooklyn along with the commercial warehouse sitting on it.

Throughout the whole painful business, Roman came to the hospital day after day, much to my surprise and delight. With me not able to speak, our conversations were as unilateral as my crush had been. His testimony precluded any further loitering on his part with Sparks or the other two; he told me that was more of a relief than a misfortune.

"You know how they are," he said.

I learned quite a few surprising things about Roman during those three weeks. For one thing, he liked classical music—and was shy about admitting it.

"Who do you like?" I wrote down excitedly on my pad.

Smiling as sheepishly as Gary Cooper in *Desire,* he said, "Brahms is my favorite. His third symphony is incredible. And Liszt. Did you know that he tied sticks between his fingers before going to bed to improve his range? And, I don't know . . . Ravel. Schubert."

What bus stop conversations we could have had!

My earlier decision to terminate my relationship with Roman now became untenable. As I saw him every day, my long-term interest evolved into something more and it disturbed me to find out that the film school he had decided to go to was UCLA—California! It had taken three years and a broken jaw to get this far and I didn't relish the idea of letting something as mundane as geography separate us.

"Why so far?" I wrote down.

He shrugged. "I've been sort of planning it. Besides, it's the best place to study film."

*   *   *

That summer after I had mended, I made certain we did all sorts of things together so that I would have a surplus of memories to draw from after we were separated. The best times were spent sailing on a small barge that had been fashioned from an old outhouse and a square-pontooned float. By day, it functioned as an aquatic hot dog stand for ravenous boaters. By night, it was . . . *borrowed* for our private champagne parties. Tying one bottle off the side to chill in the water, we would drink another and I'd entertain Roman by improvising parodies of Ronald Reagan movies, a redundant exercise.

We would swim naked in the starlight and, exhausted, would crawl back onto the barge for a last bottle. While the breeze dried us, I'd memorize the look of his body stretched across the dark boards, the words used when we toasted our friendship at midnight, the drone of a lone motorboat in the distance. I was able to ignore our impending disunion, except for one time, late in August, when the alcohol coaxed me into crying. I loved Roman so hard.

The memory of our evening voyages is clear to me even now: two naked shadows in the dark, the sky and sea sparkling in their own ways.

Once, after I had drunk half a magnum of champagne, I told Roman of my sexual proclivities. In his characteristically boyish way, he shrugged. We never spoke of it for the rest of the summer.

My life has always been a quest not for wealth or power, but for a propitious niche. From my comfortable vantage point, Tufts looked promising. Its age appealed to me; its facilities and staff piqued my intellectual appetite. I was sure that its students would be more sensible than those of Gingold. But even if they weren't, it was encouraging to read in the college bulletin that physical education was not a required subject.

I decided to put my twenty thousand dollars in trust for four years. New York City was my destination after Tufts and I didn't want to start out living there in some hovel on Avenue C. Besides, I could earn a high interest on the fund while the college loan could be paid back with minimal usury.

During the summer, I visited the campus and was taken on a tour by an undergraduate who offered more in the way of personal trivia than I'm sure even his mother would have found interesting. As part of the circuit, we visited his living quarters, a rather small but quaint nineteenth-century house just off campus, which I was appalled to discover he shared with fifteen other students. He showed me points of interest, including the bathroom floor, on which he had first seduced his present girlfriend. But he seemed most proud of a kitchen refrigerator that he had modified to be a beer dispenser. The shelves had been replaced with a heavy metal platform that could hold the weight of a keg, connected to which was a tap that protruded from a hole in the door. Although this eliminated the tedium involved in opening individual cans, it precluded the storage of food. My tour guide assured me he was unconcerned with that since the members of his house did all their dining in a nearby Woolworth's. The living room furniture was either broken or deflated; the bedrooms were small, with single beds and Salvation Army bureaus; the walls were cracked and peeling.

"Isn't this great!" he said.

"Very nice," I replied, but upon parting I taxied into Cambridge to look for civilized accommodations. After two days' search, I found a six-room flat overlooking the Charles River. Though there were other communities closer to Tufts, I felt I would be more than compensated for the commuting time by the architectural and aesthetic delights of Cambridge, not the least of which was a nearby patisserie open twenty-four hours a day with free delivery.

Apartment found, I went to Tufts housing to inform them that I would not be taking advantage of their rather droll offer of *room and board*.

"I'm sorry, sir," a clerk replied blandly. "All freshmen are required to live on campus."

"Can I talk to anyone else?" I asked.

"I'll send you to Mr. Freemont."

Mr. Freemont was able to provide the page number and subparagraph containing the rule but neither dispensation nor any reason for its existence.

"Can I talk to anyone else?"

"I'll send you to Mr. Grace."

Mr. Grace, the supervisor, was of the opinion that half the benefit of a college education during the first year was derived from "drinking with buddies."

"Can I talk to anyone else?"

"I'll send you to Mr. Morton."

I asked Mr. Morton, director of housing, if I might be at least given a private room. He replied indignantly that the housing shortage was much too severe to allow that sort of thing. I pointed out that letting me live off campus might solve both our problems. Faced with having to make a decision, Mr. Morton suddenly remembered a dental appointment.

Upon arriving in September, I was given a housing assignment, keys and a name tag reading BURT which I promptly deposited in a trash can. The building to which I was directed was a concrete monstrosity, the embodiment of that architectural dictum that form should follow function. The halls were long and ugly. Small windows at each end provided only enough light to see the decorative fire hoses hanging from the ceiling. Walking into my room, I was immediately struck by the designer's generous use of cinderblock and noted the obvious influence that the shoebox had had on his spacial theories. Along the length of one wall was a formica board meant to be used as a desk and, above it, pegboard shelving—a horrible reminder of Mr. Parker and his Rhythm Kids. On the opposite wall was a bunk bed. Next to that were two closets which *together* couldn't have held my Bermuda shorts collection. I sat on the edge of the bed and quietly began to hyperventilate.

Any vestigial hope of peace was compromised by the other one hundred sixty-two people billeted on my floor. Most evident was my roommate Charley, small and thin and moody. Whenever I felt like reading, Charley would sit at his desk and recite poems of his own creation with titles like "Sweet Suicide" and "Angel of Death, Come to Me" while accompanying himself on the sitar. Although this sparked the hope that I might yet have a private room, it did little for my reading comprehension. Charley was both a Marxist and a sports enthusiast: While waiting for the revolution he believed would wrest control of a lucrative television tube factory from his father, he would shout profanities at inept hockey goalies on the color set in our room.

Joining him were several others; one was our next-door neighbor who, having been seduced by his stepmother at age fifteen, was in his second year of primal therapy. He had a secondhand mattress hanging on the wall dividing our rooms, positioned next to my eardrum; his psychiatrist had suggested he buy it and scream and pound on it whenever he felt anxious or unloved. He often felt anxious or unloved at four o'clock in the morning.

I detested the lack of privacy. All sorts of people descended on my room bearing bottles of wine selling for under a dollar; they would celebrate with puerile, bacchanalian enthusiasm. I do not mean to imply that I hate parties—but I prefer sardonic conversation to indoor touch football games. Nor do I mean to imply that the aforementioned distaste was unilateral; it is simply *amazing* how much prejudice can be generated by wearing a silk Chinese bathrobe and wooden sandals into a shower room.

During orientation, an upperclassman called a dorm meeting in the common room to give us information about restaurants selling hamburgers to students at a discount, and to give a personal appraisal of the sexual morals of women in nearby schools. He also warned us that an establishment called Lord Alfred's Bar & Grill was not the sort of place to bring a date. This sounded promising.

Once when my roommate Charley was spending the weekend at Radcliffe with his girlfriend, a Trotskyite, I decided to go there for a drink. I was libidinous and wanted to do something about it. The bar was small and decorated with brass railings and potted palms. I met a handsome chap there, a twenty-six-year-old medical student with a Clark Gable mustache. We had a few drinks and talked and realized we had at least one thing in common, then went back to my room on campus.

When I awoke the next morning, I discovered that my roommate, Charley, probably having had an ideological clash with his girlfriend, was snoring away in the bottom bunk. Not wanting to wake up my bed partner, I rolled over and went back to sleep.

The next thing I knew, someone was violently poking me in the back. I raised myself up off the mattress. Squinting, I could see Charley flanked by several of his friends—all drinking beer and looking rather ominous. My companion was still asleep.

"So what's going on here?" Charley asked, taking a sip of beer.

Rubbing my eyes and smiling, I asked if everyone had a coaster. I was invited to move out forthwith. Of course, I could have put up a fight about it—after all, more than one fellow's *girl*friend had been seen in the shower room. But since it enabled me to move to the off-campus apartment that I wanted in the first place, I let the inequities stand.

The worst thing that happened during my four years at Tufts was witnessing a violent rally in Cambridge Common by a religious zealot named Sister Ivy, who was agitating against forced busing. A child was crushed under the feet of the crowd she had harangued into a frenzy. The police had to break the riot up; several cars were overturned in the process. Sister Ivy was subsequently sued by the city but was held unaccountable for the destruction.

The best thing that happened was that I discovered I had a knack for writing. For two years, I criticized the campus's Torn Ticket theatrical productions and occasionally wrote movie reviews for the Tufts newspaper, the *Observer*. Imitating the style of James Mason Brown, I could be nice—"Michael Thropp was a corpulent triumph last week in *The Man Who Came to Dinner*"—or nasty—"Rena Parafon's performance last night was so wooden that during her love scenes one got the sense she was being felled rather than seduced"—but eventually I became bored and turned to writing screenplays.

My first one took place in the South and concerned a rich and genetically evil plantation family. The plot was ridden with drama, pathos, boll weevils—but more than anything, clichés: a domineering patriarch, a mysterious room he kept locked, a no-good son, his barren wife and a family fortune that so preoccupied everyone in the clan that I wonder how, reading it over now, they ever managed to get from room to room without bumping into walls. I pictured Charles Laughton playing the Big Daddy part, Ann Blyth the barren wife. I called it *Sweet Decay*. Mr. Randall, one of my professors at Tufts, said that while reading it he had "the most peculiar urge to swim in salt water" and that the use of twenty-three characters was beyond my abilities.

The next, *Second Wind,* had four main characters. It opened with a shot of a rich old man in a wheelchair (Alec Guinness?) taking a revolver from a desk drawer and hiding it under his blanket. He removes a letter from his pocket, reads it over and tucks it under the desk blotter. The viewer at first thinks he is planning to murder his youngish business partner (Anthony Perkins), who pays him a visit and subtly badgers him to retire from their concern—then it appears to be his wife, a beautiful but cool cookie (a Jane Greer type), who serves them tea while they talk. When the partner and wife leave his room, the old man yells at his nurse to take him downstairs to the garden where the two have rendezvoused for cocktails. He has her position him inside a hedged maze where he can observe them, unseen. The nurse leaves. He watches them. They toast each other. He raises the gun. The hammer is cocked, violins play a tense A-minor-seventh chord in the background, and then—surprise!—he points the barrel at his own head. His hand trembles; perspiration beads on his brow. He closes his eyes and— nothing. He can't do it. He yells like an upstaged star and the nurse wheels him upstairs for a mineral bath. At the end of the scene, the camera focuses on the forgotten letter; the viewer realizes it is a suicide note.

A few days later when he is in his bedroom furtively reading a book about poisons, a niece (Tuesday Weld) from the poorer branch of the family, who is an aspiring actress, comes for an extended visit. Her infatuation with the stage and life itself eventually prompt the old man to put aside any thought of making a poisonous purchase.

Meanwhile, the wife—who *is* in love with the business partner—finds the suicide note and realizes that the niece is the only thing standing between her and an inheritance of three million dollars. At first, she tries to get rid of the niece by making her feel uncomfortable.

"Have you *really* only been here three weeks, dear?"

Failing with that approach, she calls her husband's partner, who agrees to put up money for a play to be staged in New York with the stipulation that the producer hire the niece to a run-of-the-play contract. When the niece gets the telegram from New York, she gives her regrets and packs.

In her absence, the old man reverts. While dictating an opening-night telegram for his niece to the nurse, the viewer sees that he has a bottle of sleeping pills wedged between himself and the arm of his wheelchair. The telegram is painful for him to compose and before he can get out the last "stop," he changes his mind and dashes the bottle of pills against the wall. The astonished nurse asks, "Will there be anything else, sir?" He replies, "Yes, call my lawyer." The old man divorces his wife, gets rid of his business partner, and tries to live as a vital human being.

Professor Randall said that the screenplay was a Capra-cum-Hitchcockian mishmash "that even Republic Studios wouldn't have produced" and "that could hold an audience's attention only if all the actors performed in the nude. Write about something you know!" he growled, handing the manuscript back to me.

Gritting my teeth, I bought a bag of fresh legal pads and wrote a story about the torment of unrequited love. Called *Silence,* it concerned an older, eccentric woman pursuing a younger man. Though it too was flawed, I was pleased with the characterization of the older woman: a vulnerable, passionate, insecure, proud creature. Randall thought I should junk the plot and move the character into another situation.

A few months before I was to graduate, I got an idea for the plot. I also contracted influenza and was bogged down with a fever of one hundred and one, but the idea grabbed hold of me as ruthlessly as the virus, so I set to work. The plain older woman became an aging movie star. I locked my door for six days against all intruders, except for the delivery boy from the patisserie down the street, and wrote the rough draft. I raced through the one-hundred-and-fifty-page manuscript, taking breaks only to eat and vomit. By graduation, I had pared it down to one hundred and twenty-six pages. I called it *Resurrection and Denial*. Randall congratulated me.

"My boy, it's rather good."

I was inclined to agree.

Romantically, I was unimpressed during my four years at Tufts. I had an agreeable amount of sex but essentially kept to myself. No one produced in me the feelings that Roman had. No one lasted more than two or three nights.

Roman came to visit me twice a year. I kept postponing trips to California. Part of the reason was that I detested the idea of flying or driving and didn't have time to go out by rail; part had to do with self-regard: Seeing Roman again meant saying good-bye again. Going through that when he came East was enough, but if I took the initiative to go out there, parting would have been agony. We saw each other in the summers back on Long Island, where I worked as an usher at a movie theater. It wasn't until his graduation that I visited UCLA.

On one of my summer vacations, I decided to take a look at the Flatbush Avenue warehouse that Bob Monroe's father, the leading authority on financial investment, had paid me in lieu of damages. It was huge and in disrepair.

I investigated its history and found out that it had originally been a shooting stage for an old movie company during the silent era—part of the old Vitagraph Company.

The Man in the Iron Mask

Roman held up his hand against the light streaming in through the train station windows. A passenger jet floated down through the streaks on the glass and disappeared behind a distant building. A girl shared the view with him. Dressed for tennis, she shielded her eyes with an aluminum racquet. Her face was healthy, if plain; her chest large. Roman checked for cigarettes in case she asked for one. The plastic wrapper crackled in his pocket and, as if offended, the girl walked away, bouncing the racquet on the heel of her hand. He thought she would come back.

"Passengers for Houston. Houston passengers—"

Static drowned out the voice. Roman looked up at the ancient speakers. The manufacturer's trademark, a lightning bolt, was barely visible under the many coats of steel-gray paint.

"—sengers. Track four. Passengers for Hous—"

He sat down on the dark wooden pew next to the window and closed his eyes. The warmth of the sun on his face and forearms made him sigh. The station smelled of damp concrete and faint traces of other odors: mothballs from the clothes of disembarking passengers, and another, which he decided was from the men's room—he could see the janitor sprinkling Ajax on the floor through the open doorway.

"Passengers for Houston. Track four. 'Board!"

The girl didn't return, but a uniformed man came in, who opened up the front of a vending machine with one of the keys attached to a ring on his belt. As Roman watched, he stocked the machine and emptied the change receptacle into a canvas bag. His uniform was baby blue except for the back and underarms, navy with perspiration.

Roman looked away when the man glanced at him.

"Now arriving. Passengers from Port—"

The vending-machine man went on to the second machine. A Coff-E-Mat. Roman watched him fill it with paper cups. Something broke in the men's room and the janitor's curse echoed out onto the concourse. The vendor laughed and looked at Roman again. He looked away again.

As the vendor continued his duties, Roman listened to the change receptacle being emptied and the face of the machine being closed. He listened to the wedged soles of the vendor's shoes as he padded away.

Roman nervously looked up at the sound of a flaring match. The janitor was lighting a cigar. Roman watched him throw the match into a urinal, then kick his mop bucket hard. The grayish-green water splashed onto his pants. He cursed at that and then went into the coffee shop.

"Passengers arriving from Portland. Portland arrivals. Gate ten please. Gate ten."

Roman sighed. The train station stood like a neanderthal in modern Los Angeles. Could any city have anything less useful to itself in its midst? The ceiling was filthy with the residue of smog and retiary insects. There were sparse flurries of passengers who quickly left, like unhappy guests at a dull reception.

Roman looked at his watch. Burton didn't belong here any more than this antiquated train station, or the withered stars who wisely stayed cloistered in the outer hills and canyons.

"Gate ten. Portland arrivals. Passengers arriving from Portland. Gate ten."

The vending-machine man returned carrying a large box on his shoulder. Roman regarded the strain of his neck and arm muscles when he put it down. The vendor wiped his brow and ripped the lid off. He opened the candy machine and stacked the bars in steel slots.

He reminded Roman of the instructor at the gym Roman had joined two years after coming to California. He had joined that particular gym in part because it wasn't the *modern* sort with carpeting and orange trees, just an old-fashioned one with mats, barbells and playing courts. And a reputation. Mostly Roman went there because of that.

Roman watched the vending-machine man rip open a candy wrapper with his teeth.

It had taken a lot of nerve to join. And a lot of time. Even after he left everyone in Long Island behind, it was still difficult. He had made the promise that all young boys make to themselves when the first apprehension of their natures brings on the terrible fear of discovery. To impose exile on oneself so that the repressed soul might be resurrected in the new camouflage of a vast city. In New York, Roman had isolated the bisexual part of his character from his other thoughts as Mr. Rochester had locked away his mad wife from the sight of other men. He hoped, like Mr. Rochester, that neglect would extinguish the feelings. But alas, the feelings continued to filter up out of the darkness like ghostly apparitions; he endured them and fled. But even with a distance of three thousand miles between him and his family and friends, he couldn't let go. It took the added distance of two years and a lot of frustration to act against the inertia.

The instructor, John Berry, was a friendly man who took athletics seriously. Roman would pretend to be resting against the far wall of an empty court while John played handball with someone else. Roman wanted to ask if he could play but was too embarrassed to do anything but watch for a few minutes each day. John was blond and had the husky build of a man more interested in the feel of sports than in the aesthetic effect of exercise on the body. As Roman sat watching, he imagined them in bed together.

Once John's handball partner didn't show up. It was ten o'clock in the evening. On his way to watch, Roman met John frowning with annoyance.

"Wanna play?" he asked, looking Roman over.

"Sure," he said.

Roman was too disoriented to make much of a showing for the first game. But warmed up, he smacked the ricocheting ball back to his opponent with ease. John slapped Roman on the back when he scored the winning point. They walked back to the lockers together and the instructor asked him if he'd like to stick around until midnight—he had to teach an old man gymnastics first.

At twelve, they went out to a diner for coffee. The instructor talked about his children for a while, which both disconcerted and relieved Roman; he said he had been separated from his wife for two years and had no plans for either divorce or reconciliation. Roman was mesmerised by the handsome, tanned face sitting across the booth from him, the movement of his full lips as he spoke. After they had three coffees, John asked him if he'd like to take a swim in his pool at home. Roman asked if he could have another cup of coffee first.

They talked about cars. It was two o'clock before they left.

John's backyard was enclosed in a wooden fence. He poured them both Scotches and they talked until three at a wicker table next to the pool and its whirring filter system.

"I'm going in," the instructor finally said. He discarded his shirt, revealing a diamond of coarse curly blond hair. He stepped out of his pants, then placed his jock and wristwatch on the chair.

Roman looked down in embarrassment at the sight of John's assertive nakedness and started very slowly to unbutton his Brooks Brothers shirt. In high school it wasn't unusual for him to run nude through the locker room pursuing or being pursued by a teammate flailing a wet towel. But that was fun unencumbered by desire. This was just the reverse and the novelty was disconcerting.

Roman listened to the clink of ice cubes as John finished off his drink. He knew he was being watched but looked up only when he heard the instructor dive in. The pool lights darted under the surface of the water as John swam to the side. His powerful arms and back were slick and

tan and his white buttocks shivered and separated as he kicked the
water into the air. Surfacing, he stretched his arms out along the lip of
the pool and waved to Roman.

"Come on in!"

Roman stopped unbuttoning his shirt and reached over for his Scotch
on the table. He had put years of thought into this moment. He had
wondered what it would be like and who would be involved. Fear
impeded the divestment of his past and he sat motionless, like a
condemned man not able to ready himself for execution.

John called again and dove under the water, swimming the length of
his pool. Suddenly Roman tore off his shirt and threw it on the ground.
He as quickly shucked off the rest of his clothes and jumped into the
water like a virgin modestly arranging herself under the covers of her
wedding bed. There was a surge of water as John came up for air near
the diving board and pulled himself up out of the water. His biceps
strained and the muscles of his stomach grew taut as he drew his legs up
at a right angle. Roman looked away from the large blond genitals
bobbing on the surface.

John swam over and reached out to Roman, who submerged.

"This is great," Roman said, tossing his wet hair back after surfacing.

John suggested they have a race. They swam free-style, four and a
half laps to the stairs. John won.

Roman waded to the stairs as he caught his breath. He looked at
John's blond hair falling slickly back, its dampness reflected in the
moonlight. His tan body was perfectly visible in the illuminated water.
Roman shyly leaned back against the incline of the stairs and looked up
silently at the stars. John approached. They talked quietly for a bit, small
talk masking lust. The instructor sat on a step, his leg brushed against
Roman. He leaned closer, his eyes scanning Roman's face. He raised his
arm out of the water and touched Roman's shoulder. Roman swallowed
hard. He looked away. John's hand slid down to Roman's slippery chest.
He touched a nipple with his fingertips. The percussive repetition in
Roman's ear matched the rhythm of insects in the flowered plants

beyond the pool. The still air was heavy with rose. Roman closed his eyes as the instructor embraced his waist and drew their wet bodies together.

The instructor led him up the stairs and onto a lounge chair where they made love. Roman had had many women lovers, but this was the best. At five o'clock, they went inside the house and made love again. The wall of denial within Roman had cracked, releasing the accumulated passion of a lifetime. John had to rock Roman in his arms after they made love the second time as Roman was convulsed with tears. When they parted, Roman thought he was in love.

During the week, he bought John a skindiver's wristwatch that confided time, date and tide information.

"Thanks," he said, putting it on.

Trying to expand John's taste, Roman also bought him a recording of Schubert's Great C-major Symphony. They played it together while having sex; John said he liked it. But he broke his date with Roman later in the week.

"That's okay," Roman said, and to prove it drove to the Mark Taper Forum to secure two tickets for *Waiting for Godot*. They both enjoyed it and ate enchiladas in a Mexican restaurant afterwards.

The following week, John broke another date with Roman via his telephone answering machine. Roman drove over to his apartment. As he approached the house, he could hear music coming from inside. Carole King. He cupped his hands against a window, trying to see into the living room. It was dark; Roman could see that no one was there. He walked through the beds of marigolds growing on the side of the house to the back. A hot tub had been built on the stone patio. It was directly under a window so Roman stepped on its edge and peered inside the house. He saw John in bed with a woman and another man, whom John was fucking. He keened at the sight of the ménage à trois. Jumping down, he stumbled back to his car and drove to his apartment, hysterical.

This unfortunate incident caused a regression. Once again Roman denied his attraction to males and, worse, he became bitter and reclusive. It was six months before he allowed himself even to have a conversation with a woman, longer before he had a date. Women complained of his feline aloofness.

After a year, he met a girl named Beverly March. She was beautiful, sexy and, most importantly, benevolent. She was incapable of lying. Her credo was happiness. She painted little rainbows on her fingernails and cooked him organic meals. Sex was good, if not earthshaking; Roman felt secure again. He bought her an engagement ring after six months, put it in the top drawer of his bureau under a pair of pajamas his mother sent him but he never used. He didn't know why he didn't give it to her.

The vending-machine man came back into the terminal. He stared intently at Roman, then went into the men's room and stood by the door. The janitor was sitting at the counter in the coffee shop smoking his cigar and talking to the cook. Roman looked at his watch and went to meet Burton at the gate in the main part of the station.

Roman Holiday

I sat atop my Stanley Steamer trunk wearing a three-button black linen suit and a black bowler hat accessorized nicely by an ebony walking stick leaning harmlessly to my right and a red carnation pinned to my lapel. Having initially been depressed by the sunny morning on the train and the resulting aggressive cheerfulness of its passengers, my mood improved at the sight of the train station.

Enwrapped in a silver coat and cloche hat, Nazimova had been here, with lily tattoos decorating her shins, waiting to reread a love letter in the privacy of her compartment. Miriam Hopkins, having divorced her second husband, Austin Parker, had smiled bravely for reporters after returning from a brief vacation in Bainbridge, Georgia. Born on October 17, 1918, in Brooklyn, New York, a moderately attractive girl named Margarita Carmen Cassino, with an excess of ambition and facial hair, would pose for photographers by gate six as the glamorous Rita Hayworth, accompanied by husband Orson Welles and daughter Rebecca. Later, Robert Taylor and Adolph Menjou would wave to fans and board a train for Washington, D.C., where they would help the House Un-American Activities Committee destroy the careers of their peers. Ruth Donnelly and Gene Lockhart and Pola Negri and Charles Ruggles—all had walked through the concourse to have scraps of paper and pencils with gnawed erasers thrust at them before boarding Pullman cars.

I unbuttoned my jacket, revealing a brightly colored Turkish vest. The initial flurry of activity caused by the rather clumsy disembarkation of my fellow passengers had died down as one by one they connected with friends, family and male nurses. Now the concourse looked depleted of life and, what seemed to me more terrible, of spirit. It was almost as if the huge edifice had wearied from its activity during the first half of the century and was awaiting some final fate.

I had mixed feelings about visiting Hollywood: that peculiar contrast of emotions one experiences when about to meet an old acquaintance again after many decades or, as a child, when walking stealthily up to view the remains of what had been a jovial uncle at a funeral. I wanted to love Hollywood because it had given me so much, including the sense of romance with which I now viewed it, but I feared sitting too close. Of course, I knew Mae Busch wouldn't be there to serve me gin from a rattan throne, Franchot Tone wouldn't wave to me from a soggy polo field; I knew no one would ever enunciate or peer at one as well as Edna May Oliver. I knew there would be disappointment. I just didn't want to see progress. I didn't want the Hollywood I knew to be an effete ruin like this train station.

"Passengers to Portland. Portland pass—"

Some of the local creatures timidly peered at me from the perimeter of the station. A girl dressed in a pastel green tennis suit walked by with the young man from the train who had made a most flamboyant use of dental floss in the dining car. A molelike creation carrying a mop head threw a cigar into a cracked marble urn. Crossing my legs, I unsheathed a cigarette and tapped the filterless tip against my black enamel case. I was wondering if Roman's tardiness might be due to some unfortunate geological confrontation when a lighter appeared from behind me and burst into flame.

"You're overdressed," a deep voice said.

"Roman!" I yelled, jumping down from the trunk. "It's good to see you again!" It was. He looked splendid, tanned a copper hue with auburn highlights in his dark hair. We jabbered excitedly for a few minutes, then had a porter take my trunk outside where we got into something called a Ford Pinto. Noticing his lack of precaution in leaving the keys in the ignition, I said, "You just leave it like this?"

"Yes," he replied. "It's different out here, Burton."

Isn't that nice, I thought to myself insincerely, people trust each other in California. "That's nice," I said, smiling. Roman shrugged.

Coldly eyeing a magnetized tic-tac-toe board on the dashboard, I asked what had happened to the Volvo.

"It's being fixed," he said. "This belongs to Beverly."

"Who's Beverly?"

"A friend of mine. You'll meet her."

I didn't think I wanted to.

We drove about thirty minutes and Roman pointed out different restaurants designed to look like objects one might wear or pet. The sides of the road seemed to be a revolving backdrop of the same drug store, liquor store, supermarket and adobe gas station. As we drove on, the altitude made it possible to glimpse a partial view of the city.

"That's the business district," Roman said, pointing to a dozen or so somber skyscrapers looking lonely and uncomfortable in the midst of the flat gray city. The incongruity was softened by the Los Angeles smog which gave the metropolis the fuzzy appearance of a cinematic image shot through a filtered lens.

At one point, Roman slowed the car down and stopped.

"Why did you do that?" I asked. "We're in the middle of the road."

He smiled and pointed to an overweight woman wearing toreador pants and spiked heels. She daintily stepped off the concrete island and walked across the street, waving thanks.

"Pedestrians have the right of way in California," Roman explained. "If you see someone at a crosswalk who looks as if he or she is even *thinking* about crossing the street you have to stop."

Isn't that nice, I thought to myself. People don't try to run each other over out here as they do in the East. "That's nice," I said, smiling.

Roman shrugged again and asked me if I'd like to stop for something to eat.

"Yes!" I replied, suddenly imbued with the contagious beneficence that apparently had infected even the provincial traffic laws. "Let's go somewhere that the local canaille frequent."

"Okay," Roman replied.

We pulled into the parking lot of a restaurant called Body Parts and went inside. The paper placemats at our table were printed with connect-the-dot games and optical illusions captioned, CAN YOU FIND A CAT, A BOOT AND A SNOWFLAKE IN THIS PICTURE? In the center of the table, next to a bottle of soy sauce, was a folded placecard faced with a cartoon of the human digestive system. A bean-shaped organ was outlined in red; underneath it read: THE GALLBLADDER. In italic print it explained how a thick, bitter viscous fluid called *bile* is discharged by the gallbladder to form a foamy solution which emulsifies fats and oils. As if that weren't offensive enough, it went on to list the early warning signs of gallbladder problems—not the least of which are "belching and vomiting." It suggested that sufferers choose the special of the day.

"Hiya, fellas!" exclaimed a big, healthy woman with platinum hair and eyebrows. She winked cheerfully at me and put menus in front of us. "The special of the day is Millet Tabouli," she said, squirting the table with biodegradable glass cleaner.

The menu was laminated and filled with little drawings of plants with parenthetical appellations such as *Avena Sativa* and *Humulus Lupulus*. Aside from the Millet Tabouli, the menu offered Soft Nutty Carob Balls, Safflower Nut Loaf, Squash-Sunflower Stroganoff, and Alfalfa Fritters. Rather than displaying photographs of these equine entrees, which would have provoked customer outrage, the management had seen fit to follow each dish with titillating imperatives such as M-M-M-M! and SLURP! Or, as in the case of a beverage such as raw milk, MOO!

I deposited a small gratuity and we left.

As we drove to Roman's apartment, he said, "You know who I bumped into out here from Gingold?"

"From high school! Who?"

"Delilah Lutz."

"No! The Jeane Dixon of Gingold. How did she look?"

"Well— I ran into her on Page Street on one of my jaunts up to San Francisco. It seems she's had a really rough time. Her parents put her away."

"You mean in a mental hospital?"

"Yeah. They just couldn't deal with her anymore."

"That's awful."

"Yeah. She told me she went through two years of shock treatments and all kinds of intense therapy. She said it almost drove her *really* crazy."

"How did she get out?"

"They had her in this arts and crafts therapy class making different things. When she was given a bunch of popsicle sticks to make a pencil holder, she kept one and carved it into a knife in her room at night. The nurses thought she was masturbating. She planned to stab the night nurse and run out of the place one night but changed her mind and snuck down to the basement, hid in a laundry bag, and was carted out the next morning. She hitched cross-country and settled in San Francisco. She's real happy now."

"How does she make a living?"

"As a mime," Roman replied, pulling in front of his apartment building. I laughed.

As we carried my trunk in, several strangers offered to help. In the East, this sort of thing doesn't happen. Strangers talk for one reason— solicitation. They ask for one of two things—money or directions. One has two alternatives—to comply or to plant one's chin in one's chest and continue walking. I think this is how God meant people to behave. I think it is unnatural for a stranger to risk a hernia and then extend an invitation to "ride bikes later."

When we got upstairs, I collapsed on a sofa. Roman had a one-bedroom apartment with a terrace. "It was furnished when I got it," he said, noticing the curl of my lip as I looked around. The walls were painted pale green and the molding was salmon-colored. Openings to rooms were arched; only the bathroom had a door. The acoustic ceiling looked like cottage cheese. The furniture was junk, or, as a local game show host might have said, elegant Mediterranean. The paintings were the sort that glorify Harlequins, huge-eyed waifs and flamenco dancers in oil on velvet.

"Who decorated this place?" I asked. "Stella Dallas?"

"Shut up," Roman replied, walking into the kitchen to make a batch of Margaritas.

Lying about the apartment were athletic chachkas like hiking boots, a kayak paddle, running shoes and a surfboard. I peered over the edge of the terrace. A gravel path wound around palm trees, swings and a bicycle rack, which had a habachi chained to it—at least one sign that distrust did indeed exist in California.

As I walked back into the room, there was a knock on the door. In strode a tall, dazzling woman with shimmering blond hair cascading down her back. A carpetbag was slung over her shoulder and large, gold-plated loops dangled from her ears. Grabbing Roman by the shoulders, she looked into his eyes in silence for a few seconds, then said pointedly, "How ya doin', man." They kissed noisily.

Disengaging himself, Roman gestured toward me and said, "Beverly, I'd like you to meet the friend I told you was coming."

"Far out," she replied. Her large breasts bounced happily underneath a loose-fitting red T-shirt as she loped toward me. The gorgeous face, tanned and freckled, was adorned with translucent blue eyes and a short, dapper nose, freshly peeled and pink. A light growth of blond hair covered her legs and peeked out from under her armpits. She exuded good health and fertility. A vitamin-enriched madonna of the New West.

"Beverly March," Roman said, "I'd like you to meet Burton Raider." I held out my hand, but she ignored it and hugged me ferociously. "Burton came all the way out here from the East Coast just for my graduation."

"Wow," she said, easing us both down on a sofa. "Like, you came all the way out here, to see a friend. Like, that shows commitment, you know? I was telling Roman just this morning. Like, my own *doctor* doesn't even show me commitment." She went on to describe a vaginal infection he had failed to cure.

Roman offered us Margaritas. I declined. Beverly said, "Wow, man, you, like read my mind." She sipped the drink and turned to me again. "Things have been so flipped out lately. My head's all messed up. I went to this encounter rap? This guy has this hot tub that seats ten in the basement of his house and, you know, people get in it and, like, talk and touch and stuff."

"That sounds very nice," I said.

"No, man, it isn't," she replied, explaining that the encounter session had done nothing except reinfect her vagina. She was planning instead to register for est, which was just becoming popular, although all she knew about it was that she would be put in a large room filled with people and humiliated for eighteen hours.

"I think they give you, like, two bathroom breaks," she said solemnly.

Roman spoke up. "We were thinking of borrowing your car this afternoon, Beverly. Maybe do a bit of sightseeing. This is Burton's first trip out here."

Beverly's eyes lit up like two thousand-point bumpers on a pinball machine. "Oh, man, so this is, like, a whole new thing for you! Wow! Like, a whole new state!" She opened her carpetbag and pulled out a plastic sandwich bag. "Have a lude on me," she said, holding out a white tablet.

"A *lude?*" I replied.

"A quaalude," Roman interjected. "A tranquilizer."

I have never been one to use pharmaceutical products. First of all, it is difficult for me to swallow them with liquids. My mother crushed aspirins in jelly for me all through my childhood and ever since I've had to pop pills into my mouth with masticated food and swallow the whole mess down together. This can be an inconvenient idiosyncrasy; it is the rare physician indeed who maintains a supply of English muffins in his office.

The idea of taking drugs to alter consciousness on a regular basis seems to me just one more manifestation of a technology geared to accommodate a people who have so lost character that they can no longer bear to be in touch with even their own perceptions. A people who, if judged solely by their manufactured food, entertainments and complaints, would be deemed craven. Or perverse. One of the reasons I took the train to California was to get a feel for the country. In a plane I couldn't have sensed the distance I had traveled or the subtle differences among the towns and the people. Taking drugs seemed an equally undesirable way to dull my impressions, making Hollywood no more interesting than a midwestern city at ten thousand feet.

"Why don't you take it?" Beverly asked, waving the pill in front of my nose.

"Thank you for the offer," I said. "But I really don't think I have to become a drug addict simply to visit Grauman's Chinese Theater."

"Okay, man. It's your own space," she said, smiling and popping it back into her bag.

Roman asked her about borrowing the car again. She said she had a few errands to run but that between doing them she would be glad to drive us wherever we wanted to go.

Beverly turned out to be a lighthearted driver. She tailgated tanker trucks marked EXPLOSIVE MATERIALS and emblazoned with skulls and crossbones. She careened across five lanes of traffic making exits off the freeway. For two days, Roman sat with her in the front seat while I sat in the back in the company of seat belts, shoulder harnesses and rosary beads.

The only tourist attraction I saw the first day was the LaBrea Tar Pits where I spent an hour looking at a recreation of the Mesozoic era replete with plastic prehistoric vegetation and dinosaurs.

Beverly's *errand* after that was to drive one hundred and fifty miles (no bathroom breaks) to a farmhouse at the bottom of one of the miscellaneous canyons with which southern California is pocked: the residence of a commune, Beverly told us, that practiced occult rituals in which were used materials like opossum blood, phosphorescent spray paint and chicken feathers.

"Most of all they, like, believe and, you know, practice the thing about equality," she said. I wondered *what* she 'could have been talking about.

As we arrived, I could see two women squatting down on the muddy ground grinding corn into meal with stones.

"The one on the left is Sunbeam. She used to do Pepsodent commercials until she got real pissed off at the, like, sexual thing. The all-you-are-is-a-piece-of-meat thing. So she told her agent to fuck off and came out here with Sage."

"Sage?" I asked.

"Sage Feinstein," she replied. "He, like, started the group. I'm picking up some ludes from him."

"Oh," I said. "Who's the other girl?"

"That's Algae. She used to be a tour guide at Universal Studios until she got tired of showing people Lucille Ball's dressing room and telling them to put out their cigarettes. Oh! There's Sage!"

A chap who looked like Paul Muni in *The Life of Emile Zola* came out the front door carrying a bucket. He lethargically strolled over to the two women who were pounding their brains out and dumped some more corn in the trough. He pointed at the pile. Glaring fiercely, Sunbeam got up, stomped into the farmhouse and, I imagine, telephoned her agent to advise him of her availability.

Beverly got out of the car to get her quaaludes.

The only other tourist attraction we visited before Roman got his Volvo back was Disneyland, that sprawling amusement park where high school students certified as clean-cut by the personnel department walk about in Mickey Mouse and Pluto drag.

"Isn't this far out!" Beverly said approximately every fifteen seconds.

The tourists there were perhaps the most petulant collection of people it has been my misfortune ever to encounter. I was always being told to "get the hell outta da way" by some middle-aged man taking a picture of his souvenir-laden family. It was amazing how nasty some women could get if they had reason to suspect one had cut in front of them on the Dumbo ride line. The average child walked around either with what appeared to be an arrow thrust through his head or wearing a felt porkpie hat decorated with a three-foot purple feather. I could imagine the benevolent Walt Disney Foundation sending out safaris biannually to slaughter innocent ostriches just so that a child who was incapable of determining where his cotton candy ended and my cashmere pullover began would be happy.

The food offered by concession stands made me long for Millet Tabouli.

"I love this place," Beverly said at the Sara Lee café, happily munching a candy apple and wearing a pair of mouse ears.

We left only after I threatened to throw myself under a moving tram if we didn't.

Dangerous When Wet

After four days in California, I began to wonder if Thorazine might be the local staple. I would sit on Roman's sunny terrace in the afternoon, drinking Campari and soda, and watch the other tenants drink milk and eat salads on their terraces. Occasionally, one of them would get up and shake out a beach blanket. Below, people played volleyball, chatted in the communal Jacuzzi, skated on skateboards and crashed into trees. With absolutely no encouragement, strangers would invite me into their apartments to see their organic tomato crops or turquoise belt buckle collections, like proud mental patients showing the results of a month of recreation periods. I couldn't wait to get back East to have an argument with someone.

Beverly epitomized this lobotomized ambiance. Relentlessly good-willed, she reacted to the world with a mixture of awe ("Wow, man, did you ever, like, really *look* at your feet?") and enthusiastic sincerity. Her most unwavering characteristic was politeness. Though I made several disparaging remarks about California, partly to goad her out of her vapidity, she would smile, nod and continue to sprinkle wheat germ on whatever she happened to be eating. It was only later, in private with Roman, that she would confess reluctantly that she thought I was crazy. Now, she humored me with smiles, narrated drives through Beverly

Hills ("There's Barbara *Eden's* house!") and gushed about the gift of a Navajo Indian blanket that was as notable for its colorful depiction of a buffalo hunt as it was for the celerity with which it induced hives.

When Roman got his car back I asked him if we might go off by ourselves somewhere. We packed cucumber sandwiches, caviar and tea and drove the Volvo toward San Francisco. At first, we took the coastal road: a narrow, two-lane highway which some enterprising dynamitist had blasted out of the ocean palisades. In the movies, dispensable characters blinded by tears often met their fates here, bursting through the guardrails and crashing on the rocks two hundred feet below. In reality it was a scenic jewel; one had merely to pry one's eyeballs open to enjoy it.

Halfway there, we left Route 1 and continued through the desert—a red, dusty plain filled with gila monsters and asthmatics; its desiccated beauty had often been used as a background for Maureen O'Hara's profile. Although I've never been one to be impressed by nature's pageantry, when we drove into San Francisco even I was thrilled. The sun was setting; the low, white buildings covering the hills around the bay were rose-colored. Golden Gate Bridge stretched across the pale, churning water and silver puffs of fog drifted underneath its span into the bay. Unlike Los Angeles, here there was little aesthetic clash between the handiwork of man and nature.

The first thing we did was eat. We avoided the tourist restaurants on the bay where we would have had to sit next to children wearing lobster bibs and armed with melted butter, coordinated parents picking at Surf 'n' Turf platters while discreetly slipping handfuls of salted crackers into their pockets, and grandmas gingerly cracking crab claws, sending geysers of hot juice onto the backs of nearby necks. Roman took me to a restaurant in Chinatown he had been to where we ate Ta Chien chicken, cold noodles with hot sesame sauce, and Pa Pao Chai. We sat near a bay window. Roman looked exceptionally handsome against the background of city lights. I was in heaven.

We talked about our families and our plans.

"Are you going to stay out here after graduation?" I asked.

"I'm not sure. My mom will be out Thursday for the ceremony. I'd feel bad about leaving her back East for good."

"What about Beverly?" I asked.

He replied with an anecdote about the eccentricities of Sausalitoans that didn't answer the question. "What about you?" he asked. "I know *you're* going to stay East."

I nodded.

"Did I ever tell you my uncle Hyam works at the same network as your father? Hyam Patchwicke?" Roman asked.

I shook my head.

"You should meet. Maybe I'll write him a letter. Ever think about working in TV?"

I shrugged. "You know me. I'm more the movie mogul type."

"That's all out here," Roman said.

"So is most television for that matter," I said.

He nodded.

I had heard these lines before and was tired of them. I wanted more from Roman.

"I really don't know what I'm going to do except move into Manhattan."

We both looked out on the busy street. It was getting late. We had gone through two pots of jasmine tea. I signaled the waiter and suggested we go out somewhere.

"What do you want to do?" Roman asked.

"Let's go dancing," I said.

"Dancing? Where?"

"Somewhere we can both enjoy. Do they have mixed clubs around here?"

"Well . . . yeah . . ."

"Let's go to one."

"Well . . ."

"Please," I said. "We've never been out here together. Let's do something we wouldn't have dreamed of doing in Oyster Bay."

"But it's such a long drive back to LA. We can't stay out that late," Roman said, checking over the bill.

"Come on, Roman. Please."

His eyes narrowed on a bowl of duck sauce. "Okay," he finally said, handing the waiter our money.

We drove along Polk Street until we came to a bar that had a midget whose T-shirt read SNEEZY standing outside distributing flyers. I got out and asked him about the place. "Straight," he said, and directed me farther up the block. Roman was reticent as we stopped in front of the club that the midget had described—no marquee, blue neon flamingo flickering above the doorway. The pulse of music inside drifted out to the street.

"Well?" I said.

Roman stared at the club for a moment, then pulled a plastic film cylinder out of his pocket. Inside were five white pills.

"Are those those lude things?" I asked.

"Yup," he said, swallowing one.

"Look, Roman, if you'd rather not—"

"Come on," he said, getting out of the car. I chased after him to the door. We went in and squeezed next to a bar lit by Tiffany lamps and jammed with people. Along the opposite wall to the back was a honeycomb of shelves where people could place drinks and shoes. In the rear, the dance floor was crowded with saltatory bodies, athletically dressed.

"Want a drink?" Roman asked.

"No, thanks." I didn't need one. Being out in San Francisco with Roman was exhilarating enough.

He ordered a Black Russian for himself and we settled against the bar. Perspiring revelers pushed by to leave while collected newcomers pardoned their way through to assume their places on the dance floor. Roman and I were jostled by the crowd, drawn three people apart by the ebbs and pushed chest-to-chest with the crush.

"Sorry," he kept saying.

"That's okay," I replied. My shirt got the benefit of his black Russian.

The role the outdoors plays in California was evidenced by the dress and conversation of the people around us: Skindiving wristwatches and gym shorts abounded. Two men next to me shouted over Donna Summer in an attempt to share information about catamaran rentals. Blond and red-headed girls wearing zodiac jewelry were draped over the necks of their surfer boyfriends. Football-jerseyed merrymakers shouted at the dancers from the upper shelves against the wall.

"You want to dance?" I asked Roman.

"Naw, naw. I'm not much of a dancer."

I smiled. I knew he could be.

Roman waved to the bartender and ordered another drink. Someone tapped me on the back. I turned to see an attractive dark-haired stranger wearing the Librium grin I had come to know so well.

"Hi," he said.

"Hello," I replied.

"My name's Blue. What's yours?"

"Burton," I said.

He continued grinning. "You're not from around here, are you?"

"No," I replied.

"I knew it. I could tell by your fedora. Wanna dance?"

I glanced over my shoulder at Roman. He was popping another quaalude into his mouth. "I'm going to dance for a while, Roman. Okay?"

"Sure, sure," he said.

For over half an hour I danced with the colorfully christened stranger, who moved his muscular body extremely well. Reluctantly we bid farewell on the floor. As I pushed my way back to the bar, a chap I recognized as a featured model in the Winston advertising campaign asked me to dance.

"Okay," I said.

The model lit a Tareyton and danced sedately, trying—successfully—to look as much like a billboard as possible. Nearby, two girls wearing cowboy hats with turquoise and silver headbands wildly threw their arms and legs about, suggesting electrocution rather than dance. A straight black couple dramatized their style of sexual intercourse for public scrutiny and two stoned hippies did the twist until they fell on the floor laughing.

By the time I got back to the bar, Roman was clearly feeling the effects of the alcohol and drugs. He was talking to an attractive blond fellow.

"Burton!" he said, slurring the word loudly. "I'd like you to meet someone." He turned and squinted at the blond. "What'd you say your name was?"

"Bill," came the cheerful reply.

"Bill! That's right! Bill, I'd like you to meet a friend of mine. The very best friend I have in the whole world." He put his arm around my shoulders and hugged me. "You know, Bill, we went to high school together. Gingold High School. We took gym together—"

Like a mental patient who had already received his Dixie cup of medication, Bill passively listened to Roman run down our high school schedules.

"You know, Bill," Roman concluded, patting me on the stomach. "I . . . I love this guy. I really do."

Bill smiled.

"Whoaaaa!" Roman lost his balance, and Bill and I had to pick him up off the floor.

"Maybe we should get going, Roman," I said, brushing him off.

"Go?"

"It's getting late and—"

"Naaah," he said, dismissing the idea with a clumsy wave of his graceful hand.

"Remember, I don't drive," I said.

He looked at me under drooping eyelids. I caught him as he swayed forward.

"Okay! Let's go!" he said.

"Do you know a hotel?" I asked.

Slowly shaking his head, he said, "We're not goin' to a hotel."

"What are you talking about? Where are we going then?"

He pushed ahead of me to the door, saying, "Somewhere we can both have some fun." He turned to wave good-bye to Bill and I helped him stagger out to the car.

"Sure you're okay?" I asked.

"Sure," he said, grinding the gears.

We drove for about fifteen minutes.

"Will you please tell me where we're going?" I said, growing more impatient with each mile. This was unlike any Roman I had ever seen.

Lighting a cigarette, he replied, "You're going to see a San Francisco landmark. Beverly loves this place. It's called the Mantra Baths."

"What in God's name is that?"

He explained that it was the only sex bath in the United States for both men and women. It had been a gigantic public swimming pool at the turn of the century. Now the mammoth pool, indeed the entire style of bathing, was gone.

"I've never been to a bath before," I said, not mentioning my sudden alarm at the thought of going to one with him.

"You can just sleep there if you like. I'm horny. We'll drive back to LA in the morning."

It was four o'clock when we arrived. We parked the car on a deserted block. Roman pointed out a small, illuminated sign next to the door across the street. "That's it. Beverly loves this place," he repeated. "Come on."

Immediately inside was a chamber that looked like the rumpus room in the basement of a suburban house. It was paneled with blond wood and there was a bar cut out of one wall with leather stools in front and Cinzano ashtrays on top. A fat man in a T-shirt stood behind, drying a glass.

"Hello," he said. "What'll it be, fellas."

Roman was drunk enough already and I was still too excited to drink.

Undernourished couches had been placed liberally around the room along with scores of overstuffed pillows. No one else was about.

"Lockers are five," the man said.

Roman took out a ten-dollar bill. The man smiled and placed two turkish towels on the bar. "Down there," he said, pointing.

Towels in hand, we walked down a narrow corridor lined with glossy wood like the lower-deck passageway of a luxury liner. The locker room was small and lit by two fluorescent bulbs. It had the competitive smell of ammonia triumphing over fungus. We undressed next to each other. Roman knocked his head against a locker trying to pull off a shoe. He wriggled out of his tight jeans and placed the belt loop over a hook inside his locker. His legs were strong and lightly covered with fine dark hair. Reaching into one of the pockets, he pulled out a small red enameled box.

"What's that?" I asked.

Weaving slightly, he slowly replied, "Cocaine." A tiny little spoon was extricated and dipped into the white powder in the box. He inhaled a small pile.

"What's that going to do?" I asked, distinctly annoyed with his considerable drug intake.

He looked at me with his eyes almost shut and replied, "Make me feel good. Want some?"

"No, thanks," I replied and continued undressing, staring furtively at the half-nude Roman.

He sniffed several more spoonsful, put the paraphernalia back into his pocket and took off his shirt. The light above him highlighted his black hair with a bluish tint and cast a shadow over his face. His voluptuous arm muscles shifted in definition as he pulled off his white Jockey shorts. Gary Cooper would have been envious. Wrapping a towel around his waist, he said, "I'm going to see if there's anyone else in here. I'll see you later." He padded out of the room.

I was glad he left. Being in this sort of a sweaty locker room with Roman made me feel extremely uncomfortable.

After I finished undressing, I went to explore. There were two floors above the locker room. The first was a dimly lit dormitory affair; pillowless beds were arranged haphazardly with less than a foot of space between. A man and woman in the corner were quietly making love. I couldn't tell if one was Roman. Two men and a woman were fast asleep on separate beds in the rest of the room. I climbed the spiral staircase to the next floor.

It was in absolute darkness. I stood listening to the quiet breathing of sleepers, then crept along with hands extended like a blind man. I tripped over the corner of one bed. The woman sleeping on it briefly stirred. Continuing more carefully, I worked my way along hoping to find a door leading to a more lighted and lively room, but there was nothing more. This floor was identical to the one below. I felt for an unoccupied bed corner. When I sat down, a winsome female voice nearby breathed a string of unintelligible words in her sleep, the reply in some imagined conversation.

I got up again and stubbed my toe. Silently cursing, I decided to go down to the bar for a drink—provided, of course, that they stocked something that didn't involve the emulsification of raw vegetables. I went back to where I judged the spiral staircase to be. As I felt for the banister, a hand suddenly touched my leg. It was eerie and exciting to realize that another consciousness was awake in the darkness. I stopped, listening. I could hear the sound of labored breathing. Arms reached up out of the darkness and pulled me down onto the bed. I came to rest on a smooth, muscular, very male form. I ran my hand along his shoulders and chest.

Suddenly I knew. I knew it was Roman. I tried to push away but he held me fast. I didn't want this to happen. Did I? I pushed once more to get up, but then surrendered to his maleness. I touched the places I had always desired. Eyes. Forehead. Palms. We grappled hungrily, almost brutally.

I didn't say a word after it was over—words would have tainted the perfection of the scene. Roman's arm fell over the side of the bed as he passed into a deep sleep. I embraced him and listened to his breathing become more settled. I lay there all night, watchful and protective, not sleeping, but savoring the memories that had led to this. I ran the past before me like a 35-millimeter black-and-white film. I felt immortal.

*   *   *

The next morning, Roman woke with a start. Sunlight streamed in through the cracks in the black paint on the windows. I smiled at him, waiting for a good morning. He looked groggily about the room, somehow different.

"Are you all right?" I asked, sensing that something was terribly wrong.

"Wha—" he mumbled.

I reached over to push his wavy hair out of his eyes but he jerked back and unsteadily rose to his feet. Tottering, he picked up his towel. "C'mon," he said vaguely, wrapping it around his waist. He stumbled toward the spiral staircase.

"Roman?" I called after him as he started to descend. Alarm bells were going off in my head. I scrambled to the edge of the bed. *"Roman!"*

"C'mon," he repeated, disappearing. I grabbed my towel and hurried after him.

"What's wrong?" I asked frantically in the locker room.

"Nothing," he replied, pulling on his trousers. "Get dressed."

"But, Roman, I—"

"Burton, please," he said, pressing his fists to his head. "Let me get my bearings, will ya?"

We dressed in silence. He wasn't taking this at all well. As we walked out to the car, I asked if he felt like eating breakfast somewhere.

"Ugh, no," he replied, putting the key in the ignition. He glanced over sourly at me.

I was horrified. I could see it in his face: He was ashamed of last night. Disgusted. He started the car. We lurched forward. My chest tightened. I eased myself back against the cold plastic upholstery, trying to be calm. We drove back to Los Angeles through the desert valley in absolute silence. Once I asked him how he felt; there was no reply. I felt shattered. I leaned back and closed my eyes. A steady stream of warm air blew through the windows and vents. Exhausted from my night-long vigil, I fell asleep.

When I awoke, I was alone in the car, parked outside of Roman's apartment building. My foot was asleep. I stumbled across the lawn, took the elevator up. Roman was sitting on his bed next to my suitcase.

"Roman—" I said, hoping, but not really thinking, that he had regained his equilibrium.

He looked up, not directly at me. "I want you to do me a favor, Burton," he said deliberately.

"What?" I asked apprehensively.

"I . . . I want you to go," he said.

I swallowed hard. "Go?" I asked, moving toward him.

He stood up quickly, drawing away. "Please," he said. "Don't make it harder for me than it already is. I have to think. I can't think with you around here. Please."

"But, Roman," I begged. "What did I do? Whatever it was, I won't do it again. Just tell me. You want me to go to a hotel? I will. I don't mind. It's okay. I have traveler's checks. If it's about last night. We'll forget it. Okay? See, I already forgot. Just ask me what happened. I can't remember. It was—"

"*Burton!* For God's sake!" he yelled. Closing his eyes, he rubbed his head. "I have to think. I can't talk about anything now. Just please be my friend. Go." Averting his eyes, he walked toward the door. "I have to see if Beverly is back yet," he said, leaning against the doorframe and facing the other room. "If you can pack, I'll drive you to the train station." I sat down on the bed, not believing this was happening. This nightmare. He glanced back at me. "I'm sorry," he said. I opened my mouth to speak but he turned and slowly pulled the door shut behind him. A child screamed from the courtyard below.

Not listening to my brain as it chattered away with opinions, I clenched my teeth, called a cab and packed. Downstairs, Beverly passed me as the cabdriver was putting my bags in the trunk. Polite to the end, I waved; not recognizing me, she blinked and bounded toward the apartment building.

"The airport?" the driver asked.

"Yes," I replied. "The airport."

The flight I took is no longer part of memory; I had seven vodka martinis before Chicago. My parents picked me up at Kennedy Airport. My mother fired questions at me all the way home.

"How was your trip? Why did you come back early? Did you bring me anything?"

I answered between sighs. When I was in my bedroom alone, I dove under my covers and cried. My best friend. Lost.

Mr. Blandings Builds
His Dream House

It was to be the last summer I would live at home with my family, but during most of it, I hardly spoke except to utter spiteful statements about the human race. My mother would be happily washing radishes in the kitchen sink or adding delicate touches to her latest watercolor, and I would suddenly appear, quoting Thomas Hobbes and John Locke in lugubrious tones.

If my own parents had kicked me out of the house for no reason, I couldn't have been more confused and hurt. Roman's very existence had, from the first, given my life a context; he was the consideration, the framework around which I would act and plan. With that taken away, I was fumbling for lines like an actor who had lost his place in a script. For weeks I came down to dinner wearing black and reading Kafka.

Lucy, who had finally begun to show a glimmer of intelligence, took to referring to me as Hamlet's father. "Look, my lord, it comes!" she would say with a mouthful of salad.

My parents were concerned about my well-being but I told them that the depression would soon pass, that I was just doubtful about the future and my place in it.

The only thing that prompted me to display any animation was the approach of the mailman. I expected a letter of explanation. An apologetic postcard. But I heard from Roman only indirectly: His uncle Hyam Patchwicke sent a letter offering an interview at my convenience. I thanked him over the telephone and asked if we could perhaps have lunch toward the end of the summer. He agreed. Instead of feeling good I felt worse than ever, swathing myself in a quilt and spending the next two days in my darkened bedroom.

One morning, for no other reason than to change scene, I decided to visit the warehouse that had been titled to me. Looking through my clothes closet, I chose a pair of black jodhpurs, a charcoal-gray shirt, black English riding boots and a riding crop. I had a cab drive me out to Flatbush, an undistinguished part of town except when considering cheese calzones and movie history.

Before Jane Fonda wore plastic G-strings in *Barbarella* and Susan Hayward threw back her head and walked into the gas chamber in *I Want to Live,* before Debbie Reynolds stopped traffic in Madrid after her divorce from Eddie Fisher and *Life* spent a day with Maria Montez and before Ernst Lubitsch showed Herbert Marshall how to hug Marlene Dietrich, the movies were silent and the biggest stars were Mary Pickford, Charles Chaplin, Gloria Swanson, Clara Bow, Richard Barthlemess, Theda Bara, Lillian and Dorothy Gish and Clara Kimball Young—deities in the new pantheistic religion being adopted by the world. Before the golden era, movies had been a relatively small business. Norma Talmadge, Mabel Norman and James Morrison went to work for the sole purpose of scratching out a living. They did their own stunts (though audiences thought them faked) and started at salaries of twenty-five dollars a week. They were paid in cash and lined up to receive their wages directly out of the producer's pocket. Edison Studios, the largest, would film ten movies simultaneously on the same stage. Biograph Studios on East 14th Street produced one-reelers to be shown in converted cigar stores and grocery stores for a nickel.

I sat in the cab for a few minutes and looked at all that remained of Vitagraph Studios. At its zenith, Vitagraph had earned over a million dollars per year. This money was split among a few owners, who quickly became greedy and hired efficiency experts to reduce costs. Ironically, they lowered productivity by limiting such things as the amount of film that could be exposed per movie.

Bad weather and lack of space precipitated a move to California, where Vitagraph became Warner Brothers. Its commodious stages in the East decayed and were eventually torn down to make room for occult bookstores, discount chandelier outlets and other modern improvements. Only this building remained. It was large and concrete with hangar doors and virtually no windows. As a warehouse, it hadn't made any money for the financial authority who had titled it to me. Before him in the 1960s, another entrepreneur had hoped to begin a New York–based film company and purchased it as a publicity stunt to attract interest and money. The press took pictures of workmen laying down acoustic floors and walls and there were little features in Sunday magazine sections that heralded the return of the movies to their home town. But the only person who got caught up enough in the excitement to give the entrepreneur any money was my benefactor, the leading authority on financial investment on the East Coast, who took possession of it after the entrepreneur decided to rethink his idea in Venezuela.

I had the driver wait for me, unlocked the huge door and went inside. It was hot and empty and filthy. The acoustic interior was intact. I scuffed around the perimeter. They had filmed the original versions of *Captain Blood* and *The Life of Napoleon Bonaparte* in this room. Klieg lights made their debut here, as did Alice Joyce, who had to douse her eyes with a damp cloth between scenes because she was allergic to the mercurial vapor produced by the lights. Arcs had to be imported from Broadway. It probably cost a few hundred dollars to produce a movie in 1911. Now the cost of a low-budget film was about a million dollars; at least that was what Roman had told me when I showed him this place.

I sat down on the floor feeling glum and lost. I lit a Dunhill. The room was silent. A breeze brushed my face, as if a ghost from the ancient cinema passed by to observe me more closely. There was a brace hanging by one screw from a beam way above me. I wondered if it might have held a light that shone down on Marion Minter. Resting my head against my knees, I sighed.

What is the fate of a pariah? To mourn his plight? To look back wistfully at a more graceful time? Forward to a more understanding one? To deny the nature that sets one apart? Obscure it with pleasure or pain? What is the fate of a pariah? Passivity? To be poked and prodded into some definite form the way nature is by the stick of technology, the way philosophy is by the artillery of politics? Or is his fate aggressiveness? To add the sights and sounds one finds missing from the world. To create. Add beauty where none existed, transform confusion. Impress the world with one's presence.

I looked around the cavernous studio. I knew what had to be done. Make a movie. Knew that was what I had always wanted to do.

I left the building and locked the enormous metal door. The cabdriver was resting with a baseball cap over his face. The material rose and fell with his breathing. "Up! Up!" I said, rapping the car door with my crop. "Take me home."

When I arrived, I gathered my parents together and told them I wanted to make a movie.

They looked at each other. "A *movie?*"

I explained that I wanted to resurrect the old studio building and film the script that I had written in college. *Resurrection and Denial.* There was a pronounced silence as I looked from face to face.

Trying to be tactful, my mother said, "Shouldn't you sell the script to someone in California and let *him* make it into a movie?"

"Of course!" my father said. "You need training to do something like that. Experience! Luck."

My father had risen in the network to the point that he was in charge of developing dramatic pilots purchased from independent producers.

He had toyed with the idea of starting his own company, but hadn't out of the need for security. "It's a real tough business, Burton. You can't just *decide* to make a movie. You have to apprentice."

I sank down in my chair. "I just thought you might be able to give me some ideas about getting started."

My mother fiddled with a canister and pinched my father's arm. He sat down next to me. I peeled the label off a bottle of club soda while he looked at me.

"Okay, so you want to make a movie," he said. It looked as if he were going to take me seriously after all.

I nodded.

"You want to make a studio out of a shell of a building in Flatbush."

I nodded again.

He rubbed his forehead. "How much money do you have left from the lawsuit?"

"Twenty thousand," I replied.

"So you're essentially broke."

I nodded.

He thought for a moment. "And you don't want to go out to the Coast, is that right?"

"Yes!" I said.

"Well . . ." he said, "if you won't go out to California to see how a studio operates . . . maybe . . . you can do it in New York."

I sat up. "How?"

"Television. Learn as much as you can from television. The TV studios at the network are the descendants of those at MGM and Warner Brothers. Work here. See how they function. That's where you can start, anyway. Maybe in a few years—"

"Can you help me get a job at the network?" I asked excitedly.

He nodded. I hugged him.

"Plus," he continued, "there are a lot of expatriates from Hollywood working at the network. They can teach you plenty. I'll introduce you."

"Thanks, daddy!" I said, hugging him again. I never loved him more.

I grabbed the classified section of the *Times* and ran upstairs to telephone superintendents. I was ready to move into my favorite city.

I have always loved Manhattan. My frequent demands as a child to be taken there were met considerably less often than I might have wished. My parents had a genius for coming up with lame excuses.

"Lucy has a temperature of a hundred and three! We *can't* take you to Bendel's for their white sale."

I would have run away to New York if I hadn't been a pragmatist. After all, that sort of thing takes money and all my funds were tied up in a savings account my father assured me existed. *Somehow* he had charmed me into surrendering all monies received on birthdays and other lucrative occasions without so much as a receipt. I acquiesced only because the man had faithfully provided free room and board for years in exchange for my keeping the rather uncomplicated promise of being a *clean plater*. I also hesitated about running away because my primary reason for doing so, autonomy, would have been impossible; even a subway token couldn't have been purchased without someone giving me a boost.

I began looking for living quarters in Manhattan on my own. Though I always set up a specific appointment with the superintendent to view an apartment, I'd inevitably end up talking to his wife through the opening of a chained door while a Doberman pinscher knocked itself senseless trying to get at me. The conversations were always the same.

"Could I see the superintendent, please?"

"Doloresdelrioannamariaalberghetti."

"Did he go somewhere? I have an appointment."

"Xaviercugatcarmenmirandadesiarnaz!!"

"Could *you* show me the apartment then?"

"Lupevelezcantinflas!"

SLAM!

There were occasions when I was shown something. But how the superintendents kept straight faces while showing me camouflaged bathtubs in kitchens I'll never know.

After a week, I engaged a broker to find something with my specifications. Most of the buildings with apartments that met my size requirements had been converted from factories and contained what landlords called *conversation pieces.* With the end of the Vietnam War and starvation still popular as topics of conversation, I felt there was plenty to talk about without relying on surrealistic pipe formations and exposed girders. It was awful. The shopping conditions alone made these neighborhoods almost uninhabitable unless one's needs were confined to magic novelties and wholesale Christmas tree ornaments.

One day I was given an address by my broker and found that it pinpointed a magnificent building near Gramercy Park, an ornate L-shaped edifice on a corner. The highest floor had nine Gothic windows: five facing the avenue, four the side street. From the center, at the crux of the L, rose a huge gabled tower with five thin, arched windows at its face. Below that stretched a stone balcony, the imposing type used for speeches by South American dictators and popes before television cameras. The agent on the premises showed me the apartments, but they were the usual industrial conversions.

"What about the top floor?" I asked her. "Are you leasing that?"

"You don't want that, Mr. Raider," she replied. "We haven't touched it. It's just one huge room with bare concrete floors and walls."

I insisted.

"All right," she replied, wagging her finger. "But you'll get your cape all dirty."

The elevator went only as far as the ninth floor, which was not renovated either. It appeared as if the contractor responsible for the project had run out of capital. We used a narrow flight of stairs to get to the top floor. The door leading into the main chamber was heavy and wooden; dust had settled into the geometric scrollwork carved around its perimeter and knob. While the agent searched for the key, I admired its intricacies and wondered why modern objects received so little attention in the making. Children perceive time to be overabundant;

adults do not: Perhaps some difference in temporal perception made it possible for earlier civilizations to create beauty everywhere while ours, finding time spare, can only manage pragmatisms like men's hairspray and innovative forms of home insulation.

The door opened rather noisily but with ease. Diffused rays of sunlight penetrated the windows, translucent with dust. I had expected the room to be filled with debris from the renovation of the rest of the building, and perhaps one or two pieces of factory equipment, but it was quite empty. I walked along the row of windows, looking at the view of the intersection below. Each window stood encased in a housing of concrete scrollwork. Graceful caryatids rose up the length of the sides, which culminated in a bestial gargoyle at the arch.

"Filthy!" the agent said, brushing her hands.

The walls were unadorned, as was the ceiling except for a huge rectangular hole in the center.

"Is that the tower?" I asked.

"Yes," she replied, frowning. "We don't know *what* to do with *that.*"

Enough light came into the room to allow me to see about halfway up into the tower. There were intertwining spans of metal braces like flying buttresses reaching up into the darkness. I used the agent's flashlight and saw the delicate pattern in its upper reaches. Properly lighted, it would be dazzling.

Grimacing, she said, "Maybe we can board it up or something."

The presence of a rather large spider precipitated our return to her office. There, she said, "Really, Mr. Raider, I don't have time to play explorer. Are you interested in one of these renovated flats or not?"

"No. I think I'll take the top floor."

"You can't be serious!"

"Why?"

"It's just a storage area. We've terminated construction. We'd have to hire another contractor to renovate it."

"I don't want it touched," I said. "Just have the water and gas lines brought up another floor."

"Well, I don't know. I'll have to call the landlord, Mr. Gibbs."

It turned out that Mr. Gibbs had indeed run out of money and was desperately trying to rent out the completed apartments in order to continue construction. He was more than delighted to lease the floor. Its income was a windfall.

Having lived in a house and a traditional apartment, I decided I didn't want much in the way of rooms. Therefore, in the small part of the L, I had a large bedroom and bathroom constructed. I commissioned an artist to paint a Pompeiian mural on the wall facing the rest of the apartment. It was done in muted tones of red, gold and gray and the furniture I purchased shared its simple style. I covered the floor with one-inch mahogany tiles of three color tones. Electric light was used only for reading and shaving; the rest of the room depended upon no less than one hundred and forty-six white candles which I regularly had replaced by the grateful proprietor of a shop in Greenwich Village. Thirty-six of the candles were used in three huge wrought-iron chandeliers suspended over a twelve-place dining table. I never had curtains made: I loved to let the city glitter through the floor-to-ceiling windows. I discovered a reproduction of a Roman throne in an antique shop on Hudson Street, which I bought and had refinished. The kitchen was constructed along the inner wall of the large part of the L. It was separated from the living room by a black granite counter bordering the bottom of a paneless picture window.

The whole enterprise turned out to be more of an extravagance than I had originally estimated. My bank account was reduced to only a few thousand dollars. My morale dipped as well: my mother had driven in from Oyster Bay with the last of the cartons that had been filled with my personal belongings. We opened them together and came across several knickknacks that set my memory going. A photograph of Roman in a football uniform (number 87) with black grease under his eyes, spitting on the ground. An unopened recording of Liszt's piano concertos 1 and 2 I had planned to give him before I left California. My mother helped me dump them down the incinerator shaft.

Seeing the depressing effect this sentimental refuse had on me, she said, "Come on, darling. We'll meet your father and go out to the theater and dinner."

At first I refused, but she talked me into at least looking through the listings with her. While she went downstairs to buy a newspaper, I wrapped myself in a quilt and sat on the floor, brooding.

Upon returning, she said, "I've got the *Village Voice!*" with an unpleasant Bonita Granville color to her voice and sat down beside me. We looked over our three categories of choice.

In 1974 on Broadway, commercial success was still the thing. Little had changed over the years except for an increase in the part played by technology in performance. Thanks to hidden body microphones and twenty-five-foot speakers, for the first time in history one could hear the scraping of an actor's beard against his collar better than one could the unwrapping of toffee candies in the audience.

"Shall we see a musical?" my mother asked.

Broadway hadn't yet taken to mounting plays that dramatized physical handicaps, or lugubrious musicals that featured demonic barbers and well-dressed dictatoresses but what was offered looked pretty depressing. We turned the page.

Off-Broadway is a collection of small theaters where artistic excellence has always been a hallmark and where high-minded artistic directors help young, attractive playwrights develop their *talents*. We looked through the critiqued list: musicals about Third World struggles composed by recently graduated Yale Drama School students and tragedies concerned with the integrity and virtue of the human spirit written by recently paroled ethnic playwrights.

"Turn the page," my mother said.

Though neither of us had any instruction in the martial arts, we thought about venturing into a neighborhood that harbored an Off-*Off* Broadway theater. Rather than artistic excellence or commercial success, the concern of Off-Off Broadway artistic directors is that there be a sufficient number of loose linoleum tiles over which to trip in the lobby and that the interior pages of mimeographed programs *not* be stapled so as easily to slip through the legs of the audience. There is no need for microphones, since Off-Off Broadway theaters are of such an intimate nature that the actors can be smelled as well as heard. And because character development, plausible plots, costumes and scenery are not considered the stuff of avant-garde theater, one is treated to stone-faced actors sitting on orange crates repeating dialogue such as:

"Go."

"A going."

"Went."

"Loan."

"Lean."

"Lent."

Though this might sound like the conjugation of irregular verbs to some, the astute critics of New York always clear matters up the next day by informing the public that it was really "a triumphant lament to the desperate confidence of language and silence."

"Oh," my mother said, fingertips to cheek, "none of these looks very lighthearted."

I agreed, doubting whether I could make it to the intermission without walking over to a refreshment stand to end it all with a swig of imitation orange drink.

"Let's at least go to dinner," my mother said.

"No," I replied, crumpling the paper. "I just want to stay home." I was more depressed than before.

Sensing I needed company, my mother turned on the television. *The Blue Dahlia* was on PBS. I would rather have seen a Marietta movie.

The Public Broadcasting System is the Off-Broadway of television, a reaction against the commercial programming of the networks. Critics often point to the products of NBC, CBS and ABC as the cause of the decline in education; they rarely mention the fact that PBS is responsible for the high rate of vandalism in urban areas.

As any fool knows, the entertainments on PBS are of a high quality. There are no commercial interruptions. There is no need to endure aging movie stars endorsing savings banks or condoning the use of domestic olive oil. There are, however, *intermissions*. Periods of time about ten minutes in length during which aging movie stars squint at teleprompters and miss cues in an effort to impress upon viewers the fact that the Chubb Group of Insurance Companies cannot be expected to pay for *everything;* that uninterrupted programs such as the one she just interrupted wouldn't be possible without membership dollars. Giving the impression that moving men are waiting off-camera with ropes and pulleys to repossess the very chair in which she is sitting, the star pleads for contributions.

"This is the last day of our membership drive," she warned my mother and me, offering us handsome tote bags with twenty-three snap-off features and *Upstairs Downstairs* commemorative posters if we pledged something.

I imagined guilty, underpaid office workers all over the city reaching for their telephones. The camera panned the bleachers of volunteers answering calls. Though we could barely hear the aging movie star's voice over the racket, she complained she did not hear any ringing. A GOAL CHART was superimposed on the screen by means of a very expensive chyron machine as she berated us for not contributing, using adjectives like "freeloaders" and "moochers." All over the city, I imagined office workers slamming down their telephone receivers, leaving their apartments and throwing bricks through glass-enclosed bus stops decorated with PBS promotional material.

I got up and turned off the set. "Let's play Parcheesi," I said. That always cheers me up.

At least watching the TV served as a reminder. I decided to go to the network for a job first thing in the morning.

The Glass Web

The Vietnam War produced, more than anything else, a surplus of media arts majors. It would have been impossible to get the personnel department to smile down on my application without the help of my father and the sexogenarious Captain Dodo, who had had no recurrence of ego problems. And my stint as a writer for the *Observer* stood me in good stead.

After swallowing my pride, I met with Roman's uncle Patchwicke and was added to the writing staff of a morning show called, not surprisingly, *The Morning Show*. Patchwicke, as he preferred to be called, was the head writer. The staff worked on the seventh floor of a sixty-story office building on Sixth Avenue. One simply walked down an expressionless gray hall past an obsolete kinescope machine and some paint cans, to a door marked WR TERS. Inside were two offices. The smaller was a conference room, the larger a reception area used by the secretary to have amorous telephone conversations with her boyfriend.

Each writer received several assignments each day. He or she might have to write a human-interest story, preinterview guests so that some agreement could be made as to suitable questions and answers, or write some of the on-air patter that the hosts of *The Morning Show* attempted to appear to have ad-libbed.

The staff members worked independently of each other except

during the hour-long conference held daily. The first half of the meeting was informal and friendly and bon mots flew across the large table. My coworkers were an intelligent group of men and women; I had never before and have never since enjoyed more concentrated and witty conversations. After that pleasant half hour, though, Patchwicke would rap on the table and say, "All right, ladies and gentlemen, time to work." The amusing wisecracks would subside and the most uninspired discussions of possible feature stories concerning creative child custody arrangements and franchise fraud cases would ensue.

Within the industry, working for *The Morning Show* was considered enviable by everyone but the writers, who all considered their work frivolous and had pipe dreams of authoring four-character plays and opening Japanese restaurants; none had the strength of his own convictions. The writers' frustrations would occasionally be manifested in uncalled-for rebukes and acts of frenzy involving pineapple danishes.

Though it appeared the secretary had no ambitions other than to make typographical errors and read twelve-hundred-page gothic romances, she shared their frustrations; indeed, she was to be the only person in the office to make her pipe dream come true. She wanted to be an actress. Each lunch hour she would attend an audition. If it had gone well, upon returning she would happily make a fresh pot of coffee. If it hadn't, she would slam desk drawers and accuse people of stealing her pens. Success would begin a year later when she would do a commercial that required her to say "Hotsy Totsy Tacos" in an amusing fashion. Taco sales would rise sharply and an enterprising television executive on the West Coast would fly her out to do a pilot in which she had to mouth dialogue of little more consequence in an equally amusing fashion. The pilot would be developed into a situation comedy series in which she'd play the daughter of a blue-collar worker. Every week Americans would roar with laughter as she ridiculed yet another of her father's prejudices. For instance:

"Daddy, Margaret is coming over."

"That women's libber in this house!"

"Be quiet, daddy. I think she's a very concerned person."

"I think she's a girl *fag!"*
(Tremendous laughter from the audience)
"Daddy! What a *disgusting* thing to say!"
(Applause and laughter.)

The show would be a smash hit for two seasons. Liberals would consider the dialogue extremely broad-minded.

Making the rounds of talk shows, the secretary would have the opportunity to tell Katharine Hepburn her various theories of acting. ("A good press agent is crucial.") After the cancelation of her series, she would drop out of sight. From time to time the public would read about her being arrested for possession of cocaine. Accompanying such articles would be photographs of her as she was released on bail—cold, tired, trying to keep her identity a secret but only succeeding in hiding one ear. Eventually, she would straighten herself out, marry her parole officer and retire to Mystic, Connecticut. Occasionally, she would be asked to be a presenter on the Emmy Awards show.

The Morning Show aired from 7:00 to 9:00. Its primary purpose was to report to its viewers the news events that had occurred during their sleep: An almost comatose housewife arising at dawn to prepare tunafish sandwiches for her children's lunchboxes could be briefed on the latest body count in a Nicaraguan earthquake; her husband, revived by his morning shower, could be told the fact that the beer he had been drinking since high school had been shown to cause cancer. Weather predictions and sports scores were included in these reports along with short features the network felt would be of general human interest.

The Morning Show was hosted by a representative of each gender. Liz Bonwit was the more popular. Born in Kansas, at eighteen she had won a statewide beauty contest. Though during the poise competition she had expressed her plan to teach retarded children, she soon left for New York City with the hopes of becoming a Rockette. During the audition, Liz discovered that dancing was harder than it looked. She would have gone back to Kansas if the choreographer hadn't sent her over to the Wilhemina Modeling Agency. The talent coordinator there discovered that Liz was very good at flashing disdainful smiles and putting her hands on her hips, so she signed her to a contract.

Within a year, Liz was a top model. Her face became associated with an expensive line of natural-ingredient shampoos containing visible nuts and berries produced by a prestigious cosmetics company. Wealthy and famous, Liz moved into a Park Avenue penthouse apartment with her psychiatrist. When that ended, she had a series of lovers, including a billionaire from Caracas who named an island after her, a Frenchwoman who owned a large nightclub in Manhattan, and an Argentinian tennis pro. The tennis pro died tragically after falling sixty-three stories from the terrace of her apartment. Liz's ordeal at the trial became legendary. Photographs of her fainting face up were run in fashion magazines. Sympathetic interviews appeared in newspapers all over the country; many included her beauty tips. Though her neighbors testified at the trial they had heard violent arguing the night the tennis pro plunged to his death, the predominantly male jury labeled it suicide. Taking advantage of the publicity, *The Morning Show* offered her a job as cohost. She accepted. It was her function to interview quadraplegic war veterans, home economists with money-saving ideas and blind jazz musicians.

Bob Schaeffer was the other cohost. He had been the star pitcher for a national baseball team until he walked too close to a batter in the warmup box. Although the concussion ruined his equilibrium, there was little other noticeable damage since he had never been very intelligent anyway. Jobless, yet popular enough to have a candy bar named after him, Bob was asked to endorse an insecticide spray on a series of television commercials, leading to an offer by *The Morning Show* to replace their retiring host. Bob Schaeffer was expected to handle interviews with child prodigies and Nobel Prize winners.

Among the minor personalities on *The Morning Show* was a woman who gave consumer affairs reports. Following news stories about such things as firebombings, rapes and murders, she would explain the dangers inherent in maraschino cherries and dispel exaggerated claims made by the manufacturers of vaginal deodorants. She had become most famous for her crusade to stiffen the safety regulations for children's toys. Thrusting a red toy fire truck toward the camera, she would demonstrate how easily the tires could be removed for consumption and how sharp the edges of the toy were. "Can you imagine what this could do to a four-year-old *face?*" she would ask plaintively while using the miniature ladder to slice through a loaf of pumpernickel bread.

Another trademark was her dramatic reportage of consumer fraud. Once, for example, she opened her report from the inside of a large hole. "Mr. and Mrs. Yablonsky of Paramus, New Jersey," she said, gesturing toward two forlorn creatures in the background, "dreamed of having their own swimming pool." The camera panned to Mr. Yablonsky, who was holding an inflatable raft for effect. "Please tell us, Mr. Yablonsky, what possessed you to give your young son's ten-thousand-dollar trust fund to a total stranger." After he did, Mrs. Yablonsky walked over to where the deep end of the pool was to have been and recalled when she first realized that her husband and she had been victims of a fraud.

"When the bulldozer failed to show up on the second day, I telephoned the contractor's office. As soon as I realized I was talking to a waiter in an Italian restaurant, I told Mr. Yablonsky I thought something was wrong."

Dr. Tom Spencer, *The Morning Show*'s weatherman, was also popular. Though all one might be interested in was the advisability of carrying an umbrella, he happily insisted on proving he had attended weatherman school. Armed with multicolored grease pencils and magnetized thunderbolts, his predictions involved drawing caricatures of high pressure systems and displaying unintelligible satellite photographs of tropical inversions.

At one point in his career, Dr. Spencer felt that his work was no longer challenging. The network, concerned with his well-being and not unaware of his positive effect on the ratings, subsidized a year of psychology courses at the New School for Social Research. He thereby expanded his role into *The Morning Show*'s resident psychologist; as such he would give advice on the air to the parents of autistic children, homosexuals and impotent businessman. Since his doctorate had been achieved in the field of meteorology, his use of the title "doctor" bordered on misrepresentation but went unchallenged.

His son, a weatherman on another network, was inspired by his father's success. He took a different set of courses and was soon allowed to give medical reports on the six o'clock news. Having inherited his father's gift for ambiguity, he often made it appear to millions of admiring viewers that he was not merely *reporting* on a new medical breakthrough in leukemia therapy, but that he had been instrumental in its discovery. Years later, he would die in the network commissary after choking on a chicken bone.

One of the most informative segments on the show featured a woman who instructed viewers how to turn household waste into attractive gift items.

"What can you do with grandpa's empty cigar boxes?" she would ask brightly. "Cut up those worn out drapes and start gluing! The decorated box will make a wonderful present for that friend who needs something to hold her loose buttons."

Her particular brand of alchemy included recipes for turning old marbles into expensive-looking jewelry and pillowcases into bikini bathing suits. She also had decorating ideas. Wielding a pair of pinking shears and yards of colored felt, she would describe how to transform two-pound coffee cans into replacements for tired lampshades and cereal boxes into conversation pieces that would make anyone's living room come alive. America loved her.

My favorite reporter on the show was Gloria Stein, the gossip columnist. Abandoned as a child, she had grown up in the drab atmosphere of an orphanage: She had had few possessions other than the clothes on her back and a tattered photograph of Ingrid Bergman scotch-taped to the wall next to her cot. But at an early age she discovered life need not continue to be dreary. Rewards were forthcoming from the head of the orphanage for merely naming food strike instigators and exposing escape plans. Her job for *The Morning*

Show was to keep housewives in Ohio up to date on who had just been made head of production at Universal Studios and what star was supposed to sign with NBC but was holding out for a larger percentage and a promise of a dramatic miniseries.

Patchwicke was a nervous, gnomelike fellow about fifty years of age. He wore dark spectacles to hide a slight cast in one eye but only succeeded in drawing attention to it. It was his job to hand out assignments to the writers and give the results to the producers for coordination. With almost sadistic cunning, he asked my opinion on a whole variety of subjects, then gave me my baptism of fire.

The first was to preinterview the winner of the Most Valuable Player Award given by the National Hockey League. Though I admire anyone who rises to the top of his profession, I do not necessarily like to smell his masculine cologne, nor do I believe that he should be allowed to think such achievement ensures his looking good in a suit. Once I became accustomed, however, to the sinewy chap's severe lisp—a condition resulting from the recent forfeit of several front teeth—we had a charming if superficial chat about, among other things, the question of violence in sports. When I asked him how he felt about winning the award, his in-depth reply was, "I feel thwell."

My second assignment was to accompany Liz Bonwit and a small camera crew to a drug rehabilitation center. While Liz gave her attention to the program director, the crew and I gave our attention, wristwatches and credit cards to some heroin addicts.

Though unqualified to handle either of these stories, I did quite well. Patchwicke congratulated me on my work but began to display a certain alarm over my manner of dress.

As one might deduce from the entertainments manufactured, television is a predominantly heterosexual business. The typical network female employee keeps up with trends, buys scented furniture polish, decoupages her favorite Christmas cards and talks about her rights as a woman in the same repetitive way a blacksmith pounds out horseshoes.

The average male employee takes pride in his handshake, reads books like *The Portable Henry Kissinger*, spends over a quarter of his day commuting and harbors a secret desire to breed race horses. Fearing for their jobs, homosexuals in the networks keep low profiles. Some blatantly read magazines about racing cars and stereo equipment to hedge against discrimination; others are less amusing. I became acquainted with one sound technician who would leave his lover of twenty-three years at home and pay a next-door neighbor to pose as his wife at company Christmas parties. I asked him if he ever felt humiliated when he rang that woman's doorbell to say it was "that time of year again." He said he didn't. I wondered what the woman thought: Did she judge his chronic secrecy to be perverse or did she laugh about it with her girlfriends over bridge?

The writers in my office never seemed to take notice of my purported flamboyance; Patchwicke, however, did and took me out to lunch at an Italian restaurant to tell me so.

"You can't wear buskins around the office," he said pleadingly.

"I don't see why not," I replied, lighting a cigarette. "If I'm willing to tolerate the fact that other people wear shoes with pennies obtrusively wedged in them, why can't I be allowed my buskins?"

During that lunch I suspected that Patchwicke himself might have feared some sort of discovery. The tone of his conversation was less reproachful than it was concerned. "You've got to be careful in a company like ours," he said, sounding very much like the sound technician.

I didn't press him to reveal any clandestine longings. Instead I listened to stories about his wonderfulwifewonderfulsonwonderfuldaughter. I know he liked me. And I think at the same time that he abhorred my latitude, he envied it. But it was plain that he feared my "shenanigans" would reflect on his staff or him or both. During our lunch he threatened me. "If you don't wear a suit and tie and behave like an adult, I'll make sure you continue to get the lousiest assignments. For instance," he said, leaning close to me, "Sister Ivy is a person we'll be doing a long feature on in the next few weeks. I'll put you on *that!*"

Sister Ivy was the wealthy evangelist who had brought on the havoc at the rally in Cambridge. At that time, she had been speaking out against busing and the women's liberation movement. Of late, she had taken to campaigning against allowing homosexuals to teach in public schools. Both issues had enlisted disciples and detractors, but it was the latter issue that put her face on the cover of *Time*. She had short dark hair; the large features of her aging tan face were gathered to the center. The cover photograph was airbrushed so that she looked a bit like Barbara LaMarr. The inside pictures were more true to life, resembling Alma Rubens toward the end of her life.

"And if that doesn't work," Patchwicke continued, "I'll fire you. I don't want to, but I will."

Leaning back, I replied, "*Mister* Patchwicke. Try to remember you're not talking to some nervous little computer programmer who is up to his ears in mortgage payments and diaper service bills. I have money and I'm not afraid to spend it *all* on a lawyer to win a case against discrimination."

Patchwicke suddenly looked like Mr. Sawyer in *Miracle on 34th Street*. We smiled at each other and continued eating our *paglia e fieno*.

During the course of the meal, there was a fracas at another table near the kitchen involving a rather poorly dressed woman and a waiter.

Patchwicke studied her with recognition, then whispered excitedly, "That's *Marietta!*"

"It *can't* be!" I said, staring at someone Patchwicke thought was one of the most beautiful creatures employed in Hollywood during the 1940s. Could it be she? My heart raced with uncertainty. The commotion had seized every customer's attention, though it was doubtful they knew who might be involved. All eyes followed the manager to her table, where there seemed to be some problem over the bill. "Are you sure?" I asked, my doubt starting to lessen.

"Positive!"

Louise Brooks, in spite of the severity of her bee-stung lips and hip-waisted shifts, was one of the most beautiful women ever to roll her eyes on the screen—she ended up as a salesgirl at Macy's. Paramount's answer to Garbo, Frances Farmer, was dragged naked through the lobby of Hollywood's Knickerbocker Hotel and eventually committed by her own mother to a state mental institution for ten years of straitjackets and shock treatments. Judy Garland had to sneak down the back stairs of a hotel in Asbury Park to avoid paying a bill; she had collapsed onstage the day before. And in a canary-yellow Pierce Arrow, Mae Murray drove from being a leading lady in films like *The Merry Widow* to a dead end: a bench in Central Park where she was arrested for vagrancy.

I have always felt that if I actually met one of these fallen stars something of the quality that made him or her special would still be intact. I leaned toward the shabby figure sitting a few tables away, straining to catch some of that incandescence. But from my angle, it was difficult to discern whether or not it really was Marietta; I could only see the woman's profile. Her hair was pushed under a brown woolen cap, her head cocked down. For someone who had to be in her mid-fifties, her face was surprisingly firm: only a slight double chin, no facial fissures. She was wearing makeup—mascara and wine-colored lipstick—but as for electricity, there seemed to be none.

"It can't be!" I whispered to Patchwicke.

A Saks shopping bag was perched on her lap, out of which she was dumping all sorts of things on the table. Because Patchwicke seemed so sure, I was inclined to rush over and pay her check. After all, how many times had she been around, if it was she, when I needed her! I had my hand on the back of my chair, preparing to rise, when I saw her stop extricating things for a moment to give a vitriolic look to a young woman staring at her from a nearby table; the woman abashedly turned her attention back to her cottage cheese salad. I stayed put. The older woman resumed her search.

Despite the compromising position, there was a haughtiness about this woman. Pride rather than the sad regality of a Norma Desmond. Finally, touching palm to chest in understated relief, she pulled out a small purse. The problem was resolved. The secretaries, mail clerks and other office personnel sitting at the tables around her tittered as she picked up the items on the table and gingerly put them back into her shopping bag. Then she tied a burgundy scarf around her neck and, throwing her head back, walked gracefully toward the door.

"That's her all right," Patchwicke said.

I believed him.

Passport to Destiny

Marietta was born Frieda Schoenburg in a small town in Germany on November 9, 1919. Her father, who had been a civil servant, was robbed and fatally beaten when she was three. Frau Schoenburg supplemented his small pension with wages as a laundress. Though she never told Frieda how precarious their financial situation was, the little girl sensed it. Even when her mother tucked her into bed at night and told her to sleep safe and sound she felt afraid. Sometimes she would wake up in the middle of the night and creep sleepily toward the light in the parlor where her mother sat alone brooding and talking to herself.

"Who were you talking to, mama?" she would ask.

Frau Schoenburg would gesture her over and they might sit together for an hour or so. In time, Frau Schoenburg would purposely wake the girl up for company, sometimes keeping her up until one o'clock in the morning. On one of these nights, Frau Schoenburg told Frieda how she met her father.

"They just brought him into our parlor. Mama stood next to me while papa shook your father's hand. He was fat. Mama squeezed my hand when his father pushed him toward me. He introduced himself. The next year I was his wife." Frieda listened without comment.

About six months after her husband's death, Frau Schoenburg became ill. Though she quickly recovered, the doctor told her it could be fatal if she continued to lift heavy burdens. Since mother and daughter couldn't survive solely on the pension, they began a nomadic existence that was to last thirteen years and seriously affect Frieda's life. Relative after relative took them in. As she had sensed the trepidation in her mother, she now sensed the reluctance of her relatives. Of course, none of these aunts and uncles and cousins actually complained about taking them in, but Frieda was aware of their resentment just the same.

"Certainly you may have a piece of candy," an aunt would say, but the expression on the woman's face would make Frieda lower her head as she reached for it. She was to see that look many times in her early life.

Whenever mother and daughter would move to a new town, Frau Schoenburg would take Frieda to a convent and ask the nuns to teach her. They always welcomed the girl and baptized her as a Catholic as the first order of business. Frieda was baptised over thirteen times, though she never told her mama. The nuns taught her well; she learned to speak French, English and Italian over the years.

The Schoenburgs' longest billeting was with an uncle, a doctor, and his family. He had Frieda enrolled in a private school with his own children and in every other respect as well she and her mama were treated as equals. This pleased everyone but the doctor's wife who, aside from being a rabid Nazi, suspected that her husband had taken a fancy to Frau Schoenburg. In any case, the brunt of her displeasure was directed at Frieda. To escape, Frieda would hide somewhere in the huge house or at the cinema. It was during these lonely times that she learned to imitate and pretend—the only training she would ever have as an actress. George Cukor would later call her a natural.

One day a telegram arrived at the doctor's house informing Frau Schoenburg of the death of the husband of her sister Liesel, who had lived in America for several years. Frau Schoenburg telegraphed Liesel that she was coming to console her but didn't mention the length of time she planned to do so. Frieda was happy to leave behind the stifling atmosphere and the frightening swastikas.

It was 1937. Frieda was eighteen. Liesel lived in a four-room apartment in the ugly little town of Culver City with her own daughter, Johanna. She had, in fact, been relieved when she had found the blue-colored corpse of her husband on the floor and was not at all pleased to discover he was being replaced by two poverty-stricken relatives. But Frau Schoenburg hadn't lived a vicarious existence for all these years without learning something. She found out that Liesel was trying to get her daughter into the movies; for years they had been going out every day for six hours to the studios. Frau Schoenburg said to her sister, "I take care of the cooking and the cleaning and you can go."

Liesel was suspicious.

"And take Frieda vis you. Look vat a pretty girl. Now you got two chances and half the work."

After a few housework-free days, Liesel decided to give it a try.

For six months Frieda went in and out of offices. No one was very impressed at first; her accent and chin were considered too broad. But something occurred at MGM that paved the way for her acceptance there.

Greta Garbo wasn't happy. She had refused to do more than one picture per year and was becoming more difficult with each of those. Once she even disappeared for several days. The studio bosses feared that she might do so for good and began a clandestine search for a replacement. When Louis Mayer's assistant Ida Koverman saw Frieda, she was dazzled. Frieda's beauty was in full bloom; she had learned how to apply makeup and wear clothes. What made her different from other girls, Mrs. Koverman later told Mr. Mayer, was the "forlorn quality that betrayed her smile. . . .Vulnerability is the only virtue that both men and women can respond to in a beautiful girl," she opined.

Of course, it took a great deal of nagging on Mrs. Koverman's part to make Mayer see this, but before the year was out he wrapped his arms around Marietta and welcomed her to his family.

Nothing could have made Frieda happier.

The MGM machine set right to work on her. Marietta was beautiful, but even she had natural defects which had to be camouflaged: She was 5'6" but had rather thick legs. Since Mayer wanted her to be a glamour girl, Orry-Kelly prescribed full-length gowns as the remedy. He also made great use of Schiaparelli's invention, padded shoulders, which Adrian had used so successfully on Joan Crawford to hide her, as he put it, "Knute Rockne physique." During photo sessions with Clarence Bull, lights were concentrated upward to give her chin more definition and to reduce the absorption of light by her black hair. (Marietta's black hair shifted the emphasis from platinum hair, which had been the fashion since Harlow: Davis, Crawford, Goddard, even Garbo, had been forced to hit the peroxide bottle at least once until then.) Though Marietta loved all the attention she was getting for the first time in her life, she disliked these photo sessions most of all. As with everyone else, her facial skin had to be pulled up and back and taped behind her ears, which was painful. And Marietta was what makeup people referred to as a "tidal wave," a heavy perspirer. Photo sessions and scenes often had to be stopped so that she could be dried off with fans, dabbed with towels and sometimes completely redone. Her favorite hairdresser occasionally jokingly wore a life preserver when working on her.

During 1939, she made two pictures. In the first, *Tangier*, she played a beautiful spy who plots against a handsome spy (Charles Boyer) until they decide to pool their resources and, in the last scene, their lives. In the second, *Run for Cover*, she played a beautiful native girl who bewitches the leader of a gang of gun runners (Robert Taylor) hiding on the island of Zanzibar. The outcome of the second movie was much different—she was boiled in oil—but the reaction of the audience was the same: They adored Marietta.

Garbo made *Ninotchka* that year. In 1941, she made her last film, *Two-Faced Woman*, then tragically disappeared from Hollywood forever. Marietta attracted the legion of her fans. When photographs were taken of the MGM Stock Company from then on, Marietta sat at Mr. Mayer's right, Judy Garland or Katharine Hepburn at his left.

By 1942, Marietta was making six thousand dollars per week. The overall top box-office draw that year was Abbott and Costello. Carole Lombard lost her life and the most beautiful ship in the world, *Normandie*, burned and sank at its pier. Americans were fighting on three continents with pictures of Betty Grable, Lana Turner, even Jane Powell folded in their helmets. Housewives were making *The Song of Bernadette* by Franz Werfel a number-one best-seller, drooling over the pink-skinned Van Johnson and wearing snoods. Everyone still loved Jane Darwell; no one ever warmed up to José Iturbi. Patti, Maxine and LaVerne were in the process of waxing nine hundred sides and selling sixty million records. Francis Langford, Ginny Sims and Jane Frazee were on the road getting applause and selling war bonds. Ceceila Parker, Mickey Rooney, Lewis Stone, Fay Holden and Sara Haden were America's favorite family. Mary Benny was telling Ann Sheridan to keep her paws off Jack.

Marietta bought a large house in Beverly Hills, a three-story Mexican mansion with white stucco walls and rust-colored tiles on the roof. It had belonged to Wally Reid before he poked his arm with the needle once too often. She moved in with her mama and Aunt Liesel. As a personal favor, she asked Mr. Mayer to give Liesel's daughter a contract.

"Anything, darling!" he said.

Johanna walked through a few hotel lobby scenes, said even fewer lines and finally ran off with a trombone player in Artie Shaw's band. After that, it was just Marietta and the two older women in the house. Frau Schoenburg and Liesel ran the mansion as if it had been the old apartment in Culver City: They cooked, cleaned, tended the garden and served the studio executives when they paid social visits. Though there was plenty of money, they were creatures of their pedestrian habits.

Marietta was no different from before either; she continued to feel like an intruder whenever she was at home. In the back of her mind was the notion that to be completely secure one needed a husband.

In 1943, she married the man who had directed two of her films, Howard Shlumin. Howard was a physically impressive sort of person, but some thought him a bit plodding. Basically, he considered movie-making an unmanly sort of business and was much more content to blast away at quails with double-barreled shotguns in the Hollywood Hills. His best buddies were Clark Gable and Victor Fleming.

The marriage was a big event in Hollywood. Louella Parsons helped her pick out a wedding gown, Hedda Hopper bullied her about the guest list. Marietta didn't like either of them; she thought them the last in a long line of insincere guardians. Louella, whom she considered the lesser of two evils, also gave her advice about men. At twenty-four, Marietta had had less than a half-dozen encounters with that particular species—a boast few girls on the MGM lot could make—and each time she had been disappointed.

"It's just kerplop on top of you and boom-boom-boom and that is all."

Lolly gave her a few hints that might help her enjoy her new husband, but he kerplopped and boom-boom-boomed just the same. Marietta accepted this as another of life's little jests. But she enjoyed other aspects of their union and did many things to try to make it last.

They moved into his house in Stone Canyon not far from Judy Garland. Marietta instructed the new domestic staff of her husband's preferences: cigarettes pointing in the same direction in the cigarette boxes, a steady diet of Chinese and Mexican food, curtains always drawn. After a long day at the studio, she would personally go through all twenty-seven rooms of the house and make sure everything was just so. On Fridays, she fussed over his tackle boxes. The couple belonged to a country club in Beverly Hills (she hated golf), a skeet-shooting club in the Palm Springs desert (she hated loud noises) and the Hollywood Democratic Committee (she hated worrying about raising money). She found out about Howard's infidelities almost immediately—Hollywood was lousy with *concerned friends*— but she ignored them, blaming herself.

Then one night he didn't come home at all. She ignored that as well. When it became a habit, she discovered she liked it better without him. Who wanted to spend all their time cleaning out gun barrels anyway? They divorced in 1945. No children. They remained friends but never worked together again. She moved back with her mama and Liesel in the Beverly Hills house.

Her new director, Joe Stein, became a lifelong pal. Tall and rather thin, with drawn, basset-hound features, he was a sensitive man and his films had a romantic lilt to them. Irving Thalberg had first brought him out to Hollywood from the New York stage in the early '30s, making him an assistant director first under Fleming and later Cukor. Pleased with the results, Thalberg gave Joe Stein his own directorial assignments; the first starred June Preisser, the second Marie Dupont. Stein was grateful to Thalberg for all he had done, but was impatient to be given an A picture. He would wait for hours outside Thalberg's office only to be ushered in and out in minutes.

"In time, in time," Thalberg would say, covering the receiver of a telephone with his hand.

Out of frustration, Stein began to mumble cracks about Thalberg to anyone who happened to be around. One day he spotted Thalberg in the Alley looking especially disproportionate in an overly padded suit, he muttered to his assistant, "Christ, it looks like he's got two dining room sets under those shoulders."

Joe Stein nicknamed Norma Shearer, Thalberg's wife, the "Persian Cat." "Irving," he would say, "your Persian Cat was wonderful in this or that." Thalberg beamed until someone tipped him off that the moniker referred to the slightly crossed eyes that his wife and the breed shared. He would have relegated Stein to B pictures after that (firing him was out of the question considering the amount of MGM's investment in him) but Marietta intervened. She was so pleased with their first collaboration that she demanded Stein direct all her pictures from then on. Thalberg reluctantly agreed, but never allowed him to do anything else. The forced lack of versatility in his career coupled with subsequent political sanctions against him robbed him of the historic stature of a Cukor or a Hitchcock; Mayer had followed Thalberg's tradition. But loving Marietta as he did, Joe Stein always considered himself a very lucky man.

"I'm the son of a man who sold pistachio nuts on Flatbush Avenue and look who I get to hold hands with every day," he told Marietta. From 1944 on, Marietta's star continued to rise. She lived for work, its international fame and its familial atmosphere. Then the locusts descended on Hollywood.

* * *

1948. Marietta held up her hand against the glare of the light in the limousine.

"Put that out," she said to the driver.

"We're here, miss."

She frowned at the silhouette through the glass partition and pulled the hood of a black cape over her tangled hair. The light went out. The car door opened and a hand reached in to assist her.

"We're a little late, miss."

"Please," she said, brushing the hand aside. They walked together to the entrance of the sound stage. The night air was cool. The chauffeur opened the door. "Sank you," she said, stepping over the frame. He closed it behind her.

Standing in the shadows of the sound stage, she removed her gloves, then stopped for a moment, detecting a slight odor of smoke.

"Hello, Miss Marietta."

She turned and saw the guard. "Oh, hello, Edmund."

"They're waiting for you in your dressing room, Miss Marietta."

"Sank you, Edmund. Tell me somesing, is this building on fire?" She put the gloves in her purse and looked calmly at the guard.

"Oh, no, miss," he said quickly.

"That's good . . ."

"It's the pagan idol. Mr. Green and some of the prop boys are testing it."

"Oh," she replied. "Of course, the pagan idol."

"I hope you slept well, Miss Marietta."

She smiled. She had had two engagements that evening. The first had been arranged by the studio, a supper with a fellow named Howard Keel. As part of a publicity buildup for him, the studio was having him seen with every eligible star and starlet on the lot. This was standard procedure: The publicity department seemed to be of the opinion that fame could be contracted through repeated exposure like a contagious virus. Loyal to the call, Marietta had donned a green Chanel evening gown, placed a few emeralds in her hair and accompanied this *Howard Keel* to Romanoff's.

As they had entered, the array of spies on duty that evening dropped their dish towels and checkpads and scurried off to phone Lolly and Hedda. Marietta introduced her escort to Mike. Drinks arrived. Then photographers. They smiled cheek-to-cheek and ordered dinner. At that point in his career, Howard Keel had made one picture for British Lyon but had left to sign with Metro. A marriage had been dissolved "in the shuffle." His first picture was to be *Annie Get Your Gun* with Judy Garland. Marietta liked him and was amused by his conversation; he was handsome and said he could sing; he appeared to be at the beginning of a fine career. She had no notion how near she was to the end of her own.

Marietta had returned at nine. At ten o'clock, she was sitting in her living room dressed in a long black skirt and a tight pewter lamé tunic decorated with a militaresque brooch. She was waiting for George Kaufman and he was late. When his car finally did pull into her drive, she went upstairs and had the maid answer the door. She let him repent for ten minutes in the library. The maid was accustomed to greeting visitors like Tyrone Power and Ray Milland and was so surprised by the unattractive figure of George Kaufman that she audibly gasped. The playwright, both perceptive and self-conscious, became extremely embarrassed. The maid installed him in the library and went back up to straighten her mistress's shoulders and stocking seams. She asked Marietta if she was very interested in the man waiting for her. Marietta said that she had spoken to him at the studio last week for the first time. "He looks like a pipe cleaner with eyes to me," the maid observed. Marietta laughed.

Their meeting was strained from the beginning. They went to Ciro's. The first time Marietta had gone there had been with her mother; aside from the novelty, Ciro's had been interesting that first night because Johnny Weismuller finally got fed up with his wife, Lupe Velez. After stopping all conversation in the place with a loud, descriptive accusation, he pushed their table over on top of her. Lupe sat there, covered with mushroom mousse. It was breakfast in bed for Weissmuller the next morning, according to Lupe ("I make eet wis my own two hends!"), but divorce soon after.

Ginger Rogers had been there tonight with her husband Jack Briggs.

Marietta didn't like the chartreuse dress she was wearing. Ginger had notoriously bad taste. Gail Russell was at the bar with Guy Madison. Martha Raye was sitting ringside with Nick Condos. Marietta and George Kaufman received the proper amount of attention upon arriving. She talked with Bruno the maître d' about the lovely autumn rains. Drinks came: a sidecar for Marietta and a Seltzer for Kaufman. Photographers did not. Kaufman sat in silence. Marietta tried to initiate a conversation. She told him she *adored* his plays though she had never really seen one. He scratched his head in reply. She mentioned Robert Benchley, knowing he and Kaufman were good friends. "Bob was in one of my films," she said, smiling, but Kaufman only managed to clear his throat. Finally, she grew irritated with his taciturn behavior and, spotting Lucille Ball and Desi Arnaz walking into the club, waved them over to join her. Everyone had a good time but Kaufman; he was eventually ignored altogether.

Lucille joked about Truman; Marietta gamely defended him. Their party had broken up at two thirty when Lucille and Desi had a quarrel, which Desi started: He couldn't understand why she hadn't brought the new carnelian cigarette lighter he had given her for her birthday to match her red hair.

"I for*got* it. Use a match," she said, shrugging him off.

He stormed out of the restaurant as Lucille, Marietta and Kaufman watched. Lucille sheepishly rose from the table, gathered a rust ranch mink stole about her shoulders and said, "Good night, kids," following after.

The chauffeur dropped Kaufman off at his place by three—they shook hands and Kaufman told her he had had a wonderful time. Marietta hadn't. Sleep would have been preferable to Kaufman.

Exhausted and a bit angry when arriving home, Marietta stripped off the lamé armor and war paint and took a bath. She toweled dry her hair but didn't bother to comb it. She put on a teal blue cotton dress and took a black cape out of her closet of wraps. Downstairs, she ate the bowl of sauteed sweetbreads the maid had left for her in the refrigerator.

Halfway through the meal, the doorbell rang. It was four thirty. The driver was waiting.

"I slept very well, sank you, Edmund," she said after arriving at the studio, blowing the guard a kiss.

Marietta walked through the dark fringe of the set. A few grips and sound men were crawling about. In two hours, the plaster-of-paris city would be filled with the full crew and the hundreds of extras who were being readied in rows and rows of chairs in the makeup department. Marietta stepped up to the door of her dressing room. An electronic chime rang as she opened it. Her maid, who had her head down on the dressing table, jumped up. Her hairdresser looked at her from behind a raised glass of bourbon.

"Bonjour, everybody," Marietta said, removing the hood.

"My God, Marietta's been gnawing on high-tension wires again," the hairdresser drawled.

"Oh, be quiet," the maid said, helping Marietta off with her cloak and dress.

"I don't know if I'm up to working miracles this early in the morning," he continued.

"I had a lousy night," Marietta said as the maid slipped an amethyst satin robe around her shoulders. She was already a bit cheered by the sight of the ruby-colored dressing room and her two friends of many years. She slid down into the leather recliner, nestling into its arms as if into those of a lover. The hairdresser eased her slowly back and gingerly placed her head on the edge of the sink. He massaged her hair with warm water and shampoo. The maid put away her clothes and prepared fresh Viennese coffee. It took the hairdresser an hour to finish. The makeup man came in and covered the small imperfections of her face with heavy pancake. A tray of brushes, creams and powders then had to be applied.

The hairdresser leaned over and whispered in her ear, "You're just lucky that my training included a course in taxidermy."

Marietta sighed contentedly. She had a sense of humor and didn't mind his jokes. When he had finished she gestured to her maid.

"Maya—" A white chiffon dress was brought out of a closet. "Are you sure that's the right one?"

"Yes, miss."

The hairdresser was on his third bourbon. He knew enough to be quiet at this point. The makeup man was dusting Marietta's neck with powder.

"That is enough," she said, waving the man away; he shrank to the side of the room.

Marietta gestured to Maya to bring her the script. It never took her more than two readings to learn the lines, one rehearsal to master the gestures and emotions.

At seven thirty there was a knock on the door. Heralded by the electronic chime, Joe Stein entered and extended an invitation to Marietta to come to the set. She blew a kiss to his reflection in the mirror and powdered her nose. He waited patiently. When she was satisfied with her face, she rose and regarded her figure in a full-length mirror outlined with brass nymphs and satyrs. She fluffed the chiffon skirt, turning this way and that. The four gray figures in the room watched her.

"All right," she finally said. Glittering in an array of First Testament jewelry and pursued by yards of white chiffon—they were making *Sarah of the Nile*—she was helped down the stairs of her dressing room by Joe Stein. Her attendants followed with the tools of their particular trades, fussing over her like pastry chefs preparing a confection.

A man in a gray trenchcoat was watching the procession. Suddenly he hurried out from behind a camera and stepped in front of Marietta. The entourage came to a halt.

"You . . . eh . . . Marietta? Formerly Miss Frieda Schoenburg?"

"Yes," she said, vaguely annoyed. Who was this cretin?

He thrust an envelope at her. She took it. "I liked that last one you were in," he said. "Eh . . . what was it . . . *The Waltz*. The wife liked it too. Well, good day," he said, tipping his hat. Everyone watched as he made his way through the heavy equipment and disappeared.

Marietta opened the envelope.

"I don't understand," she said, disturbed by the government agency letterhead.

"Here, let me look at it," Joe Stein said.

Marietta watched his face whiten as he read. "Well, what is it, Joe?" she asked worriedly.

"It's nothing," the director said, slipping it into his pocket. "Nothing. Let's rehearse this scene, shall we?"

Pocketful of Miracles

The image of Marietta in the restaurant haunted me for days. That gray silhouette passing out onto brightly lit Fifth Avenue played over in my mind like a Möbius strip.

What had brought that star crashing to earth? An MGM undoing, alcoholism, drugs? A calculating business manager, a breakdown? Research into the matter proved futile. Out-of-print bookstores had no biography. Libraries provided only newspaper clippings of two openings: one of a movie, the other of a marriage. Both inscrutable MGM propaganda.

I did manage to find at the network a videotape of the first of her glorious movies that I had seen and which had not been shown in years.

In *The Waltz,* Marietta played a naïve young lady of Louis XIV's court who takes part in its decadent imbroglios—to her own ruin. At the beginning of the movie, we find out she is the daughter of the Marquise de la Marquette, a rival of du Barry's. Her mother dies of tuberculosis when she is twenty and Madame du Barry adds the naïve girl to her roster of spies at court. When Marietta realizes she is being used, she must decide whether to run off with a poor footsoldier (Tyrone Power) with whom she has fallen in love or take her mother's place as du Barry's rival. She chooses the latter course, despite the warnings of Power, and is framed by du Barry, then imprisoned. Power manages to free her only moments before she is to be removed from her cell beneath the palace and executed. Melodrama notwithstanding, it was wonderful to watch *The Waltz* again after all these years. Marietta's dark, forlorn beauty was dazzling.

But *The Waltz* provided no clue as to what had happened to turn its velveted star into the shoddy creature Patchwicke and I had seen. I wondered if perhaps there were no one spectacular explanation, if Marietta's present state were the result of a thousand small defeats, mundane compromises that appeared dramatic only in retrospect. If that were true, Marietta's undoing was prosaic, the fate of the disciple rather than the divinity. Perhaps the gradual surrender of the innocent in *The Waltz* had been as prophetic as it was sad.

My ruminations on this subject had to be put aside for more important considerations. I had to indulge all sorts of untidy people with my presence in order to get a sense of how the different studios within the network functioned. This led to my being introduced to the stage manager of a private television movie production house that developed pilots for the networks, who gave me an overview of how a project is planned on paper. He asked an associate producer to give me an idea of some of the common problems from pre- to post-production; she was helpful. It was a start.

For a while, Patchwicke and I got on a bit better. He promised that though television viewers might bray for three-minute features glorifying the human spirit, I did not always have to be the one forced to write them. It was a relief to get a break from reporting on such triumphs as the determination of a geriatric jogging club in Arizona to run to New Mexico and the success of a feisty paraplegic in navigating the rapids of the Colorado River in a kayak. As a gesture, he gave me two assignments he assumed would be more suitable.

The first was to preinterview a thirty-seven-year-old avant-garde artist and his wife. In girth and temperament, he was as thick as she was compendious; side by side they looked like the Eugene Pallette and

Mildred Dunnock of conceptual art. It seemed that as a struggling young artist living on the Lower West Side, he had toiled to express "allegorical injunctions exalting the implications of life and death by manipulating splashes and drips on wide monochromatic spaces." He grew angry when his landlord refused to accept this in lieu of the rent, bitter when the New York critics virtually ignored a private showing of his work in his living room, which featured a technical and ideological tour de force juxtaposing mosquito netting and basketballs. Frustrated, he and his wife fled the commercial barbarism of New York for the "raw, creative spirit of Nebraska." There he conceived a new art form, which he called free-form sculpture. It involved the rigging of large cloth sails from forty-foot poles erected on a harvested cornfield and letting "the breath of nature" do the rest. Pointing a chubby finger at me, he explained how all this digging and hammering surpassed the work of Rodin and Calder while his wife nodded her head like a dog ornament in the rear window of an automobile. For all his self-congratulation, I imagined that his work would do more to influence the lactic cycle of midwestern cows than it would the New York art world. I asked him, however, to tell me what had inspired the creation of this new form of sculpture. Laughter erupted from deep within his corpulent frame. "The artiste cannot make his mind clear to ordinary men," he said. This confirmed my suspicion that he had been inspired by watching his wife hang his boxer shorts on a clothesline to dry.

The second assignment was also a preinterview. Edward Villela, star of the New York City Ballet, was appearing on various television programs to promote the upcoming season. I was very excited about having the opportunity to talk with such a virtuoso performer. Praised for his classic lines and forceful attack, Villela had been described as "Dionysian" and "mercurial" by the critics. He was well known for dancing, among other roles, the part of Oberon, king of the fairies, in *A Midsummer Night's Dream.*

Ironically, until Mr. Villela appeared at my office, I had forgotten that there was a particular stigma attached to the *male dancer.* It was immediately obvious from his behavior that he was sensitive in this regard and was determined to demonstrate to everyone that he was really a *good Joe*.

"Do you play ball?" he asked me.

I replied that I most certainly did not and then asked if on the show he might like to make a comparison between his style and that of another performer, say, Nureyev.

"I coach the Seventy-eighth Street stickball team," he replied, and went on to talk about the fighting prowess he had acquired as a result of being brought up in a tough neighborhood, and about his unfulfilled dream to play third base for the New York Yankees. The interview climaxed with his making an analogy between jetés and drop kicks.

When he got on the air, it was more of the same thing. The premier star of the New York City Ballet and Dick Schaeffer had a wonderful time "giving each other five" and discussing the pros and cons of AstroTurf. I think Mr. Villela expected blue-collar workers watching the show to say to their wives, "Hey, Marge, that Edward Villela looks like an all right guy. Let's pile the kids into the station wagon and go see *Le Lac Des Cygnes* tonight."

Despite the fact that I maintained my composure in the face of such pretense, I must have done *something* that bothered Patchwicke because in my presence he once again became as tense and uncomfortable as Dick Haymes in *My Blue Heaven*. Assignments that he considered to be terrible he resumed giving me. The first was writing and filming an account of a day in the life of a rock-and-roll star. The crew, *The Morning Show*'s music critic and I were admitted to the star's dressing room at Madison Square Garden where he was busy painting lightning bolts on his face. While the crew set up, I talked to the musician, Tim Zeggo, about his life with the interpretative aid of his sixteen-year-old girlfriend. From what I could gather, he had been the lead singer of a group in the 1960s that had recorded four hit albums. At one point, however, there was an ego clash among the musicians and the group was disbanded.

Depressed, the lead singer turned to hard drugs. A divorce from his wife of six months followed, along with rumors of illegitimate children and cocaine-related nose operations. Broke and faced with a $600,000 IRS lawsuit, he wisely committed himself to a Los Angeles sanatorium. In six months he left the hospital completely cured. His only problem was what to do with the rest of his life.

He decided to take acting lessons. After three weeks at the Actors' Studio, Lee Strasberg told him he was a natural genius and suggested he register for more classes. After spending a year and much money, he was still undiscovered. It was only with the support of the lead bass player in his old band and a priest that he was able to go back into the music business. Now, at twenty-eight, he was making a comeback. The alternative, his girlfriend told me with a shiver, was to finish high school.

It was an arduous day's work. For revenge, I wore a lemon flannel Zoot suit into the office the next day.

In retaliation, Patchwicke made good his previous threat and put me on the Sister Ivy story. "You fly down to Charlotte in six weeks!" he spat.

"But—"

"And stop twirling that watch chain!"

The next day, armed with my Tufts education and my movie mogul ambitions, I found myself scouring different department stores to gather material for a report on unusual Christmas gift items. *The Morning Show* did at least four such stories each December. Knowing how I hated department stores, Patchwicke assigned me to every one.

Perhaps it was the magnanimous atmosphere of Christmas, or just my ill luck, but I tripped over more than my share of bums that day. There was a hag of a woman outside Altman's, another one at the door of Lord & Taylor, and two red-faced men collapsed in each other's arms near Saks. As I entered Bloomingdale's, a man who looked like John Emerson doffed his hat, descended to one knee, and performed *Perfidia* for the crowd.

In Manhattan, schizophrenic bums litter the streets like discarded copies of the *New York Post*. Of course, Manhattan is a busy place; there are bound to be a few mental casualties. Those who are rich and famous will write books on Valium addiction. Others will be institutionalized and become part of the city's origami work force. But why do others forsake their jobs, homes and families for sleeping accommodations on subway gratings and black overcoats that give off gothic smells? As I walked around Bloomingdale's watching women jockey for positions at scarf counters and men register expressions of abject self-pity after not being able to find YSL mock-pleated trousers in their size, I realized that the fashion industry is the cause of this last type of bum.

Mental deterioration begins when New Yorkers buy one of the outgrowths of the fashion industry: the fashion magazine. Though New Yorkers may flip through its glossy pages merely to discover where they might buy a decent bathrobe, they must endure a photographic advertisement in which it takes ten muscular models depicting a high school swim meet to sell a protein skin moisturizer, an interview in which a famous designer—hailed as a genius for his beachwear—talks honestly about life, love and mixing plaids, and an article that traces the evolution of fashion from the bearskin loincloth to the sequined elbow pad.

Some New Yorkers need only put down a cat-o'-nine-tails and unchain a famous designer from a wall to get a new spring outfit. Others must go to department stores. It is there that the real mental undermining takes place. The New Yorker must fight through the crowds. Blocking the aisles are professional perfume sprayers dressed beyond their means, sloppy women who apparently do not have the time to wash their sneakers but can spend hours sitting in highchairs to get free mascara-application lessons from black men wearing magnifying visors and powder blue tunics, and large groups of people watching frying-pan experts spin cooked eggs around the incline of no-stick pans like balls around a roulette wheel. The strain begins to show as the New Yorker squeezes past these people while trying to remain polite.

Tension builds as he searches for the proper department. Finding it is not always easy, since the men's shirt department of yesterday is often being renovated into the voile broomstick skirt department of tomorrow. Working behind plywood partitions that read EXCUSE OUR APPEARANCE BUT WE'RE WORKING DAY AND NIGHT TO BRING YOU A PRETTIER STORE, beer-bellied construction workers bang resonantly on mylar two-by-fours while recreating an exact replica of the spaceship interior of a top-grossing science fiction movie—with the addition of computerized cash registers and twenty-first-century clothing racks.

By the time the New Yorker finds the correct department, an unsightly tic has developed. A salesclerk is asked for help. Unfortunately, salesclerks are often struggling writers trying to earn enough money to pay their rent. Though they can easily find symbolic meaning in their work, they are hard pressed to find anything in a medium size. Muttering, the New Yorker has to take the initiative to search through the racks of clothes created by heiress/designers and former pool boys. By now, it is almost too late to save his sanity; the New Yorker suffers an identity crisis. Seeking to reestablish his ego, he frantically searches for the shocking-pink wool gabardine shirt with looming shoulders and cryptic pockets that John Travolta was photographed wearing last week. Nearly arrested for taking the shirt to another department for a color match, something in his mind snaps. Passing the gourmet food department, the knitted hat boutique and the chocolate St. Moritz running shoe display case, he leaves the store, saliva dribbling down his chin. In a matter of weeks, the poor soul is walking the streets, arguing with fire hydrants, pointing an accusing finger at park benches and laughing hysterically over the jokes of an invisible friend. He will have to rely on the contributions of strangers and will have to carry his solicited earnings in Big Brown Bags at all times since banks have a policy of not accepting deposits made in the form of lime green shower caps and plastic yellow snow boots.

Having come to these conclusions, but finding nothing of use to *The Morning Show,* I was just about to leave Bloomingdale's when I caught sight of a familiar face. I stopped abruptly.

Standing at a counter, examining a bottle of perfume, was Marietta. In the full light I recognized her immediately: the black hair and

Himalayan cheekbones were evident. She wasn't dressed as poorly as she had been in the restaurant: her black lambskin coat was somewhat worn, but stylish; her hair was partly hidden under a matching black turban. To get a closer look, I joined the vociferous customers standing at the counter who were spraying samples at each other and demanding the attention of an overly madeup saleswoman, who seemed to be waiting for Marietta to make a decision. Marietta put down the spherical bottle she had been examining and picked up another which looked like a Burmese pagoda. She unscrewed the roof, sniffed, sniffed again, then replaced it. She said something, but I couldn't hear what. Setting the bottle back on the counter, she picked up the spherical bottle and gave it another olfactory examination. Several customers away, a large, well-dressed woman, obviously a long-standing member of the East Side gentry, began to pound the counter with her fists. The saleswoman excused herself. Marietta nodded and waved her away.

Delighted with my good fortune, I decided to approach her as soon as she had transacted her business. Since her performances had given me so much pleasure over the years, I thought the very least I could do was reciprocate with lunch. It would be marvelous. I was mentally running through a list of alimentary possibilities when a curious turn of events took place. The expression on Marietta's face changed completely, to one of wary alertness. She seemed to lose all interest in comparing the two scents. Looking around her, she slipped her pocketbook down between her midriff and the counter, glanced toward the saleswoman at the opposite end busily laying an array of bottles before the petulant customer, took a handkerchief from the pocketbook, covered her mouth, coughed, and put it back. The bag was left open. Her eyes slowly moved to the left, then to the right. She put the spherical bottle in front of her on the edge of the counter. With a flick of her black-gloved hand, she pushed it off the edge and into her purse.

Shocked, I immediately looked down in embarrassment at a box of designer soap powder in the glass display case. Had I actually seen *Marietta* purloin perfume? No one else had noticed: Other customers were pointing and cooing at the toiletries inside the case; the saleswoman was still at the other end writing up a receipt. When I looked at Marietta again, she had already positioned the Burmese pagoda bottle. Oh God, I thought, she's going to do it again! She'll get caught! Suddenly I found myself casing the immediate vicinity for security guards, plotting diverse escape routes.

Marietta looked around. The saleswoman was putting merchandise in a bag. The customers around her were even less curious. Plop! The Burmese pagoda tumbled over into the black opening of her pocketbook. She snapped it shut and glanced around. No one had seen her. She slowly walked away. I edged my way along the counter to follow. She was about ten feet away when the saleswoman returned to take care of her. I was passing that part of the counter when the saleswoman looked at the shelf where the two bottles had been, realized what had happened and picked up the house telephone.

I quickened my pace. A man with an unbecoming manner bumped into me; I lost sight of Marietta. Behind me, the saleswoman was craning her neck over the customers to see if she could spot the thief; she came out from behind the counter. Two security guards jabbering away on walkie-talkies sauntered up to her.

Jostling my way past hordes of people, I finally caught sight of Marietta again. She had stopped to fondle a mauve silk necktie in the men's department. Exhilarated by the excitement, I walked right up to her, slipped my arm through the crux of her elbow and quickly whispered, "They're on to you. Follow me." She was startled but I didn't give her time to protest. The saleswoman, flanked by the two security guards, was squeezing her way through the crowd. She was still too far away to spot Marietta; I could see her because I have eagle vision in addition to a photographic memory. Fortunately, I also had an extensive list of movie plots at my disposal. I knew three ways to navigate through the dangers of the Amazon River, fourteen methods for smuggling important documents out of Berlin and an infinite number of ways to deduce murders at black-tie dinner parties. I pushed Marietta into a corner between the men's slippers counter and a pajama display.

"What are you doing!" she whispered angrily.

Before she could say another word I pulled her toward me and kissed her. She tasted smoky, aromatic. She tried to push me away but I embraced her more tightly. She squirmed in my arms. The saleswoman and guards came bounding along and stopped only a few feet away.

"I *know* she came down this way," the saleswoman said.

One of the walkie-talkies sizzled with static. "Uh, yes, uh, this is Boyd. We have followed suspect to pajama department. Will continue search. Ten-four."

Marietta heard that and stopped struggling. We both held our breath. If they made an arrest and discovered her identity, the publicity would be ugly. I, of course, would be arrested as an accessory. I was paralyzed with fear. There was more static. Finally, the other guard made a decision.

"Boyd, you go that way. I'll go around this way. We'll meet in socks."

"Ten-four."

The static diminished as they walked away. Relief streamed through my body. I counted to ten, then looked around out of the corner of my eye. Marietta was shaking.

"Let's go," I said. "Put your arm in mine. The exit we'll use is straight ahead toward Third Avenue. Do you see the one I mean?"

She nodded.

"I'll turn around. Keep up with me. If you see them, just keep going."

Like Marie Dressler and Wallace Beery on their way into dinner, we escorted each other casually through men's shirts. Then jewelry. There was a security guard with a walkie-talkie clutched to his cheek directly in our path. I held tight to Marietta's arm.

"Keep going," I whispered. "He probably doesn't know what you look like."

We walked by him, then four dozen pairs of men's shoes, finally out through the revolving door onto the avenue. Marietta didn't say a word, just stood there, staring straight ahead. I felt intensely sorry for her. I hailed a cab, pushed her inside, and directed the driver to my apartment. I wanted, needed her to come back for a talk. Not once looking at me, Marietta rummaged through her pocketbook and extricated a Sobranie cigarette and holder. Her hand trembled as I lit it for her. She inhaled deeply.

"Sank you," she said, as she had to Paul Henreid, Humphrey Bogart, Tyrone Power, Dennis Morgan and many others. Her voice was deeper now, but the accent was as I remembered.

"Are you all right?" I asked.

She bit her lip and looked out the window. "You know who I am?"

"Yes," I replied. She pulled the collar of her coat higher. Her eyes surveyed the scene on the street. "You have me at a disadvantage," she said, exhaling. "Would you mind introducing yourself?"

"Burton Raider," I replied.

She seemed unimpressed. "I am so stupid," she said. "I forget and become careless."

"You do this often?" I asked.

She turned abruptly. "These are *presents,*" she said, raising her plucked eyebrows regally. Her fright disappeared with her indignation. I admired her vigorous spirit of self-defense. She turned back toward the window, then sighed. "Sank you again."

Age had mellowed her beauty but had certainly not destroyed it. The gray-violet eyes were intelligent, deep and quick, unmarred by evidence of habitual drinking or drug taking which I supposed she might have indulged in. The face was slightly sallow; but the fine lines on it were no more dramatic than those on a porcelain figurine. The cheekbones faithfully held the almost Slavic configuration of her face, seeming more prominent in contrast to the drawn contours around her mouth. The amber tint was gone. Her lips were not as full or deep as I remembered, but then she was wearing little makeup. She spoke without turning. "If there is somesing I can do to repay you . . ."

"I'd like you to have a drink with me at my apartment." I had to find out more about this gorgeous relic of the past.

After a moment's silence, she turned and exhaled a cloud of smoke in my direction. "I don't drink," she replied with glacial elegance.

"Perhaps you would like to talk. Just for an hour. I have spent many hours of my life watching your wonderful films. I am a fan. Could you spare me an hour?"

She looked at me the way Vivien Leigh must have regarded Marlon Brando whenever he scratched his testicles on the set of *Streetcar*, and said resignedly, "Very well."

Bathed in candlelight, we sat down together at the dining table in my apartment as the violet glow of dusk played at the windows. Shaking with excitement, I iced some Perrier Jouët and caviar and laid out breads, cheeses and crackers. I suspected it had been a long time since she had tasted such good champagne—I had taken to imbibing daily—but she said nothing to indicate so.

"So, Mr. Raider, What is it you wish to know?" Her tone was still cool, but slightly looser after the first two sips of the wine.

I dabbed my lips with a napkin. Caviar is divine but *so* sticky. What did I want to know . . . ? What *didn't* I wish to know? Hollywood was my religion. I wanted to know dirt, of course. And more. Did she know if William Randolph Hearst had really murdered Thomas Ince? If Shirley Temple was a pain in the ass? Were Lana Turner and Ann Sheridan as beautiful in person as they were on the screen? Did a visit to the Eiffel Tower stir fond memories of Gary Cooper in Marlene Dietrich? Did *anyone* get along with Miriam Hopkins? Easy, easy, I thought as I looked at the frosty legend sitting across the table, a celluloid companion of many years. I was eager and a little afraid. I wiped a bit of perspiration from the side of my cheek and asked, "What was it like at MGM? It's so hard to separate the reality from the press releases and gossip which have been passed down over the years, and have been distorted in biographies. What was it like? Everyone on talk shows says it was nothing but hard work or—"

"It was *wonderful*," she said simply and slowly raised her long-stemmed crystal glass to her lips, a reflection of candlelight glinting on the rim.

I smiled wanly. "Yes, but . . . Well, what did the place look like?"

She sighed and looked off to the side. "It was divided in two parts by an avenue called the Alley. The main section had Mr. Mayer's offices, the sound stages, makeup departments. That sort of sing. Laboratories, dressing rooms."

"What was your dressing room like?" I asked, topping off her glass with more champagne.

She shrugged. "At first it was in a two-story wooden building. In the silent days before I came, the top floor had women: Marion Davies, Norma Shearer, Garbo, Crawford, Lillian Gish and Sally O'Neil. Men were on the bottom floor. Uh . . . John Gilbert was there." She pulled a pack of cigarettes from her pocket. Taking one between her fingers, she waited for me to lean forward with a lighter.

"Sank you," she said in a cloud of smoke. "For most of my time at Metro it was in my contract to have a dressing room on the set. It was comfortable. Scarlet velvet. But nossing like you see in the movies." She smiled for the first time, a radiant smile.

Seeing it, I let go with a you-were-wonderful-in-this-you-were-wonderful-in-that gush, refilling her glass and mine at regular intervals. She did not seem bored by the praise. "I saw *The Waltz* just the other day at my television station," I said.

"Oh yes," she said, shaking her head wistfully. "Ty Power. Such a nice man. A gentleman. So many of them were conceited. Ty always had a sense of humor about himself. In front of the whole crew he would laugh and point to a run in his stockings." She sipped her drink. "The costumes I had to wear were terribly heavy and uncomfortable. I wore tennis shoes underneath whenever I could get away with it. You know, Metro would always use the same costumes over and over again—like the people. I wore a black gown in the first scene of *The Waltz*. Next time you watch *Marie Antoinette,* look at the gown Norma Shearer wears in some ball scene or other. It's the same one. I sink *I* looked better in it." She said this quite seriously. "And there is a dream sequence in *The Waltz.* Remember?"

"Yes!" How could I have forgotten?

"They had all these tubs of dry ice around me for it. The dress weighed enough as it was! But the vapor soaked it srough and I could hardly stand. It took twenty women wis ironing boards to dry it out."

"More champagne?" I asked. This was my favorite kind of conversation.

"Please," she replied. "Crawford was supposed to be in that picture. But they sought she was too . . . too harsh. She was. We *were* in one picture together, but it was not as good as *The Waltz*. She was very nice to me. Remembered little sings. How was my mother? How was Howard? That sort of sing. She was . . . perfect. But not in the best sense." She paused. "Perhaps that is too harsh. I tell you. I remember two sings about her. One was that she would close her eyes when someone lit her cigarette. Like a kiss. The other was an embarrassment for me. It was Christmas. She invited me to a party at her house. In the afternoon, we all got together in the living room. Margaret Sullavan, Walter Pidgeon, and . . . I sink Mary Astor were there. Crawford gave me a Titian. A tiny, beautiful nude. I gave her a blouse. I remember mumbling 'sank you' as she smiled and went on to another guest. How could she give up a masterpiece? I went to the basroom wis it under my arm, ready to cry. I sat in there forever wis that little reddish painting on my lap." Sipping the champagne, she stared off into memory. "I sink I knew more about Titian after looking at his painting for five minutes than I *ever* did about Joan. And we were at Metro together for four years. She was a mystery."

As if Marietta weren't. She picked up a caviar spoon, piled a healthy portion onto a cracker, nibbled slowly at it and looked about my living room. "Lovely," she said of the Pompeiian mural. So, she had taste. She held up another cigarette and I lit it for her. The tiny blue flame illuminated the famous face; without moving her head, she looked up at me seductively, into my eyes as she had on the screen with Clark Gable, James Craig, and even Sidney Greenstreet. I was so overcome having this old and dear friend all to myself that, one of the few times in my life, I couldn't speak. Instead, I watched every nuance: the way she crossed her legs and leaned back in the chair, her habit of using a cigarette to emphasize names and situations, the way she blinked her eyes. It was too much to appreciate at one time, so I memorized it for later.

"It was a family at Metro," she said, pointing her cigarette at me. "Mr. Mayer took care of you. You didn't have to worry. You didn't ever have to feel . . ." She stopped and looked at me, then fanned herself lightly with a napkin as if relieved that she had caught herself in time before divulging some clue to her personality.

"Is it too warm in here for you?" I asked.

"No," she replied. "I tell you how it was a family. Everyone ate lunch in the studio commissary. Mr. Mayer made sure the food was excellent. Lamb, veal, duck, snapper, smoked salmon. He hired a gourmet chef for us. At lunch he'd come to our tables to say hello. They always had chicken soup that Mr. Mayer personally supervised. The apple pie was his mother's recipe."

I knew Mayer had done this to avoid the problem of grumbling actors leaving the lot to eat decently. Time was money.

As if Marietta sensed my cynicism, she continued, "And for birsdays! At five, after work, a big cake would be rolled onto the set and Mr. Mayer and Ida, his assistant, would come down. He'd raise up his arms and lead everyone in 'Happy Birsday.' On weekends, sometimes he'd invite us to his beach house for a picnic. It was so lovely. Mama loved it."

I refilled her glass. I wondered if her mother was still alive.

"My mama and aunt and I lived on Lexington Road in Beverly Hills. All the streets were lined wis different trees—maples, magnolias, sycamores, eucalyptus, jacarandas. So beautiful. Sometimes on weekends I would pack Mama and Liesel into the car and we would ride up to Arrowhead or Venice. So for me, Metro was good. For others, no."

Marietta was a bit tight by now. She wriggled out of her coat and let it fall from her shoulders onto the chair. She had on a simple black house dress. "That fellow, uh—" She sipped. "Walker, his name was. Robert. He did not enjoy it. Love. Work. Somesing. Once I went wis Judy and Dottie Ponedel to look for him in bars in Hollywood. We found him at two A.M. and brought him home for coffee and a massage so he could get to work on time. Judy did that night after night. We made one movie togeser, you know. But that picture was the first in which they let Judy be a woman. The grips would whistle at me when I came on the set, but they still treated her like a child. It hurt her and she complained to me about it. We were good friends. She could be *so* funny!" A catty look came into Marietta's eye. "I tell you a story about Judy. She was supposed to make *The Barkeleys of Broadway* wis Astaire. Judy got sick and couldn't do it. She was great friends wis Ginger Rogers up to then, but was *furious* when she found out Ginger was replacing her. 'That bitch!' she yelled at me over the phone from the hospital." Marietta leaned forward. Judy Garland has always been another favorite, and I was enraptured. "Ginger was very sensitive about having so much hair. You know—" She patted the sides of her face. "Like a peach, she was. People were always making jokes about it—*and* the way she dressed! But she was afraid to have it removed. 'It'll leave spots,' she said. So they took it off all of her photographs instead. Well, Judy knew all this. When *Barkeleys* began filming, she sent Ginger a gift. It was wrapped in bright red paper, Ginger's favorite color, and placed on her dressing table before the first day of shooting. When Ginger found it, she was thrilled; she thought Judy had forgiven her. But they said you could hear her cursing all the way to Paramount when she opened the box and inside found a huge shaving mug inscribed GOOD LUCK!" We roared. I hadn't known Garland was so . . . considerate.

Lighting her cigarette, I asked how she came to this country. She simply said she had moved from Germany with her mother into a house in California owned by an aunt Liesel and her daughter. She added that she had married and divorced a director named Howard Shlumin. I had known all this. "I dated Howard Hughes after that."

I raised my eyebrows. Hughes, the most reclusive weirdo in the world?

"Oh," she said with a wave of her cigarette, "he was *boring*. Always talking about business. And *germs.*"

I laughed, delighted she could joke with me.

"I didn't sink he was serious about me until he offered me a taste of his soup at the Colony!"

We laughed.

"But after Howard Shlumin, I decided I had had enough of marriage. I live wis friends in Manhattan now." She suddenly looked sad. What kind of friends? Lovers? "Mama and Liesel are dead now. Liesel died during a fight wis mama. A stroke. Mama soon after." She folded her hands and rested them on the table. "Did you ever hear of a man named J. Parnell Thomas?" she asked.

I nodded. "The House Un-American Committee."

"In 1948, I was subpoenaed to go to Washington and explain why I was a registered member of the Hollywood Democratic Committee. I didn't even know I *was* a member until they told me. But I was a liberal. I *hated* the Nazis. I had only joined the committee because Howard did—not Hughes, my husband. Mr. Mayer sent six lawyers to help me defend myself against the committee. That idiot Nixon was on the panel. He was the youngest-looking one. And *ugly*. The rest reminded me of Ward Crane and Claude Gillingwater."

I smiled. So this was what had brought Marietta down. And it wasn't her own fault.

"The whole lot of them were *terrible*. The committee yelled at me. My own lawyers yelled at me. They all talked like I was a criminal! Insinuating awful sings, bullying me. No one had talked to me that way since I was in Germany as a little girl. The lawyers Mr. Mayer sent were worse than the committee some of the time!" She took a sip of wine. "What could I do? Let those . . . those *clerks* tell me what I should do? I said, yes, I *was* a member of the Hollywood Democratic Committee and was *proud* to be. I guess I was nervous. They wouldn't let me smoke or anysing. I told them I knew *dozens* of Communists but that I wasn't going to tell them one single name! Mr. Mayer's lawyers ripped my dress trying to get me to sit down." She paused, looking down at the table. "There was banging at the committee's desk. The gallery booed me. Photographers crowded around taking pictures. I had no idea how stupid I had been.

"I sought Mr. Mayer would protect me. He either could not or would not. I met wis him in his office a few days later. He told me how sorry he was to have to settle my contract. He cried. *I consoled him!*" She laughed and drained her glass. "Then he brought in a new batch of those damned lawyers and it was over. The next week, one came to my house and told me I owed the government eighty thousand dollars in back taxes. Of course I didn't. But he said the IRS wanted it and that it would cost that much just to prove my case against the government. I sold my house to pay for it. I called Jack Warner for a job. We had met at Ann Sothern's house at a party. He wouldn't talk to me over the phone and his secretary said a meeting in his office was out of the question since Mr. Warner would be at sea for several weeks. At *sea!* That was the best he could do. Well, my friends were all at sea too. Overnight I was poison. Everyone was afraid to be seen wis me.

"There was nossing for me to do but go abroad. Mama refused to come. I settled her and Liesel in a large apartment on Santa Monica Boulevard. They bose died while I was living in Italy wis my friends. I arranged their funerals but didn't attend them. I took my director Joe Stein, my accountant James Carmichael, my maid and my hairdresser all to Rome. It was ironic. The only one of us who was really a Communist was Maya, my maid. And she hadn't kept up her dues! My hairdresser was lucky to find work in the home of a rich department store owner and his wife. Maya worked as a seamstress. They were so loyal. They still are. I love them. Poor Joe directed movies like *Eterna Femina* and *L'Amante di Parigi*. He *hated* working wis the Italians. So disorganized. So—" she waved her arms in the air frantically—"so . . . *crazy!*

"'Christ,' he would say to me after a bad day, 'Mayer wouldn't even have put the star of this piece of crap in his chicken soup!'"

She leaned forward, laughing. "Dear Joe. James, my accountant, was never able to learn the language. I tried to teach him but it was no use. We found him a job as a night watchman in a museum. I worried about him doing such menial work but he insisted he liked it. 'It's less boring than accounting,' he said. But I sink he was just trying to spare me. I was miserable. Joe wouldn't let me make any pictures. He said it would be embarrassing for bose of us. I didn't know how to do anysing else. So I just cooked and made sure everyone had clean clothes."

I filled her glass, feeling awful for her. A star like this doing the laundry for her own maid!

"And then when the Red Scare was over, we talked about coming back and then finally did. To Hollywood first, not here. That was 1963. I expected to start working right away. Ha! The studios were gone. People looked at me like a prehistoric dinosaur had walked into their office." Marietta became more animated, her tone bitter. "I was told the world was more sophisticated now! That no one wanted to see me talking about love to Hank Fonda in the moonlight. We were beyond all that. They wanted *realism*. Twenty-nine-year-old kids were telling *me* about *sophisticated* and *realism!*" She stabbed out her cigarette, the way she had in *River of Love*. "So we left. And came here. Joe wanted me to go on the stage but I—" She stopped abruptly and looked questioningly at me. I sensed that the Perrier Jouët had prompted her to say a bit too much and that she was embarrassed. I was in seventh heaven and didn't want her ever to stop. "I sink I should go now," she said, reaching behind her for her coat.

While listening to Marietta's sad tale, I must confess I had been imagining her in several different scenes of the screenplay I had written. She was even dressed a bit like the main character in a scene about two-thirds of the way into *Resurrection and Denial* and she had that vulnerable quality about her that was just perfect. But I was petrified to bring it up.

"Are you satisfied, Mr. Raider?" she asked.

"Just stay a few more minutes," I begged, reaching for the champagne bottle.

She put her hand over her glass. "I am afraid I can't. I must go. My friends will be worried about me if I am too late."

There are perhaps two or three times in one's life when one finds opportunity staring into one's face less than four feet away. Realizing that it was now or never, and bolstered with alcoholic confidence, I said, "Please, just wait here for one minute. I'll be right back." She had to read my screenplay.

"Mr. Raider, I really—"

"Please—" I yelled as I flew out the room. I found what I was looking for in the bedroom and came back. Panting, I handed her a red-bound copy. "Here," I said, "I want you to have this."

"A script? Mr. Raider, I don't sink that—"

"Please, just read it through. That's all I ask."

She read the title aloud. *"Resurrection and Denial . . ."* She frowned, as if not quite sure what it meant.

"My telephone number is on the cover," I said eagerly. "In case you'd like to make any comment on it. I'd be honored."

She looked at me for a moment, then rose from her seat to indicate that the audience was over. I held her coat; she slipped into it with practiced ease. We walked downstairs and I offered to pay for the cab back to her hotel.

"That is not necessary, Mr. Raider. Sank you for the champagne. Adieu." Proud to the last, she walked up Broadway with my script under her arm and disappeared.

The Fountainhead

The more I talked about movies to the people at the network and the independent film companies around the city, the more I realized that the aloof fifty-six-year-old woman I had let escape up Broadway was essential to my plan to make *Resurrection and Denial*. For one thing, she was the perfect person to cast. For another, the idea of Marietta making a comeback would be a tremendous audience draw, I felt, providing, of course, that the film was released; the public now had the macabre curiosity of the archaeologist when it came to relics of the cinematic past. But most importantly, she could help me raise the money needed to hire the people who would actually make the movie. I had compiled a half common sense/half inside-information manual with which to oversee the production, but I didn't have enough cash or expertise to produce it. The angels in New York certainly wouldn't give an unknown commodity like me a dime, but with an appealing asset like Marietta in the deal, what angel wouldn't risk a paltry thou to be in on such a deliciously glamorous and potentially tremendously profitable come-back? We would naturally alert the descendants of Parsons, Hopper and Grahame of her impending return to the screen: A profile of her in their periodicals was the sort of publicity that was both priceless and gratuitous. It thrilled me to think that Marietta might be able to make up for the years the HUAC had taken away from her, that she could feel some sort of equity had been attained, and, appealing to me, that she could get her hair done and buy a new coat. I felt like an adopting uncle, only what child was as glorious as Marietta?

Besides the pragmatic reasons I had for wanting to see her again, there was also the fact that I simply wanted to further our acquaintance. I sensed we shared a certain incompatibility with our environments. True, she had been adored by millions of people around the world, but what does fame accomplish except to make one a beloved outcast? And now, with public affection behind her, she was simply an aberration who stayed in hiding, not wanting, perhaps not able, to live with the housewives and busdrivers who had once adored her.

I looked up the names of all the people she had mentioned as living at her hotel: none were listed. That made me uneasy. With a project of this magnitude, I wanted to have confidence that anyone who might be involved in its completion would be reliable. If she did call back, I wanted to know something more of what had happened to her during the last twenty years. I checked with *The Morning Show* gossip columnist, who only had a few old photographs and a bio compiled in 1951, stuffed in a file marked INACTIVE.

After a week of frenzied searching, I gave up, realizing there was nothing to do but wait and hope for a telephone call.

I envied Marietta the relationships she had with her old friends from MGM. Aside from Roman, I had almost always been devoid of friends. Until now, I had been angry that his memory could still depress me, could still dominate my thoughts, but, inspired by Marietta, and frustrated waiting for her call, I decided to try to find someone with whom I could replace him. I set out to explore Greenwich Village.

In the past, homosexuals had led clandestine existences, fearing that the world might discover and punish them for their sexual proclivities; now, they congealed in their own communities because of them. Both styles of living seemed unnaturally contrived to me. I knew relatively little about homosexuals except for what I deduced from myself, observed in a handful of others and read in the biographies of people such as Wilde, Tchaikovsky, Shakespeare and Colette. Still, I had formed some definite ideas and images in my mind. It took me two months before I went to a gay bar in New York. As I walked down Christopher Street that first night, I was struck by the incongruity of myth and reality—the way someone might be observing a movie star in person for the first time. That evening, and during many later ones, I observed the tremendous effect *liberation* had had on the homosexual way of life.

For instance, I was always under the impression that homosexuals had more than their share of good taste. Of course, before liberation, male homosexuals did not have much to do. Unwelcome in sand lots because of a tendency to scream in the face of line drives, unable to stomach the inferior brands of liquor used in adolescent drinking games and tepid in regard to dating and marriage, they had had plenty of time to ponder pattern-on-pattern compatibility and mixed color harmony. Though this garnered them a reputation for excellent taste, it established them as epicene fellows with unmasculine concerns.

In 1969, communal solidarity was established when a group of drag queens stood up to police harassment at the Stonewall Bar in Greenwich Village. Suddenly homosexuals had lots to do. There were parades to march in, referendums to vote on and ears to pierce. Special interest periodicals had to be established and Edith Piaf memorial albums had to be pressed. No longer having time to worry about minimal contrasts in color, homosexuals exchanged their individualized tastes for faded jeans, baseball caps and T-shirts of various colors and platitudes. But the world still thought their underwear too fancy and continued to make fun of them on television.

Wanting to establish their masculinity once and for all, they took to participating in traditionally masculine activities. They formed moving companies and baseball teams, had playoffs, wore jockstraps and pitched overhanded. With regard to clothes, they adopted all the traditional masculine images of heterosexual society. No longer would the world see them prancing about in tweeds and gabardines like a bunch of English fops. Now they would stand on piers wearing five-ring utility belts, exuding the animal magnetism of the telephone repairman.

I suppose whenever there is a repression of human sensibility there will be a reaction in expression. This often takes the form of the translation of unacceptable impulses into tolerable acts. In ancient Greece where one could be banished or executed for asking a lot of questions about the Absolute Good, the world saw the flowering of physical science, mathematics, theater, philosophy and the baklava. At a much later time, when the pope could have a man's head removed if he used it to ponder the existence of God, the Renaissance happened, producing exquisite paintings, sculpture, architecture and music.

Certain people had not only to face this general repression, but the stigmas given to certain physical or emotional characteristics. Women were kept politically impotent and educationally limited, yet were able to do pioneer work in radioactivity, compose novels and musical scores, and be the first to photograph such diverse subjects as the East Side immigrants and the DNA molecule. Ethnic and religious minorities were tarred and feathered, robbed, beaten and denied admission to toilet facilities, but reacted by giving the world great works of art, banks, technology, new forms of music and creative uses for the peanut and poppy seed.

Perhaps because homosexuals were put at the bottom of the societal scourge scale right below baby eater, they made the most substantial contributions to art and science. Sand, Hawthorne, Michelangelo, Alexander and Plato made incalculable contributions to the fields of painting, sculpture, architecture, poetry, music, engineering, mathematics, science and interior decorating.

To the extent that liberation movements educate people, repression subsides, affecting the creative output of all historical pariahs. Women now do flush sets of arm curls, minorities form block associations, and after two thousand years, homosexuals have advanced from glorifying the human form in marble to depicting the human penis in devil's food cake.

As I walked toward Hudson Street to my first leather bar (I have always been attracted to a rougher circle than my own), I couldn't help but think how alienated and alone homosexuals of the past must have felt. True, they wrote, painted, said witty things and dressed impeccably, but they perceived themselves to be lone stains on the fabric of life. There were no gay newspapers to read with editorials printed opposite lasciviously illustrated Key West motel advertisements. There were no books with in-depth articles about the pros and cons of foreskin piercing nor pictorial essays called *Asses: An International Art Form*. Any film containing a gay character was either pornographic or suggested that the rosiest fate homosexuals could look forward to was to be an entree for Spanish adolescents in front of Elizabeth Taylor. Sexual encounters were erratic; love relationships were at best guarded secrets, at worst inconceivable.

In those years preceding the establishment of leather bars, homosexual men were forced to guess about the sexual proclivities of other men before making any sort of advance. They had to ask themselves such questions as: Does that hand frantically waving at me from under the wall of the next bathroom stall belong to a person in desperate need of toilet paper or interested in going out for drinks? Since a miscalculation could lead to life imprisonment in thirty-six states, many chose to suppress their desires and sit at home jotting down things like *Oedipus Rex, Cat on a Hot Tin Roof* and *Pal Joey*.

Liberation took the guesswork out of meeting people. No longer did one have to sit for hours in a bus station with a copy of *Giovanni's Room* perched obtrusively on one's lap. Leather bars were places in which one could safely choose from an assortment of libidinous ideals, all with glandular inclinations to complement one's own. Naturally, there was little more in the way of brooding at home over unrequited passion, so the world saw a marked decline in such chefs-d'oeuvre as *Prancing Nigger, Remembrance of Things Past* and *Moby Dick*.

Perhaps, I thought to myself as I entered my first leather bar, the world has been more than compensated for this by the advent of the adjustable tit clamp.

"Are you a member?" a rough-looking chap with a blond crewcut asked me at the door, looking over my unorthodox burgundy suede bomber jacket and raw silk jeans.

"No," I replied, terrified.

"Three dollars, please."

Most of these dank drinkeries are nestled in the West Village, conveniently located next to gangs of Italian adolescents trying to convey the heterosexual point of view through baseball bats. Their interiors are modestly decorated with a bartender, pool table and, for balance, a hitching post. Bathrooms are usually neglected but often have spectacularly colorful mold formations. Frequenting these bars are mostly *New York* magazine reporters doing research incognito, and a slightly smaller percentage of men clad entirely in leather. As these chaps search their pockets for bottles of synthetic amyl nitrate, a noise similar to that of balloons being twisted into a poodle sculpture punctuates the air. The uninitiated like me that night might feel a little intimidated surrounded by all this masculinity, but veterans of these caliginous cantinas know that what appears to be an ominous, bald-headed storm trooper is in reality only an amiable salesclerk relaxing after a hard day behind the perfume counter at Macy's.

What chisanbop did for mathematics, the leather bar does for human relationships. After a sufficient amount of beer-can crushing and wall leaning, the most aggressive in the crowd grabbed someone by his studded dog collar, applied a genital tension device and proceeded to get acquainted in a way that wouldn't have been attempted by even the most thorough proctologist. Sensing a relationship in the making, the crowd around the two invited them to intensify their satyric gymnastics by offering braided jockey bats, rubber thumb shackles and leather ping pong paddles. I walked on, aghast and amused. If a good impression were made, the two might have gone to the full limit of human endurance and introduced themselves.

I expected to hear a few amusing wisecracks as I walked around the bar. Traditionally, homosexuals have enjoyed a certain reputation for prowess in the derisive dexterity department, a direct result of having to share a world garishly populated by heterosexuals. For centuries, homosexuals tried to understand the problem of heterosexuality without making any moral judgments, looking at heterosexuals' odd behavior patterns as something they would just have to struggle through life with, like a birthmark or a clubfoot. But heterosexual attitudes have been consistently annoying. For example:

> After being given birthday tickets to see Birgit Nilsson in one of the most spectacular performances in opera history, the heterosexual will become animated only when recalling what the bar charged for Raisinets.

> The heterosexual not only wears clothes made of artificial fibers, but will also draw attention to the fact by confidently pointing out to his concerned hostess that the soup he just spilled on his coat sleeve is beading.

Homosexuals had no choice but to develop a habit of passing the scathing remark, devastating epigram and witty invective. The absence of any such amusing conversation this evening was puzzling at first. I finally attributed it to liberation as well. It is simply a physical impossibility to get off a scornful remark when one has a rubber ball gag padlocked to one's jaw. Of course, not *everyone* had such a device clamped to his mouth. But many patrons do complain that people become unnaturally aloof inside of leather bars. I think this is more a matter of lighting than personality. It is not surprising that customers want these places kept dim—not everyone looks good in a one-piece balls spreader—but it is unrealistic to expect to get a conversation going when for fifteen minutes one has been mistaking a hot water pipe for a Latino.

Having spotted no one of Roman's caliber, I went home. Was I always going to be hung up on him? I tried again the next evening at the baths.

The Romans gave us a lot. Aqueducts, arches, law, the calender, Latin and oregano. Though barbarians from the south of France had the unmitigated gall to destroy most of the empire, subsequent cultures were able to enjoy these artistic and scientific inventions because the Romans used materials like marble and granite rather than lucite and

Congoleum. The Roman baths were the prototype of our present franchised models, but the average Roman did not have sex there; he bathed there. Homosexuals had to sit in the Forum all day with a copy of the *Phaedo* perched obtrusively on their laps if they wanted to meet somebody. Since a miscalculation could lead to being drawn and quartered in thirty-six city-states, most chose to stay home to decline nouns and invent the Artesian well. But we can still compare how the Romans got their steam to how we do.

In the modern bath, one is expected to trust one's wristwatch to a financially insecure-looking attendant who will grudgingly put down his comic book and give one a key to a private room that would be judged cramped by the most easily accommodated hamster. In the Baths of Caracalla, magnificently structured centurions relaxed after a hard day of cohort forming by sitting on mounds of cushions in awesome pink marble chambers. Lithe slaves bathed them with warm scented mineral water and massaged perfumed oils into their skin. Looking about the antiseptic auberges of today, one experiences a sense of loss seeing barefoot public accountants step on live cigarette butts, slip on water-soluble lubricant and apply strawberry-flavored prolongation cream.

The largest of the ancient baths was built by the Emperor Diocletian in the late 300s and could serve as many as three thousand plebeians at once, providing the towel supply from Turkey was uninterrupted. This opulent structure had huge square-shaped swimming pools surrounded by lush gardens, columned porches and extensive libraries—what is the equivalent in modern baths to the simulated waterfall and prefabricated jail cell. There were no weight-lifting facilities in the Roman baths. After all, when one has hordes of Visigoths with which to contend, there is no need to do superfluous parallel-bar dips. The decorations of the ancient baths included such things as precious marble statuary and mosaics of colored glass and tiles; this has given way to grainy charcoal murals of blindfolded Nazis wielding rectal extenders.

As far as food was concerned in the ancient baths, one pictures young boys from Judea and Greece carrying bowls of luscious fruits and wines, hirsute barbarians trained to convey boards laden with fishes decorated by shells, and seven-feet-tall Etruscans offering platters of roast wild boar, peacock and clams oreganatto. Today one sees more of the automated snack bar/truck stop: Vending machines tempt the towel-clad purchaser with barbeque-flavored corn chips, cupcakes injected with an unconscionable frosting and vitamin-E-enriched desensitizing cream.

Occasionally, the ancient baths were rented out for private orgies. But when it came to sex, the Romans sorely lacked ingenuity. Oh, the baths were filled with hundreds of bodies writhing in Dionysian abandon—limbs intertwined, genitals aflame with desire, mouths stuffed with grapes. Diaphanous Persian boys were handed out as party favors, golden German boys were carried out on silver plates and served on beds of linguine noodles with side orders of adolescent Moors. Talented lutenists wildly played popular iambic tunes of the day while black slaves danced madly among the nude revelers, demonstrating an early facility for the time step. But not much else went on.

One wonders how they *ever* got along without deluxe enema kits, chrome anal balls and vibro-butt plugs.

If there had been a strictly homosexual bath in Roman times, one has to wonder if meeting people then might have been done with a bit more panache than now. It is much more pleasant to imagine Cicero walking languidly through a garden and engaging a young Roman poet in witty conversation than an experienced greeting card cashier beckoning one into an artificial truck cab by means of excessive nipple tweaking. And it is infinitely more agreeable to think that if someone in whom Cicero had no interest peeked into his private bath chamber, he would communicate his lack of interest in a direct and civilized manner rather than to pretend to be in a coma.

In my one Sunday night foray to the baths, I did manage to meet four rather boring individuals. The first was short, dark, and talked of nothing but how dissatisfied he was with his sexual orientation. For me, wishing that the presentation of a grandchild could be made to one's seventy-five-year-old mother before she dies does not fall in the domain of verbal foreplay. If she still prays for such an event after seeing that one has continued to have male roommates long after it is financially necessary to do so, she is probably too senile to play patty-cake anyway.

The second was a blond in his late teens, attractive but with the affectation of a Lippizaner stallion. It is understandable that one should want to brag a little after saving a patient's life; it is, however, inconceivable that anyone would want to brag about being on the cover of a male pornographic magazine simply for being born with oversized genitals and having no desire to seek political office.

The third was dark, thin and interested in politics. I don't think thoughts on Soviet imperialism should be expressed when one is being eagerly led to a second-floor room. In fact, one should not feel qualified to speak at length about *any* world problem and its possible solution simply because one is employed in the United Nations gift shop.

The fourth was in his mid-thirties and wanted to tell me his life story. The date of his birth, anecdotes about a favorite uncle and the influence Joan Didion has had on his life might have been of interest to some future biographer but not to someone who had to interview a hit man for the Mafia early in the morning.

Depressed by this lack of satisfying companionship, if not of physical activity, I went home and took two showers.

I invited my family out to dinner the next night: I needed to feel their warmth and hear some intelligent conversation. My mother and Lucy drove in from the Island and we met in my father's office ten floors up from my own at the network, even though I rarely saw him. We went to one of New York's many pretentious restaurants.

The pretentious restaurant is such because it boasts a certain percentage of celebrity patrons. If one happens to be starring in a television police drama, seating will be at a comfortable table in the front where one's order will be taken personally by the owner. If, however, one is a brain surgeon who saves several lives per day, seating will be in the rear next to a cigarette machine where one can easily observe busboys filling water glasses and hear large pots being dropped in the kitchen. Fortunately, I am the type who insists on a good table—and gets one.

Our order was taken by one of New York's pretentious waiters. Since he had spent his day being rejected by big Broadway musicals, the last thing he wanted to worry about was the banality of bringing menus or supplying rolls. Of course, he eventually did appear. Claiming that his name was Tristan, he announced the specials of the evening in the sort of bored tone of voice George Sanders might have used in reading his suicide note aloud for sense. Asking him to repeat any of these specials resulted in pencil-tip breaking; requesting a wine list caused jaw-muscle movements.

The pretentious menu is limited: cold, pastel-colored soups, entrees reflecting the latest influx of Asian refugees, and desserts lacking both girth and icing.

Some New Yorkers feel that watching Woody Allen, who was there that night, eat creamed spinach more than compensates for all this. Others are compelled to steal the salt and pepper shakers. I am one of the latter type.

Thank God we had lots of laughs anyway. I filled them in on how the *Resurrection and Denial* project was going and repeated my Marietta story—and told them of my ambitious plans for her should she call.

"Sounds good," my father said, clearly excited by my friendship with one of the biggest stars in movie history.

"Big deal," was Lucy's only comment.

Requiem for a Heavyweight

I vy Caitlin North was born in Peapack, New Jersey, on December 7, 1939, the only child of the Reverend Joshua P. North. Familiar with God's thoughts concerning propagation, the reverend had originally planned to have a large family. After two years of concentrated industry directed toward realizing this ambition, however, his home still lacked any sign of an impish grin or a crayoned wall mural. Though the reverend believed this to be God's Will, the local gynecologist was of the opinion that it was due to a blockage in the uterus of his wife, Rebekah.

While Rebekah shared her husband's faith in divine intent, she was nevertheless devastated by the report and became severely depressed as they drove home from the doctor's office. She felt as if she had failed her husband. "I am so sorry, Joshua," she said, looking to him for comfort.

The pastor grimly shifted gears and said, "Put not faith in the advice of men. For the Lord said, 'Thy wife shall be as a fruitful vine by the sides of thine house, thy children like olive plants round thy table.'"

Unable to control herself, Rebekah sobbed all the way home. That evening, she begged her husband to allow her to sleep alone, but he replied, "The Lord said, 'Thy wife hath not power of her own body, but the husband.'" Thereafter, he doubled his conjugal efforts and had

Rebekah kneel down with him before and after intercourse to pray for fertilization.

"Please, Heavenly Father, help my wife to be Thy useful servant rather than as barren and inutile as the parched desert of Sinai."

For Rebekah, these incantations gave the act of making love a somewhat baroque quality. Added to the guilt she already felt for not being able to multiply was guilt for no longer wanting to try. Notwithstanding, she dutifully continued to submit herself to her husband.

After five years, the congregation could find no other subject so delicious to gossip about.

"I think it's *him.*"

"No, I heard *she* had an abortion in Newark when she was fourteen."

The pastor's wife was supposed to be exemplary. But how could good Christian mothers take counsel about child-rearing practices from a woman who had no such experience? And how could they take her advice about familial problems seriously when she had no family of her own? The whispers reached Rebekah's ears; she felt as if she had failed not only her husband but the entire congregation as well.

To assuage her guilt and compensate for her inadequacy, Rebekah put all her energy into doing good works for the church. She acquiesced to the demands of the pulpit committee and agreed to teach preschoolers about sin in Sunday School. She memorized information about all the people who regularly attended her husband's services and made it a point to remember their birthdays and attend their funerals. She put up over three hundred jars of strawberry preserves and sold them in order to put a down payment on the congregation's second organ. She even typed her husband's Deuteronomy Seminar notes and painted the inside of their house when he went to Hawaii for a reformed-theology conference.

She was on a stepladder painting the kitchen ceiling when he returned. "How do you like it, Joshua?" she asked, wiping a blot of paint from her nose.

The reverend looked around the room solemnly and replied, "The

Lord said in Proverbs fourteen: one: 'Every wise woman buildeth her house, but the foolish plucketh it down with her hands.'"

A resilient and determined woman, Rebekah tripled her efforts. The congregation still gossiped about her inability to contribute babies to the world, but they *were* pleased to note that she suddenly had time to contribute gourmet dishes like potatoes au gratin to every pot luck supper, give speeches about the devil at luncheons, cheer the congregation's peewee baseball team, teach the women's Bible study, and still have time to look well groomed. Things went on like this for several years. Naturally, everyone came to take Rebekah's frenetic laboring for granted. When she declined a wedding invitation for the first time in five years because of a scheduling conflict, the mother of the bride rebuked her in front of several women after services the following Sunday.

"I don't see *why* you don't have time to attend," the mother said coolly. "After all, you don't have any *children* to take care of like the rest of us." Assorted smirks followed.

Rebekah cried the rest of the day.

When medical research accidently discovered a way to help women with Rebekah's problem, she got down on her knees in the gynecologist's office and thanked God. The Rubin Test was really designed to determine whether a woman's tubes were perforated by injecting air into the cervix; an unforeseen benefit was that the air sometimes opened the constricted uterus.

"There's no guarantee," the doctor warned, "but it has helped a fairly high percentage of women."

Rebekah crossed herself.

"However, Ms. North, I think I should tell you that given your present state of health and your age, I wouldn't advise undergoing any treatment that might facilitate pregnancy. I hate to say it, but there is a chance you won't survive."

Rebekah went to her husband for guidance. "Tell me, Joshua, what should I do?"

The reverend looked at her bleakly and said, "It is your decision with

God. But remember that He said, 'Be fruitful, and multiply, and replenish the earth.'"

"But what do *you* say, Joshua?" she asked, searching his face.

"I would have what God would have!" he said, looking at her angrily. "In Ephesians five: twenty-two, it is said: 'Wives, submit yourselves unto your own husbands, as unto the Lord.'"

Rebekah's cervix was injected with air the following week. Three months later, she was pregnant. The news spread through the congregation and the reverend beamed with pride as the members of the church congratulated him.

Rebekah was chronically ill during her gestation period. She stopped all church activities and fell behind in her domestic chores. The reverend found it difficult to be constantly understanding. Sticking a finger though a hole in his sock, he would quote liberally from Proverbs about her wifely duties. Pointing at the lumps in his mashed potatoes, he would remind her of God's purpose in creating Eve. Rebekah's tendency to vomit after these reprimands left the pastor no alternative but to accept dinner invitations elsewhere. So Rebekah spent the latter months of her pregnancy mostly alone, comforted only by the knowledge that she was fulfilling the paternal wishes of her husband. She prayed that God would make her baby well and whole.

On the evening of December 6, Rebekah began to experience labor pains. The pastor had gone to Miami Beach to lecture on sex sins at another reformed-theology conference; Rebekah had to call an ambulance herself. When it arrived forty-five minutes later, she was writhing in agony, terrified. They carried her out on a stretcher and notified the hospital on the way. It was touch and go, but a few hours later she gave birth to a five-pound girl.

"Joshua will be so *pleased,*" she managed to whisper to the doctor before plunging into a deep sleep.

The physician had her moved immediately to a private room, where he examined her thoroughly. He had a nurse telephone the reverend to return from Miami Beach at once. Rebekah's blood pressure was low; her respiratory functions were uneven. Directing a nurse to administer a stimulant, he arranged an oxygen tent around the upper portion of her body.

He attended her all night trying to stabilize her condition, but she became weaker. Her body was slowly running down like a neglected five-and-dime windup toy; the doctor couldn't find any physical reason why. At seven A.M., Rebekah awoke from the coma and calmly asked the doctor if the baby was alive.

"Yes," he replied. "A girl."

"Is she healthy?"

"Yes, she's perfect."

"Good," she said and closed her eyes. The doctor reached for her hand. Before he could take a pulse, Rebekah North sighed and passed into immortality. She had fulfilled her last obligation.

Giving the eulogy at her funeral, the reverend said he envied Rebekah her place in the presence of God while he was left behind to endure the hardships of the world. The congregation thought that despite his grief, the reverend looked very handsome with his new tan.

Ivy Caitlin North was not a terribly bright child. All children will miscalculate in their attempts to imitate daredevils like Douglas Fairbanks, Harold Lloyd and Bebe Daniels, but Ivy fell off more than her share of roofs. Her father naturally took complete charge of her religious education and, though she was a slow learner, he taught her with the same single-minded determination and relentless patience that he had used to acquire her in the first place. He told her all about Rebekah, whom he held up as the Christian ideal he expected Ivy to emulate all her life.

Because of this concentrated instruction and the fact that she was a pastor's daughter, Ivy felt set apart from others at an early age. She noticed quite early that people took life too lightly—it was apparent that the devil was at work everywhere, at every minute. She considered it her moral obligation to point out his handiwork. Thus, seeing Officer Marlowe steal an apple from Plutarch's Fruit Stand precipitated pants-leg pulling and the relating of an anecdote from the Book of Judges.

Losing at tag prompted liberal quotations from the Old Testament. Since young children do not like to hear parables about Elijah the Tishbite when they are trying to choose sides, Ivy had few friends. Everyone in town, in fact, took to ducking behind mailboxes upon seeing her approach. She was soon nicknamed "Poison Ivy."

At first this upset the little girl: After all, her intentions were charitable. But her father consoled her.

"It is not easy to be a good Christian. You are a pariah in a fallen world. But your rewards in heaven will be tenfold."

Ivy would draw strength from these words later when, having harassed large segments of the population, she would be pelted with lemon meringue pies during press conferences.

Ivy withdrew from the world and led a Charlotte Vale sort of existence, not buying fashionable clothes, the latest record albums or eyebrow tweezers. She tended to her father and her Bible. Then, suddenly, in the middle of her adolescence, she developed a secular passion for the cinematic presence of Pat Boone. She scotch-taped his picture to the back of her bedroom door and sent him a fan letter every month. He never answered but her devotion remained strong. When he made *April Love* with Shirley Jones and refused to kiss her on camera because he didn't think it was proper, the newspapers made a joke of it. Ivy wrote him a sixteen-page letter applauding his decision, and received an autographed picture six months later. Ivy promised God at the mailbox after ripping open the envelope that she would only marry someone with Pat Boone's looks and convictions; she prayed that He would deliver him to her.

In 1957, when she was eighteen, God fulfilled the physical half of her request. His name was Roy Semple and he was the proprietor of the Peapack Used Car Emporium located on the other side of town. Reverend North invited Roy to dinner after buying a hardly used Hudson from him. Ivy almost dropped a bowl of mixed vegetables when she saw Roy: About twenty-six, with a crew cut, disarming smile and blue eyes, he was the image of her white-bucked idol. Roy was immediately taken with Ivy as well; for although her intellectual acumen was almost nonexistent, her mammarial topography was more than evident. Ivy asked her father if she could invite Roy to dinner again the following week. Pleased to see that his daughter was taking a renewed interest in life after all these years, the reverend agreed.

Ivy and Roy continued their masticatory romance for six months. When it appeared to be getting serious, the pastor asked Roy what his feelings were about Jesus. "Have you put your life in the hands of the Lord, my son?"

Roy Semple may have *looked* like someone who wouldn't kiss on camera but the resemblance ended there. Since he was able to convince hundreds of used-car customers (including the reverend) that *he* "didn't hear any thumping noise under the hood," he easily assured the pastor that he was a devout Christian. To impress the reverend further, he cut up construction paper and made a set of Biblical flashcards so that he could memorize and recite short passages. Roy made such a hit that within a few weeks Reverend North agreed to announce his daughter's engagement. Ten months later, Ivy North became Mrs. Roy Semple and honeymooned in Roy's small house on the other side of Peapack. Out of respect for her new husband, she had solemnly burned all her Pat Boone photographs on the eve of her wedding.

Ivy knew little of sex except for what she read in the Bible. Since her favorite passage was Corinthians 12:21, "I shall bewail many which have sinned already, and have not repented of the uncleanness and fornication and lasciviousness which they have committed," she was horrified when Roy told her what he planned to do with the can of whipped cream on the nightstand and spent a miserable night shivering in the bathroom with a meat cleaver lying across her lap while Roy pounded on the door. Eventually he was able to catch her off guard and consummate the marriage, but because he could never adjust to hearing tearful prayers to the Holy Ghost during intercourse, their sex life was rather unsatisfying.

Like her mother before her, Ivy tried to compensate for disappointing her husband by taking an interest in his business. Hoping that humoring her might lead to fellatio, Roy taught Ivy everything he knew about selling used cars: how to use her voice and hands to avoid being brushed off with a "we're-just-looking"; how to use psychology on the customers by playing on their vanities and exploiting their weaknesses; how to make old gears sound like new with an application of sawdust and olive oil. Though this all sounded a little like lying to Ivy, she remembered that, according to Ephesians and Colossians, the wife was expected to support her husband in financial matters regardless of whether or not she thought he was right. So in no time she was successfully selling broken-down Plymouths to unsuspecting spinsters.

Like her mother in another respect, Ivy discovered that work was no substitute for fulfilling the desires of her husband. No matter how many used Thunderbirds Ivy sold, Roy still kept insisting on having sex.

Soon after their marriage, Roy committed adultery with a waitress in the men's room of a diner. He truly did not want to be unfaithful—at least not before his wife had finished unpacking the dishes from her trousseau—but he simply could not contain his sexual desire. He continued to have sex with the waitress in various motel rooms, then went on to other women.

Feeling guilty telling Ivy he was going into town to buy sparkplugs when he knew full well that he would be enjoying cunnilingus while she innocently poured sawdust into their latest acquisition, he began to drink to lessen his anxiety. Women chased down with alcohol soon became a chronic addiction.

Unlike her mother, Ivy was quite fertile. Although her sexual encounters with Roy were rare, brief and austere, she became pregnant during the third month of their marriage. Roy was overjoyed at the prospect of having a child, but came down to earth when Ivy told him he would be sleeping on the lumpy couch in the living room during her gestation period.

He continued to whore and drink.

In 1958, the couple was blessed with a boy. They named him Claude. Their sex life resumed, Ivy muttering prayers to the Virgin Mary between sobs.

Roy added gambling to his other vices. He rarely came home.

Not able to count on her husband anymore, Ivy had to take care of the Peapack Used Car Emporium, Claude and the small house single-handedly. She felt herself growing bitter and angry toward Roy but, knowing this was sinful, suppressed it. Her efforts notwithstanding, the business suffered and Ivy prayed fervently to the Lord for guidance.

"Please, O Lord. Show me how I might best serve my husband," she would say through clenched teeth, but the Lord ignored her. It became more and more difficult for Ivy to control her hostility when Roy stumbled in the door with liquor on his breath and betting stubs in his pocket.

Within a year, Roy developed a duodenal ulcer and collapsed coming out of a black prostitute's apartment. Her pimp delivered the unconscious Roy to Ivy at home. Though the pimp made up a story about being an ex-army buddy of Roy's (who had been a good customer), Ivy could tell from his quilted red satin jumpsuit that he was lying. She deduced a lascivious explanation.

"Lord, please show me how I might best *serve* my husband," she said, seething with anger.

The doctor told her Roy had a bleeding ulcer and had him installed in the hospital for six weeks, which further weakened Ivy's precarious financial situation. She worried night and day about her little Claude's future and prayed that God would show her a way out of the mess she was in.

When Roy was discharged, he had to remain in bed for several weeks and be fed bland dishes and special medicines. The business continued to suffer because Ivy had to attend to Roy's every need and whim; the doctor had warned her that any frustration could be fatal to him. She controlled her enmity by praying. She even told Roy that she knew about his infidelities and forgave him.

Roy immediately sat up in bed and demanded a bottle of Four Roses.

Ivy thought for a moment. The doctor had made it quite clear that he was to have no liquor under any circumstances. But the Lord had said, "Ye wives, be in subjection to your own husbands." Since her father had often told her to put faith in the words of the Lord rather than men, she happily made Roy a double. The next morning, she served white bread soaked in skim milk to a cadaver.

Though Reverend North gave the service and eulogy for free and got a discount on the embalming from the Peapack Funeral Home, the ceremony still cost a great deal of money. Ivy was too poor to stall off the creditors any longer, and they descended like locusts, leaving her with only the large tent under which the used cars had been displayed, and a passenger van. She packed the tent and little Claude into the van and drove home to her father, who was overjoyed to have them.

Ivy would later tell interviewers that at that point in her life God had provided the tools for her life's work but not the spark that would catapult her like a piston throughout the world. That ignition would take place when she was speaking to a young Christian bride in 1967.

Reverend North had asked Ivy to assume some of his duties, the most responsible of which was the job of marriage counseling. Ivy met the young member of the reverend's congregation in her father's study as she had many other brides over the years. It seemed that she and her husband had been quarreling.

"I inherited a lot of money from my grandmother before we were married," she began. "I've kept it in a savings account for the last two years. My husband is a soda jerk at a drugstore. He doesn't like it much. He's always looking for ways to advance himself. He saw this ad in *Variety*. Seems they're looking for investors in this all-star movie. Elizabeth Taylor's in it. Tennessee Williams wrote it. It's called *Boom!* He says it's a sure thing and will double our money, but I don't know. I don't like the idea of risking twenty-five thousand dollars in one place. But he's all fired up about the idea. Keeps begging me to withdraw my money. I keep saying no. We argue about it all the time. What should I do?"

Ivy smiled and told the girl that she was lucky to have come to her about this. She quoted a line from the Bible that had given *her* guidance during bad times: "Ye wives, be in subjection to your own husbands."

The woman frowned and pulled out a copy of *Cosmopolitan* from her grocery bag, which she showed to Ivy. "I've been hearing a lot about liberation lately. Here's an article by Gloria Steinem that says a woman has rights too. That we should have a say about money matters and even practice birth control if we want."

Ivy's mouth dropped open. Pulling the King James Bible from her father's shelf, she quoted from it extensively.

"In Esther one: twenty it says, 'And when the king's decree which he shall make shall be published through all his empire, (for it is great,) all the wives shall give their husbands honour, both to great and small.' In Proverbs eleven: sixteen: 'A gracious woman retaineth honour: As a jewel of gold in a swine's snout, so is a fair woman which is without discretion.'"

After forty-five minutes, the young woman remembered she had Popsicles in her grocery bag. "I've really got to go," she said. "You've been very helpful."

Ivy was too shocked by the things printed in *Cosmopolitan* to gather any satisfaction from helping the woman. She asked her to leave the magazine with her. After a close reading, she decided that the filth between its covers was against everything she and her mother had believed about marriage and family. There were despicable stories about men cooking shrimp marinara while their wives ran about earning M.B.A.'s—and blatant padded-bra advertisements.

Wondering just how far this sort of thing had gone, Ivy bought and read a newspaper for the first time in her life. It was worse than she imagined. The federal government had passed laws geared to break up the family unit, grants for women to go to secretarial schools instead of PTA meetings, food stamp programs for college students that would weaken their dependence on their parents. Where would it end? Who would be the savior of the ideals upon which this great country had been founded?

"I'm going to bring the nation back on the path to righteousness," she told her father after a week of introspection. She explained how God had led her to that decision and outlined her plan to take Claude and the tent on the road to speak out against abominations like the women's liberation movement and such devil's disciples as Bess Myerson.

"But you'll be all alone," her father said. "Who will pitch the tent?"

"God will be with me. We'll find a way."

"And what about Claude? His education?"

Holding up the Bible, she said, "Everything he needs to know is in this book."

With her father's blessings but only a few hundred dollars in cash, Ivy was off on the most important errand of her life. On the Jersey Turnpike she decided to call herself Sister Ivy. She dubbed her efforts against feminism the Rescue Democracy Campaign and worked her way south, putting up handwritten posters in supermarkets, shopping malls and automotive centers in order to solicit help and an audience. At first, her assistants were few and the crowds sparse, but as she criss-crossed a path down the coast she built up a word-of-mouth reputation. Sister Ivy seemed to strike a chord in the psyche of the great mass of Americans sick of radical change, liberal propaganda and eating leftovers. Applying the same principles Roy had taught her to sell poorly preserved four-door convertibles, she fanned the emotional flames of her audiences.

"The women's liberation movement is an *abomination!*"

She would illustrate this axiom with dramatic predictions of what an application of its philosophy would bring: frightened women hiding in foxholes; communal public toilets in which women would be forced to urinate in plain sight of perverts, exhibitionists and Negroes; pregnant women compelled to stand on buses and open their own car doors. Sister Ivy's most vivid prognostication had to do with babies being yanked from the loving arms of their mothers so that the women could be trained to operate tanks and bazookas.

"This fits right in with the Communist plan to take over our beloved country by weakening our military strength!" she reasoned for her audiences.

The coup de grace, preceding an appeal for donations, had Sister Ivy hoisting little Claude up over her head and explaining in colorful detail how feminists would like to have doctors with dirty hands rip innocent children like Claude from their mothers' wombs and throw them into trash cans. To prevent this, she suggested each member of the audience contribute five dollars or more to help her continue her work.

It was an effective campaign. As her popularity grew, she invested money in fluorescent paint and had SISTER IVY printed on both doors of the van. She also bought a primitive sound system and strings of Chinese lanterns to decorate the tent. In town after town, with little Claude standing by, she continued to speak passionately about lust, abortion and the practice of burning female underapparel. She raised the consciousness of thousands of people: housewives who paled at the thought of learning how to operate an M-2 rifle and crane operators who feared they might come home some day to find their wives pursuing a medical career rather than heating up dinner. Though many groups supported the women's liberation movement, including the Girl Scouts of America, she maintained it was part of a Communist plot and that no *real* women were feminists—only oddballs, misfits and Communist lesbians. She ignored the fact that the Communist party of the United States and the John Birch Society HOT DOGS (Humanitarians Opposed To Degrading Our Girls) applauded her efforts; she eventually managed to stall a major legislative bill that would have especially benefited the many poor women who subscribed to her warnings.

"What would you rather have, happy homes with healthy families or a Communist takeover?"

Sister Ivy discovered that people responded to other issues as well: prostitution, pornography and tax laws. But what really brought the attention that would catapult her into the limelight was the issue of homosexuality, which she called the Rescue the Babies Campaign. Its purpose was to prevent homosexuals from teaching in school. Pointing to Claude—now seventeen and still not able to multiply or divide—she would describe a scenario in which a sex-crazed geometry teacher might trap him in a supply closet and fondle his genitals with a protractor.

"Not only should we take homosexual teachers out of our schools, but we should take out the books they write as well."

Her adoring audiences grinned at the thought of bonfires being fueled by the works of Shakespeare and other homosexual authors they had been forced to read in high school.

"Homosexuality is an abomination in the eyes of God!" she never tired of chanting, though every Biblical scholar knows that neither God's Ten Commandments nor any of Jesus' teachings even *mentions* the subject. And whereas there were people in her audiences who did break the Commandments on a regular basis (lying to and cheating on their spouses and the IRS), their sins seemed to pale in comparison to Sister Ivy's image of an English teacher masturbating in front of innocent seventh graders while discussing *The Red Badge of Courage*.

Impressed with her growing popularity, a radio station in Charlotte, North Carolina, offered Sister Ivy a fifteen-minute spot on Sunday mornings. Twenty thousand people were able to listen to her at one time after that; contributions came to thousands of dollars.

As Claude grew into a handsome but rather imbecilic young man, Sister Ivy's radio spot grew into a three-hour program with local high school choirs and guest evangelists, and she opened up a permanent headquarters for the Rescue Democracy and Rescue the Babies campaigns in a converted furniture store. She came to ally herself not only with God, the family unit and national security but also with the democratic principles expressed in the Bill of Rights, world peace and the free enterprise system, so that the heterosexuals and homosexuals who fought against her campaigns were thus perceived by millions of Americans as being against democracy, peace and capitalism. *Time* magazine helped to promote this notion by juxtaposing two photographs in one of its cover stories: a picture of bearded transvestites in fishnet stockings raising up their fists in protest, the other of Sister Ivy and Claude peacefully kneeling down on a collapsible pew in their living room to pray for the country.

Some Christian newsletters condemned her as an egotist who misquoted God, Jesus, and Masters and Johnson, but Sister Ivy just smiled at these accusations and humbly reminded people that she was merely God's personal messenger on earth.

"I just want to save the children," she would say at the end of each of her three-hour radio programs before bursting into tears. Contributions from parents who did not want their children to perform fellatio before their twelfth birthday increased until Sister Ivy was able to buy time on television, a local program she called *The Sister Ivy Club.*

Although she was prone to grab a crucifix off the wall and thrust it into the faces of lawyers and accountants bearing bad news, she was soon able to turn that hour-long television program into an evangelical empire.

A Date with Judy

Patchwicke filled the weeks before I was to go to Charlotte to interview Sister Ivy with a numbing amount of work. But tired as I was, stumbling home at nine or ten o'clock each night, my need for companionship was greater than my fatigue, so, after taking a bath and a meal, I would often put on some fresh clothes and walk the dozen or so blocks to Greenwich Village.

I was already aware of one of the bad aspects of bringing a stranger back to my apartment: My choice might attempt to speak. While this could be interesting if I had picked up Tennessee Williams, more likely it would not be; the odds were in favor of my picking up a graphic artist or male model.

The first person I met one Tuesday evening was red-haired and tall —though I knew him for less than fifteen minutes, he reminisced about his childhood. Since I had little tolerance for all the complaining Shirley Temple did in her movies ("I *hate* this orphanage"; "I don't wanna be sold to the gypsies"), I did not enjoy listening to even less interesting complaints about the parents of a less disarming person. It is natural that a father who served in the Marine Corps should punish his son after catching him applying lipstick. It is unnatural that his son should remember the incident long after reaching middle age and cite it as the main cause for his failure to make a go of an Art Deco clothing boutique on Bleecker Street.

That Friday, I talked to an attractive seventeen-year-old on Barrow Street. It was not understandable, but it was at least tolerable that he hoped to have been included in a photograph taken of Princess Caroline doing cartwheels at Studio 54. But I thought his referring to over fourteen celebrities as personal friends was in poor taste considering he was a sophomore at the Parsons School of Design.

When a blond sitting on a stoop told me he was really straight and only went to leather bars because they were close to his apartment and the music was good and besides one blow job didn't make him gay since girls were where it was really at as long as he smoked at least three joints and anyway he never went more than once a week, I was appalled by his hypocrisy but admired his breath control.

The next Wednesday, I finally brought someone home: a swarthy chap. He seemed intelligent, but eventually became tiring. We had a drink on my couch. I thought it was laudable that he should want to become a fashion designer and be bursting with innovative ideas, such as marketing clothing heretofore worn exclusively by Palestinian terrorists. But I did not think it was laudable to beg me in annoying tones of voice monetarily to back such dreams simply because I had a large livingroom.

Around 1:00 A.M., we retired to the bedroom.

"What do you like to do?" he began.

Being concerned about pleasing a sexual partner is all well and good. Homosexuals have had to redefine their roles in intercourse because traditional attitudes and positions based on gender do not apply. "What do you like to do?" is a reasonable question and its answer should have provided all the information necessary for us to proceed. I think spontaneity was sacrificed a bit when he opened a Socratic dialogue about bondage mittens before I had the chance to remove my socks. Later, he came to a sudden realization. But 4:00 A.M. is not the proper time for anyone to inform me he thinks he is in love; all I care about at

4:00 A.M. is whether or not my toes are sticking out from under the covers.

Conversation has not been the only element to ruin a potentially amorous evening. Not knowing something about the character of the person I was picking up has also turned out to be a bother. For instance, there were times when I have been in a hurry and brought someone home only to discover that he was a psychotic.

New York is a city of over nine million people and has a high proportion of mental defectives. Some of them are obvious. Others appear to be no more than excellent librarians or soft-spoken UPS delivery men when in reality they are destructive fiends. It is one thing to allow these people to walk the streets, another to allow them to walk into an apartment filled with expensive art objects.

Nothing is more disheartening than realizing that the muscular guest sitting on one's couch is a lunatic. Perhaps it is the references to *voices* or the paranoid outbursts or the claims to have enjoyed all of Germaine Greer's books that tips one off. But powerful twenty-eight-inch arms take on a whole new meaning when they are flailing.

Trying to escape is of little use. Psychotics are sensitive to people inching their way out of a room backwards. Once he is there, it's too late to regret not enrolling in that karate course or sending away for that inexpensive ballpoint pen filled with napalm. All one can do is reassure the ranting guest that no one has put a time bomb in the armoire, and calculate the distance to the nearest blunt object.

I once brought home someone's husband. Most homosexuals who marry women do so because they need them as props in completing an image of heterosexuality. A suburban life-style is established and any temptation toward infidelity is suppressed behind thoughts of buying smoke alarms and plastic lawn decorations. Sooner or later, though, the need to satisfy his sexual hunger becomes overwhelming and he finds it impossible to concentrate on even the simplest home repairs. Telling his wife he is going to comparison-price automatic garage doors in town, he dons a London Fog trenchcoat and sunglasses and heads for Greenwich Village.

On the way, a husband will berate himself for succumbing to his lust and experience a feeling of cosmic injustice for being forced to lead such a complicated life. Then paranoia will set in. Visions of being arrested in a men's room make it difficult for him to avoid hitting iridescent detour cones. Images of his wife tearfully handing over bail money and of the subsequent exposure of his perversion in screaming headlines make the extrication of toll fare from his rear pocket virtually impossible.

When brought to my apartment, this particular husband, a thirty-five-year-old blond, nervously apologized at least seventy-two times before sitting down. I excused myself from the room to make cocktails. Judging from the amount of noise coming from the living room, I realized that a frantic search for hidden microphones was in progress. Inquiries as to his name were regarded as highly suspicious; friendly questions concerning occupation were viewed as a prelude to blackmail. When he was finally satisfied that he was not to be the foil in a confidence game (after four Scotches), he smugly confided that he was married. My reaction of pressing palms to cheeks in shock prompted him to provide proof in the form of wallet-sized Kodacolor prints of children riding Shetland ponies.

Sex took approximately fifteen seconds and was followed by a great deal of hand washing on his part.

After a thorough round of doorknob cleaning and polishing other surfaces possibly dirtied with fingerprints, he inquired as to my availability next April. It was September.

On another lucky evening, I dragged home a sychophant. I consider myself to be a fairly decent person and am more than willing to treat my guests hospitably. Food and drink of many varieties will be provided, as will a fresh toothbrush and a superb breakfast upon my awakening the following afternoon. I did not, however, appreciate a tearful, middle-of-the-night confession from my guest that he did not attend the School of

Visual Arts nor did he live with his parents in Canarsie. That he was, in fact, from Ohio, had been kicked out of the house by his stepfather, was hungry, penniless, and would nominate me for sainthood if I allowed him to sleep on the kitchen floor for one or two nights. I don't imagine anyone likes to hear such stories, but only a movie critic could turn out such a person into the night.

So I lent my Midwest refugee a few dollars to rescue a suitcase from the clutches of a Port Authority baggage clerk, allowing only a minimum of genuflection and hand kissing.

Of course, there is a difference between staying in my apartment until a room at the YMCA is financially feasible and running up bills unprecedented in the annals of telephone history, between being thankful for every scrap of food charitably offered and criticizing the Daquoise that took three hours to make, and there is a point when hogging the covers becomes intolerable. It was at that point that I was sorely tempted to make the high percentage of runaway deaths in this country increase slightly.

Once I even brought home a thief.

One of the saving graces of thieves is that they are often very attractive. Beautiful smiles flash when another hubcap has been successfully pried off a tire; biceps expand to a majestic level when a color television set has been removed from amid the shattered glass of an appliance store window. Of course, *anyone* could have highly developed musculature if, like a thief, he combined staying away from carbohydrates with running away from the police. And it's almost impossible not to have a healthy glow if, at least twice a week, one runs down the street as fast as one can carrying an armload of stereo components.

The magnetism of thieves is not confined to the physical; it includes several attractive personality traits as well: a simplicity of speech that could only be the result of knowing less than fifty words; a boyish quality—thieves will rarely ruin one's day by suddenly discussing the artistic contributions of Andy Warhol; a cocky manner—the result of knowing that the mailboxes of Social Security recipients can be opened in less than ten seconds; and an inventiveness—such as the ability to adjust car horns to play the melodies of popular songs and wedding marches.

Of course, there are drawbacks to inviting such people into one's apartment. They are, after all, *poor* and as such can always use an extra Art Nouveau snuffbox.

I realized my visitor was a thief when he, in moving about the apartment, noticeably rattled. I sent him away forthwith.

Four Jills in a Jeep

"They will not!"

"Yes! Yes, they will!"

"No!" Joe Stein stubbed out his cigarette, Joan Crawford fashion, and burrowed his hands into the pockets of his gray baggy pants (they had actually once been navy blue). "No, they will not!" he said.

Marietta sat erect in the red velour chair she and Joe had snuck out of the Pierre Bar through one of the downstairs lobby exits. She had a green cotton robe, a legitimate present from Joe, pulled around her neck. She hadn't changed since morning; it was now 4:00 P.M.

Their little group lived in one of those Upper West Side concrete confections, a wedding cake marvel that had been eaten away at the bottom and from the inside by time and neglect. She and Joe shared a four-room flat. The landlord had liked her movies enough to take fifty dollars off the rent. The other three friends—her maid, her hairdresser and James Carmichael—shared a nearby five-room apartment. Also at a reduced rent. They pooled their incomes and their filchings, *all* being light-fingered. Once, while watching her maid put ten dollars into the "pot," Marietta was prompted to remark, "The committee was right after all. We *are* Communists."

All their rooms were quite nicely decorated, considering the circumstances. They had dragged what they could with them from Hollywood to Italy, accumulated more there, stole a great deal when they returned to Hollywood and had it all arranged now in New York. There were magnificent paintings: the Titian from Crawford, a Picasso from Picasso. They all had satin or velvet bedspreads to cover their beds. One had been a present from Cecil Beaton; the hairdresser treasured that. ("I *must* have it! I slept with Cecie once, you know. He said I was simply *dreadful!*") Another was from Gene Tierney—Joe Stein got that one. The rugs all had to be left behind because they were too cumbersome and expensive to transport.

All of Marietta's antiques had been sold with the Hollywood house. She remembered being in Rome and reading about the MGM auction: Fairbanks's tights. Judy's shoes. She crumpled the paper when she read that one of the dresses she had worn in *The Waltz* had been auctioned off for eight thousand dollars. How they could have used that money!

Suitcases full of mementos made it all bearable. Sometimes unbearable. A little porcelain dog begging for attention, a gift from Van Johnson. A wooden cigarette box from Bing Crosby. Three silver-framed oil portraits: one of Dietrich in a man's suit; one of Bill Powell, looking very young, thin and serious; the last of a person she did not recognize. "I sink it's John Carroll," she said. "Anyway, the frame is pretty."

Joe Stein now put his leg on the radiator and looked through the window down Broadway to the Food City at the bottom of the Ansonia. "I promise you," he said quitely, "they will not laugh."

Marietta stared straight ahead with "that wonderful numbed look, darling," which Clarence Bull had asked for many times during their photo sessions. The expression crumbled again into one of terror. "They *will!*"

This scene had been played daily since Joe Stein had handed her back the manuscript of *Resurrection and Denial*, along with the telephone, to ask this Burton Raider person if he was offering her a part. A good script had finally come along and he wanted the lowdown.

"How did you meet this guy?"

She told him but wouldn't call.

"Look," he said, "I wouldn't let you do that horrid stuff in Italy, would I? This is the sort of thing we've been waiting for, isn't it? *Isn't it!*"

He had listened to excuses for days on end. She couldn't act anymore. ("I'll be worse than Paulette Goddard.") She didn't have the strength. ("It's too much to go srough again. I feel so empty.") She was terrified of the critics. ("I don't know them anymore. It used to be if they said somesing bad about your picture, they were cutting their own sroats.") He had almost succeeded in convincing her to pick up the phone when a nightmare brought a latent fear to the surface, one she had never mentioned to him outright: How would she look if she went back? It was the first dream she had had that related to making a comeback in all their years together.

She said she had floated through the dream like a ghost. It was a premiere night in New York. A line of people stretched from the Baronet theater down and around 59th Street past all the avenues to the very edge of the river. It was pouring rain and they were huddled against the red brick walls of buildings and under the tattered overhangs of storefronts. Invisibly, she flew over the crowd and swept down to listen to what they were saying. Despite the grotesque weather conditions, they were excited.

"I can't wait!"

"I love her!"

"Remember *The Waltz*?"

"I heard she hated Tyrone Power."

"I heard she *spit* on Greer Garson."

"Oh! I can't wait!"

She slowly floated over their heads toward the theater.

"She was stupid to turn down *Gaslight.*"

"And *Laura.*"

"Remember when she strangled Miriam Hopkins in that picture . . ."

"Yes! I heard that was the easiest scene she ever played!"

Giggling to herself (she did *hate* Hopkins), she flew through the lobby of the theater and perched herself atop the railing of the balcony. The audience began filing in. Coats were removed and umbrellas shook out.

She sighed. It wasn't like the old days: Searchlights. Velvet ropes. Screaming fans. The same limousines going around and around the block to deliver the movie star fare to the hungry public. Now the people just went in and that was it. Ker-plop on top of you and boom-boom-boom.

The music came up and Marietta drew her knees up to her chin, wrapping her arms around her legs. The lights went down. Stragglers searched frantically for seats.

"Oh . . . we can't sit together."

"Shit."

The MGM lion roared on the screen. Marietta's skin tingled. The orchestra on the soundtrack rose in a crescendo and exploded in a cymbal climax. Her name appeared on the screen in huge block letters. MARIETTA! The audience whistled and applauded. Marietta clutched at her wrist and, still perched lightly on the railing, looked at the audience. It had been twenty-five years and *listen* to them, she thought. Some stood up and more joined them. She put her fingertips to her mouth. The spontaneous ovation reduced her to tears. Joe was right, she thought, dabbing at her cheek with the hem of her ectoplasmic gown.

Suddenly there was silence. The audience froze and in unison sat down in their seats as if on cue. Startled, Marietta turned back toward the screen. The movie had begun. She could see the opening shot that had been in the manuscript of *Resurrection and Denial.* Oh, she thought to herself, I have missed Joe's name. But she arched her neck, waiting in communion with the stone-faced audience for Marietta.

Suddenly a hideous face appeared on the screen. Something straight out of a horror movie. Rondo Hatton in an Edith Head dress. Marietta screamed.

"That's her!" someone yelled.

"It *can't* be!"

"It *is!*"

"I don't *believe* it!"

"*Oh, My Gaw-w-w-w-d!*"

The audience began to laugh. Marietta stood on the railing, holding her hands over her face. *"That's not me!"* she screeched. The crowd around her continued to laugh with an intensity rarely heard outside of a revival theater showing Maria Montez in *Cobra Woman.*

Marietta had sat up screaming in bed. Joe Stein had awakened and ran into her room, nude. He found her drenched in perspiration, eyes wild, still screaming. He tried to shake her out of it, but to no avail. Flinching, he hauled back and smacked her across the face. She stopped screaming instantly and looked up at him.

"Joe . . ." she said hoarsely. He put his arms around her and she began to sob.

It was now late afternoon and he had managed to get her wrapped in the green robe and out into the living room. She was shaken, but listening to him again. "Forget it!" he said. "You remember the nightmares I had when Thalberg and I had that first fight. A dream is a dream."

"I know. I know. It is ridiculous. But I don't know if I have the strengs."

"Here we go again. You're like a horse! You know you want to go back. You know I wouldn't let you get involved in anything bad. Did I let you in Italy?"

She shook her head stiffly.

"In Hollywood?"

"They didn't want me in Hollywood."

He moved from the window and kneeled at her lap. "Darling. This may be our last chance. It's a good script. If it's an offer, you must do it. This will mark your return as an *actress!* And God knows they're starved to see a *star* again."

"But, Joe. I look at some of them. Remember when we were in Hollywood? When we were watching that fruit parade on television. And Betty Hutton came riding along in that convertible, sandwiched between those two gigolos. She was so drunk she could barely *wave.*"

"I remember." He had heard this many times.

"And that idiot came up to the car to ask her questions. She hit her toos on the microphone and garbled somesing—"

"And she almost slid backward down the trunk. I know . . . I know . . ."

"Oh, *don't*. I'm so afraid. And poor Judy. They srew *breadsticks* at her in the nightclub."

"Talk of the Town."

"I don't want that."

He looked up into her frightened eyes. "You take care of yourself. You're not a drunk."

Marietta looked away. He squeezed her hands and she looked back at him.

"You're scared," he said. "You were scared in 1939. You were scared in 1949. You could always act." He leaned closer. "I can't force you to pick up that telephone. I don't want to. I just think you should, that's all. I'm just trying to remind you to."

Marietta smiled. "Dear Joe," she said, and pulled his head gently down onto her lap.

"It's up to you to decide," he said. They stayed that way as the afternoon turned into twilight.

It was night. Roman had finally decided. He sat at the formica bar in the apartment he shared with Beverly, drumming the countertop with one hand and fondling a little velvet box with the other. Where the hell was she, anyway? He opened the box, looked at the quarter-carat diamond engagement ring and popped it shut. Should he call his mother before he changed his mind again? She would cry and hang up and start knitting booties and that would be good. Roman flicked the velvet box with his finger. Beverly, he thought, should know first. He wondered what her reaction would be. One of those bear hugs? Roman frowned.

He reached for the telephone to call his mother. No, that's not right, he thought, and replaced the receiver. His mother would enjoy another trip out to California, though. She loved coming out for the graduation. They went to Disneylandknottsberryfarmthemoviestarshomesand- graumans. Or maybe he and Beverly should be married on Long Island.

No, California was better. He thought about the restaurant to which he had taken his mother on a cliff at Big Sur.

"Look, ma, seals!" he said, pointing.

"Where?" she asked, turning about.

"On that big rock over there!"

"Oh, my," she said, sipping her first Margarita.

Roman had debated for a long time whether to marry Beverly. Sex with her this morning had given him a jolt, had made him finally decide to go through with it. He knew their marriage would be far from perfect. His passion for Beverly had deteriorated from the tropical to the torpid, and sex now was just something to get over with. But Beverly gave continuity to his life and provided an emotional straitjacket for his libido.

He had tried to sneak into the shower this morning before she woke up, but she caught him.

"You're up early again," she said seductively.

"Yeah, well."

"Wait, let me get it," she said, rising from the bed.

It was a pair of black crotchless underwear she had bought at Frederick's of Hollywood. Loping nude across the room, she pulled the panties from a tissue-lined pink box. While she slipped them on, Roman searched for a fantasy. He had almost always included a stranger in their lovemaking, running images of girls he had seen around town like a loop through his mind; it was impossible for him to have an orgasm if he didn't think of someone else.

He fondled the velvet box. Where the hell was Beverly?

Of late, he had started to let himself think of men.

"Okay!" Beverly had said that morning, jumping back into bed. Roman looked at her bovine frame spread out before him, the black see-through underwear looking silly on her. Grabbing her knees, he pulled them apart and dove in head first.

"Roman . . ." Beverly said impatiently. "Not *that* way." She pulled his head up by the hair.

He wiped his mouth and gasped for air.

"Fuck me, Roman. Just plain old *fuck* me, man."

Roman bought time by rubbing her crotch and turning his thoughts to the blond guy who had been sitting behind Beverly at the next table in a bar the night before.

"Oh!" she gasped as he entered her. He closed his eyes and began the ritual. The muscles in his body tensed as he tried to bring their ménage à trois clearly into his mind.

"Roman . . ."

But it didn't work. He couldn't come. He clenched his teeth, sweat pouring off his forehead onto Beverly. Gasping for breath, he did something he hadn't done in a long time—he let the gym instructor appear in his mind.

"Beverly! I . . ."

Then, almost as unavoidably as one frame follows another on a strip of film, Burton appeared. The sex at the Mantra Baths, the best sex he had ever had, all night long—

"Beverly!" he screamed, coming. He collapsed on top of her, exhausted.

After a moment, he felt her squeeze out from under him. He looked up weakly. She was stepping into a pair of jeans. "Where are you going?" he asked.

"Out," she said. He hadn't seen her since.

He stopped drumming his fingers on the counter and put the velvet box into his pocket. The hell with it, he thought. I'll give it to her tomorrow. He picked up her car keys and went downstairs. His Volvo was in the shop again. He decided to take a ride down to the beach.

Walking across the lawn of the apartment complex, he turned down the side street where she kept her Pinto parked. He stepped into the street to the driver's side of the car and slipped his hand around the handle. It was locked. As he looked for the right key in the light of the streetlamp, he heard something bump inside the car. Then he heard a voice. Bending down, he looked into the window. There were people inside! He inserted the key and threw open the door. Two people sat sheepishly staring at him in the back seat. Both nude. He had obviously interrupted lovemaking.

"Beverly!" he gasped.

She was with one of the maintenance men from their building.

"I can't believe it!" he said.

"Look, Roman, I—" Beverly began.

Roman dug into his pocket and pulled out the velvet box. "You see this!" he shouted, opening it. Beverly and the maintenance man leaned forward and peeked into the box. "I wanted to marry you, you goddamn bitch!"

"Marry!" Beverly said with almost burlesque shock.

"Yeah, marry! Do you see, do you see!" Roman shouted, thrusting the box at them. The maintenance man cupped his hand over his bulging crotch. Some children playing handball against the building stopped to watch.

"Look man," Beverly began.

"After the great sex we have," Roman ranted, "you have to fuck a janitor!"

"Hey, watch it there," the maintenance man began.

"Shut up!" Roman spat.

Beverly looked at him incredulously.

"I'm fucking humiliated, Beverly," Roman yelled. "I can't believe it! I'm sitting upstairs with an engagement ring and you're down here fucking a janitor."

The maintenance man looked for an escape route, but was stuck between the two of them.

"Do you think I'd be fucking this guy if we had great sex, Roman?" Beverly yelled.

"What are you talking about!" Roman spat.

"At least I feel like this slob *wants* me!" she replied.

"Hey, lady—" the maintenance man said, hurt.

"Shut up!" Beverly yelled. She leaned toward Roman. "I feel like I'm

. . . I'm *forcing* you to fuck me. I feel like you're thinking, oh, my God, man, she wants it again! I feel like—"

Roman slammed the door. He hit the hood of the car with his hand. Beverly pounded on the front window shield, shouting more of what he didn't want to hear. He stumbled down to the next car and leaned against it. The velvet box fell from his hand. Staggering forward down the street, he finally kneeled down between a van and a station wagon and began to cry.

The Clock

All things contain the seeds of their own destruction. Before one girder is thrust into a riverbed, the potential weakness of a bridge lies in two dimensions on the architect's drafting table. As a child prepares to blow out the five candles flickering atop his birthday cake, the faults that will lead him to corruption forty years hence fill him as invisibly as his breath. The poison that will end a relationship is there from the beginning, hiding in the lovers and camouflaged by love; the reasons for starting are often the same as for parting.

It was a Friday and I was preinterviewing the mayor of a large eastern city. His fraternity with organized crime was all but proved, yet over the years he had managed to become a national political character actor, transmitting an image of proletarian joviality and gaudy cheapness. The alleged atrocities of his administration included the mismanagement of funds earmarked for a severe-burn clinic and his repeated capitulation to the absurd demands of trade unions. Yet the publicity that resulted from his sophomoric antics and tasteless manner of dress had his constituents poking each other in the ribs as if he were an adolescent cad rather than a middle-aged extortionist. For a time television found him fascinating, but as with any attraction, his demand had waxed and waned. During the past five years, he had been virtually ignored by the talk shows. His popularity had only lately been renewed because his campaign manager had been discovered floating in a reservoir, riddled with bullets.

I was in no mood for corruption that morning. I tried to cover my business with the mayor as quickly as possible, but he continually interrupted my questions with anecdotes about his recently failed marriage to a former cocktail waitress from New Jersey. Regardless, I cut our interview short and had the receptionist telephone a page to escort His Honor to the executive dining room for lunch. While we were waiting in the outer office, the mayor clenched a cigar between his teeth and through a flurry of ashes told me the secret of making good spaghetti sauce. "Oregano," he whispered.

None too soon, the page walked into the office. "I'm looking for Mr. Raider," he said politely.

The grotesqueness of the mayor, which had filled and depressed my morning, paled to a gray inconsequentiality, vanquished like any darkness by a sudden light.

The epicene beauty of the page's face was framed by large curls of champagne-colored hair. He was flushed and animated; perhaps he had run. He looked intensely challenging. Royal-blue eyes shone above prominent cheekbones and a strong jaw. The corners of his mouth were like dimples and accented full pouting lips.

"I'm Mr. Raider," I said, stepping forward quickly.

One look at the page's uniform was enough to inspire the mayor to recall a story about his humble beginnings as a pinball salesman. He rolled the cigar from one side of his mouth to the other. When it became necessary for him to put out a small fire on his lapel, the page and I got what Ann Sheridan used to call "a load of each other." He looked interested in me, too. I encouraged the mayor to go into another story but the receptionist interrupted.

"Mr. Raider, your eleven-thirty appointment—Mr. Seawald?—is here."

"Mr. who?"

"Seawald."

I reluctantly sent the page off with his charge and asked the receptionist what she was talking about. "What eleven-thirty appointment? I have got to have a break or I shall *stab* someone!"

"But Mr. Seawald came all the way from Massachusetts, Mr. Raider."

"Who *is* he?"

She handed me the short article that had led some benighted staff member to think he was of national human interest.

> BOSTON. Richard Seawald, 27, has been collecting comic books since he was six. At present, a third-year student at Harvard Medical School, he has built his hobby into a profitable mail order business which supports his wife, Sybil, their son, Dick, Jr., and his seventy-two-year old mother, Grace. Profits to date total $50,000. Sybil Seawald admits that there *are* problems maintaining a stock of over 11,000 comic books in a two-bedroom apartment. However, looking at her new washer-dryer, she admits, "I can't complain."

Disgusted, I put the article down and left the office. The malaise that had been dispelled by the brief encounter with the page now returned to disconcert me. I walked down the hall with no destination in mind, just to walk a maze of passages until my head cleared. The walls of the corridors had been carpeted as well as the floors, so the extraneous sounds of typewriters and telephones were absorbed by the worsted material. Conversations, too, were dimmed by the acoustics. The network seemed to change the nature of everything—creativity itself became a dim echo. I lit a cigarette and pictured the studio in Flatbush and Marietta dumping my screenplay in a garbage can. I walked up a flight of stairs and down a maroon-carpeted hall.

Someone bumped into me and I found myself in front of the executive dining room. Following my unconscious lead, I went to the entrance and peered in. The mayor was immediately obvious, railing loudly and gesturing with broad sweeps of his arm to a table of grim, silent vice-presidents. The page wasn't anywhere in sight. I had no idea at the time how crucial it was to my future that I find that blue-uniformed page; I merely thought it would be pleasant to have lunch with him. Almost without thinking, I walked down the corridor and up a flight of stairs toward Guest Relations, the headquarters of all the pages.

About halfway there, in front of a glass wall displaying the inner workings of the network's local radio station, I caught sight of a page. He was around the corner before I could determine whether it was the one I was looking for. Trying not to appear too eager, I sauntered after him at a restrained pace and made it to the corner in time to see the men's room door close. I used my key and went inside but he was already securely locked in a toilet stall. I waited ten minutes listening to the most *atrocious* noises and enduring olfactory assaults that *defy* description, only to find that the creature who emerged wasn't the right one after all. In a way, I was relieved.

Since Richard Seawald had to be taken care of, I decided to walk back to the office. Existential dreariness began to assert itself again: The decaying odor of the receptionist's perfume awaited me, as did the relentless pounding rhythm of the Xerox and the brown-tipped leaves of the dusty potted palms.

Then, at the end of the corridor ahead of me, I saw him. The blond curls tumbling down to his shoulders, the dancer's body, tall and diamond-shaped with broad shoulders tapering into a trim waist. He was talking to the associate producer of network news who seemed very amused by a story he was telling. The page waved his arms in the air wildly; it was one of his eccentricities. I edged a bit closer, remaining unobtrusive. I was quite interested. He continued blathering on at a frantic pace, prodding his fingers consecutively as if listing the characters in his tale. The associate producer laughed through all of this, rubbing the sparse surface of his head with an empty clipboard. Suddenly the page stopped, gasped and yanked up the producer's arm so that he could see his watch.

Letting out a yelp, he turned and ran down the hall with the earnestness of Arthur Lake going to work in *Life with Blondie*. The producer frowned and I, perhaps one of the three times in my life, began to run. I couldn't catch up but was able to keep him in sight down three *long* corridors until he finally stopped, caught his breath and walked composedly into Guest Relations. My cardiovascular system in a state of near anarchy, I leaned against the door in an attempt to bring my unattractive wheezing under control before going in.

I had almost succeeded when the stainless-steel doorknob turned with a clack. Thinking it might be my prey, I retreated far enough so that our encounter would seem incidental. To add to the air of casualness, I pretended to be admiring a nearby water cooler. The door opened, and as if someone had suddenly turned up the volume of a television set, a din of childish voices poured out into the hall followed by a veritable flood of second or third graders. They carried in their wake two disheveled women.

"Ladies and gentlemen!" one of them, tall with silver-blond frosted hair, yelled at the cherubic faces around her knees. The other woman was squatty with dark, closely cropped hair. She stood silently against a wall holding an unlit cigarette. The blond clapped her hands over her head, *"Ladies and gentlemen! Please form a double line behind Mrs. Raposo."* As if this were a cue, three boys with neckties tied around their heads ran down the hall and a girl wearing an organdy dress primly turned several cartwheels. The women conferred over strategy for a moment, while the blond temporarily focused her desire for order on her hair; the brunette sucked pointlessly on her cigarette.

Then I saw him again. He strode out of Guest Relations and waded through the children swirling around his legs like a school of guppies. Holding up his hands, he jubilantly yelled over the cacophony, *"Who wants to meet Captain Dodo!"* Thirty-odd arms shot up into the air accompanied by rabid pronouncements to the affirmative.

I was amazed. The decrepit prince of pies and puppets evidently had more fans than ever. *"All those who want to,"* he exclaimed, pausing with an impish expression, *"pick a partner!"* Suddenly, the mob found itself in the midst of a terribly exciting game and there was a riotous rush to claim a friend. Two girls jealously fought over a third, tugging her arms in opposite directions. The noise rose to an even louder level, and the dark-haired chaperone, who was really only a civilian mother assisting the teacher and who had been wrestling with a certain temptation since boarding the school bus early that morning, rummaged through her purse and pulled out a container of bright yellow capsules: *ten* mg. Valium. The teacher, seeing her swallow one, glared priggishly. The harried class mother ignored her, swallowed a second capsule, lit the damp cigarette, and went to the back of the line. Her defection left the page and the teacher to cope with the mob by themselves.

"Does everyone have a partner!" the page yelled.

The deafening clamor that followed suggested that everyone did indeed. *"All right then!"* he said, embracing the shoulders of two girls. *"Let's line up behind these two movie stars!"* The feminine half of the class giggled abashedly while the masculine half made vomiting noises. In a few minutes, he had the entire mob lined up. The blond teacher leaned against the wall with a sigh of relief. The brunette crushed her cigarette into the carpet.

His name, I was soon to find out, was Winston Walker. His charm—and there was lots of it—was based on his complete allegiance to the present: He never regretted a neglected opportunity or treated life as a rehearsal for a subsequent performance. It was his great fortune to feel all the ebbs and tides of emotion intensely and his great gift to share his enthusiasm with all those in his presence. Never have I seen anyone so deft at drawing people into a web of excitement. His entire life, acquaintances felt they had had a personal renaissance for having known him. Theatrical people are often thought to have such an aura, but alas, their vitality is often the result of craft. If one approaches too closely, one can see the calculation, and too often, seemingly spontaneous conversation can be seen to be revival. Winston's spell was pure and he cast it freely. He had no ambitions. No pretenses or loyalties. And he harbored no malice toward anyone.

"Today, boys and girls, we are going to explore all the different parts of a television network. We'll see the machines that broadcast your favorite shows. A cameraman will tell you what he does. If one of the news reporters is available maybe he'll talk to us for a few minutes. But best of all, we'll visit the set of the *Captain Dodo Show*—"

Pandemonium followed.

"Calm down now. The taking of photographs is permitted. In fact, Captain Dodo himself will give autographed pictures to each and every one of you."

Cheering. Winston waved everyone forward, and the double line that had been so painstakingly achieved dissolved into a shapeless mass around his legs.

I followed them down the hall. Employees jumped out of the way of the oncoming crowd and Winston shrugged his shoulders apologetically. As promised, he took them to the videotape department and through a glass wall showed them the taped reels of shows and the heavy machines that edited and played them. He pointed out the small red cassette boxes that contained commercials and explained how two of every-thing—shows and commercials—were broadcast simultaneously in case a machine should fail or a tape should break. He took them to the set from which the news was aired, but it was empty and much smaller than it appeared on a television screen, so few of the children appreciated it.

During their travels, the bevy accidently crossed paths with a veteran game show host carrying a lunch tray. An audible flush of excitement swept through the group, and the host, balancing his tray on one hand, favored them with a wave and an overexposed smile. The stampede was immediate. Though the host was used to talking to people of such limited educational and intellectual background, he was not accustomed to talking to so many at once. He clutched his tray and ran down the hall leaving behind an overturned Styrofoam cup of Cling peaches. Winston thought this was hilarious but the incident made the children so rowdy again that he finally had to suggest they adjourn to the commissary for a snack of ice cream. It was an off hour so confusion was kept at a minimum as the children bought their fill. I had a cup of tea at another table.

"All right, everyone!" Winston announced to the tables of sticky juveniles. *"Let's go meet Captain Dodo!"*

A discordant symphony of scraping chairs and immature yammering followed. *"Throw all milk containers and wrappers in the receptacles to your left!"* the blond teacher bellowed. The brunette opened her purse and took another capsule. Before everyone filed out, there were a few minor fights, a couple of chairs were overturned and insults were exchanged.

"You dirty pig face!"

"You stupid pineapple nose!"

They followed Winston out of the commissary and into a stairwell, where their boisterousness became almost unbearable due to the echo created by the cinderblock walls.

"Please keep your voices down!" The shrill voice of the teacher punctuated the din. I followed patiently.

I was at the bottom of the stairs when a series of infantile events took place that completely changed my life. A boy in the group reached up toward the girl on the next step and yanked her ponytail as hard as he could.

"Eeeeeeyyyyuuuhhh!!"

Losing her balance, the girl instinctively grabbed for the support of the boy in front of her who, after turning about, unsympathetically punched her in the stomach. She fell backward with a scream and the crowd reacted to her push with a general surge forward. Meanwhile, on the top step, the girl who had managed to turn several cartwheels had also managed to smuggle an ice cream cone out of the commissary. It was quite pliable and only half finished when the domino effect of the crowd reached her. Someone crashed against her back and the cold vanilla cone was thrust between Winston's legs.

"Aarghhh!"

As I said, Winston was a delightfully spontaneous person who lived almost solely by susceptibility to his own impulses. His behavior for the most part was cheerful, but whenever he suffered any irritation—such as having an ice cream cone shoved into his gonads—his manner became egregious. All control drained from him and the world merely became a floor on which to throw a tantrum.

"You little bastards!" he screamed on the landing above the crowd of upturned faces. Shaking with anger, he picked up the girl who had

assaulted his groin and held her at his side as if he were going to use her to bludgeon the rest.

"Don't hurt her!" the teacher bellowed at the bottom of the stairs. *"I'll lose my job!"*

The children who had been dragging passively at the back of the group all day began retreating out of the stairwell. Winston shook his fist at them and yelled obscenities. Several children screamed; panic overtook the entire group. They pushed each other to get back down the stairs away from their raging tour guide.

The teacher at the bottom of the stairs helped the children who had fallen down. Winston kept yelling. A good portion of his neck's circulatory system was visible. The girl who had been dangling from his side managed to wriggle free. Showing no sign of fear whatsoever, she went down the stairs holding on to the banister and the empty ice cream cone. The teacher took her hand at the bottom of the stairs and turned toward Winston.

"You haven't heard the last of this!" she yelled and left to round up the rest of her charges.

Suddenly it was as quiet as a movie theater that had just played its last feature. Winston stood at the landing with his hands at his sides. I was at the bottom of the stairwell. The class mother was standing in a corner embracing a water pipe. She smiled goonily at me and began to giggle. "God, tha' 'as good," she said and drew herself up to rejoin her entourage.

After a few minutes, Winston regained his wits and began to descend the stairs.

"Excuse me," I said. "I couldn't help noticing that you share my regard for children." He stared at me. "Why don't we go turn in your uniform. It's improbable that they'll want to keep you on, what with you assaulting entire tour groups. And afterwards I'll buy you a drink."

He agreed immediately.

During the following month, a more predictable procession of events took place. Winston took a fancy to me as I had to him, and in the throes of our mutual infatuation we debauched ourselves on one another. This was the first time I had felt strongly about anyone since Roman and I found it an immeasurable improvement to have my affections reciprocated. Of course, it was quite clear to me that Winston was no Roman: A first love is a first love. But one can ruin one's life waiting for hopes that linger in the back of one's mind to come true, as one can ruin one's life lingering in the back of a movie theater, motionless, while other people live and move on a two-dimensional screen.

Winston was the golden boy caricatured in imagination. To be in his presence was to participate in a celebration of life as something awesome and wonderful; to be parted was, at first, unthinkable. We spent every night in my apartment. For several days, I couldn't bear to release him from my glance. While the world went busily about its business beneath my windows, Winston and I would spend hours touching and talking. We were in a state of euphoria, rejoicing in the good fortune of having discovered one another.

Suddenly, I began participating in the most bizarre activities in the name of romance. At various times, I was surprised to find myself in the abdomen of the Statue of Liberty; stepping over a monumental bowel movement in front of the Plaza Hotel so that we might be carted about Central Park by a woman wearing a polyethylene top hat; and, worst of all, renting roller skates. Experiencing a moment of intense affection while on the swings in front of a housing project, we decided that ours was no mere beguine; we were in love. For some reason, we celebrated this declaration by going horseback riding. A discussion of the pointlessness of paying two rents ensued.

It should be obvious that one's thought processes are not quite up to par when one suddenly finds oneself ducking branches while perched atop a galloping palomino. At this stage of a relationship, the parties involved should not be allowed to purchase a vacuum cleaner attachment together, let alone make any momentous decision concerning cohabitation. But, of course, one looks at all the irrefutable evidence proving compatability—a mutual admiration for Bette Davis and a distaste for telephone answering machines—and one immediately begins flipping through the Yellow Pages for moving van services. We decided to move in together three weeks after we met. My apartment.

After Winston made arrangements to terminate his lease, we went over to his apartment to pick up his belongings. I had never been there before. All I knew was that it was a one-bedroom in the east thirties. The *very* east thirties. Winston said he had hunted for two months before making an inquiry there. Coincidentally, one of the tenants was being removed to the city morgue. The superintendant had told him about the accident.

"Old broad o' ninety. Fell outta da window. Ba-boom!" he said, chuckling and dramatizing the event by smacking his fist against his palm. Only in New York would such a callous comment be followed by an inquiry as to closet space.

His was an ancient, tiny apartment. The computer printout of its history showed that the old woman had been renting it since 1921. No relatives claimed any of her possessions. Winston had kept what the neighbors didn't filch.

"I never spent much time here," Winston said. It was immediately apparent why. The living room was dark; the furniture had been depreciating since Calvin Coolidge was in office but would never come to be considered antique. There was a maroon and gray Oriental rug on the floor that I thought about taking until I lifted up the corner and it tore off in a dusty cloud of fibers. An upright piano stood neglected in a corner with a framed photograph of Virginia Woolf on its music stand.

We went into the kitchen where it appeared a good deal of eating had taken place but not much in the way of dishwashing. There was a biology project growing in the sink. The refrigerator had absolutely nothing in it except for one plastic packet of soy sauce and something I deduced must once have been a banana. If my mind had been functioning normally, I might have taken a few minutes to consider whether I wanted to live with a person of such environmental laxity, but I was operating at such a perceptual disadvantage that I found it all, even the colorful fungi, quite enchanting.

The bathroom had a tub on legs and walls covered with swan decals as dried and cracked as DaVinci murals. "Isn't this cute?" Winston asked, jiggling the pull cord of the ancient toilet. "It fits with the mood of the apartment." If that apartment had a mood, it was suicidal.

Our final stop was the bedroom, which, like the rest of the apartment, was a shrine of neglect. A television set was perched on top of a dusty dresser next to combs, brushes and bottles of cologne—the only modern intruders aside from us and the rumpled sheets on the floor. Winston slid three large suitcases out from under the bed and began to transfer his wardrobe out of the drawers. It was incongruous, but with the aid of hindsight, quite predictable, that his clothes should be in order. He pulled out dozens of shirts with blue ribbons tied around them—the hallmark of a French laundress. Trousers that covered the spectrum of popularly sanctioned looks were also transferred, along with sweaters, shoes, a Betty Boop doll and a Mattel model car. Winston was feline: Personally, he was immaculate; contextually, he was a slob.

He moved in forthwith and I continued to find joy in the simplest things. So severely had the infatuation affected my brain that I refused to send his laundry out. We would do it together as if it were some sort of domestic adventure, whacking each other with wet towels like common physical education students and sorting socks in the evening so we could giggle over the pyrotechnics of the static electricity. We seemed incapable of passing a park without building a snowman, or of using shaving cream without writing a love note.

It was bliss and seemed to go on forever. Roman could have been on Mars for all I cared.

Hellzapoppin'

W e existed in this bizarre state of infatuation for about two months. Then it began to go sour.

The same magic that makes *Citizen Kane* more than a two-dimensional image flickering in a shabby revival theater also makes the object of one's affection a nonpareil. Such alchemy can be sustained for two hours for an audience, but it cannot be perpetuated indefinitely between two lovers. The ergodic period must eventually begin—that dreadful stage between novelty and necrology when something happens to break the spell. Only if the two lovers can adjust to the realization that they are mortal and flawed will the relationship continue.

For me, the spell was broken on a day we decided to go to the supermarket together. Another domestic adventure. Food shopping is something for which I have never had any patience. I avoid it by making generous use of ethnic delivery boys. Winston had never even been *in* one thanks to maternal cosseting and the opening of large numbers of coffee shops by Greek refugees, so we decided it would be great fun to explore one together. We went on a Saturday afternoon, a convenient but somewhat congested time.

I cringed at the first sight of those humorless customers peering over their reading glasses at packages of creative frozen side dishes. Winston, however, seemed fascinated by all the activity. My tension increased when I noticed that the only available carriage was the type with the wobbly wheel that either jams, causing sudden right turns into fluted cake mold displays, or vibrates, making one feel as if one is test-piloting experimental aircraft. "Let's get out of here, Winston," I said, sensing disaster.

"Aw, come on," he cajoled, pulling at my shirt.

Reluctantly, I backed the carriage out into the aisle. We passed a cardboard display of children's encyclopedias which asked the question HOW MUCH IS YOUR CHILD'S EDUCATION WORTH? and made an introductory offer of volume I for three cents. A heavily armed security guard stood menacingly nearby, scanning the store for six-year-old Hershey-bar thieves and abandoned food carriages. We strolled into the produce department.

Whether one patronizes a supermarket or a vegetable stand, there is little resemblance between fruit sold in Manhattan and fruit as originally designed by God. New Yorkers buy it merely out of an eagerness to avoid bleeding gums and softening bones. Fruit weighers are an elusive breed: They are rarely in the produce department and no amount of banging one's cucumber on the scale will make them materialize. When they are nearby, they are usually preoccupied with affixing adhesive price tags to laminated heads of iceberg lettuce. The menacing looks that accompany any request to interrupt this routine to weigh one's vegetable account for the preference of many New Yorkers to rely on gifts sent by retired relatives in Miami Beach.

Though I explained this to Winston, he insisted on procuring cherries. I stood grimly by, drumming my fingers on the carriage handle while he had a wonderful time ringing the bell for service and chatting with the women waiting by the scale.

Continuing on, we were accosted by a woman standing on tiptoes and making straining noises.

"I'm too short to reach that can on the top shelf," she said belligerently, as if it were my fault.

Though she appeared to be above average in height and looked rather robust in her designer jogging suit, she demanded that one of us get a toehold on a shelf of peanut butter jars and hoist himself up to retrieve a can of fancy whole Kadota figs in heavy syrup, grade AA.

Supermarkets are stocked with many such annoyances. Terribly narrow aisles are made completely unnavigable by inconveniently positioned ceiling braces and unpacked cases of tomato paste and imitation mayonnaise. Further complications are caused by mothers pushing tandem perambulators and slow-footed senior citizens with no pressing appointments. When one is sufficiently frustrated trying to pass these obstructions, a child whose mother has been amiss in giving him carriage-wheeling responsibilities will barrel up behind one and say an exasperating thing like "Beep-beep."

Winston began to get on my nerves by tirelessly pointing out all the products he had seen on television. As we walked through the store, I found it increasingly difficult to listen to him reenact thirty-second comedy sketches written for bathroom bowl deodorizers and hum scores composed for fast-acting drain cleaners.

"Look," I finally said to him, "this isn't turning out to be as much fun as I thought. Let's just leave."

"Okay," he replied cheerfully.

We abandoned the carriage. Unfortunately, on our way to the exit, we passed the freezer.

"Can't we get some ice cream at least?" Winston whined.

I sighed.

"Please?"

"Okay. Okay. What flavor do you want?"

"Carob."

Certain flavors are never immediately visible through glass freezer doors. It is not enough casually to move a few undesirable pints to the side; unusual flavors are always hidden in the back and encrusted with several months of accumulated freezer frost. Extraction involves sticking one's head in the freezer and pummeling the desired pint with one's fists while being blinded by clouds of condensing air.

"You get it," I said, opening the door.

Winston cheerfully rummaged around the inside and came across a childhood memory. "Look! Eskimo pies!" he squealed and effervescently recalled the part they had played at his ninth birthday party.

"Is *that* what you want?" I asked, gritting my teeth.

"Yes!"

"Come on then." We went to the front to pay.

The supermarket checkout is a real challenge to one's mental well-being. Interminable delays from all sorts of complications are typical. For instance, there are customers who remember to cut out hundreds of coupons from magazines and newspapers but forget to present them to the cashier until he has totaled the order, bagged it, and is doing an intricate dance step while waiting to be paid. Though there may be policemen on line pressed to return to shootouts, such customers insist that the cashier spend ten minutes making the necessary four-cent adjustment to their receipts—for tax purporses.

There are other customers who wait until there is a flu epidemic in the city that leaves only one cashier able to report to work before they decide to purchase every item their families may eat for the next several months. With the line behind them stretching back to the frozen food section, they present an out-of-state check for payment. Such customers should be forced to eat every can of fancy whole Kadota figs in heavy syrup grade AA that the store stocks.

Cashiers often delay things as well. Waiting until the last minute to replenish their quarter supply, they consult loudly with their associates in the vicinity of one's ear.

"*Hey, Bobo! You got quarters?*"

"*No!*"

"*Hey, Uretha! You got quarters?*"

"*I ain't got quarters. I got dimes! You want dimes?*"

"*Did I ask for dimes? I got dimes. I need quarters!*"

"*I told you! I ain't got quarters!*"

Such conferences never fail to include recently naturalized store managers.

"*Mr. Vascopolos!*"

A conclusion to this business is further delayed because he is invariably on the telephone with an irate customer who is convinced that the store's frozen fish filets are lethal and has the dead cat to prove it.

The longest delays are caused by unobservant customers who do not notice that their containers of milk are leaking—loud crashes and people sprawled on the floor in their slippery wake notwithstanding. They only discover their predicament when the cashier points out the puddle on the black conveyor belt, resulting in fifteen-minute safaris to the dairy section. As a further annoyance, one has no choice but to look at the covers of tabloids inviting one to read features describing how country-music legends lose weight; amazing articles written by Jeane Dixon in which she predicts half-million-dollar shopping sprees for Jacqueline Kennedy Onassis, further UFO sightings in the South, and political corruption in Washington; and exposés on regular people such as a married couple living in New Jersey who discover that their fourteen-year-old son is a latent Nazi when they find him goose-stepping to a recording of "Deutschland Über Alles" in the rumpus room of their basement.

Winston borrowed some change from me and went over to the gum ball machines. I got on the express line with the box of Eskimo pies pointed in the direction of the cashier. There were only two customers in front of me. Both were holding cash; neither seemed to have a hole in anything he was carrying.

"Burton!"

Winston held up a rubber shrunken head in triumph. I breathed a sigh of relief that I would soon be out of the store. The cashier rang up the price of the ice cream.

Claaaaccckkk!

Everyone on line behind me immediately realized that the receipt tape mechanism had broken and only a repairman from Amityville, Long Island, could fix it. They scrambled to redistribute themselves on other lines.

"I'm sorry, sir," the cashier said, plopping down a plastic CLOSED sign. *"Mr. Vascopolos!"*

Winston pranced over and put an aluminum engagement ring on my finger. "What's taking so long?" he asked airily.

I was a model of self-control. I didn't strangle him or anything. But after that day, the pancakes in the shape of a heart he made me never tasted the same.

Our relationship was far from over. I concentrated a bit more on my duties at the network; Winston took charge of domestic affairs. We stepped out at night together with gusto, but were no longer transported on a cloud.

I gave up trying to find Marietta or hoping she would call; instead I toyed with the idea of approaching Betty Hutton. An article had appeared in a magazine saying she had gone through her share of woes but was now peacefully residing at a rectory in Rhode Island. Winston was all for riding down to say hi, but my father wasn't too excited about the idea.

"Leave her alone," he said. "If she's found some sort of sanctuary, don't barge in. Remember her reputation—you couldn't afford delays due to temperament or whatever. The pressure of making a movie could start that stuff up again no matter what priest she's been talking to."

I agreed but decided against Hutton for another reason. Though her life in some ways paralleled that of the main character in *Resurrection and Denial,* I couldn't see her playing the part, which called for a subtle mixture of nobility and bitter capitulation. It was Hutton's frenzied mugging in her films of the '40s that prejudiced me against her.

My disappointment at how things had bogged down with *Resurrection and Denial,* and Patchwicke's petulance at the network, brought Winston's frailties into an even clearer focus. His insatiable desire to meet and see and do took me to places I would never have gone otherwise. If impulsiveness was the characteristic that most appealed to me about Winston, it was also the underlying theme of the idiosyncrasies that, at times, made him invidious.

For instance, his extreme reactions to things were maddening. In

New York City, fortitude is a requisite virtue. One is expected to walk under flimsy wooden safety arches while economically unviable hotels crumble against the impact of two-ton demolition balls above one's head; side-step ambulances that recklessly barrel through red lights in an effort to deliver living rather than merely fresh goods; and get into elevators with people who do not appear to be country club material but have seven-irons dangling from their belt loops nonetheless. These encounters are as common as they are potentially dangerous.

The cockroach is a blatterian insect characterized by rapid movements, nocturnal habits and the flat bodies necessary to take refuge under toasters. They are an accepted part of city life and, though generally acknowledged to lack the charm of the butterfly, are more of an annoyance than a menace.

I was never able to adjust to Winston's extreme reaction to these little creatures. While frantic pointing and coloratura screams can be highly entertaining in kabuki theater, in real life such surprises tend only to bring on heart infarctions. Of course, everyone gets *angry*. Adults swear; children pull arms off of dolls that urinate tap water. I am essentially an irenic person but, fated to live in a world that allows Yankee games to preempt *Thin Man* movies, I too do my share of fist shaking.

Some people learn to put their anger to good use. For instance, Joan Crawford was often able to get her entire mansion sparkling clean in a matter of hours with the help of the kids and a few toothbrushes. Other people do not have this ability; their anger leads only to destruction. Winston was of this latter variety. Whenever he lost his temper, he would abuse inanimate objects. Over the course of our relationship, I learned to sit quietly as vulnerable crystal ashtrays crashed to the floor, defenseless record albums broke over his knee and unsuspecting gladiolas were throttled in their vases. I pointed out to him that punching a wall might be somewhat less expensive. It took him a while to redirect his anger, but he did. I had to stop him, however, when it became apparent that we would soon be able to go from room to room without opening any doors.

A visit from Winston's parents could sometimes evoke this level of rage in me. His mother was an imperious woman; his father was a retired bank officer with nothing to say. One would think that after forty-one years of stability in Fort Lee, New Jersey, they would want to take in the Parthenon. But no. Every Sunday they preferred to visit their son and his "good-looking friend who cooks."

When Mrs. Walker wasn't sticking her fingers into pots simmering on the stove, or her nose into my personal life, she was telling her husband to watch his cigar ashes and sit up straight. She also attended a little yap-yap dog named Chrysanthemum that she took downstairs for a walk at regular intervals. Though Mrs. Walker cut a menacing figure, she insisted that Winston and I accompany her in order to foil any mugging attempts.

"Boys?" she would say, lifting her eyebrows and her pet.

Downstairs, she would gingerly place the dog on the sidewalk. If there was not immediate action, she would start barking, "Do it, Chrysanthemum! *Do* it!" The tiny creature would look up at her with a panicked expression on its pileous face, its four little legs would start vibrating and, well, I guess I wouldn't have been able to go until I was alone in an obscure corner of my apartment either.

Like the curbed Chrysanthemum, Winston started a thousand projects he never finished. Bookshelves, French lessons, record-to-tape transfers. One day he got it into his head to build up his body. We visited a health club and were shown rooms full of serious-minded men grappling with octopodinal machinery. It appeared, from the glint in a few bugged-out eyeballs, that some fellows were lifting too much—I could almost hear the little blood vessels in their brains popping as our guide ran through the advantages of signing up for the club's twenty-year plan. We were introduced to an instructor who regarded Winston's physique and wrote down a tailored weight-lifting schedule. He also showed Winston a dietary program scientifically designed for bodybuilders, consisting of nuts, cornmeal, sunflower seeds and other items normally thought to be the nutritional favorites of squirrels.

Winston decided he would rather exercise in the privacy of our apartment, so we had a sporting goods store send us the necessary equipment. By the time our (exhausted) mailman delivered it, Winston was engrossed in taking guitar lessons. I forced him to assemble the barbells anyway, but it was no use. The only time the weights got off the ground was when I lifted them to vacuum. I should have gotten angry with him but I didn't. I regarded him with understanding and truss.

I started collecting all sorts of clothing at an early age. Winston was my size at every contour and borrowed liberally. William Randolph Hearst was also a collector of clothing and gave fabulous fancy-dress balls to which he invited movie stars from nearby Hollywood. They were allowed to choose appropriate costumes from the huge warehouses he maintained with every sort of netherhose, hennin, doublet and liripipe. On a typical Saturday night at his castle, one might find Tallulah Bankhead dressed (if at all) as a Siamese dancer, Oscar Levant as a Zamoran peasant and Lana Turner as an Elizabethan lady-in-waiting. With all this borrowing going on, no doubt the clothes incurred a great deal of damage. Still, I am almost positive that if Olivia de Havilland burned a cigarette hole in a redingote, she would have the decency not to roll her mistake into a ball and stuff it under a mattress.

Since I was working and Winston was not, we made our deal that I would pick up the tabs if he would pick up the clothes. This worked out for a while until Winston found it impossible to stay cooped up in the apartment all day long doing domestic chores. Thereafter, it was up to me to pick up our refuse. The shoes. The shirts. The squished donuts ground under heel in the bedroom carpet. The crumpled telephone messages stating the address and time of an al fresco lunch with someone named Bucky. The untidy lines on my MasterCard invoices that stated *someone* had enjoyed a $161.97 dinner at Lutèce. The hints of bisexuality in the folds of the bed sheets in the form of Sperm-O-Jelly Con-Ception Cream. The unfamiliar brands of cigarette butts. The spirochetes.

I didn't mind so much. Men are by nature untidy creatures. I did, however, mind Winston becoming offended if I called him a slob.

"I'm just as neat as you are," he'd say. To prove it he would leave the apartment to purchase some cleaning products. Still, I think everyone knows that it is unnecessary to put on a cockring to buy a box of Spic and Span.

Winston's value system was sometimes inscrutable. For instance, I loved to cook extravagant things for him. A certain Chef Deblieux invented a fabulous dessert called Le Gateau des Trois Mages, a layer cake filled with crème Chantilly, fruits and liqueur syrup, all enclosed in a caramel cage. The cake is relatively simple to make, but the cage involves the use of three saucepans and a pair of very heavy rubber gloves used to prevent third-degree caramel burns. The syrup must be heated and cooled and reheated until its consistency is such that thick, heavy threads can be formed. Using a spoon, one must make a network of interlocking swirls over an upside-down bowl. Depending on one's agility, this will either be the dome of the cage or a cleaning problem that will involve the use of dynamite.

After spending three hours constructing Le Gateau des Trois Mages, it was depressing to see Winston look straight at it and then extricate le Ring Ding from le kitchen drawer.

Winston and I had divergent musical dispositions. Well, polytonal harmonies aren't for everyone. A short walk down any Manhattan street will testify to the eclecticism of musical tastes: A strain of Copland drifts through the windows of a brownstone apartment on Horatio Street; the Beatles disdain the life of the junior executive in a song wafting out the open door of a fish market with the smells of cod and perch; ethnic rhythms rise from the sidewalks like ripples of heat. I think this is great, but cannot deny the fact that I am happy to live in an apartment with immobile windows. In sharing a flat with another, one must relinquish dictatorial control over one's stereo. A lover brings his tastes along with his suitcases and one must indulge them. I do, however, think that both parties should be sensitive to and considerate of each other's cochleas. There is, after all, a point when a difference in musical opinion can become intolerable. I don't think it is terribly inflexible to believe that this point is reached when the wails of Elvis Costello are allowed to knock sentimental pictures off living room breakfronts.

Everyone has bad habits; we ignore our own and sometimes are able to endure those of others. My own habit of mentioning Roman more and more each week certainly was not nice. It is a shame that a relationship can be ruptured by such mundanities, an inevitability that it will be eroded by them.

It is a statistical fact that most murders are domestic affairs: A wife will shoot her husband; a lover will stab his beloved. To avoid this sort of thing, Winston and I thought about seeking professional counseling. Traditionally, this would have meant lying on a couch in a darkened office next to a box of tissues. Recently, it has come to mean being humiliated in front of large groups of people while not being allowed to know the time.

I talked to two lovers who had taken est. They had not been getting along and, hoping to avoid a violent conclusion to their relationship, had signed up. During the weekend it took place, the trainer of the group often interjected stories about the fabulous relationship he was enjoying with his "lady"—of four weeks. He explained that they had an under-standing between them that transcended jealousy, making it perfectly permissible for either to have a sexual encounter with a stranger.

"We've weighed the considerations," he told them. "As a matter of fact, she's out at the Hamptons by herself right now!" the trainer boasted. *Uh-ohs* and *ahs* were heard throughout the auditorium. "I'm not worried," he said, sticking his hands in his pockets and strutting across the speaking platform. The crowd envied his confidence.

After the weekend was over, many people—including the est trainer—went out to the Hamptons to relax. The two lovers who had just graduated were walking happily down the boardwalk holding hands and enjoying the rebirth of their relationship when they spotted the trainer on the deck of a beachhouse, screaming at a woman who fit the description of his "lady."

"I'm not gone three days and you have to jump into the sack with somebody! You couldn't wait!" He was purple with rage. But, aided by the wisdom

derived from all the psychology courses offered by USC, a deep friendship with Werner Erhard, the creator of est, and the clinical experience accumulated from having a successful private practice for many years, the trainer weighed his considerations and decided that the only way he could cope with his frustrations was by diving into the nearby swimming pool to cool off. The lovers looking from the boardwalk went on.

Weeks later, in their Manhattan apartment when the initial euphoria produced by taking est had worn off, one of the two lovers did something that infuriated the other. He wanted to work things out, but since no swimming pool was available in the apartment, he decided to strangle the other instead.

Winston and I decided to work things out on our own.

"I'll stop talking about Roman if you'll be more neat," I said. "Deal?"

"Deal," he replied. We hugged and went off to the movies.

Cat and Mouse

A s exasperating as Winston could be at times, I still considered him a refreshing contrast to most other people—especially the somnambulists working at the network. Strangely enough, the only person I was really fond of there was Patchwicke; though his premeditated personality was the antithesis of Winston's, I came to harbor a grudging affection for the man. His plea at lunch to adopt his credo of conservatism and his censures in the form of unpleasant assignments struck me as disguised signs of affection. There were times when I was prompted to transgress the unspoken rules of our relationship, but he was the sort of person who would have been more embarrassed than pleased. I always hoped that something would happen to bring us together, but it never did. In fact, just the opposite occurred.

It began about a week before I was to go to Charlotte to interview Sister Ivy. My financial outlook was dim. I had only a few thousand dollars left in the bank and most of that had to be saved to pay the property taxes on the studio in Brooklyn. At times, my movie mogul ambitions seemed as preposterous and airy as James Stewart's preoc-cupation in *Harvey*. To maintain the Manhattan apartment, Winston had to channel eight daily hours of his energy into the respected field of table busing while I took on extra assignments for the overtime and added expense vouchers. I was working late on one of these assignments in *The Morning Show* conference room trying to organize the recorded thoughts of a pornographic film director into thirty interview questions for Liz Bonwit. Most of them had to be contrived because all he had wanted to talk about during our preinterview was how the art of Sternberg and Renoir compared to his own *(The Doorknob, In the Kitchen)*.

About eleven o'clock, I heard voices in the hallway. Though the outer door was locked, I listened for any unsavory quality in their inflections—hoodlums were always charming their way past the geriatric security guards downstairs. The voices came closer. Someone tried the doorknob. I stood up, looking at the blurred movements behind the frosted pane of the door.

"Come on," a muffled voice said. A key was inserted and turned with a click.

Though he had left five hours earlier to catch a train bound for Westchester, Patchwicke walked through the door. He squinted at the lighted conference room and saw me immediately.

"Raider! What are you doing here?" he said, shocked.

"Working," I replied.

Nonplussed with a key in his hand, he looked somewhat like Ray Milland in the last scene of *Dial M for Murder*. A sheen of perspiration burst over his forehead.

"I forgot my book of railroad passes," he said with an odd strain in his voice.

The reason for his unease was standing in the doorway behind him: a handsome blond boy wearing a T-shirt and jeans. The boy took a few steps into the room, a *Playbill* dangling from his hand. He said nothing but spindled the program while Patchwicke went over to the coat rack and extricated the railroad passes from the pocket of his sports jacket. Smiling foolishly, he held them up to show me he was ready.

"All set," he said. "Had to walk all the way from Eighth Avenue. What a bother." He grinned at me, then at the boy. After an awkward silence, he said, "I don't think you've met my nephew Jeff here." The boy slipped his thumb through a belt loop and shifted his weight to one side.

"No, I don't think I have. Hello." I said.

The boy nodded.

"We just saw a very funny musical. Didn't we, Jeff?"

The boy said nothing.

"Yes . . . well . . ." Patchwicke said as his glasses slid down the bridge of his nose. "We have to get along. Jeff here has . . . er . . . you know . . . *school* tomorrow."

"Of course," I replied.

The boy turned and walked out into the hall.

"Nice meeting you!" I called after him.

There was no reply. With a little wave at me, Patchwicke closed the door gently behind him. "See you tomorrow, Raider."

I put up my feet and laughed to myself. I had always suspected Patchwicke had a touch of the pederast in him but apparently he wasn't as frustrated as I had surmised. Still, it was hard to imagine that nervous little man walking among the nocturnal carnivores attracted to the neon glow of Times Square—and to ask a hustler out to the theater, no less! It made me even more fond of him.

I thought it would be awkward between us the next day, but Patchwicke never showed up at work at all, which was unheard of. The secretary called his house and his wonderfulwife said he was sick but would be in the following morning. To celebrate, everyone spent the day at Charley O's.

"It's a miracle!" one writer toasted.

"He'll probably be in this afternoon," a more pessimistic one said gloomily.

But Patchwicke didn't show up for two days. Even then he was only glimpsed a few times during the course of the day. He looked terrible and spoke to no one except the secretary; work was doled out through her. This routine went on for three more days.

The writers joked about his erratic behavior and tried to guess what was causing it. A few of the less neurotic ones grew concerned about his health, but that concern dissipated when everyone became irritated as the organization of the office broke down. They all crowded around the secretary's desk complaining about poorly coordinated interviews and mismatched assignments. She periodically left in tears. *The Morning Show* associate producers finally appeared, inquiring as to Patchwicke's whereabouts. We were able to cover for him only because the writers department worked six weeks ahead of the aired shows.

Between bursts of anger, the writers continued to postulate possible reasons for Patchwicke's curious behavior. Cancer was a recurring possibility; so was the idea that he had heard a rumor about being fired. I kept the knowledge of the blond boy to myself.

On the fourth day he was back; everyone was given a clue: Patchwicke began to borrow money. He would accost people in the men's room or pop out at them from around corners, always asking for exactly one hundred dollars. After this happened three times, everyone reconnoitered in the conference room to gossip about it.

"He's probably got the first dollar he ever made," one wag said. "Why does he need *my* money?"

"His wife probably cut off his allowance," another replied, yawning. I listened to everything and said nothing, but I thought his behavior did seem to suggest that he might not want to explain any bank withdrawals to his wife.

When he was up to six hundred dollars, I decided that blackmail was the only explanation. The blond boy was obviously a street hustler who lived from twenty-five dollars to twenty-five dollars. No doubt after Patchwicke had left the office that evening, he wiped the perspiration from his brow and told the boy what a close call running into me had been. A confession of his assorted fears probably followed, and before he was able to compose himself he had been given an ultimatum. It was possible that he and the boy had a standing appointment and the boy knew not only where he worked, but also where he lived in Westchester and how well off he was. Patchwicke would do anything to keep his job and reputation intact. I suppose I could have gone to the police but, after all, I wasn't sure I was right. If I was, however, I knew Patchwicke would want to take care of the matter as quietly as possible. I wondered how much money the boy had demanded. Probably what he considered a large sum: a thousand dollars or so. Realizing what Patchwicke must be going through, I looked in vain for him the rest of the day. When I left the office, his reported borrowings from the writers amounted to eight hundred dollars.

I called his house that evening. His wonderfulwife curtly told me he was in Manhattan attending a *Morning Show* dinner. There was no *Morning Show* dinner. He had probably collected all the cash and was paying off the boy in some roach-infested hotel room. I told her to have him call me as soon as he returned. He never did. The next day, he was out again. I had the secretary call his house but no one answered. She tried all that day and into the next but never got through.

I finally had to put my fears aside to organize my trip down to Charlotte. Because of the confusion and added work, the secretary hadn't made any arrangements. I was going to take Winston along and I needed flight information to buy his seat; hotel accommodations had to be booked and expense vouchers had to go through a battery of approvals. I also had to talk to the producers myself about the emphasis they expected the piece on Sister Ivy to have; Patchwicke usually did that sort of thing. They told me that the trip was for preliminary research and that the on-air segments would be taped when she came to New York. I took the opportunity to express my concern over Patchwicke's behavior to them. They told me that they were on top of things. Knowing the television producer sincerity quotient, I doubted they even knew his home telephone number.

On the morning I was to go, all I had managed to get were the plane tickets. Winston and I were bouncing on the lid of a suitcase trying to get it closed when the telephone rang. Thinking that the secretary had finally obtained the expense vouchers, I slid off and grabbed the phone. "It's about time!" I yelled.

There was a silence on the other end. Then a voice said, "I beg your pardon?"

"Oh . . ."

"May I speak to Mr. Raider, please?"

Winston shouted in triumph as he clicked the locks shut. I held my hand over the receiver and told him to shut up. "This is Mr. Raider speaking," I said.

"Oh, hello, Mr. Raider. This is Marietta."

Shocked, I picked up the body of the telephone and began to pace. "Uh . . . hello! How are you?"

"Quite well, sank you. I'm calling about the script you gave me."

"Yes?" I squeaked. She must have hated it. Winston frowned at a shirt tail sticking out of the suitcase.

"I've meant to return it to you. It's been sitting here for several weeks and I am afraid I might lose it."

That didn't sound promising. I looked at the piles of clothes on the bed that had to be packed. "Could we meet?" I blurted out.

"Yes, I sought perhaps tomorrow—"

"No, no. I'm leaving . . . tomorrow is impossible."

"Then when you return."

"No! I mean, I'd like to see you before I go. Would it be terribly inconvenient to meet early this afternoon?" I asked, pacing on top of some of Winston's clothes.

"Well . . ." She thought for a moment, then gave me the address of a restaurant on the Upper West Side.

"Is one thirty all right?" I asked, looking at my watch.

"I shall see you then," she replied and rang off.

"Hooray!" I yelled, ecstatic. If she wanted to see me she must have liked it!

"C'mon," Winston whined. "We have all this to do. We gotta take the stuff out of this one and put it in that one. And get those socks out of the drawer. Look," he said, holding out his finger, "I got a blood blister."

I ignored him and called the office. The secretary told me that the hotel accommodations were being arranged for by the Sister Ivy people. At least that was done. I told her to send the expense vouchers over to my apartment by messenger.

"What's the holdup?" Winston asked testily.

I told him I had to go out to meet Marietta and that he had to do all the packing himself.

"What!"

"And after the messenger comes with the vouchers, take the suitcases out to the airport."

"Why do *I* always have to do *everything?*" he moaned, throwing himself down on the bed.

I took a shower and changed. "And don't forget to check the baggage and get our seat assignments," I said, zipping up. "I'll meet you at the gate around four thirty."

Winston sulked. "I don't want to go anymore."

"I'm sorry I'm leaving all this to you," I said. "But please don't let me down." Winston threw his shaving kit on the floor in a show of discontent. I had to leave.

Marietta had picked an uninteresting Italian restaurant on Columbus Avenue. It was long and narrow, and rather than a dining room it had a single row of formica tables pushed against the wall from front to back, decorated with faded yellow-checkered tablecloths and black plastic ashtrays. I smiled to myself, noticing that she had chosen an extremely dim place to meet, then walked slowly along the file of tables, looking at the few customers in it. A waitress asked if she could help me. I told her I was looking for a middle-aged woman.

"There's only two people in the back," she said, chewing on a strand of hair that had loosened from her beehive coiffure.

"Well, I'm a little early. I'll wait at the bar."

I ordered a martini. Five minutes passed, then ten. I called my apartment at one forty-five, but no one answered. I went back and ate my olive. I became anxious. Each time the little bell over the restaurant door tinkled, I turned to see the customers coming in; fifteen minutes passed and Marietta was not among them. I called my apartment again, then Patchwicke's house in Westchester. Neither answered. Just after two fifteen, I threw some money on the bar and went into the back to pee. The two people the waitress had mentioned were sitting at a table, their figures just outside the glow of a centerpiece candle. Their hands were resting on the bases of their empty wine glasses.

As I was opening the men's room door, one of them spoke. "Mr. Raider?"

I stopped short. "I—"

"Please come here, Mr. Raider," a voice I recognized as belonging to Marietta spoke firmly. "You are late." I walked uneasily toward the table. There was a man in a business suit sitting next to her. "Mr. Raider, this is Mr. Carmichael." We nodded to one another. "Please sit down," she said. To make matters simple, I apologized for being late.

"Will you have a drink, Mr. Raider?" Mr. Carmichael asked. He leaned forward into the light.

"No, thank you," I replied.

He was about sixty years old. His face was pleasantly avuncular, adorned with a gray mustache. A Charles Farrell type. The suit he wore appeared to be expensive, but upon close inspection, a fraying shirt collar suggested that he shared Marietta's fiscal fate. She reclined away from the light. The manuscript was placed on the table; Marietta pushed it toward me.

"I sought it best to return this before I misplaced it," she said. Mr. Carmichael nodded. Marietta lit a cigarette.

"Did you like it?" I asked, not wanting to beat around the bush.

"Oh, yes," she replied. "Very sad story. But amusing at times as well. Mr. Carmichael read it. I hope you don't mind."

I turned toward him, radiantly happy.

"Yes. I liked it," he said.

I waited for more but apparently that was the extent of their criticism. Well, they liked it. My pride bolstered my confidence.

"Some people are very interested in producing it," I suddenly lied. "But I'm going to do this one myself."

"Oh?" Mr. Carmichael said, leaning closer to the candle. "Are you an independent producer, Mr. Raider?"

Without hesitation, I replied that I was indeed. He and Marietta shifted slightly in their chairs. Mr. Carmichael quickly glanced toward her. She remained in the shadows. It suddenly struck me that the dark site of our meeting might not have been chosen for vanity's sake at all, but rather to disguise any eagerness on their part in regard to work, should any be offered. That realization further bolstered my confidence.

Marietta fiddled with her hands, then removed them from the table. Mr. Carmichael continued. "What have you done?" he asked.

Pulling names out of a hat, I told them I had been producing television pilots in Burbank but was now only interested in feature-length films. I described the studio in Brooklyn: its history and how it would be utilized for the filming of *Resurrection and Denial*. Of course, I had to imply that it was fully operational. Marietta stabbed out her cigarette.

"The production schedule is all planned," I lied. "I'm in the process of raising funds." After a little more propaganda, I looked at my watch. It was already three o'clock. Pressed for time, I decided to make a proposition straight out. "Look. I would very much like Marietta to play the lead in *Resurrection and Denial.*" I stopped for a moment, surprised at the sound of the words. "I have to leave the city this afternoon, so I can't go into details or show you a contract. I would, however, like to know if you are at all interested before I leave." I bit my tongue. No one spoke for a moment.

"We are interested," Mr. Carmichael finally managed, looking at Marietta. My heart surged; she said nothing. "But let us be frank with you, Mr. Raider. Marietta will not do another film unless certain criteria are met."

"Oh?" I said, taken aback. "For instance?"

"For instance, you cannot employ *her* unless you also employ some others."

"Others?"

"People she worked at Metro with and remains friends with today."

"And how many people does that involve?"

"Five. Three would be of little consequence to your production: her maid, a hairdresser, myself—I am an accountant by profession. One, however, would. Joseph Stein, her director." He stopped, looking for a sign of recognition or perhaps protest.

I knew that Joseph Stein was a veteran of MGM of the '40s, that he was not in the same league as Hitchcock, Mankiewicz or Wyler, but was a very respected craftsman. I pretended to mull over his words for a few minutes as if unsettled by the unexpected stipulation, but I was really quite relieved. After all, *I* didn't have anybody. Plus there were advantages to using someone like Joseph Stein: He knew a lot about sound-stage filming and would be loyal to the production because of Marietta.

"What else?" I asked. He named some of the working conditions that Marietta would need and said that Stein would probably want to choose his own cameraman and staff. It all sounded quite reasonable. "What about salary?" I asked.

"That can be negotiated later but seventy-five thousand dollars plus a percentage seems reasonable."

I gulped. Mr. Carmichael smiled and leaned back into the shadows once more. "Of course, we have to go over these details with your lawyer, Mr. Raider, but those are all the *unusual* points."

I folded my hands and leaned back, pretending to brood. This was all going much more easily than I had expected. "I think we can work out a deal," I finally said. Mr. Carmichael looked at Marietta. Inscrutable as always, she looked from him to me, then stood up. Chairs scraped.

"I *must* be going," she said, holding out her hand. "Mr. Carmichael has one more detail to talk over with you, Mr. Raider."

"Oh, yes?"

"When will you return to New York?" she asked.

"I would like to meet in my apartment in about a week."

She nodded. "Here is my telephone number," she said, handing me a small yellow card with only her number printed on it. "Call me when you return."

I picked up the manuscript and handed it to her. "Why don't *you* keep this now," I said.

"Good-bye, Mr. Raider," she said graciously, taking it. The heels of her shoes clicked against the linoleum tiles as she walked along the row of tables and out into the sunlight.

"Charming woman," Mr. Carmichael said as we sat down.

"Yes," I replied.

"Quite sure you won't have a drink, Mr. Raider?"

"No, thank you. What is this *detail* she mentioned?"

"Oh, yes. It's very simple, really. I am Marietta's business manager. She would like a small payment to be made from you to her as a sign of good faith."

"Without a contract?"

"Precisely."

"As a kind of retainer?"

"If you'd like to look at it that way. Yes."

I looked at the candle sputtering in its own waste. "How small?"

"A thousand dollars."

My eyes drifted to his frayed collar, and then to the yellow card in my hand. Looking up, I saw that Carmichael was smiling. I thought of Patchwicke suddenly. Then of the blond boy who was now inexorably connected to him. Of Marietta tipping the perfume bottle into her purse. I looked at Carmichael again. "Is a personal check all right?" I asked.

"Fine," he replied, touching his fingertips together.

It was quarter to four when I left the restaurant to meet Winston at the airport. I was already flying. The movie would be a reality.

But first, Sister Ivy was expecting us.

Bwana Devil

When Winston and I arrived in Charlotte, we were greeted at the airport by a limousine and installed in a suite in one of the finest hotels. Complimentary religious products and promotional material were provided along with a note instructing us to be prepared to attend a live broadcast of the Sister Ivy Club the following morning. Winston and I looked through the many pamphlets. There was a financial report for the preceding fiscal year showing the assets of the Sister Ivy Club to total over fifty million dollars. There were many Rescue Democracy and Rescue the Babies brochures, one of which for the latter campaign was faced with an illustration of a wretched creature lying in a gutter, unshaven, labeled HOMOSEXUAL. Below that was a cartoon of a peaceful and handsome young man looking up toward heaven from the palm tree serenity of his Olympic-size swimming pool, labeled GOD-FEARER.

I could sense disaster. I knew I wouldn't be able to interview the woman or her son. I tried to ignore my predicament by amusing myself with the Sister Ivy Club Mail Order Catalogue.

The first section advertised Bibles. The old-fashioned King James version was offered at a range of prices from $12.95 for regular hardcover editions to $1,000 for handmade models. The Sister Ivy Club had its own edition for $20.00 which the promotional copy proclaimed was now available in paperback and contained none of that "Shakespearean gibberish" of more traditional Bibles. For a limited time only, the catalogue offered a compact book of psalms and a convenient totebag for "Christians with on-the-go life-styles" with every $10.00 purchase.

Another literary product was the *Loaves and Fishes Cookbook,* which apparently contained the information needed to turn the most paltry leftovers into gourmet meals. It also gave recipes for the dishes served at the Last Supper.

The Christian with a bank account could purchase the *Book of Revelation Checks.* Each check was numbered. Six color scenes were depicted, including one of the fiery consumption of New York City and another of God wearing a powdered wig while judging sinners. Written on each check was a quotation from Holy Scriptures that could be shared with the many people who look at the checks one writes as they are processed.

On records and eight-track tapes were hymns sung by Dale Evans and Jane Russell. On video cassettes were a score of feature-length films produced by a subsidiary of the Sister Ivy Club. A western called *The Gold Nugget Gospel* was about the lucrative friendship between a blind prospector and a one-legged preacher. Another, called *Heaven's Heroes,* was about two police officers in Manhattan who discover Jesus while in the middle of a shootout with corrupt discotheque owners.

Cruises and chartered flights to Biblical lands were offered at low, low prices so that ministers and seminary students could walk the lands where Jesus strode and ministered. Included in the deal were penthouse accommodations at the Tel Aviv Hilton, continental breakfast, free admission to all nightclub shows and extension tours to Paris, Rome and Bermuda.

Pastors were offered Sister Ivy Club products as well as lay people: Designer choir robes and pulpit gowns made of synthetic blends in a variety of primary colors; attractive and modern formica pews, pulpits and chancel furniture. The Sister Ivy Club also offered a large variety of Fiberglas steeples, stained-glass windows and heated or nonheated baptistry swimming pools.

In the back of the catalogue was a picture of Sister Ivy herself, surrounded by a display of all the products offered (except the Fiberglas steeple). The photograph was captioned INVEST IN GOD and was followed by an order blank.

The next day, Winston and I were whisked off to the Sister Ivy Club studios. We met Sister Ivy and Claude in the green room. She was shorter than I expected, attractive but somewhat hard-looking, with a deep tan, shrewd hazel eyes and permed dark brown hair. She had the look of an animal that has just been spayed. She didn't have time to talk to us because it was only a few minutes to air time. She did, however, have a spare moment to pin a button on my lapel which read WE WILL WIN THE WORLD, the Sister Ivy Club slogan. After she left, I promptly deposited it in a garbage can. Claude talked to us for a while. He was extremely attractive, a young Ramon Navarro type, but it took a minimum of conversation for me to realize that he had the intelligence of a gerbil.

"He's cute," Winston whispered to me as Claude zipped up his fly at my suggestion.

Claude offered to take us on a tour of the television complex. Winston accepted, an old hand at TV tours, but I said no and made myself comfortable by a monitor. The two of them went off by themselves.

The show began with Sister Ivy smiling and asking the studio audience, "What will we do, everyone?"

They replied fervently, *"We will win the world!"*

This despotic exchange cued a fifty-member choir to burst into a melodic interpretation of that sentiment accompanied by a thirty-piece orchestra. When they finished, the camera moved over to Sister Ivy, who was seated at a desk in an elaborate talk show setting. She acknowledged a group of ladies from Minnesota in the audience, then explained how much money it took to run a ministry like hers. She suggested that each viewer help support God and ensure salvation by sending in twenty-five dollars each month to the Sister Ivy Club so that she might continue to spread the word of God.

"Just look what we have done already," she said, and a short video documentary began to roll on the screen. It showed Buddhists wearing strange robes and setting themselves on fire, then cut to a shot of Muslims kneeling in the dirty streets of Medina and bowing in the direction of Mecca. The narrator explained how these multitudes would never find everlasting life if they didn't know Jesus. Then it showed healthy-looking teenagers drinking Pepsi and putting Bibles into corrugated boxes earmarked for Thailand, China and Israel. The narrator suggested that this was only the beginning of Sister Ivy's efforts to win the world for Christianity. The final segment showed the work being done to convert a secluded army barracks into a treatment center for admitted homosexuals. I wondered what the "treatment" consisted of. The narrator hailed this as proof positive that Sister Ivy did not "hate queers" as her critics had contended, and as further proof quoted relevant passages from Dr. David Reuben's *Everything You Always Wanted to Know About Sex*. When the show was over the audience gave her a standing ovation. The choir sang "America the Beautiful" as the show went into a commercial break.

The first commercial showed all sorts of clean-cut people building a four-lane highway while they held up babies and American flags and sang a song entitled "The Road to Salvation Ain't Cheap." Then there was an advertisement for Sister Ivy College, which promised a serious Christian education, a fully equipped gymnasium, tennis courts and skeet shooting. Finally, there was a commercial that showed a recent widow being thrown into the street by her landlord; while looking at her Hamilton Beach blender lying broken in the gutter, she thought how she could have saved herself this heartache by joining the Sister Ivy Annuity Plan, which would have had her money working for God and her in her old age.

That over, the rest of the program was devoted to guests who sat on a couch next to Sister Ivy and witnessed for the audience how it was they came to find Jesus in this secular world. The first was an accordion player/singer named Joe Kruspchezk. He explained that, though he had seen other important stars like Efrem Zimbalist, Jr., Rhonda Fleming and Tippi Hedrin abandon successful careers to put their lives in Jesus' hands, it took him a long time to see the light.

"I didn't have time for that stuff. I wanted to be a big singer like Frank Sinatra," he told the nodding Sister Ivy.

It seems he was working in a nightclub called the Aly Baba in Brooklyn. One night he was singing "Goldfinger" when a drunken woman got up from the audience and started miming the lyrics and wiggling. Furious because the audience was paying more attention to her, Joe Kruspchezk stormed drunkenly out of the club and went home where he bludgeoned his wife with his accordion. He woke up the next morning—his wife gone, his beautiful crushed velour tuxedo split up the back and his accordion in adjoining rooms. Going into the kitchen, he found an empty refrigerator, a note from his wife saying she was suing for divorce, and stacks of unpaid bills—including an invoice for the last installment payment on the accordion. Depressed beyond imagination, he lay in bed for three days. Eventually, he got up enough energy to lean over and turn on the television.

"And the Lord saw to it that the Sister Ivy Club was on," Sister Ivy prompted.

"Yeah," he replied. "But I still wasn't ready for da Lord. Still immoised in my own sorrow, I listened ta ya speak and trew tings at da TV. Den I hoid da witnesses come up an' I tought it was all bull. I got up in da middle of a commoicial and called my agent. His numba had been disconnected. I went nuts. I trew everting out da bedroom window. I was pushin' da mattress trough when da Sista Ivy Singas and da toity-piece band got on. I stopped and watched. Dis feelin' of excitement came over me. Den I saw da audience give dem a standin' ovation. I felt so happy!"

"And that's when you accepted Jesus into your life?"

He nodded vigorously, adding, however, that he had done so only after a telephone conversation with her musical director.

"And soon Joe Kruspchezk will be one of the Sister Ivy Singers!" she told the audience. This was followed by assorted hallelujahs.

Through the rest of the show was a parade of witnesses: cardiac patients who had found Jesus directly before open heart surgery; people who had had accidents with wheat threshers, losing the lower portion of their bodies but finding God; and overweight singles who had traded in the bar scene for the scene at Calvary. Each segment of the show culminated in an appeal for money.

As the audience became more carried away, I became more bilious. I decided to call New York and tell Patchwicke or somebody that I just couldn't do it. This woman was a fraud, a greedy crook. I looked for Winston, but he was nowhere to be found. A small group of stagehands smoking marijuana said they had seen him go off with Claude but couldn't pinpoint where.

I tried to avoid Sister Ivy but ran smack into her as she came off the set.

"Well, Mr. Raider, what did you think of *that!*" she said, eyes wild and nostrils flaring.

I couldn't hold back. I told her exactly what I thought of her perverse manipulation of religion and human beings. The smile on her face slowly disappeared. She frowned at the security force around her, pushed me out of the way and left. It became very crowded backstage as the orchestra and choir came off the set. In the shuffle, I suddenly found myself pinned against a wall. One of the security guards punched me hard in the stomach, then disappeared into the crowd. I went outside in time to see my limousine speed off. I hailed a cab and waited at the hotel for Winston. It was several hours before he returned and we flew back to New York.

The Great Lie

I expected to be fired from the network and *The Morning Show* producers did not disappoint me. I spent my last half hour in Charlotte sitting in the hotel room, holding a telephone receiver several inches away from my ear as one of them bawled me out.

"*. . . unprofessional . . . jeopardized the whole idea . . . possible lawsuit . . .*"

I was prepared to find a pink slip in my pay envelope when I returned. I was not, however, prepared for the shocking news that awaited me.

"Patchwicke's dead!" the secretary blurted out as soon as I walked through the door, actually standing up and yelling it at me as if the news had to do with a five-percent raise. One of the writers took me aside and told me what had happened, at least what was known so far.

The night before I had left for Charlotte, Patchwicke had taken a pistol from his wife's night table. He had given it to her for protection because, having to commute to the city for work, he often left her alone. He told her that he was expected to attend a *Morning Show* dinner. She and the kids dropped him off at the train station about seven o'clock, then went to a local movie. No one knows what he did for the next three hours. There were no distinguishable fibers on his shoes, no matchbooks or ticket stubs on his body. His last stop was *The Morning Show* conference room.

A cleaning woman found him a little after midnight, seated in a chair, the upper portion of his body sprawled across the table, blood spattered over the wall behind the chair and a pool of blood drying on the table. The police still had the room padlocked.

Apparently, Patchwicke had entered the room about ten o'clock. As was his habit, he hung his sports jacket on the coatrack and transferred keys, Lifesavers and a railroad passbook from his trouser pockets to those of the jacket. Clutching at the pistol, he went into the conference room, sat down, put the barrel into his mouth and blew the back of his head off. The mutilated body slumped forward and spewed blood until the vessels coagulated. There was no note, no explanation. At the moment, it was being considered a suicide, but the police had been advised of the money Patchwicke had borrowed right before his death and were pursuing the possibility of foul play.

I went into the men's room after he finished telling me these gruesome details, locked myself in a stall and cried.

"You missed the two viewings," the secretary told me as I left *The Morning Show* office for the last time. "The funeral is tomorrow morning." She handed me a photocopy of the necessary information and went back to her crossword puzzle.

Because Patchwicke had always been appalled by my manner of dress, I wore a black Brooks Brothers suit to the funeral. I arrived early, before the family, in fact, and sat by myself in the back after saying a prayer over the body. Patchwicke appeared as everyone does after a session in the antiseptic wings of a funeral parlor: as overly made up and mum as a silent screen actor. There was no sign of a wound. They had scraped his brain off the walls and stuffed it under an unobtrusive wig.

People strolled in little by little. From the way they almost calculatedly ignored the body, I assumed they had displayed all their grief during the previous two days of viewing. I was vaguely irritated by the cheery murmur of relatives getting reacquainted and gossiping about the circumstances surrounding Patchwicke's death. No doubt they had never before been to such an intriguing funeral. I recognized several people from the network but said little to any of them. The secretary was escorted by one of the writers. When she walked back to say hello to me, I couldn't help but notice her eyes were red and puffy from crying.

Among the last to arrive were Patchwicke's wonderwifewonderfuldaughterwonderfulson. The son's head was wrapped in bandages; I overheard someone say he was in the middle of a hair transplant operation. His mother and sister were both wearing wigs, so it was impossible to tell just how far their own hairlines had receded. After a brief prayer, they also ignored the lifeless centerpiece of the room. The wonderfulwife walked along the banks of flowers barely filling the front of the room, lifting up tags and squinting at names, pursing her lips as if calculating the price of each arrangement for any reciprocation that might be necessary at future funerals. The children, both in their twenties, followed behind her. The three of them were dowdily dressed: The two women had dark sweaters draped over their shoulders and reading glasses dangling from chains around their necks; the son's jacket sat back on his shoulders—he had tried unsuccessfully to complete a dark suit by combining a navy blue jacket with a pair of black trousers. The alliance among the three was manifested in their gestures as well as their dress: They all walked at an obtuse angle to the floor and picked at their upper lips. The slowness of their movements suggested they were not particularly bright. The three conversed with relatives but for the most part whispered among themselves. It seemed likely that they included Patchwicke in their business as much now as they ever did.

Poor Patchwicke.

Since I held them partly responsible for his death, I had no intention of paying them my respects. Going to the cemetery was out of the question as well—but only because I didn't think that Patchwicke would have approved of the idea of a yellow Checker cab in the procession.

As I sat there frowning at them, one of my least favorite coworkers from *The Morning Show* came over and sat down next to me. "Sad, isn't it," he said. I bit my lip. "You know, he wasn't such a bad guy," he continued and waited for me to acknowledge his succinct eulogy. I shifted in my seat. He looked around the room. "I guess he didn't have a lot of friends. Not much of a turnout."

I started to excuse myself when I happened to glance to the front of the room and saw Mrs. Patchwicke lending her cheek for a kiss, greeting someone I hadn't seen since the end of college—Mrs. DeMarco! I had been so upset I hadn't even thought she would be here. Would Roman? My stomach tensed.

"Did you like Patchwicke?" the writer asked me.

I craned my neck to see her. She looked the same: a gray Claudette Colbert hairdo with round, white mother-of-pearl earrings. I don't know why her presence surprised me so; Patchwicke was her brother. I grasped the back of the foldup chair and pushed myself forward, looking to see if Roman had come with her. I didn't see him. Mrs. DeMarco talked solemnly to her sister-in-law, who was flanked by the two children.

"Well, *I* liked him," the writer said.

I strained to see, through the double doors toward the front of the room, if Roman were among the crowd milling in the hallway. A priest came striding through, escorted by a small group of people eager to get his attention. He walked across the front of the room and reached his hands out to Mrs. Patchwicke. As soon as she saw him, she put her hand to her face and began to shake as if the whole ordeal of her husband's death was about to overwhelm her. The children inched their way closer to share his sympathy.

Mrs. DeMarco was slowly edged out and took a seat in the front row. With a priest in the room, everyone began to look for a place to sit for the service. A red-faced gentleman tried to get the chair next to Mrs. DeMarco, but she smiled and shook her head. A pair of gloves was placed on the seat. The only person she could have been saving it for was Roman.

I shifted uneasily in my chair. What would it be like to see him?

"I don't think I'll stay for the service," the writer said. "I've got all this stuff to do and with the office still all screwed up—"

Mrs. Patchwicke had slipped her arm through the priest's and they were walking along the bank of flowers, fondling blooms. Like two shadows, the children somberly followed.

". . . and does anybody care?" the writer asked.

"Hmmm?"

"Does anybody care how much work I get stuck with?"

"Excuse me," I said, getting up. I certainly didn't. Funerals are never agreeable, but the lack of sorrow in the room made this one positively offensive. I walked up the aisle and gave my condolences to Mrs. DeMarco. A tributary of tears was on her face. We kissed.

"You know, I worked with your brother."

She nodded.

"I was really quite fond of him—"

She squeezed my hand. "Roman's here somewhere," she said, dabbing her nose with a tissue, obviously not wanting to talk about it.

"Is he? How about if I call you later in the week to see how you're doing?" I said. She nodded and kissed me quickly on the cheek. "Good-bye," I said.

Having every intention of leaving before bumping into her sinewy son, I walked through the double doors. But as I peered down the shadowy corridor toward the front door, I spotted him standing in the foyer. Alone, he had his foot propped up on the edge of an umbrella stand. He looked rather pale, but was as handsome and shapely as always. His hair had grown a bit. Having long since ceased to allow myself to grieve over the remains of our friendship, I turned and headed for the lounge downstairs. I would slip out when the service had begun and he took his place inside next to his mother.

This particular funeral home was built like one of the many peculiar split-levels in Scarsdale meant to resemble Georgian mansions. The main floor and stairs were hidden under a consoling powder-blue carpet. Downstairs, the floor was covered with dark green linoleum and had veins of lighter green running through to match the painted walls. Lining the perimeter were more foldup chairs and a variety of lopsided ashtray stands. No one was around. I sat down in a corner and lit a cigarette. Moments later, I heard someone on the stairs. I squeezed the edge of my seat tightly as Roman peered into the lounge.

"I thought that was you," he said, striding over. I swallowed hard and looked away. "How are you?" he asked.

Suddenly, as if they had a life of their own, my hands were scratching shins that didn't itch and adjusting pieces of clothing that had been quite well off. "Grieved," I said, trying to seem unflustered. Fighting the impulse—to no avail—I finally looked up at him. Those Tony Curtis eyes stared at me sadly from behind long lashes. My metabolism accelerated immediately and I berated myself for not being able to outgrow my Pavlovian reaction to his presence.

"Can I sit down?" he asked gently.

I shrugged.

He positioned himself on the edge of a chair and folded his hands. I turned my concentration to the irregular shape of my kneecaps.

"I've moved back here," he said.

I sucked on my cigarette. "Yes?" I said. "Is Beverly here too?" The smoke mingled with my words. He brushed back a clump of that black hair and I turned away.

"No. She . . . we decided . . . we don't see each other anymore," he said, lowering his head.

"Oh," I replied with a distinct jab of pleasure.

"I think she moved to Santa Barbara."

"I heard there was a big earthquake out there a few weeks ago. I thought about you. For a minute," I added quickly.

He looked down uncomfortably. "I've been back for a while."

"Oh?"

"About a month."

I frowned. So nothing had changed. He was still ashamed. Damn him! It was about time Roman DeMarco got told off.

"I wanted to call you . . ." His voice trailed off. "I don't know, Burton. It's weird . . . it's like I—"

"I'm sorry about your uncle," I interrupted. "He was really a very nice gentleman. I'm glad I had the opportunity to meet him."

"Oh, yes . . ." Roman turned his chair to face me. "You see, Burton, with me it's—"

"I got to know him fairly well," I said, gathering steam.

He leaned back. "Yeah?"

"Um-hmm." I glanced over. "Haven't you heard all the talk? No one seems to be sure of what happened. The police haven't decided whether it was a suicide or murder."

He regarded me silently.

"I have a few thoughts on the matter, though."

"You do?"

"Yes. Would you like to hear some?"

He peered at me. "All right . . ."

I stabbed out my cigarette and stood up. Resting one foot on the seat of my chair, I faced him. "It has to do with a boy."

"A boy?"

"A hustler. An attractive youngster who sells his body to older, not-so-attractive men on an hourly basis."

Roman leaned back. "What does that have to do with my uncle?" His tone already had a twinge of defiance to it.

"I saw him with a boy like that."

"What! When?"

"A week before he died."

He looked at me for a moment. "So?"

"It was accidental—our meeting."

"My uncle wouldn't—"

"Wouldn't what?"

"He was *married!*"

"So?"

Roman looked toward the stairs. I grabbed on to his sleeve and told him about the circumstances leading up to Patchwicke's death—the borrowing and the absenteeism. The possible relationship he had had with the hustler.

Looking around the room anxiously, Roman spoke up, "You think this kid murdered my uncle or something?"

The organ blared upstairs as the service began. Roman started.

"I think that your uncle was sickened by the feelings he had for that boy. I'm sure he spent most of his life denying that such feelings even existed within him." I paused and leaned closer. "But he kept them locked inside and went about leading what he considered to be a proper sort of life. He did well by his family. Married over twenty-eight years. Did well by his job, though they're probably interviewing replacements for him right now. A laudable person."

Roman looked panic-stricken. "I should get up there."

I held his sleeve tighter. "The thought of anyone finding out he was a pederast was completely repulsive to him, Roman. God, he used to become apoplectic if I even mentioned Oscar Wilde."

"Look, Burton, I—"

"You want to know how your uncle died? It wasn't murder. They'll find out that it *was* a suicide. I think the boy probably wanted more money after Patchwicke gave him the thousand. I think that, rather than risk exposure, he killed himself. Do you understand what that means, Roman? If I'm right, your uncle preferred death to discovery!"

"I can't believe what you're saying." He pulled away and got up. I grabbed hold of his elbow.

"And who did he protect in the end, Roman? Do you think anyone really cares what he was? You see your aunt up there and your cousins. They don't look too upset. The priest? He's wondering how large his tip will be. The writers from *The Morning Show?* To them, he was just a boss. So who benefited from this lifetime of self-denial? Your uncle? He's not saying much."

Roman tried to shake me off. "Let *go.*"

"Tell me, Roman. Where is the perversion in all this? Is it in *being* a homosexual? Or is in in feeling so *ashamed* of oneself that death seems preferable?"

Roman pushed my arm away and ran toward the stairs.

"Who are *you* doing it for, Roman?" I called after him, exorcising my resentment.

The organ blared above.

"Who are you doing it for!"

The Catered Affair

The check I had given Mr. Carmichael returned to my bank
with designs on my life savings. My debits now amounted to a little less
than three thousand dollars; my credits, including a college loan,
amounted to something over twenty-four thousand. I had never before
seriously considered taking advantage of my father's finances, but now
as they took on a deus-ex-machina quality I began to regard them with
an almost incestuous yearning. I broached the subject of their possible
application at dinner one evening.

Disdaining the telephone, I had kept abreast of my family's business
by dining with them at least once a week. My parents had been smitten
with Winston's effervescence immediately and, after satisfying our
appetites, the four of us often stayed up past 3:00 A.M. in my apartment
playing cribbage or Murder. Lucy's attendance at these get-togethers
was erratic. She was eighteen then, quite attractive and pleasantly
cynical. She visited less than I would have liked because she was never
able to adjust to Winston's loquacity.

"God, he *never* shuts up," she would say, disregarding his proximity.

Since Winston was incapable of anything even approaching reticence,
Lucy chose to stay in Oyster Bay most of the time.

The evening I asked for parental help, however, we were all dining
together in my apartment. I served chicken in pomegranate sauce;
Winston entertained everyone with busboy anecdotes. After a third

story, Lucy said to him, "If you don't shut up, I'll go out of my mind!"

I asked them both to behave but during dessert Winston told two more stories. During the second, Lucy threw a spoon at him. He left the apartment in a fury. "Now maybe I'll be able to digest something," Lucy said. I bawled her out.

It was not a particularly dignified first meeting of the staff of Raider Productions.

My family knew everything that had already transpired concerning the making of *Resurrection and Denial.* But as long as no contracts had been signed, they treated it more as an intellectual game than a reality. We talked for hours and hours about how we could pull it off, who we could actually get to film it and star in it. My father's interest had magnified enormously as I told him about the meeting with Marietta and Carmichael. After we had solved what we had all decided was the other major problem in making the film—getting a decent director—the enterprise took on a serious tone for the first time. My father had always promised to share his legal resources if the project ever reached this stage. Now, the first question that we had ever asked ourselves was the only one left to answer: Where was the money going to come from?

"The banks won't touch you," my father said when I brought up the subject. "You're unknown and have nothing. And I have no intention of giving you any substantial fraction of what you need."

My mother kicked him under the table. "That doesn't mean your father won't help you at all, darling," she said, smiling brightly. "Your idea is not as idiotic as we first thought."

"Thanks," I said gloomily.

"You have to be very cautious," my father warned.

"I think you're crazy, Burton," Lucy said, resting her elbow on the table.

"It's a tricky business," my father continued. "Marietta has confidence in you, but only because she has confidence in the director you have promised to hire. My lawyers, of course, would add to that confidence, but she must never have an inkling of how broke you are. You're finished if she does."

"But I can only raise money with her help."

"That's all right," he said, holding up his hand. "Nowadays everyone has to expect to be part of that crapola. Just don't ever let her see your bank book."

On previous occasions, we had discussed the many tried-and-true methods producers employ to raise money. Now the only option for Raider Productions seemed to be to sell shares in the production, each share selling at a thousand dollars. Though even the most dégagé angel would be reluctant to give me anything without a thorough perusal of the script, we were counting on Marietta's reputation to win them all over.

"After all," my father said, "why do these people invest money? Two reasons. To reduce their taxable income and, more importantly, to be a part of the glamour of show business, however vicariously."

"When are we going to meet her?" my mother asked. "You talk about Marietta but we never see her. I'm dying of curiosity. She's one of my old favorites."

"I'm not dying to see her," Lucy said. "If you've seen one shoplifter, you've seen them all."

"Please be quiet, Lucy," I said.

We talked it over for a while and decided that the best idea was to give a series of cocktail parties to which we would invite well-known New York angels who could meet and invest in Marietta.

"Imagine the curiosity of the women," my mother said. "They'll be dying to see how she's stood up."

"Well," my father said, "she's got a great track record. She made millions for her discoverers. Never a bad picture."

We each interjected other positive aspects of pursuing the enterprise. Finally my mother gasped, "I'm getting excited! I really am!" She looked at Lucy, who was resting her head on the table. "Aren't you excited, Lucy?"

"Galvanized," Lucy replied sourly.

We worked out the outline of the plan that very evening. My father and a few friends would pool their contacts; then he would list groups of angels who were not likely to gouge each other's eyes out upon social contact. Each group would number seventy-five investors and would congregate in my apartment.

"If Marietta can summon up some charm, you should be able to count on suckering in about twenty to twenty-five per party," my father said. "That means you'll have to give at least ten of these wingdings before you can even equip the studio. And once you start, you're in big trouble if you turn back." He promised to give me five thousand dollars toward getting Marietta in shape—clothes and an extended visit to a beauty farm in Manhattan—and to buy office supplies, engrave invitations and retain the services of a caterer. My mother was to organize everything about the parties; my father would go about them, cajoling people into getting drunk and writing checks.

"We'll have to watch the budget very carefully," he said. "But because you'll be overseeing everything, the waste should be minimal. In Hollywood, the system of making movies has built-in incentives to piss away money. They increase costs sometimes by as much as a third. I look at some of the pilots we buy and compare them to the budget sitting in front of me—tens of thousands of dollars never appear on the screen. You shouldn't have that problem. But it's important to have people around you trust."

My mother started to say something, hesitated, then thought better of it. "You know, I was talking to Mrs. DeMarco the other day in town. She told me—"

"I don't want to talk about this, mother."

"Well, I just don't understand you two. Such good friends and you have some sort of spat and, well, I just think you're a pair of jackasses."

"Mother—"

"Well, you are. Here you have an opportunity to help each other. Did you know that he graduated very high in his class? He's a graffer or something . . ."

"Gaffer," my father corrected.

"Whatever he is, he's in town. Why don't you call him?"

"No."

"Well, why not! What is it? Pride or something? You can walk down the street in Oyster Bay wearing a pith helmet or a burnoose and you still have some *pride?*"

"Don't complicate the poor soul's life, mother," Lucy spoke up. "He's got enough to handle with that blabbermouth who lives in this mausoleum with him."

"Lucy, shut up," I groaned. "You come in here and criticize the movie, this apartment, my chicken. You drive Winston out. What do you want, for Christ's sake?"

She looked at me for a moment and, twirling her hair, said very seriously, "I want to be the script girl."

We all threw up our hands and played a round of Murder.

The following day, I went to *The Morning Show* office and picked up my belongings. The secretary told me that my last paycheck was in the mail and that Sister Ivy was in the executive dining room.

"I read in the *Times* she was in town," I said.

The writer who had been so annoying at Patchwicke's funeral was doing the piece on her. "I guess you don't want to say hello," the secretary said with a smirk. "From what I hear, she almost canceled the whole deal because of you."

"Never," I said, thinking of the free publicity she would have lost.

The conference room had been opened once more. I shuddered at the sight of writers working at the long table.

"Have they found a replacement for Patchwicke?" I asked.

"Not yet," the secretary replied.

"How about me?"

"They replaced you right away," she said, pulling some dead leaves from the ruby-colored plant on her desk.

When I got home, Winston was gone. Having waited for such an opportunity, I pulled the taped yellow card with Marietta's telephone number off the refrigerator door and went into the bedroom. The meeting with my father's lawyers had to be arranged. The relationships of everyone involved had to be defined formally in legal contracts. I dialed part of the number and, feeling queasy, hung up. I hadn't been able to bring myself to call her since my return from Charlotte. What if she had changed her mind? What if she did some checking and found out I wasn't a bona fide producer? Would she take my thousand dollars and deny she ever met me? Would she try to get more money and then disappear? My stomach rumbled. I picked up the receiver and dialed again. The line was busy. I bit my lip and went into the living room. Winston had bought a copy of the *Post*. A story about Sister Ivy's arrival in New York was on page five. It had a photograph of her and Claude disembarking from the plane as a mob picketed, with signs reading THE SISTER IVY CLUB IS S.I.C. My sentiments exactly. Some protestors held up photographic statements: On one placard was a composite photograph of Sister Ivy, Hitler and Genghis Khan (played by Omar Sharif).

I went back into the bedroom and called again. This time, a male voice answered. "Yes?"

"Hello," I said apprehensively. "This is Burton Raider. I'd like to speak to Marietta, please."

There was a moment of silence. The voice said, "Oh, yes, Mr. Raider. This is Joseph Stein speaking. We've been expecting your call."

Relieved, I sat down on the bed. "I'm happy to speak to you at last, Mr. Stein. I'm a great admirer of your work."

"Thank you." He seemed to be friendly. "Marietta isn't here now."

"That's all right. This concerns you as well. I want to set up a meeting at my apartment to negotiate contracts."

"Yes, yes. I know all about it. When would be convenient for you?"

It was as simple as that! Two days later, my parents, sister and a battery of lawyers were sitting side by side with Marietta, Joseph Stein, James Carmichael and the rest of their contingent. Marietta looked wonderful. She had used the thousand dollars I had given her to buy a beautiful black suit and white silk blouse. Her friends had evidently also renovated themselves somewhat: Carmichael had bought a new suit and put a blue rinse through his gray hair. Stein was short, with salt-and-pepper wavy hair. Surprisingly, my mother was unflustered when she met Marietta: She was already deeply involved in planning the parties and, I think, viewed her now more as an obligatory centerpiece than a celebrity. Lucy, however, had gone to the Museum of Modern Art to view all of Marietta's films and when she met her, fell to pieces.

"She's beautiful!" Lucy whispered to me. "But watch your wallet anyway."

The meeting went very well. It took a little over two weeks to hammer the lumps out of all the contracts, but when everyone was satisfied, it was signed. Marietta agreed to be present at the fund-raising cocktail parties at a minimal salary. The first was to take place two months hence. My parents were to get eight percent from the movie grosses, Stein five percent, Carmichael some fraction.

My father began to send out a series of press releases to the media—any publicity we could get would legitimize the enterprise. My mother had two more telephones installed in my apartment and commuted into Manhattan every day from Oyster Bay to man them. Caterers and decorators appeared and were interviewed. Budgets were worked out and cut and cut again. My father quickly compiled lists which my mother, Lucy and several office temporaries transformed into engraved invitations. I began to work on the script with Joseph Stein, who had been at it alone since Carmichael waved my thousand-dollar check in his face.

"The structure is very good," he would say to me, then proceed to cut scene after scene. "This whole monologue can be expressed by just having this character do that," was another favorite expression that preceded further pruning.

Slowly, the manuscript was transformed into a rough shooting script, then into a story board—sketches of each separate scene. It would take at least four months to raise the money necessary to begin, so we took our time. It all had to be converted back into a final shooting script. Painstakingly, we drew over seven hundred still-action scenes and hung them in order on the walls of my apartment. When we had finished, Stein and I stood in the center of my living room and looked at the single row of drawings stretching around us.

"Well, they should like that," he said, referring to the angels who would see *Resurrection and Denial* for the first time in that form. Stein wore voluminous pants and smoked filterless cigarettes. He looked as content as an old man puttering around in a rose garden as we worked.

I had tried to get Winston just as interested in the enterprise but he would have none of it. He detested the intrusion of so many strangers. I was really getting tired of his selfishness.

My father got away from the network as often as he could. Marietta was exiled to a beauty farm in a townhouse on East Sixty-second Street. My mother spent more time in my apartment than at home: Sometimes she put in an eighteen-hour day. Later, she would use the experience to start a catering business of her own which would employ girlfriends whose child-rearing days were also over.

Able to see other people at work on the project, I felt more assured of its plausibility, its reality. After all, it's one thing to talk about inviting Alexander Cohen to a fund-raising party and another to see a gamy tongue actually licking the envelope containing his invitation. But the magnitude of what we were attempting often threatened to overwhelm us. My father would have to give me periodic pep talks and my mother would try to cheer him when the financial prospects looked especially grim.

The times I felt lowest were usually after Winston and I had a fight, which were becoming more and more frequent. Among the ashtrays and invectives he would hurl at me were also predictions of doom for the project.

"I bet not one jerk shows up!" I would hear as something breakable whizzed by my ear.

These arguments would terminate with his storming off somewhere and my going into a deep depression under the covers of my bed.

One such bout took place a few days before the first cocktail party. After it was over, I felt ready to surrender the whole idea back to the realm of imagination. After news from my mother that the caterer was suddenly demanding more money, I could barely speak. I turned off all the telephones in the apartment and went into the bedroom to assume a fetal position. About eight o'clock, the doorbell rang. I was so deeply submerged in self-pity and quilts that I barely heard it. Hoping that whoever it was would go away, I rolled over. It persisted. Finally, I pushed myself up and with a sheet wound around my body, groped my way to the door.

"Whoizzit?" I asked.

"It's me," someone said. Not even thinking, I opened the door. Standing there, in the poorly lit hall, was Roman. Oh my God.

"Hi," he said quietly.

"Mmmph!" I replied, pulling the sheet up around my shoulders. "Uh . . ." I was shocked to see him and slipped on the sheet, stumbling backwards.

"Can I come in?" he asked.

I nodded, still too sleepy and confused to put together a sentence. He stepped through the door but no farther. I closed it behind him and turned on the lights of the living room. Gesturing to a seat, I had enough presence of mind to excuse myself in order to go into the bedroom for a robe. I dashed my face with cold water and went back to the other room to make sure I wasn't in the throes of a dream.

"Nice place," Roman said, looking around and nodding.

We glanced at each other. With hands suddenly aflutter again like Zasu Pitts's, I nervously asked if he wanted a drink.

"Okay," he said. He was perched on the edge of a chair like a would-be child star waiting to audition. I walked into the kitchen and asked him what he wanted.

"A Scotch and water will be fine," he said, rising and slowly walking over to sit at the black granite counter separating the two rooms. I poured myself a straight Wild Turkey, not daring to hope what this visit could mean. I handed him his Scotch and water.

"Thank you," he said. "I—" he looked to the side, fumbling for a word. I took a slug of the bourbon and stared at him over the rim of my glass. "Look," he continued, turned back toward me but eyes downward, "you were right. I mean what you said at my uncle's funeral was right." He looked up suddenly. "Will you forgive me?"

Forgive? Ten years of sighing notwithstanding, I was incapable of anything else. I lowered my glass. Through that framed opening, he could have been Tyrone Power in *The Rains Came* with me in the first row. I lifted up my glass. "Let's toast," I said. He eagerly raised his Scotch. "Not so serious," I said.

He blushed, then smiled. Our glasses met and I quoted a line from *All About Eve*. "There are few moments in life as good as this. Let's treasure it. We have never been closer; may we never be farther apart."

I think he thought I was terribly witty.

The first party took place at seven o'clock on a Thursday evening. On hand were two bartenders, three waiters to serve hors d'oeuvres and drinks, a small band and a distinguished-looking chap sitting on my Roman throne behind a desk, whose job it was to collect checks and distribute coupons. All were hired from the Islanders Club.

The candles in the apartment had been changed and ignited; a few tango-colored lights had been added to the others already installed in the tower. With the exception of two ice sculptures decorating the dining room table and dozens of Vaseline glass bowls filled with all sorts of dried this and sugared that, the apartment remained humbly unaltered.

I changed my shirt three times before the festivities. My mother sat barking orders at people while her hairdresser harriedly tried to perform a miracle. She was thrilled to see that I had invited Roman, who had helped with some of the last-minute details. My father walked around with his shirt cuffs unfolded and unlinked, drinking from a quart container of buttermilk. The plan was for him to maneuver Marietta from clique to clique and instigate (a) nostalgic conversation and (b) investment counseling. My mother was to attend to the party itself. I was to stay out of the way. My father didn't want to make a show of the fact that I was the executive producer.

"They don't like kids. Makes them nervous."

Marietta was to be the only object of interest: She was to arrive after eight thirty so that a proper entrance could be made in front of a sufficient number of people.

I expected Winston to be excited about the party now that it was a reality, but after eating some angels-on-horseback, he disappeared. Things were rotten between us.

A dramatic finish to an affair is more the stuff of movies than real life. Sophia Loren running over Anthony Perkins twenty times in *Five Miles to Midnight* is all very dramatic, but the parting of the ways usually comes with a yawn rather than a grinding of gears. In this case, I was mostly to blame. Winston wasn't interested in the movie and that's all I seemed to have time for. I didn't listen to his incessant banter anymore. I kept thinking I would make it up to him after the whole thing was over, but Winston wasn't the sort of person who could endure any sort of estrangement.

Lucy was relieved when she found out he wouldn't be attending. "Good. Now I won't need these," she said, holding up a jumbo-sized bottle of Empirin.

The press releases my father had sent out about Marietta's comeback were slow in getting results. There had only been a small blurb in Earl Wilson's column and an article about Marietta in *Photoplay*'s nostalgic section. I was terrified that the number of guests at the party would be just as sparse.

"Calm down," my father said, belting down the last bit of buttermilk.

"Yes, darling," my mother said, turning her head and demolishing a wave that her hairdresser had completed after an arduous fifteen minutes.

At seven, we were all put together and ready for whoever showed up. A little after the quarter hour, a woman wearing a sort of sequined housedress and a feathered hat came in. She immediately inquired about food.

"What kind of people did you invite to this thing?" I asked my father.

"She's on the board of directors of the parent company of the network," he whispered. "Mrs. Hartford!" he said, smiling and reaching his arms out in greeting.

A few more dribbled in. Waiters bearing hors d'oeuvres and taking requests for cocktails appeared and disappeared. The band struck up an arrangement of *"What Is This Thing Called Love?"* Things seemed to be humming along nicely: More and more people kept coming in, Roman checking off their names. At eight thirty, he told me that about eighty percent of the invitees had shown up.

Hallelujah!

I was thrilled to hear the harmonious sounds of voices and music fill the apartment. Heeding my father's advice not to introduce myself to anyone, I whirled about, ducking under uplifted trays of champagne glasses and squeezing between dark-suited businessmen to snatch a piece of *anguilles au vert* or a dill-stuffed egg. There were one or two recognizable faces: a well-to-do senator and a sometimes-actress-sometimes-wife-of-a-Broadway lyricist who had been popular in the 1950s. Someone from *Variety* crashed the party, to my delight; a feature writer from *Vogue* came in with a photographer. They were immediately offered liquor and plied with laban and marinated salmon.

I was in the kitchen talking to Roman when my mother burst in. Smiling, she whispered to me in an alarmed tone. "Where is she!"

I looked at my watch. "Oh, my God!" I gasped. It was almost nine o'clock. Marietta was half an hour late. I squeezed through the crowd in the living room to my father, wedged between a textile manufacturer and the inventor of Liquid Paper. "Pardon me, Mr. Raider," I said calmly, "but there's a matter that requires your immediate attention."

"Excuse me, please," he said to the guests, following me to an uninhabited corner of the room.

"Daddy!" I whispered. "Where the hell *is* she!"

"She'll be here, don't worry," he said, nodding and smiling to someone passing by.

"But look," I said, shoving my wristwatch in his face, "it's after nine o'clock already."

"Probably caught in traffic," he said.

"Suppose she doesn't come!" I whispered apoplectically.

"Then you're up shit's creek," he replied, waving to a socialite across the room. "You can't blame her for being a little late. This is her first public appearance in twenty years, for Christ's sake. She's probably been getting ready since last Tuesday." He squeezed my arm. "Chin up," he said, and rendezvoused with a nearby reporter. I grabbed Roman and dragged him to the bedroom. He sat on the bed while I paced back and forth.

"She's not coming! She's not coming! I can feel it! I can sense disaster!"

"She'll come," he said, trying to sound off-handed about it.

"What'll we tell them? Oh, God, my life's over. Everything's falling apart! I've dragged my parents into this fiasco! Where is she? Where is that bitch!"

He consoled me valiantly until nine thirty, when there was a big commotion in the next room. We ran out together in time to witness Marietta make a spectacular entrance in a sequined black gown. The crowd stood back as her glittering form swept into the room. Her hair was arranged as it always had been on film: parted in the middle, flowing to the shoulders. It was covered with a netted shawl, also sequined. She wore no jewelry; she didn't need to. She was flanked by Stein and the rest of her little group, all dressed to the nines. Noises of recognition and admiration filled the room as she let the shawl fall to her shoulders. A man broke from the crowd and rushed up to her. As if time had stood still since her days at MGM, Marietta casually extended her hand. The agitated man bowed and kissed it, and the photographer from *Vogue* pushed his way forward. Flashbulbs popped. At a signal from me, the orchestra played the theme from *The Waltz* and people buzzed and squealed as Marietta drifted in among them.

I watched dumbfounded from the wings as she drew in the attention being paid her. Her appetite for acclaim had been insatiable, because of her deprived childhood; now she was starved, from her long banishment. She was a star absolute.

She tossed her head back regally as my father took her hand to make an introduction to Mrs. Hartford from the network board of directors.

"My dear, you look divine . . ." the odd-looking woman cooed.

Marietta waded farther into the crowd and they stepped back as the Munchkins had from Glenda.

"Marietta," my father would say to a pot-bellied or sagging-breasted angel, "I'd like you to meet so and so." She would smile and the most hard-bitten among them would stammer and try to express their admiration. Some hesitated in shaking her hand, as if doing so would burn them, but all came under her spell that night. Thirty-two did in checks!

One bounced.

The parties thereafter averaged between twenty-five and thirty thousand. As word reached the ivory towers of the New York cognoscenti, I noticed an increase in the numbers of famous faces— many were wangling invitations from members of the moneyed gentry they despised. Andy Warhol came to one party with Sylvia Miles. He said nothing but made a fuss later in his magazine, calling Marietta the greatest star in movie history; Miles flirted expertly with my father. Arthur Bell appeared and did a piece for the *Voice*. Rex Reed gave Marietta an autographed picture of himself. By the sixth party, Marietta's comeback had taken on the sort of surreal tone that must attend any event in New York that is to succeed. Red-faced lawyers indulged their wives and went over to corners where Dustin Hoffman, Robert De Niro and Francis Ford Coppola—unshaven and sloppily dressed—stood brooding, pontificating on the metaphysical reasons for not giving autographs. I was dazzled by the stars but accepted their presence with a minimum of ceremony. People who had donated entire medical buildings stood by while young producers with one hot play to their credit blew cigarette smoke in their faces. This was a dadaist swirl of furs, diamonds, combat wear, heavy black capes, frizzy hennaed hair, geological and emotional jade, absurd makeup, mandarin clothing and bologna. Different strata sneered discreetly at one another from across platefuls of pâté—but all deferred to Marietta, unquestionably the center of it all.

She smothered me with kisses at the end of each party. "Oh, sank you, Burton," she said. *"Sank* you!" Joe Stein hugged me after the first party and sent me one of Gene Tierney's old bedspreads. Unfortunately, it fell apart at the dry cleaners.

For all our success, there never seemed to be enough money. As soon as it came in, it turned into studio equipment and set designers and accountants and pencils and legal pads and God knows what else. I had to give Joe Stein permission to start hiring people. Our storyboard was transposed back into a shooting script and sets began to be built. The project had finally taken on a life of its own—though at times it seemed more cancerous than controlled. But no matter how scary it became, we stuck to the original plan and budget. No one but my family and the legal and business people knew the financial mess we were getting ourselves into. My father kept telling me not to worry, but an ulcer matured in my stomach nonetheless. At least I thought so. By the end of our ninth party, we had managed to collect and spend over three hundred thousand dollars!

All we needed was about three-quarters of a million more.

Duel in Durango

Sister Ivy had none of these pecuniary problems. During the course of the five *Morning Show* segments in which Liz Bonwit interviewed her, it was revealed that the assets of the Sister Ivy Club had risen to fifty-seven million dollars. In the last segment, Sister Ivy apprised Liz and several million local viewers of the terrible moral situation she had discovered in Manhattan during her stay.

"It's nothing but a sty filled with pigs," she said as Liz nodded pensively and crossed her legs. For a moment, the cameraman took her out of focus. "This unholy city is leading the country down a one-way street away from God. Drugs come by the shipload into New York harbor and are trucked in broad daylight to the rest of the country. Homosexuals are allowed to parade their perversion. Women's lib magazines are published here. It's dis-graceful!" Liz's eyelashes fluttered cryptically. "But I see the starvation!" she continued, raising her voice and a finger toward the camera. "And I hear the unhappy voices of its lonely inhabitants. And I promise those people listening to Sister Ivy right now who have accepted Jesus Christ as their one and only Savior—I promise those souls that I will not forsake this sinful island, this modern Sodom. The Sister Ivy Club will stake its claim right *here.*" She leaned back and disclosed her plan to buy a ten-story office building on Fifty-seventh Street for the purpose of (Sam Goldwyn couldn't have put it better) "establishing a beachhead in Satan's front yard."

It was later revealed in an article in the *New York Times* that she planned to stay in Manhattan for six months to supervise the establishment of the new headquarters for the Sister Ivy Club. No doubt her imperial religious network had reached the point where a more accessible location than Charlotte was necessary. The article also said that she had purchased some apartment buildings in Brooklyn, the bankrupt Klein's department store on Fourteenth Street and a pneumatic drill factory in Queens. I dreaded to think what influence she might eventually be able to wield. Financial prestige could buy a great deal of political power in a city intermittently teetering on the edge of bankruptcy. If she set her mind to impressing her moral standards on the rest of us, which looked likely, Ivy's influence could precipitate police harassment and renewed hostility and violence against homosexuals. It was not a happy prospect.

Sister Ivy's despotism was not the only thing that depressed me as I geared up for cocktail party number ten. My relationship with Winston had reached its lowest ebb. It was apparent, in fact, that Winston had fallen for somebody else. I had long been accustomed to finding the telltale signs of his chronic infidelities, but of late I noticed a similarity of evidence: the same brand of skinny brown cigarette in the ashtrays, the repulsive odor of Old Spice lingering in the apartment (a scent neither of us liked) and ticket stubs for admission to the Statue of Liberty and Radio City Music Hall. A romance was definitely brewing. But because I partly blamed myself for our state of affairs, I decided not to ask Winston to leave unless I caught him cavorting with his new flame in the apartment.

The Saturday before the party, I had been out to Flatbush with Stein to supervise the installation of the last of the overhead lights. The six interior sets that would be used for the movie were nearing completion in different parts of the studio and the cameras we had rented were pushed against a wall and wrapped in plastic canvas. It hardly resembled the warehouse in which I had sat gloomily pondering cinematic ghosts. Its cavernousness was now filled with mechanisms; my awe was replaced by anxiety—when I looked around, all I saw were invoices and canceled checks. Stein, a sympathetic soul, realized that I was rather depressed and sent me home to get some rest.

When I entered my apartment, I found Winston standing nude in the kitchen, dunking a tea bag alternately in two cups of boiling water. Understandably, it was difficult for him to camouflage his surprise.

"Didn't you say you'd be home around *six?*" he asked, furtively placing one cup in the sink. The jig was apparently up.

"I couldn't stand it anymore. I thought I'd go into the bedroom and take a nap," I said tauntingly.

"A nap!" Winston piped.

"Want to join me?"

"Well . . . I—" he stammered, blushing prodigiously.

Hearing voices, his friend stumbled out into the living room. Winston and I both turned as he bumped into a chair. He was also nude. One of the reasons of Winston's interest in him was immediately apparent.

"Hi," he said, stepping behind the chair to cover himself. It was Claude.

I couldn't have been more flabbergasted if it had been Vera Hruba Ralston. Obviously, Claude had given Winston more than just a tour of the Sister Ivy Club baptistry swimming pool.

"It's not what you think," Winston squeaked as I walked out the room.

The bedroom was a mess. Clothes were everywhere and one of those skinny brown cigarettes was smoldering in an ashtray filled with other skinny brown cigarettes. Sheets lay twisted on the floor, dresser drawers were opened and cocked downward and a store-bought (green!) cake was sitting half-eaten in its box on the floor. Thoroughly depressed, I pushed some clothes over the edge and sat down on the bed. I was trying to figure out how long I'd give Winston to pack up and get out when I felt something stabbing at my back. I rolled to the side and pulled a processing envelope filled with photographs out from under me.

I picked one picture out. It was Winston. I flipped over to another. It was of Winston and Claude holding hands and smiling in front of the

Statue of Liberty. I sat up and looked at the next. It was of them as well—this time in a park. Almost *all* of the pictures were of the happy couple together. I looked out the window. A lightbulb lit above my head.

"Fellows . . ." I said, going back to the living room. They had been whispering fiercely to one another and jumped apart at my approach. "Did you ever think of entering the exciting world of male modeling?" I waved the envelope.

Winston blanched. I don't think Claude was able to grasp the situation immediately but after I pointed out how eager the *New York Post* would be to find out that the son of America's most rabid opponent to homosexuals was himself one, he realized the gravity of his indiscretion.

Winston packed; Claude went to pieces. They installed themselves in a nearby hotel and discussed their predicament. Winston soon grew tired of talking about the same thing over and over and suggested they go disco dancing. Claude panicked. He went to his mother's hotel and told her everything. After satisfying herself that Claude was not playing a practical joke or drunk, she chased him around their suite with one of her handmade King James Bibles, worth $1,000, trying to kill him. Using a plastic coffee table to fend her off, Claude managed to escape and hobble back to his hotel.

Winston was waiting there, munching on a hamburger that room service had sent up. "Want to go to the Cloisters tomorrow?" Winston asked brightly.

Sister Ivy telephoned me at two o'clock in the morning, calm and unctuous. I told her curtly to come to my apartment at three the following afternoon.

She appeared at my door early, flanked by two of her security goons. "Hello, Mr. Raider," she said in a businesslike tone.

"Come in," I said cheerfully, my depression now gone. I would enjoy this.

"Wait here, boys," she said over her shoulder. I closed the door and gestured to a chair. She looked terrible: pale with dark blue circles under her eyes. She was wearing a pink dress and black patent leather pumps. She obviously had something playing on her diminutive mind.

"I'll get right to the point," she began. "I understand you have some pictures."

"Yes."

"I want them."

I shook my head.

"All right," she said, drawing herself up. "How much?"

I smiled. "Why don't *you* name a figure?" I asked politely.

With an expression on her face that would have unnerved the Holy Ghost, she said "Five thousand."

I laughed. "How much are you worth?"

"Ten thousand then," she said without hesitation. "Are the pictures here?"

"No," I said, chuckling. "And I wouldn't *give* them to you anyway. No matter how much you offered."

"Be serious, Mr. Raider. What are we doing here then?"

I leaned forward. "I want two things from you. If you comply, I *promise* no one will ever see those pictures."

"Promise! What's that to me? How do I know I can trust you?"

"Well, for one thing, you have my word," I said, a gentleman to a harridan.

Now *she* laughed.

"Also . . . you have no choice. You have a lot more to lose than I have to gain by my handing those pictures over to the press."

Her eyes narrowed. "You know, Mr. Raider, God sometimes punishes people who stick their noses in other people's business. He just *strikes* 'em down before they even know what hit 'em."

"That so," I said, lighting a cigarette. So now she was threatening me.

The movies once again came in handy. I had watched dozens of hard-boiled detective films; the hero always used the same method for safeguarding the evidence. "It would be a shame if anything were to happen to me," I began and then explained how the photographs were in the possession of the U.S. Postal Service at that very minute. "They're addressed to a friend of mine and contain instructions for disposal should I suffer a gunshot wound or an accidental fall from an apartment."

"Two hundred thousand."

"Come, come, Sister Ivy. You have fifty-seven *million* dollars in assets—that the government knows about. Only God and you know how much else there is buried in the hills of North Carolina."

"Two hundred and fifty thousand dollars."

"Warmer and warmer."

"Let's stop this, Mr. Raider. Just tell me how much you want so I can go on about my business."

I exhaled a cloud of smoke in her direction. "The first thing I want is a cash deposit in my bank account *today* in the amount of three-quarters of a million dollars," I said deliberately.

She angrily waved the smoke away. "You're out of your mind, Mr. Raider."

"Please . . . Think of those banner headlines," I said with a sweep of my hand.

"Oh, Hell's bells!" she spat. "Done!"

Hosannah! Now I could make my film!

She clenched the arms of the chair. "You said there were *two* things. What *else* could you possibly want?"

"Oh, it's something much more important than money," I said.

She eyed me suspiciously. "What?"

"I want you to drop your Rescue Democracy and Rescue the Babies campaigns."

"Impossible!"

"Keep everything else. The show, the college—build an empire the sun never sets on if you like! But not at the expense of a bunch of people you don't even understand."

"No!"

"Think about it."

"People need me! They need to hear the Word of God. You're asking me to make a bargain with the devil. No! I won't. It's against my conscience. It's against—"

"Oh, pipe down!" I said. She sputtered out and I continued. "You've made fifty-seven million dollars by exploiting the prejudices of the dumbbells that live in this world. That's enough to spread the Word of God from here to Mars. I'm not telling you to stop the evangelical part of your work. People do need you, though God knows why. I'm just giving you a warning: If you *dare* say one more word about women's libbers, fags or dykes, those photographs will be on the front pages of every newspaper around the country faster than you can say damnation. Can you imagine what would happen to your credibility then? Think of the conflicts that would go on in the minds of your audiovisual congregation. How much longer would they watch your TV show? Or listen to your speeches? Or buy your Revelation Checks?"

She stood up. "Remember this, Mr. Raider," she said, pointing a narrow bony finger at me. "Don't think God won't punish you. For in Revelations 21:8 it is said, 'The unbelieving, and the abominable, and murderers, and whoremongers, and sorcerers, and idolators, and all liars shall have their part in the lake which burneth with fire and brimstone.'"

Pushing her finger to the side, I got up and went to a bookshelf. I pulled a Bible from the shelf and opened to the place I had marked last night.

"Yes, and Jesus also said, 'Woe to you, Pharisees and other religious leaders. Hypocrites! For you won't let others enter the Kingdom of Heaven and won't go in yourselves!'"

I don't think she heard me. Carried off by the ring of her own words, she looked through the walls of the apartment to her place in heaven. "I must go," she finally said. We walked to the door together; suddenly she started. "Do you know where that idiot Claude is?" she asked, scowling.

"No," I replied. "But I don't think I'd tell you if I did."

At that very moment, Claude and Winston were at the Cloisters, consoling themselves over the unfortunate turn of events and trying to pick up the momentum of their infatuation. After the Cloisters, it was dinner at the Plaza and a movie at the Baronet—Claude had a large bank account of his own. At Winston's suggestion, they took up permanent residence at the Pierre Hotel.

"God, I always wanted to live here!" Winston squealed, bouncing like a child on their king-size bed the first night.

They explored the city just as we had. There was one slight difference, though: They had a man following them.

In New York, lots of people are employed to do lots of things. Some are even paid to take photographs of Jacqueline Kennedy Onassis buying low-heeled pumps at Bendels' and Mick Jagger sprawled over the back seats of limousines. Such people, called paparazzi, are constantly on the lookout for famous faces so they can continue to put clothes on their backs and bubblegum in their mouths. Claude and his mother had appeared in every notable periodical in the country. They had won awards, spoken at political conventions and launched aircraft carriers. It was only a matter of time before *someone* recognized him. Luckily, it happened after the three-quarters of a million was deposited in my bank account.

The *Post* got the scoop after all. The headlines over the photograph of Winston and Claude kissing behind a dogwood tree in Central Park read CLAUDE QUEER!

The Squaw Man

W e used the last cocktail party as an occasion to celebrate my coup rather than to buttonhole investors. It was a grand affair. Afterwards, my parents wished me luck and retired to Oyster Bay to await residual checks. I was obliged to take my place as executive producer, a position to which I had planned to bring the enthusiasm of Warner Baxter in *42nd Street* but only managed the naïveté of his costar, Ruby Keeler.

Moviemaking turned out to be a tedious business. From 6:00 until 9:00 or 10:00 A.M., I sat dropping Visine in my eyes while the forty-eight technicians who populated the studio behind the camera did their specialized tasks in preparation for the first scene. Gaffers would plug a thing in, sit down, sip coffee, look at the ceiling, get up and unplug the thing; others leisurely performed similar choreography with their respective materials. I tried to change the time signature of their movements by pitching in but was yelled at immediately.

"Get the fuck away from my fucking fixture!" the fucking fixture man screamed.

I talked to Stein about the man's insolence. "Unions," he said knowingly. "There's nothing you can do."

I am a liberal-minded person and believe the proletariat should be protected from exploitation. I do not, however, understand how that noble sentiment evolved into a situation where an exorbitantly paid soundman has the right to threaten my life simply for pushing his boom out of my ear. But there was nothing to do. Stein told me his old friend John Huston, while filming *The Night of the Iguana* in 1964, had even been forced to hire a member of the Mexican S.P.C.A. to look after the iguanas.

"The beach boys looked after Ava Gardner," he added with a laugh.

Not wanting to infringe on the duties of sensitive 270-pound crane operators, I decided to watch and let Stein handle everyone.

Resurrection and Denial was a psychological study of the rise and fall of a movie star named Gloria Mars. The first shot was of Gloria's mother in the attic of their home, rummaging through a carton of mementos, searching for a prop to give her little girl, who was to be photographed that afternoon in a Shirley Templeish getup. The result would be sent to all the studios in California. Mother, Gloria and her father all lived in New Jersey. In the first shot, the camera slowly panned up from the mother's ankles to her waist, shoulders, and finally, to her panicked face. This matched another shot toward the end of the movie when Gloria herself is middle-aged and frantically searching through a garbage can on Third Avenue for rotten clothing and stale food.

Gloria's mother leaves her husband and drives herself and the little girl out to California—even though the studios haven't beckoned. Her husband doesn't follow. Gloria is unwittingly suffering from an identity crisis because of her mother: She is a function of her talent and seems to exist only when she is singing, dancing or acting.

The domineering mother manages to get the girl a contract at one of the studios. Gloria matures into a star, and yet still has no personal identity of her own. She tries to find herself by emulating the major stars. She plays opposite Robert Taylor, Gary Cooper, Charles Boyer.

Later, she tries to find an identity through love, but sadly, she picks equally displaced personalities to marry. She has two children; her mother offers to care for them while Gloria works. There is a vicious cycle between her personal life and her life at the studio: insecurity leading to jealousy leading to hysteria leading to looking and feeling awful leading to warnings from her mother and the studio leading to renewed insecurity. Resulting temper tantrums cause Gloria to be fired.

When dropped from the studio, she first kicks her mother out of her mansion (literally), then attempts to find herself through motherhood. But her children are already seven and eight and reject the attentions of this "stranger." Gloria has a breakdown. The children are awarded to their father, an alcoholic screenwriter, while she is in the hospital.

Upon her release, she attempts to find her own identity again—again through love but this time through a lot of casual sex as well. She admits the wrong person into her apartment one night and is almost killed when he tries to shove a black enamel Art Deco dildo down her throat.

Gloria Mars attempts a comeback—work being life—but with the wrong manager: A sleazy opportunist, he picks the wrong theatrical vehicle for her and the critics laugh her off the New York stage. So that their relationship isn't a total disaster, he takes the money she has left and skips town.

It is a short walk for her to the nearest bar. Eventually, Gloria drinks her way to the Bowery and declines to the level of tramp. While searching through a garbage can one cold morning, she comes upon a discarded copy of the *Daily News* and reads in a headline that Marilyn Monroe has committed suicide. Unable to work, still emulating bigger stars than she, Gloria finally finds identity in death.

Most of the action of *Resurrection and Denial* took place on the sets built in the studio; the rest was shot either in the outer regions of nearby New Jersey or on the streets of Brooklyn. Marietta and the other performers in the movie spent those early-morning hours getting into makeup and character. Stand-ins would take their places on the set for lighting checks and camera setups.

In one line of command, for instance, the director of photography would tell the chief cameraman what "look" he wanted for the scene and the C.C. in turn would tell his assistants how he wanted the camera positioned to achieve it. The key grip, soundman and gaffer would delegate work to their own assistants and coordinate the efforts between themselves. After hours of moving this light an inch and that camera angle a degree, the chief cameraman would check the results in the viewer. When he was satisfied, places would be called for all the technicians. The stand-ins would disappear. And out would come the director and his cast.

The first day, I looked for signs of terror in Marietta's face as she walked out to the set with Stein. It had been over twenty-five years since she had worked in front of a camera, and I was a little concerned. Stein whispered encouragement to her while a makeup man patted her forehead with a flesh-colored pad. She was still a tidal wave. She was dressed in the clothes of a bag lady for the scene late in the film I had decided to start with; her maid rebuttoned the oversized sweater hanging limply past her waist. If there *were* fear lurking underneath that cool, gorgeous exterior, it must have melted in the warmth of the spontaneous ovation given by the crew as she walked onto the set. An old gaffer standing above in the flies threw his rabbit's foot to her. Smiling, Stein squeezed her shoulders. Her maid sniffled back tears. Marietta turned about, waving to everyone. For the first time since I had met her, I saw her cry.

Stein asked the actors to take their places. There was a camera rehearsal. Some light setups were changed.

"Okay, save 'em," the lighting director yelled.

"Right!" Roman called back, at work on the catwalks above. His education had prepared him to be a professional gaffer, but only after we paid a small bribe to his guild was he allowed to become a third assistant.

An audio rehearsal followed. The boom had to follow the actors from mark to mark so that the dialogue could be recorded clearly.

When all was ready, Marietta took her place on the first mark. Stein gave a signal; red lights flashed above each exit in the studio. A warning bell rang sharply. All conversation and extraneous noise suddenly stopped. Overhead lights flooded the set. At a nod from the recordist sitting at a monitor panel, an assistant darted in front of the camera with the hinged slate. How I had longed to see that. And Roman here with me. He and I were seeing each other now that Winston was out of the picture. We hadn't slept with each other again, though; our relationship was too precious to move too fast.

"Speed!"

"R and D. Tenement. Take one!"

Clack!

The routine was to get a master shot of the whole scene and then later the cover shots: close-ups, two-shots and medium shots of other characters talking together. Time was consumed by a number of things: Marietta would forget a line, though not half as often as I had feared she would; another actor would not do a scene to Stein's satisfaction; the camera might be dollied up too slowly or quickly; there might be an unexpected cameo appearance by a large fly.

"Okay, print four!"

It was Lucy's job (I had made her the script girl) to check for continuity between scenes. Thus, if Marietta was holding a broken-handled mug in her left hand when we stopped shooting a scene at the end of the day, Lucy had to make sure she was doing so the next day. She loved the work but was subdued as always. "Well, it beats working at McDonald's in Oyster Bay for the summer," she said.

My role in all this came at the end of the day when Stein, his film editor and I took a gander at the day's rushes. Our deliberations over the best shot to go into the rough cut could last from five minutes to (I almost died) *seven* hours, yet it was exciting, satisfying work. Eventually, the editing would be passed down to assistant editors, sound editors, cutters and negative cutters. While still shooting, a composer was brought in to complement Stein's visual conceptions with musical ones. It was odd to watch my original conception of the film mesh with Stein's own ideas and the composer's; the result was an intellectually richer film than I had originally imagined. The composer was inspired to write a haunting theme which not only heightened the poignancy of Marietta's character, but also pulled the entire film together in a way that mere dialogue never could.

There were assorted problems. For example, Marietta fainted one day on the set; as she was carried into her dressing room, I thought for sure she had contracted some dreadful disease that would force us to close down. A doctor was called; luckily, her collapse resulted only from a combination of dieting and prolonged exposure to the hot overhead lights.

But as demoralizing as these fleeting jabs of disaster could be, there were also moments of pure elation when drudgery turned to magic. One such time occurred when Marietta, as Gloria Mars, had to walk grimly into her hotel at six in the morning after the disastrous stage comeback attempt. Everyone watched in awed silence as her anger turned to irritation, then unease, finally panic as she desperately tried to push aside a heavy bureau to see if the money she had hidden under the floor boards had disappeared with her manager. God only knows what personal misfortune Marietta drew on to make the scene so raw and real, but there were bravas from the nearly illiterate technicians afterwards. All of us had forgotten ourselves for a moment and *believed*. For me, such moments of suspension are what make real life bearable.

Another time, filming was delayed until late in the afternoon because of technical problems. Marietta grew more despondent with each passing hour—she was still weak from her collapse. We were shooting the scene when Gloria Mars had to throw her mother out of her house in Hollywood, pushing her to the ground and threatening to run her through the neck with the spiked heel of her shoe.

"Places," Joe Stein finally yelled. He wanted to go through the scene a few times to get Marietta and the other actress warmed up, but Marietta refused.

"Let's just do it," she said, kicking off her soft slippers and putting on the heels.

"Speed!"

"R and D. Foyer. Take one!"

Marietta exploded into her role. *"Bitch! Bitch!"* she screamed, coming at the actress playing her mother. It had been such a languid day that the unexpected fury and conviction in Marietta's demeanor almost caused the actress to forget to respond. When Marietta had her on the floor and was bringing the high-heeled shoe to bear, the actress instinctively screamed and rolled over to protect herself—ruining the shot.

"Cut!" Joe Stein yelled.

The actress sat up shaking as Marietta subsided back into her own personality. "Anyone have a cigarette?" she asked.

Once, the entire production came to a halt when a fire inspector appeared on the scene and told Joe Stein that the building was in violation of several ordinances. I was down the street having my usual gourmet lunch in a drugstore. Stein's assistant came to fetch me. Christ, I thought to myself, everyone's got to exercise a little bit of power. Some asshole making less than two hundred dollars a week was going to stop my million-dollar production.

"All right, what's the problem!" I snapped, approaching the inspector from behind. He turned around.

"Raider!" he gasped.

It was Sparks Compton, the would-be assassin.

I almost puked. "Sparks! How great to see you!" I said, a consummate actor myself. He looked puffy in his ill-fitted uniform. His hair had receded at the temples a bit.

"You're in charge of all this?" he asked.

"Yeah, well, sort of . . ." I said, wondering what approach to take with him.

He looked around and cleared his throat. "Well, according to code—"

"Hey, Sparks—" I said, slapping him on the back. "Forget all that for a minute. Tell me how you're doing. You ever get married?"

"Yeah," he replied.

I smiled and nodded though the very sound of his voice resurrected all the memories of being in the hospital with a broken jaw. "Anyone I know?"

"No," he replied. "We're divorced now."

"Too bad," I said sympathetically. My smile was in reality clenched teeth. I hated him as much as ever.

"Now about code number—"

"Whatever happened to Bob and Howard Joslyn?" I asked cheerfully. No doubt they were doing time somewhere.

"Uh, nothing," he said eloquently.

"Do you see them?" I asked.

"Not much," he said with a shrug. "They're lawyers, you know."

"Isn't that great!" I said, slapping him hard on the back. He stumbled. "Did you see Roman?"

"DeMarco?" he asked.

I pointed up into the flies. *"Hey, Roman!"* I yelled.

He emerged from the back and hung over the railing. *"Yeah?"*

"Look who's here!" I yelled, pointing to our former classmate.

"Who?"

"Sparks Compton!"

Roman came down and, seeing me with a diplomatic grin, shook his hand. "Sparks," I told him, "is a big city official now and wants to close down our production."

"Well, I wouldn't put it that way, Raider," Sparks said.

"Oh, you must be kidding, Burton," Roman said. "Sparks wouldn't want to do that."

Using everything we knew about abnormal psychology, we talked Sparks around in circles while an assistant surreptitiously went out to buy two fire extinguishers and an asbestos tarpaulin to hang on the wall. When he had done so, we pointed them out casually and joked that Sparks's eyes might be going as well as his hair. He looked bemused and grinned at us sheepishly. We told him how well he looked and told him we would just *have* to get together real soon. When he left, we lamented his physical decline, congratulated ourselves, and got on with wrapping up the picture.

Sunset Boulevard

W e were barely able to finish *Resurrection and Denial* after four months before we had to pack up to go abroad: For publicity, we had decided to debut the film at the Cannes Film Festival. Only a handful of us got to see the marvelous film we had produced before we left; Marietta was asleep in her apartment the only time we ran it. I was as proud as Rhett Butler watching Bonnie mount her chestnut.

My mother, father, Lucy and Roman flew over with me. It was my first trip to Europe and going with my parents and Roman enhanced the novelty. Marietta and Joe Stein followed the next day.

The city of Cannes is located in southern France in the department of Alpes-Maritimes, situated on a slope backed by a series of hills. In 1815, it was near Cannes that Napoleon landed after escaping from Elba. In 1834, Henry Peter Brougham, British chancellor and Baron of Brougham and Vaux, fell in love with Cannes and had a villa constructed there. His social standing prompted others to follow suit and Cannes soon became a fashionable resort to rival Deauville to the north. The older part of the city was built on Mont Chevalier, newer sections on the lower coastline.

We checked into the magnificent Hôtel Carlton. There was much to see—the Musée Rothschild, filled with engravings, sculpture and paintings, the Church of Notre Dame d'Espérance, the classical antiquities in the Musée Lychlama, and the remains of the ancient Château des Abbés de Lérins—but there was no time for any of it. Not even more than a five minute gander at the Mediterranean—a contrivance of extraordinary blues that can be found nowhere else on earth.

We drove along the wide avenues lined by palms and white buildings to meet Marietta and Joe Stein at the airport on our second day. The terminal was jammed; we had to fight through a mob to get past her gate. Anticipation over Marietta's comeback had been snowballing since the fourth cocktail party. Her presence in Cannes now ignited the mass of hysteria that we wanted. Her entrance was spectacular.

The paparazzi were everywhere. We installed Marietta in her suite at the Hôtel Carlton and one photographer even popped out of her closet! Others canvassed our corridors and peeped through our keyholes. Even I had become a celebrity. They were always bribing bellhops and hotel clerks; my father had to hire a guard to stand at Marietta's door. But then he spent most of his time in the bar downstairs. The paparazzi accosted us in restaurants on La Croisette and jumped in front of Marietta's car in the middle of boulevards. Since this was a dream come true for all of us, especially me and Marietta, it was wonderful. Up to a point . . .

The first showing of *Resurrection and Denial* was bedlam. The local police could barely contain the crush of fans trying to get a glimpse of Marietta as she walked into the theater to watch the final cut of her performance for the first time. A woman had to be rushed to the hospital because she fell and was trampled by the crowd. After the showing, word had it that *Resurrection and Denial* was *the* film of the festival and Marietta the only touch of glamour.

Glowing with the marvelous reception, we all reconnoitered in Marietta's suite and got drunk while ex-models making their film debuts tried to save face when questioned by reporters.

"Is she still alive!" one said, when asked about Marietta.

"It's amazing what those monkey-gland injections can do," another cooed, batting her eyelashes.

Bolstered by the critical acclaim, Marietta was impervious to cracks about her age. "There have always been bitches," she said. "Remember, I knew Miriam Hopkins!"

Marietta and I got to be great friends during our stay in Cannes. In the States, our fraternization had been limited by the hectic scheduling involved in the financing and making of *Resurrection and Denial*. Here, Joe Stein and my father dealt with most of the press relations work. Marietta, Roman and I would jump into a car and head out of town—sometimes for a picnic, but more often to get sloshed in a charming bistro up north. No one knew who we were; Marietta did all the translating. With a bottle of wine making a foursome, Roman and I would raptly listen to Marietta gossip about the infamous.

"There was this little assistant director on one of my pictures," she began once, filling our glasses with Pouilly Fumé. "A little bitty man— but wis the biggest schwantz in the world."

We laughed at her candor. I hadn't known Marietta had a bawdy side as well.

"He was after everyone. A pig, like Harry Cohn at Columbia. He tried to get me in my dressing room but I kicked him in the balls and he left me alone after that. He attacked my maid too. Maya couldn't resist a big schwantz. Still can't. She said when the poor man had an orgasm, he passed out! Apparently, there wasn't enough blood in his body to accommodate *bose* his heads." She sipped her wine while Roman and I roared.

I don't think I have ever been happier than during those afternoons, the three of us laughing and talking and drinking. It was like being in the darkness of a movie theater during a matinée, secure against the appalling bland brightness of the noonday sun.

"Remember Aly Khan?" she asked. "There were certain ones everyone wanted—Gable, Cooper, Dietrich, Turner. Ali was one of those. He was a Moslem, you know. His father used to have his weight matched in jewels every year. Anyway, I was invited to a party on his yacht one evening. Mr. Mayer didn't want me to go. He knew we hadn't met and was afraid I'd get pregnant." She laughed. "I went anyway. *Every*one was there. Oleg Cassini introduced us. The Prince and I had a glass of champagne on the deck and then he invited me to see the rest of his 'ship.' I was . . . relieved, I sink. I was very curious about him. We spent most of the evening 'below decks.' I had heard he could fuck for hours and not have an orgasm." She filled her glass as Roman and I looked at each other—surprised and delighted at the language. "He could, too! You know how? I tell you. After we were in bed for twenty minutes, he reached over to his nightstand and pressed a little button. The doors of the room burst open and in rushed a servant holding a silver champagne bucket!" She looked from one of us to the other. I couldn't imagine what was going to happen. "I almost fainted! The bucket was filled wis *ice* water. The servant stood there and Aly turned on his knees and put bose hands into it. Then the servant bowed politely and left. Aly did this every time he felt close to having an orgasm. I asked him why and he said it was against his *religion* to impregnate an infidel." She lit a cigarette. "One time of *that* was enough for me," she said, blowing out a cloud of smoke.

Roman and I cracked up. Her humor was bringing us even closer together, and I was grateful.

Marietta told us that affairs in Hollywood were often brief and took place between costars during the weeks of filming a movie. "Marlene was always falling in love wis the men in her pictures. Except Ray Milland. She *hated* him! But Gilbert, Cooper . . . Stewart. Them she loved." She smiled at us slyly. "Marlene was very fond of me also," she said.

"Really?" we replied in unison.

"But I don't sink I will tell you about it. She was a lovely woman, though. A hard worker. I idolized her."

We toasted Marlene. I thought of her marvelous costumes in *The Devil Is a Woman.*

"Marlene loved Olivier, you know. But he was mad for Vivien Leigh. They had already cast Olivier in *Rebecca* and he was determined to have Vivien play opposite. Selznick was sympathetic to them. At the premiere

of *Gone Wis the Wind,* he sent Olivier down to Atlanta to promote *Rebecca*
in a trailer so they could be together—but he felt Vivien was all wrong
for the part of Mrs. DeWinter. He gave her a test, I sink, but Joan
played it. Poor Joan. Olivier made her miserable." She took a drag on
her cigarette. "You know, Mr. Mayer let me test for Scarlett O'Hara."
Roman and I looked at each other. *This* was news.

"The accent. I know." She was too tight to get very indignant. *"Vivien*
had an accent, too. She did fine! They had me to do that scene where
the servant is pulling her corset tight. Wait, I show you." She got up
and turned sideways. "'Mammy, ah've gotta have it tighter, ah've
just . . .'" Although she wasn't half bad, the German accent still showed
through. Marietta dissolved into laughter and fell back into her seat.
"You know, I'm surprised Garbo was worried about me coming along.
My predecessor, by the way, had a size *eleven* shoe. I adored her and still
sink she is the most beautiful star ever, but Harpo Marx didn't like her.
We were at a party together right before she disappeared in 1941 and
he sought she had snubbed me in front of a group of people. The next
day he hired an elephant and brought it down to Sid Grauman's. He had
a picture taken of the animal wis its foot on Garbo's block. It was
delivered to the set of *Two-Faced Woman* wis a message from Harpo:
'Dear Greta. Don't worry. No one can fill your shoes.'"

While we were whooping it up, my father was back in Cannes
working on a distribution deal for the States.

"We'll give you this and that and you get a such-and-such percentage
of the Japan situation."

He finally made a deal with Warner Brothers, but as things turned
out the U.S. State Department would not even allow *Resurrection and
Denial* to be released in the United States.

"There are some political problems," a spokesman said later. Hadn't
they ever forgotten? We brought the issue to court after the festival, but
to no avail. The film was, however, released abroad and was a huge hit
in France, Italy, Spain and Germany. At least I could stop worrying

where the money was going to come from to pay the rent on my apartment.

When the festival was over, I decided to take a holiday. Nice, Venice, Amsterdam. I drove my parents and Lucy to the airport. We congratulated ourselves yet again and kissed good-bye. "See you in a few months," I said, wanting to savor my freedom and artistic spirit forever.

Marietta, Joe Stein and I had a tearful scene at the train station three days later.

"*Sank* you," she said, hugging me fiercely on the platform, smelling of a rich perfume.

"What will you do now?" I asked. I had really gotten to love her and Joe.

"We've had offers," Stein said, smiling broadly, "but for now it's just going to be a rest in Paris." I wished them well.

I met Roman back at the hotel. We had decided to vacation together and, if that worked well, live together in New York on returning.

"All packed!" he said, his eyes sparkling like aquamarines. The hotel brought a car around for us and had our luggage stuffed in the trunk.

"Where to?" Roman asked, idling the motor in front.

"Just floor it!" I said, opening the bottle of Louis Roederer Cristal sitting in a bucket on my lap. I filled our glasses and laughed as we drove up a cobbled street and out of the city. Trees and peasants whizzed by.

"Here we go!" Roman said in his deep voice, shifting into fourth.

The hills of Cannes turned to rose as we drove into the sunset. Together at last.